Starship

– OBLIVION –

Sanctuary Outpost

USS Hamilton Series Book 5

Mark Wayne McGinnis

Other Books By MWM

Scrapyard Ship Series
Scrapyard Ship (Book 1)
HAB 12 (Book 2)
Space Vengeance (Book 3)
Realms of Time (Book 4)
Craing Dominion (Book 5)
The Great Space (Book 6)
Call To Battle (Book 7)

Tapped In Series
Mad Powers (Book 1)
Deadly Powers (Book 2)

Lone Star Renegades Series
Lone Star Renegades (also called 'Jacked') (Book 1)

Star Watch Series
Star Watch (Book 1)
Ricket (Book 2)
Boomer (Book 3)
Glory for Space Sea and Space (Book 4)
Space Chase (Book 5)
Scrapyard LEGACY (Book 6)

The Simpleton Series
The Simpleton (Book 1)
The Simpleton Quest (Book 2)

Galaxy Man Series
Galaxy Man (Book 1)

Ship Wrecked Series
Ship Wrecked (Book 1)
Ship Wrecked II (Book 2)
Ship Wrecked III (Book 3)

Boy Gone Series
Boy Gone Book 1

Cloudwalkers
Cloudwalkers

The Hidden Ship
The Hidden Ship

Guardian Ship
Guardian Ship

Gun Ship
Gun Ship

Hover
Hover

Published by: Avenstar Productions
Paperback ISBN: 978-1-7372475-2-4

To join Mark's mailing list, jump to:
http://eepurl.com/bs7M9r

Visit Mark Wayne McGinnis at:
http://www.markwaynemcginnis.com

Prologue

Sol Solar System, Leaving Jupiter's Moon, Callisto
Grish Recon-Rover — *Rage in Battle*

Grish bridge commander Dromp Gam was doing his best to look casual and nonchalant, even under the watchful eye of the Varapin contingent. For the most part, they had stayed out of sight, stayed in their cabins these last few days since they'd come on board back at the Cygni system.

Dromp didn't like how the three creepy robed ghouls hovered about the way they did, always watching, but never saying much of anything. And those faces. Obsidian black skulls with those protruding white jaws. Unnerving the way they just lurked about like fucking death incarnate. But orders were orders. He was to treat his Varapin guests with the utmost respect.

The *Rage in Battle* was not a large ship. Upgraded with the latest cloaking capabilities, the recon-rover was here to assess Earth's defensive capabilities. An attack on the humans' home world was imminent, although what had been planned for the coming days was now on hold. Apparently, their Varapin allies had their own thoughts on the matter. Their plan would provide for fewer high orbit-to-surface bombardments and more of an on-world attack.

That would mean *Ghan-Tshot*. The Varapin in-your-face feeding process—where one's life force was viciously extracted—would potentially leave behind millions upon millions of lifeless, drained human husks in their wake. The mere thought of it sickened Dromp.

Approaching the blue world, Dromp Gam saw there was a fair amount of space traffic about. Some were simple commerce vessels, but many were warships. A small contingent was just now heading off toward the world's lone moon.

"Tell your helmsman to slow our approach," the Varapin said.

Dromp said, "Yes, let's give those other ships a wide berth." But he shot the Varapin a quick glance. They were second guessing his every command. He nervously snorted, which instigated several others of his bridge crew to make the same sound. Dromp inwardly chided himself. Then he was irritated with his own inner response. *We have nothing to be ashamed of!*

The Grish were hairless, pink-skinned, and snout-nosed. They stood upright for the most part. They had accomplished much, being an intelligent and spacefaring civilization. A civilization of warriors. Unfortunately, the species was remarkably similar in appearance to that of Earth's swine animal family—the domestic pig. And like most Grish, Dromp, too, was well aware of the interstellar slights—the constant insults, the comparisons to the dim-witted, mud-slopping animals down on Earth's surface. *Fucking pigs!*

The Varapin contingent moved as one, hovering closer to the virtual display.

One of them spoke, his voice like two metal files rubbing together. "Wait! Follow that small formation there."

Dromp made an incredulous expression. "That's not our objective. We're here to—"

"Do not presume we are abettors here, Ship Commander. We are not. You will do as I say, and do it promptly. Now, have your helmsman alter course for that moon."

Another of the Varapin moved fast, grabbing one female Grish junior officer by an ear and yanking her from her seat, leaving her writhing in pain on the deck. Squealing, she scurried away from the hooded alien.

Settling in behind the vacated station, the Varapin began tapping a bony finger at the controls, zooming the 3D display onto the fast-departing group of warships. One large ship in particular came into sharp focus. He looked to his two brethren. "It is indeed the same vessel we seek. That is the USS *Hercules*…"

Dromp Gam still didn't get what all the fuss was about. He looked at the attached metatag readout for the vessel. "What is so special about this particular heavy battleship?"

"It is not the ship, you fool," the Varapin said. "It is the captain of that ship. Captain Gail Pristy. She will know where he is. She alone can lead us to Quintos. We find Quintos; we find the *Oblivion*. We have a new objective, piglet ship commander: follow that strike group. And on your life, ensure we are not detected."

Chapter 1

Eta Carinae Star System
Starship *Oblivion*, Low orbit over Haven
From the personal journal of Captain Galvin Quintos

I sat there within the captain's ready room on board the starship *Oblivion*, staring out through the floor-to-ceiling bank of portside windows while contemplating what lay ahead for me later in the day. *It'll be an epic shitshow; that's what it'll be. I'm going to die today, and there's little I can do about it.*

I used the gym towel draped over one shoulder to wipe my brow. I'd come from a fairly intense early morning MMA training session with Wanda. We'd been working on multiple opponent strategies of late, using my combat avatars—avatars that were far more than simple action holograms. When Curly, Larry, and Moe, as they'd unaffectionately come to be known, connected with a punch, chop, or kick, it hurt like the dickens. But I was so distracted today that Wanda had cut our training session short—told me not to come back until I got my shit together.

For weeks we'd been keeping a low profile, and for good reason. Everyone was looking for us. The Varapin, of course; we'd hijacked their most prized warship. The Grish—multiple attack groups had been spotted in local space. And then there was the US Space-Navy. The *Oblivion* would have made quite the prize—an asset that would help turn the tide in a war that the Alliance was losing.

I thought of Gail Pristy, my executive officer (XO) and friend for the last several years. Had she been more than that? She'd opted not to join me. *Or hadn't I given her that choice?* She was going to make a fine ship commander—she had her whole career ahead of her. Why throw it all away going AWOL with my band of coconspirator deserters and little more than a half-cocked plan to take down the enemy?

A loud *clang* disrupted my reverie. There was construction going on next door—the bridge's layout was being transformed from a weird multitiered affair back into something more like what I was used to, with everything and everyone on one level. Additionally, an adjoining but separate combat information center (CIC) was being constructed. Fortunately, there was no shortage of construction bots on board this vessel. I just wished they were more considerate of the noise they made.

The *Oblivion* was possibly the most powerful warship within the known galaxy. It had been suggested by Porter, my chief of engineering and propulsion, that the ship's capabilities were well beyond anything the US Space-Navy had come up against prior. The big problem was…no one among my crew had much of an idea, other than the bare-bones basics, of how to take advantage of those capabilities. Leave it to say, this five-mile-long, highly advanced dreadnought hadn't exactly come with an operator's manual. She'd been appropriated from the Varapin while in the midst of a recent, long-drawn-out battle.

But the *Oblivion* wasn't of Varapin design. Previously, the Varapin had appropriated her from another alien adversary. Which begged the question—if this vessel was such a behemoth, powerful starship, *warship*, why the hell had she been vanquished—now on multiple occasions? We suspected the ship was of Gorvian design. A highly advanced alien race of people stemming from somewhere within the Andromeda Galaxy. How the ship had gotten here, I had no clue.

I continued staring out through the window at a view that was nothing short of spectacular. In the foreground, an emerald green world, lacking grand oceans such as those found on Earth; instead there were hundreds upon hundreds of small azure blue lakes that sparkled and glistened like so many individual diamonds. As the exoplanet slowly turned counterclockwise on its axis, I could just now make out a darkened brown area, which I knew was a patch of cleared land perhaps several hundred acres square. That was where the Pylor encampment lay sheltered within a surrounding cluster of mile-high trees called evertalls.

Diverting my eyes, looking off to the world's celestial surroundings, I saw there was constant movement. Here there were countless massive, somersaulting asteroids—all held at bay by some kind of unfathomable force or energy field, a force nobody had been able to adequately explain to me.

I spun back around to face my desk, where my worn, leatherbound journal sat opened to its approximate middle pages. I let out a measured breath. I'd been writing old-school of late—with pen upon paper. A process that had been both therapeutic and calming. Writing this way offered me a better perspective as I chronicled my day—not to mention, it helped me maintain a certain level of sanity among so much craziness.

Then again, I had chosen this life. There was no one else to blame. I also liked that there would be no electronic record being stored by the ship's ever-watchful artificial intelligence (AI)—one commonly known as MORROW. *More on that later.* I'd encouraged subordinate officers to follow my lead with this form of archaic journaling. Not everyone shared my enthusiasm for the practice.

Anyway, I'd been journaling about my time on board the starship *Oblivion*—living and working among my small crew contingent, but also among the most ruthless, brutal, cold-blooded, downright barbaric collection of people I'd ever had the misfortune to be associated with. And look—there was a difference between a group calling themselves pirates in ha ha jest and those who actually WERE real-life space pirates. So yeah, this Pylor clan were pirates, which came with all the terrible rancorous bad behavior you'd imagine any true space marauders to exemplify.

Let me start by giving you a little insight as to how the Pylors first got here. Some sixty years prior, the Pylors had chosen a home-base star system called Eta Carinae. At about twenty-three parsecs distance—that's about seventy-five light-years from Earth—this was, for the most part, a completely uninhabited quadrant of space. And uninhabited for a damn good reason. You see, Eta Carinae was designated as a luminous blue variable. This star, as its designation so aptly suggested, had an inconsistent, annoying level of brightness. That, and it was expected to explode as a supernova sometime in the near future. Then again, at least in astronomical terms, near future could be anywhere from a few years to a few million years from now. And because the gas cloud nearest to Eta Carinae produced ultraviolet laser-like radiation emissions, a rarity within the cosmos, it made for a hostile environment for any kind of organic life.

Back to how they got here…A small Pylor squadron had been desperate to escape their angry pursuers—a fleet of seventy-five Helcon-Reich gunships in this case—so the pirates had chanced entering what was the most perilous of asteroid fields that any of the Pylors had previously encountered. Making their getaway deeper into the field, they had soon realized the life-threatening ultraviolet emissions were starting to lessen—were being refracted or even absorbed by those millions upon millions of asteroids.

The trek had not been without its price. The Pylors' ragtag squadron of twenty-eight vessels had been eventually reduced down to twenty-one. It was then, some sixty years ago, that they'd discovered this small, ultra-hidden world buried deep within all those spinning and tumbling rocks. It was within a habitable Gold-ilocks zone—*an area in space where liquid water existed.* There was, of course, the uncharacteristic brightening and dimming of sur-rounding starlight. Eta Carinae could bring spontaneous daylight or nighttime without much rhyme or reason.

The Pylor ships' sensor readings described a world with an ecosystem that was much like that of Earth and seemingly sus-taining its own breathable atmosphere. The arriving Pylors orbited the bright green exoplanet while soon discovering the Eta Carinae star system was not, in fact, completely devoid of life after all. And because those within the Pylor clan were primarily of human lineage, an Earth-like environment would be just fine with them. Sure, there would be animal life of a sort, mostly herbivores and some carnivores, but nothing the Pylors figured they wouldn't be able to deal with.

One ship was sent down to the surface as a test. A week lat-er the rest of them followed suit. Soon after, put to a vote, the world was named Haven. And from that day forward, Haven had remained the Pylor clan's most hidden, most sacred stronghold base of operations.

It is best if you think of the Pylors as a clan, but really more like a disjointed extended family. Today, clusters of Pylor pirates were spread out within this quadrant of the Milky Way. Places like the small world of Vebose within the TRAPPIST-1d star system, or Chinal 5 within the Gliese system, or Ironhold Station within the Pleidian Weonan territory—which we all knew now was firmly back within Pleidian control. But have no doubt, Haven here, within the Eta Carinae system, was the pirates' home base and the true seat of Pylor power.

After leaving the US Space-Navy, I'd seized a temporary leadership role of a small band of Pylor miscreants by besting their leader, one captain Cardinal Thunderballs. But I suspected that might very well change later on today. I'd been given a reprieve after the battle with the Varapin, one having taken place back within the Perseus Arm of the Milky Way. Apparently, the Pylors had not expected me to prevail—thus my true battle to maintain leadership had been put off until today, down on Haven. My future, my crew's future, was to be determined by the organization's presiding authority.

I shook my head. I had a strategic plan. But without the help of the Pylors, my chances of success were nil.

As I was completing my journal entry, it struck me just how bizarre my life had become of late. *What has it been now…three weeks…no, four.* Prior to that I was the decorated commanding officer of the USS *Jefferson*—a powerful dreadnought in her own right within Earth's EUNF Space-Navy. The war was not going well for the Alliance—that being the humans, the Thine, and the Pleidian Weonan. Our collective enemies were both the Grish and Varapin, but mostly the Varapin ghouls, who were methodically and all too quickly vanquishing Alliance territories.

The writing was on the wall. We were losing. Humankind was in dire jeopardy, and nothing we were doing was making any damn difference. So, I'd decided not to play by the rules anymore. The enemy certainly had no qualms about playing dirty. So, I had quit the US Space-Navy, absconded with the starship Oblivion, and made a pact with a band of ruthless Pylor pirates. *All in a day's work, right?*

Apparently, my plan to fight fire with fire, so to speak, must have had some merit because a good number of my fellow USS

Jefferson crewmates had decided to jump ship and come along with me, even knowing they, like me, would be considered deserters and would surely face courts-martial, inevitably leading to lengthy prison stints if they were ever caught.

Let me tell you, a day didn't go by where I didn't feel the weight of my decision to become a criminal. And I'd dragged so many others into this wayward life along with me.

The fourth finger on my right hand started to tingle. I glanced down at the somewhat oversized, albeit impressive-looking ring situated on that finger. Each *Oblivion* crew member now wore one of these same kinds of rings. Black and shiny as obsidian, each ring was a piece of art unto itself. Engraved with intricate swirling details, and perched upon the ring's top crown, in my case, was a six-carat brilliant blue sapphire. This was the only indication of my captain's rank since none on board wore a regulation uniform.

The other officers had similar rings but had different jewels, depending on their ship ranks. For instance:
Ensign (ENS/O-1) – Ruby
Lieutenant (LT/O-3) – Emerald
Commander (CDR/O-5) –Fire Opal
Captain (CAPT/O-7) – Blue Sapphire

In contrast, noncommissioned crew had clusters of small diamonds. One's rank determined how many diamonds were mounted atop a ring. But none of that explained why my ring was currently tingling upon my finger. You see, the real reason we wore these unique and beautiful pieces of jewelry was for a far more pragmatic purpose than simple vanity. No longer could we wear our US Space-Navy standard-issue TAC-Band communicators. Those could be too easily hacked into by my former employers.

Our onboard Thine scientist, Coogong Sohp, had engineered our new *Jaadoo* rings—the name coming from the Hindu word for magic. What our Thine genius had engineered was nothing short of brilliant. Among other things that I won't go into right now, our Jaadoo rings provided crew members with a projected 3D halo display, an encrypted peer-to-peer comms package, along with an interface that coupled to the *Oblivion's* quansporter—a physical matter quantum entanglement transporter device.

I used the tip of my thumb to double tap the bottom of the ring, which triggered a foot-high 3D projected image of Dr. Vivian Leigh's pretty face. I tapped again.

"Hey, Doc…what's up?"

Her 3D image came alive above my hand. "No. You don't get to *hey, Doc* me…you know exactly why I'm calling."

"Shit. I missed my appointment."

"Uh-huh, you missed your appointment. So…what? You have a death wish?"

"No, of course not. It just feels…I don't know. Like cheating."

The suspended, all-too-real-looking Doc Viv rolled her eyes. "Cheating is what pirates do. Or did you forget that Thunderballs had a projectile firing weapon down his pants?"

What Viv was referring to was the genesis of my, of all of our, current predicament. It was a hand-to-hand fighting bout, more like a mixed martial arts match, between me and the charismatic leader of the band of Pylor pirates I spoke of earlier, Thunderballs. About mid-fight he'd shot me with a hidden pistol, one that was discreetly located in his pants in the general area of his ball sac. How I'd still managed to overcome my injuries, including being shot in the shoulder, while going on to triumph over the pirate leader—well, that still astounded me to this day. And as Pylor code stipulated, to the victor went the spoils—in that case, we had been fighting to the death for the right to lead his band of killer marauders.

"Of course I haven't forgotten…I still have the scars to remind me. What exactly are you proposing that will give me an upper hand?"

"A trifold approach. First, a cocktail of bio-stimulants to enhance your metabolism. Second, an infusion of regeneration nanites, and¬—"

"Hold on there. What's this about nanites?"

"Oh…yeah. Just one of the many discoveries I've made since coming aboard the *Oblivion*. Found them in the Gorvian's Health-Bay medical vault. Discovered a whole slew of them…and these aren't the typical intravenous micromachines we're all used to. No, these little bastards take quantum mechanics to a whole new level. Operate primarily within another paradigm or dimension. Leave it to say there are certain anatomical healing or recuperative restrictions dictated by the physics of our reality that simply don't exist within other realities. These Gorvian nanites can pull from those realities exactly what's necessary to expedite rapid healing here. Anyway, that's the simplified explanation."

"Fine. And the third aspect of your trifold approach?"

"Before I get into that, I want to remind you that if you are bested down on that world, it doesn't just affect you. We're all screwed. And I'm sure I don't need to remind you what we've all given up by following you here."

"No, you don't need to remind me."

"The third aspect will be a hard pill to swallow, Quintos. And I mean that figuratively, not literally."

"Just go on…"

"I want to replace a portion of your neural synapses."

"I already don't like this suggestion."

"Look, most synapses in your body are basically chemically based. And these synapses communicate using chemical messengers. While other synapses are electrical…these synapses utilize ion flow to communicate directly between cells."

"Okay."

"It's a relatively slow organic process."

"As mentioned, I don't like where this is going," I said.

"Don't be such a pussy. It'll be painless. Listen to me. Consider that a given thought, say wiggling your big toe, can be generated and then acted upon in about a hundred and fifty milliseconds. That's about half the time of the blink of an eye."

I wiggled my big toe. "That seems pretty quick—"

"It's pathetically slow! What if I could bring that response time down to a fraction of that?"

I thought about it. "So…my reactions, my reflexes would be faster?"

"Cumulatively, you'd be lightning fast."

"What exactly would this entail?"

She hesitated. "Here's the rub. It's never been tried before on a human. But honestly, it's a straightforward procedure. Take about an hour." She smiled in a way that was less than believable and somewhat creepy.

"What will it do to my body? No bullshit. Tell me the truth."

She shrugged. "It introduces variant biology into your physiology."

"What kind of variant biology?"

She held up a small glass vial of glowing green liquid. She gave it a little jiggle. "From a DNA perspective…it's totally compatible with humans. It's Gorvian plasma."

"As in the alien race that built this ship?"

"Exactly. Been studying them…fast little fuckers. And Quintos, this is all I have. I've spent a lot of time on this, more than I'd like to admit. There's only this one vial. There's no more of this stuff. So I hope it helps."

I let that sink in. For all the friction the two of us had, I knew she cared about me. The feeling was mutual. "Thank you, Viv. Truly, thank you. And I'm sure it will help. Give me an hour to get over to HealthBay. But I have to be somewhere in five minutes."

Leaving my ready room, I glanced into the bridge. The renovations were nearly completed, and some of the bridge crew were sitting at their stations. How they could work with all the ruckus—noise and swirling dust—I couldn't fathom. We'd set up a temporary bridge in one of the nearby conference rooms, where all the bridge console's functions had been mirrored, but space was tight, and everyone was being forced to work elbow to elbow. The bridge crew was more than ready to have an operational command center again.

Beyond the newly laid out bridge space, I could see the CIC, which was already completed, and I could see a number of crew members busy at their stations through the heavy layer of construction dust.

Leaving the ship's command center, I headed aft down the ship's main corridor artery.

"Captain! Captain!"

I turned to see Bosun Johanna Polk. One of the *Jefferson's* bridge crew who'd opted to come with me to the *Oblivion*. She was one of the few that opted to still wear her US Space-Navy uniform. More than anyone else, her decision to become a wanted criminal had surprised me. She and I had rarely gotten along, her being a rule-follower and I being anything but a rule follower. But that actually had worked out well—had enabled a strange balance on board the ship.

I stopped and waited for her to catch up to me.

"Captain, didn't you hear me?"

"Hear you?"

"Back at the bridge. When you looked in."

"Sorry, no. A lot of banging and clanging. What's up, Bosun?"

The middle-aged woman huffed before her lips narrowed into

a straight line.

"I'm not a mind reader. Please tell me what I've forgotten to do or what I've done wrong."

The *Oblivion* was a vast ship. The length overall was five miles, and we were notably undermanned to operate such an enormous vessel. My list of fix-it items to address was growing by the day. There just wasn't enough crew to address them all.

"It's the night ghosts, Captain. We lost another of the crew. This time a Pylor."

I looked up, letting my eyes fix on overhead girders some thirty feet above me. Letting out a breath, I inwardly cursed the Varapin for the thousandth time. Having been victorious in battle, we had taken this ship as a prize of war. The thousands of Varapin warriors on board had mostly died in combat. What few prisoners had been rounded up were now spending time within a EUNF brig back on Earth. But apparently, that wasn't the last of the Varapin that had remained on board this ship. It had been estimated that close to fifty of the robed ghouls still remained. They were hiding within their coffin-like beds, called Ebom-Pods. Once a Varapin was snuggled up within one of those things, even Hardy's sensors had a hard time detecting the ghoul's presence within.

"They're coming out during the late-night shifts when passage-ways are practically deserted."

"I'm well aware of that, Bosun." I shook my head. Night ghost sightings were becoming more and more frequent of late. But now they were feeding—Ghan-Tshot? "Thank you, Bosun Polk. I'll take care of it."

"That's it? You'll take care of it?"

"What else can I say? It's on my list. Until we can form an ad-equate onboard security department..."

"I think we should have something like a neighborhood watch. Just in the meantime, before that onboard security department that will never happen can be assembled."

I rubbed my tired eyes. I mentally pictured a team of little old ladies with flashlights prowling through the ship's vast passageways at night. "Fine. You want to put something together, I'm all for it. No less than groups of five or six. But a Varapin is never to be approached. Call Sergeant Max or Hardy. That clear?"

Bosun Polk nodded her head with vigor. Apparently I'd given her the answer she'd been hoping for. Why she was so excited to take on this issue, I wasn't sure. She saluted and hurried back toward the bridge.

I yelled after her, "And you don't need to salute me, Bosun!"

Chapter 2

I sat outside the physical provisions compartment, gazing up at Hardy's scorched and cratered outer plating. I shook my head. His face display was a total mess and impossible to read. He still wore a black leather vest, which concealed what I was sure was extensive damage around his torso area. He'd been keeping an uncharacteristically low profile these last few weeks. I knew looking like this was an embarrassment to him. So much of his self-esteem came from his typically mirror-like reflective surface. After that last harrowing battle with the Varapin, where he'd taken a bad beating, he currently looked more like a blackened tower of lava than what he actually was.

"Hey…they'll do a good job. You'll be back to normal in no time," I said.

Hardy stood, mechanical shoulders somewhat slumped—he said nothing.

The physical provisions compartment was a kind of onboard foundry and machine shop. But not like any machine shop I'd ever encountered prior. The level of intricate prototyping and full-on manufacturing capabilities provided by this area of the ship was beyond anything comparable found on similarly sized vessels. And it was perfect for what was needed at this moment. My good friend, perhaps my best friend, was a seven-foot-tall robot called a

ChronoBot—one designed for war—for battle.

My knowledge of ChronoBots was limited. I only knew that ChronoBots had been purchased from an alien race called the Sheentah some three hundred years ago. Integrated with multiple, usually hidden-away energy cannons, Hardy had one component that was dissimilar to the maybe one hundred other ChronoBots estimated to still be in existence. And that was his all-too-human consciousness.

ChronoBots came standard with a partial biomatter AI, a zero personality psyche called LuMan. And to make a long story short, through a series of unexpected mishaps two years earlier with the DNA of a long-dead USS *Hamilton* ship-wide maintenance worker (SWM) named John Hardy, a cross-contamination had taken place within LuMan's biomatter AI brain. Thus, the Boston-accented, highly outspoken, and never subtle character had become an integral part of the crew. LuMan had already been programmed to protect me—to risk his own life, as it was, to ensure I was safe. Although I was sure this influenced Hardy—they did share that biomatter brain, after all—Hardy's sense of loyalty, I suspected, was on a much more personal level.

The automated door to the physical provisions compartment swooshed open, and Coogong Sohp stepped into view. The scientist was a five-foot-tall Thine being—beings that typically looked like large maggots. As an alien race, they were profoundly intelligent—just not anatomically well suited to protect themselves against other invading forces. For that, they had joined the Alliance along with the humans and Pleidians. But Coogong had dramatically altered his physical appearance of late.

He had undergone a kind of genetic upgrade, which even now caused me to do double takes. His lower body was a stick figure. His brain's neural junctures had been reassigned connections to a formulated torso, arms, and legs of what were called Tendril Albicon–formulated constructs. What hadn't changed was his worm-like head, which was encased in an environment suit's helmet. His wide smile radiated behind the faceplate. Ambiogell, the goo-like substance the Thine breathed, distorted his worm-like features.

Coogong said, "Ah…Captain Quintos…Hardy. So good to see you both. The facility is ready. The equipment is prepped for the procedure."

"What exactly will you be doing in there, Coogong?" I asked.

As if on cue, a familiar-looking spindly MediBot, one not near-ly as imposing as Hardy, stepped through the door. Doc Viv had brought a number of these seemingly dull-witted bots over from the *Jefferson* along with her.

"Well…the MediBot will assist with removing the craters and carbon buildup from all of Hardy's damaged metallic surfaces. Once those are cleaned, we will begin the chrome plating process. This is a method of applying a thin layer of diamond chromi-um onto his metal substrate through an electroplating procedure. This is an old-fashioned, tried-and-true process, where the flow of electricity between two electrodes deposits multiple layers of diamond-chromium atoms, thus providing Hardy with that hard, ultra-shiny surface he so deserves."

Hardy turned his encrusted, blackened head in my direction. "If I die in there…never to return…please take care of Iris for me?"

I rolled my eyes. "Don't you think you're being just a tad dra-matic? It's not like I'm sending you into battle. And this is what you wanted. You've been nagging me to make it happen for weeks now."

"Just saying…you never know. Surgery…well, it's a tricky busi-ness."

"This isn't surgery, and there is virtually no chance you, as a ChronoBot, can be harmed by this."

He lowered his head and shuffled through the door. Something bright with a trail of sparkling, dare I say, fairy dust darted up and out of Hardy's front vest pocket, circled above the ChronoBot, and eventually came to rest upon my shoulder. I heard the medieval Symbio-Poth fairy named Iris let out a tiny breath.

"How I dost love Hardy, but he is an overdramatic idiot at times...Nay?"

No taller than an inch, the magical little fairy was just one of many Symbio-Poth–manufactured creatures currently on board the *Oblivion*. Created by the Pleidian Weonan equivalents of the old Walt Disney's Imagineers, the Symbio-Poth characters were what now remained of an elaborate interactive, medieval crew game that had taken up the top two decks of the *Jefferson*. And before that, other Symbio characters had helped to recreate my childhood hometown of Clairmont. All gifts to my crew and me from Shawlee Tee, empress of the Pleidian Weonan Empire. Which reminded me, I had to find a way to speak with Shawlee soon. She was upset with me, and rightly so.

Hardy was out of view now. With a raised voice, I said, "We'll be right here when you get out, Hardy."

Coogong smiled and turned to follow the ChronoBot.

"Um...how long do you think this will take?" I said. "I have to be down on the surface in a few hours."

Coogong turned to look at me. "Ah yes, your meeting with the Pylors. Hardy should be back in good form within...Mmm, maybe two hours? I know you will want him at your side."

I nodded. It would be close, but that should give me just enough time, barely, to head down to HealthBay.

***

Two hours later, I was back within the antechamber of the

physical provisions compartment with Doc Viv at my side. She'd said I'd need to be closely watched for the next few hours for any adverse reactions. Having completed the trifold medical procedure within HealthBay, I was still a little shaky on my feet. Nauseous and a bit dizzy, I was feeling the effects of the multiple injections—the cocktail of bio-stimulants to enhance my metabolism, the quantum regenerative nanites that theoretically pulled from other dimensions, and the neon green alien plasma shit that promised to make all my neural synapses lightning fast. There was no indication any of that had worked. Instead, I just felt sick.

Looking around, I was surprised to see this improvised waiting room area was now so crowded with other crew members. Much of the bridge crew was here, including Grimes and Chen, as well as Bosun Johanna Polk. SWM chief LaSalle and several of his maintenance department guys were milling about. I spotted Captain Wallace Ryder on the other side of the compartment, talking with Lieutenant Akari James. A number of other Arrow fighters were here as well. Chief Craig Porter was here, as well as all four of Sergeant Max's marines—Wanda, Grip, Hock, and his twin brother, Ham.

Viv gave me a pat on my upper arm before disappearing into the crowd. *So much for keeping me under close observation.*

Arms crossed, Chief Craig Porter casually leaned against a nearby bulkhead. He was wearing board shorts and a Hawaiian shirt with oversized parrots, or maybe they were macaws, each punctuating the wild jungle design.

"Sorry, Galvin…standing room only." He gave me an appraising look. "You're looking a little peaked, buddy. Heard about your, um, treatments."

"Interesting how fast word spreads within such a large starship," I said unenthusiastically.

He shrugged.

Looking about, I counted no less than thirty of my crew here. I said, "What's going on?"

A familiar female voice answered. "Hey, this is a big deal to Hardy. So we're showing him a little support. Did you think you were the only one who cared about him?"

It was Lieutenant Akari James. The bold and brassy Arrow Fighter pilot with the callsign "Ballbuster" looked up at me with a bemused expression. And like Porter, she was dressed casually—in her case, she wore a pink tank top and skimpy cutoff jeans. I had to force myself not to ogle her somewhat exposed ass cheeks along with toned, golden-tanned legs. *Where on board did she get a suntan?*

"I'm well aware Hardy has a lot of friends…people who care about him," I said.

She said, "This is like a coming out party."

"I thought that was for young debutantes being formally introduced into society?"

She laughed, "Oh yeah…I guess he's not so much a young debutante. But come on…you've seen him of late, right? All quiet and staying out of sight. Lurks about in the shadows like some kind of castle monster."

"I guess he just takes pride in his physical appearance, that's all."

She nodded while arching her back. A casual stretch that inadvertently attracted my gaze to two orange-sized breasts beneath taut cotton fabric. Clearly, she wasn't wearing a bra. *Should I implement some kind of dress code? Has the crew embraced this whole going rogue thing a little too far?*

I didn't like procedures and regulations. I rarely played by the rules, which had gotten me in trouble with my US Space-Navy superiors on multiple occasions. But there had to be some level of etiquette, didn't there?

She swiped at the bangs of her short tomboy haircut. Interesting. I'd never noticed just how large her eyes were prior to this moment. And so green. An exact match to the sparkling emerald perched upon her Jaadoo ring.

She took a step closer and spoke more softly. "Captain…have you ever been to the rotunda?"

"Rotunda? I don't know what that is."

She pursed her lips. "Thought not. It's just a place the crew has set up to get a drink. To let our hair down, so to speak."

"A nightclub."

"Kinda. Nothing as formal as that."

I shrugged and shook my head, feeling uncomfortable with where this was going. Akari was drop-dead gorgeous and dangerous in more ways than one. She was well-known for being a daredevil in an Arrow Fighter, but evidently Ballbuster's risk-taking wasn't exclusive to a cockpit.

"Hey…you were the one that brought us into this wayward life. You're a full-fledged scoundrel now, Brigs. Best you start acting like one."

She'd used Brigs, my own fighter pilot callsign.

With another laugh, she spun away—gone within the throng of the awaiting crew. It must be that glowing crap Doc Viv had pumped into my veins. *Caused a metabolism imbalance. Maybe affected my hormones. What have I become, a love-starved teenager?*

I heard a faint swooshing sound. A hush fell over the crowd. All eyes were locked onto the open physical provisions compartment hatch door. I noticed Iris was standing on my right shoulder, her little eyes also pinned to the opening.

Then Hardy stepped into view. Arms raised over his head like a victorious champion boxer, he strode forth. "I am Hardy, and I have returned. Now, feast your eyes upon my magnificence!"

Indeed, the seven-foot-tall ChronoBot looked brand new. His new face display exhibited brilliant and colorful firework animations, while his chrome surface was as pristine and reflective as a mirror. But still no one uttered a word.

Iris put a tiny hand to her mouth. "Oh my, what have they done to him? Nae longer silver…he's…pink."

Hardy, who was capable of hearing far better than any human, looked directly at Iris. "No…not pink. It's rose gold…It was one of my diamond chromium color options…definitely not pink."

The silence hung in the air like a bad smell. Hardy's fireworks display faded to black. He slowly lowered his arms while looking about the stymied crowd.

"You look fantastic!" I yelled over the heads of the other onlookers. "Good choice, Hardy."

Others, now recovering from the shock of his most definitely pink chrome plating, began shouting out their own positive sentiments. "Well done!" "Awesome choice!" "You're a trendsetter!" … none of which sounded at all believable.

Surprisingly though, Hardy was eating it all up. And once again, thick articulating mechanical arms were thrust up high overhead—yes, he was now pink, but a champion just the same. Iris was now flittering about him, making sparkling fairy dust circles in the process.

Wanda tapped my arm. "It's time, Cap." She hitched a thumb over her shoulder.

I looked behind her. There, standing at the compartment's entrance, was none other than Little Vince. At four-foot nothing, the rodent-faced pirate offered me a crooked smile. Just the sight of those rotting teeth made my already queasy stomach start to turn. I nodded to him and mouthed the words, *Just give me a minute.*

Chapter 3

Thanks to Doc Viv's well-intentioned cocktail, I felt terrible. Not only sick to my stomach, but dizzy. *Perfect. I'm heading off to meet Pylor eminence, and I can barely keep my balance.*

I looked about the grimy interior of what I'd recently learned was a Pylor flyboat, just one of a thousand historical terms originating from fifteenth-to-eighteenth century Earth pirate lore. The vessel was old, far older than me. Some kind of repurposed lander craft, the flyboat's interior was dark, but ample enough for our contingent of seven—me, of course, Hardy, and Max's five marines, along with the ten Pylors accompanying us. There weren't seats, per se, but there were enough upside-down buckets, barrels, wooden crates, and so forth for us to be seated. Hardy stood, his stance wide to compensate for the craft's less than smooth ride.

"G-force compensators are shot," he said, staggering backward as the flyboat abruptly began to slow.

"We're here," Vince announced from the adjoined cockpit area. "Stay where you are."

The craft landed with a jolt. Vince rapidly flipped down a number of old-fashioned dash switches to the off position, and the craft's drive began to wind down. Vince got up from his seat and turned to face us. "Welcome to New Petite Goave. The capital of Haven. As of right now, Quintos, you remain our interim leader. You bested Thunderballs without much hornswoggle…commendable…Henceforth, there will be a parley with the House of Lords. Only with their approval will you be permitted to jaw with Admiral Alistair McMasters."

I stared blankly at the rodent-faced pirate. "I understood half of what you just said."

Hardy said, "Hornswoggle means to cheat, as in you didn't cheat much. Jaw means to talk…To parley—"

"I know what parley is, Hardy," I said.

Vince continued, "What you're looking to get out of this is a letter of marque. It will give you license as a privateer to attack non-Pylor merchant and war vessels within the sector."

"I thought I already won that right by besting Thunderballs."

"That gave you the right to lead his men, his fleet, for a year. But only the dandy pants here can give you a license to pirate," Vince said.

The other Pylors glowered at me. Something Vince had said brought a whole new level of hostility.

"You don't get that letter of marque…we don't get paid."

I looked to the others in my group.

Wanda said, "It makes sense. It's not like pirates get a regular paycheck or anything."

I nodded. "I get that; they get a piece of the winnings."

"The booty or bounty," Hardy corrected.

I scowled at the pink robot. "And how is it you're a walking talking pirate jargon thesaurus?"

"Well, matey…I loved reading about pirates as a kid."

I brought my attention back to Vince. "So I'm first meeting with this House of Lords. What will they be looking for? What do I have to do to make them happy?"

"With them…it's all about convincing them you will be filling their individual coffers. It's all about sharing the wealth that new ship of yours can provide."

"That shouldn't be too difficult. And this McMasters fella?"

Something I said further ruffled the feathers of the Pylors. Two of them let their hands slide closer to their holstered shredders.

"Only a bilge rat speaks of the admiral that way. A direct descendant of Black Bart Roberts himself, he is."

I looked to my pirate aficionado. "Hardy?"

"Black Bart Roberts is the most famous pirate of all time. Took over four hundred prizes, ships, mostly off the coast of Africa, in the 1700s. Admiral Arlington McMasters is looking to best the record of his distant blood relation within his lifetime."

Nods and grunts of approval emanated from the ten Pylors.

Little Vince sniffed and then spat something onto the deck. I thought it was a tooth. "The admiral, sure, he'll be looking to you, to us, for profits, but he'll be measuring you as a man. That you won't spoil the ship for a ha'porth of tar."

I let out a weary breath, my eyes going to the ChronoBot.

"Means leaving a job half done. More importantly, you'll do what you say you're going to do."

Vince said, "You're a foreigner here. The lot of you are. Trust is earned. And as of right now, we'd all be just as inclined to give you a woolding as to call you our mates."

Hardy said, "I have no idea what a woolding is."

It was the first time one of Vince's men spoke up—a chubby, disheveled Pylor with curly red hair. "It's where we stab and cut a man with our dirks and daggers; then we hang him high with a robe about his neck. Then we beat the bastard until his eyes pop out of his head."

The other Pylors laughed at that.

"Sounds like a piñata celebration," Ham said under his breath.

I actually knew this rumpled-looking, bad-smelling pirate since he'd been staying aboard the *Oblivion* with the others, "Well, Sloppy Joe, hopefully…in time, we can earn your trust and avoid the whole woolding thing. But let me make things perfectly clear to you. You work for me, and I don't take kindly to being disrespected. Have I made myself perfectly clear?"

I, too, wore a tagger upon my thigh and, feeling as irritated and shitty as I did, was more than ready to draw down on the pirate. Respect went both ways, and there was no time like the present to make that point. One of the other Pylors moved, or maybe simply twitched, but without a conscious thought, I drew my tagger. No. I didn't just draw the weapon. That would be an understatement. I drew the energy pistol lightning fast. It was a blur of motion that had even me staring down at my hand in surprise. I guess Viv's Gorvian neural synapses enhancer was actually starting to do something.

Little Vince slowly raised his palms. "There's no need for that, boss. We're all on the same side here…right? Sloppy Joe didn't mean no harm. Ain't that right, Sloppy?"

"Uh…yeah. I was just flapping my gums, is all. No harm intended. We're good, Captain."

All eyes were on me. I holstered my tagger and smiled—doing my best to shrug off the incident as an overreaction.

***

We hurried down the flyboat's aft ramp, experiencing the warm and humid air of New Petite Goave. We'd set down atop a flat plateau adjacent to the town, alongside no less than thirty or so other Pylor crafts. We followed Vince and his team down a series of hand-crafted flagstone stairs. I couldn't help but notice the fine workmanship.

Laid out before us, the capital of Haven was not what I'd expected—perhaps that of a crude assemblage of various prefab building constructs. But this was anything but that. Here was a town with actual buildings. Most were multistory affairs made of brick and timber. I took in formal-looking entrances, some adorned with ornate Roman columns; others had overhanging balconies with baroque wrought iron railings. Mature weeping willows lined both sides of the wide cobblestone street.

All in all, the place had a southern, New Orleansy vibe to it. But there were notable differences to Earth. Beyond the clearing in which the town was built were those surrounding blue-green evertall forests. Trees so tall, they made the California Redwoods look tiny in comparison. And the sky, yeah, it was blue, but it was more of a teal blue than the robin's-egg blue found back home. Both modern hover cars, as well as horse-drawn carriages, shared the busy road.

Some of the locals were dressed in what I'd guess to be nineteenth-century formal attire—frilly button-down shirts along with white stockings and just-below-the-knee dress breeches. The few high society women I saw moving about wore colorful long dresses. Most had low-cut necklines revealing various degrees of cleavage. Raised parasols blocked Eta Carinae's ever-dimming and brightening rays.

Exemplifying two distinct populace classes, there were also those like us that were dressed far more casually. Pylor pirates here were typically dressed in their brown or tan to-the-knee trousers, a kind of buckled shoe, and always a dark-colored button-down shirt. All Pylors here were armed with daggers and dirks. Many wore a holstered tagger strapped upon one thigh, and sometimes, both.

A hover car, more like a hover cart, was waiting for us on the street. Vince and I took the forward seats while everyone else piled in behind. Hardy was the last to step aboard, causing the vehicle to wobble and drop several inches. Vince made an annoyed face before directing the onboard AI to take us to the New Cabildo building.

The hover cart set off, and soon we were weaving in and out of traffic. I had to raise my voice to be heard over the *clop clop clop* of metal hooves upon stone cobbles. "What should we expect from this…meeting? Any suggestions for addressing the House of Lords?"

Sloppy Joe snickered behind me. I ignored him. "It's not like any of us here spend time among the likes of the lords."

I nodded and waited.

Finally, Vince said, "The only reason you're here is because of that big, beautiful ship you've absconded with. She's a real prize, and the House of Lords will be more than happy to take her off your hands, one way or another. They'll be calculating what kind of threat you are…sizing you up. They do not trust outsiders, so don't assume you will be granted a letter of marque any time soon."

"Any time soon? I want that today."

More chuckles emanated from behind.

"Then I guess you better be prepared to make your case."

The hover cart began to slow, then made a right turn into a circular drive. In front of us was the largest building we'd passed thus far. Having more of a Gothic architecture, the castle-like structure looked to be made entirely of stone blocks. A thirty-foot-tall battlement wall surrounded the perimeter of the place, and multiple spires pierced high into the sky.

"Welcome to the House of Lords," Vince said. "Chop chop… Everyone out."

Twenty armed guardsmen stood erect upon wide circular steps leading up to what were easily fifteen-foot-high timbers with black ironwork doors. I headed for the steps but soon noticed Vince and his band of Pylors had stayed behind.

I looked back. "Aren't you coming?"

"Nah…we're not invited. You're on your own, Captain. My advice, don't get yourself killed in there."

I exchanged a quick glance with my crew. "I thought this was just a meeting. A mere negotiation."

Vince said, "Pylors in there may dress all fine and proper. Talk all hoity-toity…but they're pirates. They'd just as soon slit your throat than give you the time of day. Oh, and one more thing."

"What's that?"

"There's no way they'll let that pink mechanical tin can in there."

The cart headed back down the drive, turned right, and disappeared behind the street lined with willows.

We continued to climb the stairs while the flanking guards turned to accompany us. The double doors opened as we approached. A small man greeted us. He wore a gold silk or satin suit—knickers, leggings, and all that. A white wig sat upon his head, completing the formal manservant getup.

"You will address me as Mr. Phillips."

We entered a grand circular vestibule with three-story-high ceilings, white and black checkered marble flooring, and more Roman columns. It occurred to me the original builders here had had issues with mixing their pompous architecture, Roman, Greek, Gothic, whatever.

"The ChronoBot will remain here."

Chapter 4

I was about to object when Mr. Phillips said in a bored mono-tone, "Not open to debate. You wish to meet with the House of Lords? You leave that thing here…up to you."

"Oh, so now I'm a thing?" Hardy said, feigning indignation.

I knew Hardy well enough to know he didn't care about such things.

I said, "We'll call you if we need you, buddy." I caught sight of a soft glow emanating from his vest's breast pocket. Iris would be keeping him company.

Surrounded by the guardsmen, we followed Mr. Phillips through a maze of hallways. Oil portraits, mostly old Pylor men dressed in their frilly outfits, adorned the walls. Life-sized statues, some marble, some bronze, stood vigil within dedicated alcoves.

We entered a large—no, a very large—room. What seemed to be a repurposed ballroom with no less than five grand crystal chandeliers hanging from high overhead, the space was filled with Pylor worker bees. Although classy and made of dark hardwoods, there were close to a hundred mini office cubicles all about—each with a business-suit-attired man or woman doing various kinds of office work.

Grip said, "Okay…not what I expected from a space pirate operation."

Wanda said, "Guess pillaging and marauding is big business. And, apparently, quite profitable."

Many of the worker bees were standing now, watching our procession pass by.

Approaching a door, Mr. Phillips turned to face us. "You will speak only when spoken to. You will address the lords with courtesy in accordance with their high station, is that understood?"

I answered for all of us, "Sure. But can we move things along?" My agitation with an apparent bureaucracy that rivaled even that of the EUNF back on Earth was growing by the second. And I still felt like shit. For the twentieth time, I cursed Viv for allowing her to make me her lab rat—her amateur chemistry experiment. Yeah, I needed the Pylors. I needed their warship fleets, and I most definitely didn't want to fight both enemy and Pylors at the same time. But there was only so much of this crap I was willing to put up with. At this very moment, the Varapin were making new inroads—grabbing up Alliance territory.

Mr. Phillips, taking note of my snarky response, narrowed his eyes. "I advise restraint, Captain Quintos. Here, you are a guest. Remember that. And remember that beneath us, chiseled deep down within solid bedrock, are our numerous dungeons. They are already quite crowded with those that contradict Pylor law. I'm sure accommodations can be made for this sorry lot."

Fists clenched, I took a step forward, but Wanda restrained me by taking my arm.

"He's not worth it. Let's just take care of business and get out of here."

Mr. Phillips, offering up a bemused and all too superior smirk, spun around and opened the door. He stood within the entrance threshold. The manservant cleared his throat before making a loud formal introduction. "My good lords, I bring you Captain Galvin Quintos and his associates from the starship *Oblivion*."

"Bring them forth!" a man's voice demanded from within.

As Mr. Phillips bowed and then stood aside, we entered. This room was set up similar to an ornate formal courtroom—more stodgy portraits on the walls, wainscotting, and crown moldings. But there was no gallery for anyone to sit in. In front of us was a raised dais, and upon that was a polished mahogany bench rising at least eight feet high—seemingly more like an impregnable wall. And up top there, like presiding judges, eleven old men could be seen, each wearing a formal scarlet robe. Literally looking down their noses at us, the assembly of the House of Lords. Each shared the same expression—that of something unsavory, a bad smell that had entered into their realm.

Off to the side, a young man of no more than seventeen or eighteen stood and began reading off a tablet. "Lords, we have docket number 1523…Captain Galvin Quintos requesting letter of marque to commence operations within Pylor territory." The boy sat back down.

There were a few moments of silence, then some back and forth murmurs from the lords. The old man in the middle of the bench, who was mostly bald on top and had bushy eyebrows, maybe was the lead lord or chief lord, said, "Denied," and then abruptly handstamped something on the bench. He barked, "Next!"

I raised both palms in the air. "Whoa whoa whoa…that's it? Just denied? How about letting me make our case?"

The chief lord scowled down at me. "Decorum! I will have no insolence in this chamber!"

This really was like a courtroom.

"Please, sir…a moment of your time so I can explain how I, we, can be of benefit to the Pylors. Our ship, the *Oblivion*, is powerful. Dare I say, more powerful than anything—"

"Silence!" the old curmudgeon barked. "Of course it is. Yes, yes, an amazing vessel. And specifically why it is being boarded, commandeered if you will, at this very minute."

Stunned, I looked to the others in my group. Max was the first to look down at his Jaadoo ring—I did the same as did the others. When I tapped at the bottom surface with my thumb, the typical small projected status readout did not display. Same for the others.

"Your comms devices have been blocked." It was Mr. Phillips from the back of the room. I looked over and observed a self-satisfied expression. I was really starting to dislike this guy.

I yelled, "Hardy!" knowing he would be able to hear through the building's walls.

The rear chamber doors opened, and I could hear distant heavy footsteps. I inwardly smiled; it was never wise to mess around with a seven-foot-tall battle bot. But the approaching footfalls were not that of a ChronoBot. Not heavy enough, and too many of them.

What *did* enter through the doors were no less than twelve straining Pylor guards, each with a hand upon a robot appendage of the horizontally laid out, clearly deactivated Hardy.

"That's not good," Grip said.

"How'd they manage that?" Wanda said.

"We've been bamboozled," Hock said.

Other doors flew open as armed Pylor guards rushed into the chamber.

Hardy dropped to the floor with a loud *clang!*

The chief lord stood and stared down at me. He attempted a sympathetic smile, but it looked more like an expression of constipation. He shook his head. "You would have made a terrible pirate, Mr. Quintos. Here you stand, among the most successful marauder organization in the known galaxy, and you just trusted us to what? Play by the rules? To not take advantage of you?" He extended his lower lip out like a pouting toddler. "We're pirates, for God's sake, young man!"

The other lords abruptly laughed in unison, as did all the

guards. Behind us, Mr. Phillips had his own unique, high-pitched squeal of a laugh that could be heard above all the others.

But my mind was on my ship—my crew. I thought of Viv and Porter, Ryder and James. I thought of Coogong. *Oh God…the Thine scientist in the wrong hands would be a disaster. The quansporter technology!*

I just hadn't thought that Thunderballs's clan would turn on me like this. They'd delivered us here like lambs to the slaughter. Sure, Vince and his outfit were a slippery lot, but what about that honor code among thieves crap he had spoken so fervently about? I closed my eyes and took in a deep breath. Shit, I'd allowed the pirates unencumbered access to much of the ship. But not all of it.

I chided myself—*stay in the present moment.* Okay…I'd left Captain Ryder in charge. I could only hope he was up to the task of defending that five-mile-long dreadnought—unfortunately, there was no one on board who had much of a clue to her functional operations. *We really are fucked.*

"Take them below to the keep. And put them all in iron! At least till we figure out where to put them long term."

Mr. Phillips did one of his little bows, then said with a distasteful grimace, "And the…robot, my lord?"

"I demand to speak with Arlington McMasters!" I yelled as my tagger was being pulled from its holster.

The chief lord had already sat down and looked to be preoccupied with whatever was on the bench before him. "Demand all you want, Captain…he is a busy man. And you, I am sorry to say, have nothing to offer that cannot be taken by force."

At gunpoint, we were being manhandled toward a side door. It was then that I noticed the small, circling, somewhat larger than insect-sized object in the air. But it wasn't a local variety of a Haven housefly or a type of honeybee. It was Iris, without her typical glittering trail of fairy dust. The tiny fairy was making her way over to me, while not being overly obvious about it.

I purposely slowed, fighting the iron hold that my accompanying two guards had on my upper arms. Iris took advantage of the moment to land upon my shoulder. Standing on tippy-toes, she whispered into my ear, "Thy ship is secure, good sir…we art being boarded. While thy ring is not working, mine is usable."

I had to crane my neck to look down at her. She held up her tiny hand. Sure enough, there was a miniature version of a Jaadoo ring on her finger. Coogong truly was amazing.

So the old windbag up on the bench had bluffed. *Not bad. I believed him.*

I said, "Can you help Hardy?"

Max and his marines were now making a commotion—giving me more time to talk to Iris. More guards were rushing into the room. I needed to hurry.

"Hardy needs…Oh, I can't remember the silly words…a regret? A hard regret?" She made a pained expression while feigning little punching gestures to the side of her head. I almost laughed. But I was suddenly hefted higher off the floor, more or less now being dragged toward the exit on my toes. Then it occurred to me. *A hard reset!* I knew how to do that.

Theoretically, by laying my flat palm upon the ChronoBot's faceplate, I'd initiate a hard reset. Only three others of my crew had the clearance to do that. I, Viv, and Pristy. But Gail Pristy was no longer a part of my crew. So just me and Viv…and Viv wasn't here. Thinking of Viv, I thought of the cocktail she'd given me. What was I capable of? Anything? What had she said about the Gorvians? *Fast little fuckers.* I remembered how fast I'd drawn my tagger earlier.

I just needed to get loose from these guards. Even for a few seconds.

I looked to the marine closest to me. "Ham! Get these guards off me. Do it now!"

He himself already had three guards doing their best to secure him. He lowered himself almost down to a crouch, then suddenly shot back up—a volcano erupting with the force of Mount Vesuvius. The guards, propelled off their feet, flew backward. Standing ready, with fists clenched, Ham roared like a wild animal—taunting anyone brave enough to make a move on him.

Interesting that none of the guards have resorted to shooting us. Clearly, they have been given orders not to kill us. At least not yet.

Hock and Grip got into the action—extricating themselves from their respective guards. Like Ham, each pinged the scales at close to two hundred and fifty pounds; they came alive with a fury that had several guards dashing for the exits. All three men, towering brawn and muscle, were an army unto themselves. With clenched fists the size of catchers' mitts, Ham, Hock, and Grip were now walloping any guards unfortunate enough to be within striking distance. Max swung an old-fashioned haymaker, catching his guard with a blow to his jaw—toppling him over. He followed that up with a pile driver of an uppercut to another guard's solar plexus, bringing that guard down to his knees.

Wanda, not to be outdone, delivered a picture-perfect spinning back kick into the face of the guard behind her, shattering what had once been his nose. Blood geysered. Using an upward-thrust elbow strike, she took out one more Pylor guard.

I heard jawbones dislocate with that one. It was lights out. The man teetered over, smacking the marble floor like a side of beef.

Those few seconds were all the distraction I needed. My own two guards had stepped back as soon as copious sprays of blood shot their way. I spun left and then right, freeing myself. I dove over one of Ham's unconscious guards. I rolled and came up onto my feet, feigned left, but then spun right around two more guards. *Why is everyone moving so slowly?*

Three Pylors came at me. I leaped forward, spun, and planted a Kyokushin roundhouse kick to the head of the closest one. Without missing a beat, I stepped and delivered a Tang Soo Do front kick into the groin of another. The unlucky recipient, I realized, was none other than snarky Mr. Phillips. If only I'd had time to snap a picture of his surprised expression as he took the blow to his crunch-berries. Even as the manservant was grabbing for his groin, I was already jumping, kicking out with a devastating Muay Thai sidekick to the forehead of guard number three.

Landing close to Hardy's right side, I made a quick scan of the room. The full-out brawl was still in process, and still no weapons fire as of yet. Good. "I hope this works, Hardy. Because without you, we're not getting out of here alive." I placed my palm down onto his reflective black faceplate and held it there for several seconds. Nothing happened.

Zing! Zing! Zing! Zing! I instinctively flinched, hearing multiple energy blasts coming from behind me. Looking back over my shoulder, I saw Ham was sprawled out on the floor while Max, Grip, Hock, and Wanda stood upright, guards pressing taggers hard into their temples.

I was surprised it had taken this long. I let out a resigned breath. I honestly didn't have a clue how we were going to get out of this situation. It was then that I heard that little voice again. The fairy was whispering in my ear again.

"Hardy says thou should lean to thy left. Now!"

I did as told and leaned to my left.

The ChronoBot immediately rose up into a sitting position. Simultaneously, compartment panels opened—two upon his forearms and one upon his left shoulder. Hidden energy cannons snapped out into place. Bright blue Phazon Pulsar fire erupted. I didn't move. Nor did any of Max's team. Knowing the precise targeting a ChronoBot was capable of, it would only be a matter of moments before the enemy would be dispatched. It took all of three seconds.

The chamber was as quiet as a tomb. Now, glancing around, I saw that any of those guards who'd been holding a weapon were now dead. Hardy's Phazon Pulsars continued to pivot, to track even the slightest movement.

Chapter 5

Immediately, my—actually, all of our—Jaadoo rings began to vibrate. Ryder's miniature image hovered above my finger. I thumb-tapped to make the connection. "Go for Captain," I said.

I could see Ryder was standing within the Oblivion's under-construction bridge. He looked more than a little distressed. "You're alive!"

"You sound surprised."

Ryder nodded. "We only found out about all our comms being hacked after you left. Coogong discovered the precise backdoor network intrusion and only just now was able to make the necessary repairs to bolster the ship's firewall. He assures me it won't happen again."

"Any idea who it was who—"

"Oh, we know exactly who it was," Ryder cut in. "In fact, we have her locked in the brig."

The Oblivion has a brig? "I suppose I was an idiot to put my trust in our Pylor cohorts."

Ryder shook his head. "I don't think she was one of Thunderballs's miscreants. Yeah, she dresses like them, and swears like a drunken sailor, but according to Benjie, she's not one of their crew."

Benjie was one of the handful of Pylors that hadn't come

down to the surface with us. Hard of hearing, the middle-aged pirate was constantly asking others to repeat themselves. Thus far, he'd refused the simple medical procedure to have his ears fixed— some kind of trust issue with the whole medical field in general.

Ryder continued, "Benjie says he thinks Sonya is a Briggan."

"That's her name, Sonya? What's a Briggan?"

"Yeah, Sonya Winters. And a Briggan is another pirate clan. They're not anywhere near as established as the Pylors, but I guess they have their place among space marauders here in the quadrant. Sometimes the Pylors subcontract small jobs out to the Briggan."

"So, what's her game? Why screw with our comms?"

"That's the interesting thing. The House of Lords hired her. Apparently our little Thunderballs faction could not be trusted to go against their honor code. They'd made a commitment to you."

"At least until the next cage battle for clan leadership takes place," I said. "And how was Hardy so easily put on his back? Was that also this Sonya person?"

"Looks like it. According to Coogong, she's a magnificent coder. Oh, by the way, he wants to hire her."

"The same woman that almost got the lot of us killed down here? Not likely."

Ryder shrugged. "I don't have a dog in that fight. Oh, by the way, Coogong says the quansporter is now operational."

Good! I liked the idea of making a quick departure. This proposition, making a deal with the Pylors, had clearly been a bust. What I didn't like was being the first to use the repaired quansporter. To say the thing was a tad temperamental was an understatement. "Any issues with the *Oblivion's* sensor array?"

"No."

"Can you scan the chamber we're standing in?"

I watched as Ryder nodded to the crew member manning the tactical station.

"Okay…that chamber has been scanned down to the molecular level," Ryder confirmed.

I took a few steps to my right and placed a hand atop Mr. Phillips's head. The manservant, still clutching at his groin area, leered up at me. "Quansport this lad up to the *Oblivion*. If he survives, you can bring the rest of us on up."

I took a step away from Mr. Phillips. I splayed my palms. "Sorry, your sacrifice is greatly appreciated."

Mr. Phillips shot to his feet. "No! Wait!"

But the quansporting process had already begun. Block by block, starting with his feet, he began to dematerialize. Within seconds, he was gone.

I waited.

Ryder said, "Okay…according to Coogong…the little pirate arrived in one piece. Although he may have been injured in the process. He's grabbing at his frank and beans."

"Nah, I did that to him," I said, suddenly noticing a new commotion at the back of the chamber.

"Shall I have Coogong bring you all back?" Ryder asked.

"Um…Hold on a second, Wallace. There may be a new development." With a double thumb tap, I cut the connection.

I recognized the face of the man who had entered the room. His portrait was one of the ones we'd passed in the hallway. It was none other than Admiral Arlington McMasters. He was wearing a stark white officer's uniform. There was a colorful array of ribbons and gold medals pinned to his chest. His shoulders had fancy gold epaulets, and he wore an officer's cap with a shiny black bill. All in all, he looked more like a nineteenth- or twentieth-century sea captain than a twenty-third-century pirate leader—but who was I to dictate proper pirate fashion?

McMasters made a quick assessment of the situation. He scowled up to the high bench. Each of the eleven lords visibly sank down into their seats.

"You had to do it…you had to go against my direct orders."

The chief lord raised his bald head. "We do not answer to you, Admiral. And clearly, you do not respect Pylor's dual branches of leadership!"

My attention was drawn to Ham, who was now getting to his feet. There was a darkened scorch mark on his protective combat vest.

McMasters responded with a disinterested wave of his hand, turning his attention to me. "Captain Quintos, I presume?"

"You presume correctly."

"I am Admiral McMasters. I apologize for this…this fiasco." He shot the lords an annoyed glare. "Please, if you will, come with me. We have much to discuss."

With the exception of Ham's injured chest and a few visible scrapes and bruises on the marines' faces, everyone seemed to have fared well enough. Far better than the dozens of dead Pylor guards sprawled out upon the floor.

"We came here in good faith. Getting caught in the middle of whatever this is, Haven politics…"

"Again, I apologize, Captain. And yes, it is true, our two branches of government sometimes differ when it comes to approving new members. But ultimately, it is my final say as to who is or isn't inducted into our clan."

Above us, I heard several lords grumble snide comments.

Hardy's weaponry disappeared into its respective hidden compartments—panel doors slid closed. The ChronoBot appraised the Pylor leader. "I say we hear him out, Cap. Just look at him. Now that's a serious uniform." A cartoon-like animation filled Hardy's face display. Some kind of warship, maybe a destroyer upon the open seas—oversized skull and crossbones flag snapping in the breeze.

McMasters gave Hardy a confused, wary look. A look, I suspected, that wasn't all that different from my own. You see, over the last few months, Hardy had become somewhat introspective—less over the top. Frankly, less of an outspoken goofball. I smiled at the all-too-human robot.

The face display of his oversized, teardrop-shaped head returned to his retro John Hardy appearance. "You know…I'm liking the effects of that reboot. A good reboot is like, well…like taking a good—"

"Let's leave it at that for now, Hardy. We get it. You're feeling good."

"Oh God," Wanda said from somewhere behind me. "Maybe we should just turn him back off."

Looking annoyed, McMasters raised a halting hand, "If you're here to make a plea for a letter of marque…to operate with impunity within Pylor territories, these antics…they're not doing much for your case."

I sent Hardy a stifling glare before offering McMasters a repentant smile. "I apologize. Um. Look, we were not expecting this kind of reception," I said, gesturing toward the old men seated atop the bench. "Hostile actions taken against my ship…the hacking of my communications, disabling my ChronoBot, not to mention the violence against my team and me…"

"I apologize. I was unaware that these decisions—actions—had taken place." He glowered up at the chief lord. "With that said, I'm not so certain I would have done anything all that different." McMasters took several steps forward while eyeing the dead guards sprawled upon the marble. He huffed with a crooked smile. "Impressive, I must say. Tricked and outnumbered, and you and your team still came out of this without so much as a scratch."

"I'd have to differ on that statement," Grip said, gesturing to the slightly hunched-over Ham with his injured chest.

McMasters ignored the comment. "I've had little time to be brought up to speed on current, uh, developments. Truth is, I was expecting to meet with you one-on-one later on today, Captain. But one way or another, that ship of yours was going to be mine. To be a Pylor asset. Perhaps more importantly, your transporter technology."

I did the slow nod thing. The contemplating his statement thing. "Ahh, no. I think we're going to pass."

Looking astounded, McMasters flashed anger. "You're going to pass, did I hear you say? Nobody passes at an opportunity at becoming a Pylor."

I shrugged. "I don't need the headache. We don't need the bullshit that's coming with all this. What you don't seem to be getting is that we were doing you the favor. Not the other way around. And I certainly never thought being stabbed in the back was a part of your Pylor code."

The chief justice from above chuckled at that. "Well, no one said pirate life was fair, sonny. But for your knowledge, your Thunderballs clan…I don't think they turned on you. They refused to be a part of this, at least from what I understand."

"Oh? And the hacking of the Oblivion's comms…my ChronoBot?"

A different, elderly scratchy voice came from the bench, "Sonya is a contractor. Brought in from a Briggan crew."

That aligned with what Ryder had told me earlier. For some reason, I was pleased to know that the Thunderballs miscreants hadn't actually screwed us.

I thumb tapped my Jaadoo ring.

"Go for Ryder."

"Have Coogong start quansporting us back up to the ship." I cut the connection.

McMasters did not look happy.

I said, "We'll remain in orbit for the next twenty-four hours. You can decide if you want to continue this discussion. If you do, be prepared to make concessions. The first of which will be where our meeting will take place. On the Oblivion."

Chapter 6

Traveling through deep space
Captain Gail Pristy

Captain Gail Pristy continued to chew on the inside of her lip while staring up at the halo display. She'd tuned out the surrounding ambient noise, the tapping of fingers upon station consoles, the background murmur of voices within the *Hercules's* bridge.

The clearing of a throat pulled Pristy away from her musings.

"Stephan. Sorry. Lost in thought. How long have you…"

"Not long," Derrota said, glancing up at the halo display and the mesmerizing starfield blur. "We may have picked up the ship's trail."

Pristy sat up straight and took in a deep breath. She observed Derrota's disheveled appearance and wondered how long it had been since he'd taken a break. Her chief science officer looked exhausted. Which was how she, too, felt.

Having just recently been elevated from a US Space-Navy temporary captain's position to the actual pay grade of O-7, she was now officially a warship captain. And not just the skipper of any old warship, but the USS *Hercules*. The warship was of the latest design and one of the most capable warships within any of Earth's EUNF's still-operating space fleets.

Her mind replayed the events from months past. It had been a mere three hours after the battle—a battle within the Perseus Arm of the Milky Way. She'd been stunned. Galvin hadn't issued an invitation for her to join him. *Would I have gone? Would I have thrown away my career to become some kind of space criminal? A fucking pirate?* She unconsciously shrugged.

But it wasn't much later, perched right there within the captain's mount, that the interstellar call had come through from the EUNF US Space-Navy's executive five-star fleet admiral Cyprian Block. And Pristy had had to be the one to tell him. To explain to him that his son-like protégé had gone rogue. She'd watched as the lines and furrows of his face had deepened. His eyes, blinking rapidly against the accumulating moisture—no, a US Space-Navy Admiral would not permit tears to fall—perhaps later when he was alone.

Now, months later, Pristy's worst nightmare had come true. She was commanding this strike group of six warships. Her orders were to find the *Oblivion*…to bring the crew back to face justice.

"You hear me, Gail? We may have picked up the ship's trail." Derrota's voice brought her back to the present moment.

She nodded. "Talk to me."

"Mostly secondhand chatter. A patrol of Helcon-Reich frigates pursued an interstellar starship. It looked new, highly advanced, and big. A dreadnought-class vessel."

"That does sound promising," Pristy said.

"It gets better. She, this large starship, was accompanied by no less than twenty-five other warships. It would be a stretch to call it an actual fleet. More like a ragtag accumulation of mismatched smaller gunships, perhaps a few frigates, maybe a destroyer or two. The words *pirate force* were tossed out."

"Okay…two questions," Pristy said. "One, where did this pursuit take place, and two, did this Helcon-Reich patrol ever catch up to them?"

"No, they didn't catch them. Apparently the pirate force, armada, whatever, disappeared, probably jumped, before entering an asteroid field within the Eta Carinae star system. The Helcon-Reich, who are local to that area of space, have lost many a ship to that asteroid field. They know to keep their distance. As far as they are concerned, no ship could have survived long within that melee of spinning space rocks."

Thinking, she nodded slowly. "Thanks, Stephan." She looked at the man. Like herself, he was torn. Having to track down Galvin, not only a colleague, but a close friend, well, it was awful. "It'll be okay, Stephan. Somehow we'll figure something out."

The *Hercules's* chief science officer nodded, turned, and headed back toward the CIC.

Pristy looked to crew member Gallaher at Comms. "Inform the rest of the strike team. We'll be jumping in ten minutes."

Dan Roper at the helm raised his thick dark brows. "The Eta Carinae star system…that will take a number of jumps. Shall I plug in the parameters?"

Pristy sat back into the captain's mount. "Yes, Mr. Roper. Set our course. And check with Engineering that jump springs are charged and ready."

Chapter 7

Starship Oblivion, High orbit over Haven
Captain Galvin Quintos

It didn't take twenty-four hours for McMasters to reach out to me. In fact, it only took four. I had twenty minutes before he said he'd be ready to be quansported on board. Apparently, he was eagerly anticipating the experience. I didn't mention that the transportation device was currently off-line again, since MORROW had detected checksum anomalies during our last quansport up from the surface of Haven. Fortunately, we had all arrived back on board the Oblivion with our limbs still properly attached—no third eye added to the middle of our foreheads.

To be honest, I was a little surprised McMasters was so eager to reengage. We had, in fact, killed a number of his chamber guards, not to mention making a mess of those shiny marble floors.

I headed down to the ship's brig, an area of the ship I'd yet to explore. I figured I'd need to hand over Mr. Phillips, whom we'd quansported up to the ship earlier as a test. The area was so quiet, it was more like a tomb than a ship's prison. Then I remembered, so scarce were our crew resources, we'd been forced to use maintenance bots for security. I saw that there were close to two dozen cells, each one the same with a sink and a kind of toilet, and three clear bulkheads made of something I guesstimated was similar to the nearly impregnable diamond glass we'd utilized back on the *Jefferson*.

It was there, in addition to finding Mr. Phillips in an adjacent cell, that I had the opportunity to look in on Sonya, the Briggan crew hacker that had disrupted not only the ship's communications but taken down Hardy as well.

She was not entirely what I had expected. She was young—maybe fifteen or sixteen. Dressed in oversized green camo pants, military-style black boots, and a black tank top. Her exposed arms were so densely inked, it was a tad shocking. There were no tats on her face, neck, or hands. Her hair was as black as her tattooed arms and a disheveled mess—but purposely disheveled, because it looked strangely styled. For all the toughness and irreverent attitude her clothes and looks tried to convey, her large brown eyes couldn't hide the fact that she was scared. She had her legs pulled up to her chest with her arms wrapped around them.

I saw her before she saw me. "Ms. Winters…Can I call you Sonya?"

Startled, her brows knit together. Anger replaced the trepidation I'd seen in her eyes just a moment earlier. "Get me out of here! You can't hold me!"

"In fact, I can."

"Who are you? Let me speak to the captain…I have no time to talk with deck flunkies. Come back later if you want to clean the toilet."

I almost laughed. She knew exactly who I was. She'd been up to her chin, deep into the ship's records. She probably knew more about who was on board the Oblivion than I did.

"Is there anything I can get for you…while we decide your fate?"

Her whole demeanor changed in an instant. Suddenly, she was meek as a puppy, big eyes filling with tears, her bottom lip pouting ever so slightly. In a voice so quiet I could hardly hear her words, she said, "Please help me…I'm sorry. I'm…" She lowered her face onto her knees and began to sob. Her shoulders began to shake. The sight of her so vulnerable was almost heartbreaking. Almost.

I raised my hands and started to clap. "Bravo, bravo, Ms. Winters. An award-winning performance."

She looked up, two spiteful eyes glaring at me through long bangs. "Bite me, Quintos. I'm just going to break out of here anyway. Oh…and have you seen any of your bucket bots lately?" She put a finger to her chin and looked up in mock wonder. "Hmm, maybe they've been reprogrammed…"

"Reprogrammed to do what?" I said, the humor dropping from my tone.

She let her feet fall to the deck and sat back with a contrite expression on her young face. "You'll see. That is…unless you let me out of here."

I shook my head. "Sorry, no can do. I do hope you didn't reprogram the maintenance bots to the point they can't deliver your three squares each day. I imagine you'll be getting hungry later on."

She did the obligatory teenage roll of her eyes, but I could tell I'd pushed a button.

"I'll check in on you in a few days, maybe a week, to see if you're any more willing to be cordial." I headed over to Mr. Phillips's cell.

"Wait! A week? Seriously? Come on…I'll talk nice. I can be nice…"

I ignored her. I found Mr. Phillips sitting upon the integrated metal bench, back straight, very prim and proper looking. I opened his cell door and invited him to join me in the passageway. As the two of us moved away, I yelled over my shoulder, "Try to be a good girl, Sonya."

***

"This ship is…so stark. So…uber-functional. Really, Captain Quintos, I don't know how you can stand to inhabit such a drab and lifeless space vessel."

On our way to the nearest bank of StreamLine lifts, the little man, still fashionably dressed in his shiny gold manservant costume, was taking everything in—his head pivoting left and right, up and down. His discerning eye physically expressed itself with a perpetual lip-curled sneer. "I could do wonders with this milieu."

"Milieu?" I repeated. "What the hell is that?"

He clucked his tongue. "Milieu…you know, your environment…give it a certain *la vie est belle.*"

"Oh, you mean like hang some portraits of stodgy old men on the walls? I have to be honest…that sort of thing creeps me out."

I glanced down at him as we entered the lift—he was overdramatically rolling his eyes.

"No! Not old-fashioned portraits of dead men…I'm talking color. Tactile surfaces. Soothing surroundings that encourage optimum work consciousness."

A minute later, the StreamLine lift's door opened, and we stepped out into the ship's primary twenty-third-floor passageway. What would have been the equivalent of the *Hamilton* or *Jefferson's* Whale's Alley, Deck 23 was just as voluminous, with even higher crisscrossing overhead beams.

Gawking, Mr. Phillips stopped and took in the space. Several crew members passing by eyed the little man with curiosity. When they locked to me, it was my turn to roll my eyes, which in turn evoked smirks and chuckles from my shipmates.

"Flags!" he bellowed with hands thrust high in the air. "Can't you see it, Captain?"

"No, not so much. What flags?"

"The huge flags you're going to hang from each of those high rafters! Can you not grasp what I'm saying? Magnificent colorful flags draping down from each of those beams. The aesthetic majesty…" He placed a hand upon his chest as if he was having a cardiac event. "Captain…you must let me have this."

"Have what?"

"The interior design of your ship! What do you think I've been talking about?"

"You want to be my interior designer?"

"By the grace of God, yes!"

"Mr. Phillips…wait, is there something else I can call you other than Mr. Phillips? Do you have a first name—"

"No…I am Mr. Phillips."

"Fine, Mr. Phillips. Can we discuss this at another time? We're about to go into a meeting with your boss."

"My boss?"

"Arlington McMasters. He's waiting for us in the captain's conference room." *That is if he survived being quansported.*

The hand was back upon the little man's chest. "I am not dressed appropriately for an audience with the grand pirate of pirates."

Ignoring him, I waved open the conference room door and walked in. Sure enough, there was Admiral Alistair McMasters seated at the far end of the long metal table. A table that looked even more industrial and minimalist than the rest of the ship. *Shit*, now Mr. Phillips had me doing it.

With a slight inclination of my head, I said, "Admiral, thank you for joining me here."

McMasters stood and nodded to me. "And thank you for the invitation."

"I take it your first quansporter experience was satisfactory?"

"One I will never forget. An incredible experience. A technology beyond words." The man had changed into a dark navy blue uniform with enough sharp creases he looked ready to sit for another portrait. He still wore the colorful array of ribbons and gold medals pinned to his chest, and his shoulders wore the fancy gold epaulets. His officer's cap was lying atop the table in front of him. The man's loose-curled hair, the color of his epaulets, was long down to his shoulders. Something I hadn't noticed before.

I gestured for the admiral to have a seat.

Mr. Phillips hurried around to the other side of the table and sat next to him. Fidgeting, he looked like a five-year-old waiting for his birthday cake to be brought out with candles aglow.

As I took a seat at the opposite head of the table, the door slid open, and three more of my crew strode in. Bosun Johanna Polk, Captain Wallace Ryder, and Chief Craig Porter. A moment later, two more, Major Vivian Leigh, followed by Coogong Sohp. They hurried into the compartment—all hastily took a seat.

Clearly McMasters was taken aback by Doc Viv's appearance. He did a double take. She was, after all, a striking woman, even wearing scrubs. And like the admiral, her long golden locks were a jumble of loose curls—although hers fell past the middle of her back.

McMasters once again stood. *Always the gentleman.* He said, "I wasn't aware this was going to be a meeting other than just you and me, Captain. But I am pleased to have the opportunity to meet your senior officers."

I made introductions around the table and was eager to get down to business. The simple fact that the Pylor leader was here suggested he would be granting me the letter of marque. But then again, he had brought no satchel or tablet with him.

McMasters splayed his palms. "You have proven yourself to

be…shall I say, resourceful? I'm not happy at losing so many good men. You will make atonement for your actions."

I made eye contact with Ryder, whose unfaltering smirk almost made me laugh.

"What kind of…atonement did you have in mind, Admiral?"

"That you must now do more to earn your letter of marque. Please, take into account, our organization rarely, if ever, grants such a privilege to non-Pylor individuals, Captain. If it was just up to me, I would be handing over the document for you to sign right now. As it turns out, contrary to what I said before, the House of Lords will need to be on board. Fortunately, they have agreed to support the prospect with one minor provision. And if I can add… having their support will, in the long run, provide for smoother operations for all of us."

Bosun Polk spoke up, "What are you talking about. Some kind of test?"

"Yes, if you want to call it that."

"I don't want to call it anything. Is it a test or something else?"

While Doc Viv barely held back a laugh, Mr. Phillips looked aghast at Polk's in-your-face directness.

McMasters, unfazed, continued. "Captain, you have spent the entirety of your adult career playing by military rules and procedures—"

Ryder shook his head. "Uh, you obviously don't know Quintos. Just saying."

"In any event," McMasters said, "You're not accustomed to being a criminal. None of you are. And while we do pride ourselves on having a code of ethics, well, still we do dastardly things."

"You mean like the actions of the late captain Cardinal Thunderballs? Do you consider his actions on Ironhold Station, the abducting and raping of the Pleidian Weonan empress and her court, simply dastardly?" Doc Viv asked with an indignant raised brow.

The admiral looked down at the table, seemingly taking a moment to gather his thoughts. He looked at the doctor with sorrowful eyes. "What Thunderballs did was unconscionable. The man, and many of his men, had gone rogue." He looked over to me. "If you had not killed him when you did, I certainly would have myself."

I nodded without saying anything. I was reminded of the fact I still hadn't spoken to Shawlee since joining Thunderballs's clan. With everything she'd done for me, the least of which was giving me not one, but two operational dreadnoughts…I felt ashamed of myself.

"So what is this atonement or test you're talking about?" Craig Porter asked. Porter was wearing one of his many Hawaiian shirts. This one was bright red with a coconut pattern.

The admiral tossed something the size of a large marble onto the table. It slid and came to rest in front of Vivian. He said, "Alexandrite, the mineral chrysoberyl, is a gem we have back on Earth. Sure, it's rare…and it's expensive. But nothing like how rare and expensive it is out here in space."

Chapter 8

Doc Viv reached over for the glistening dark blue gem. Looking at it in her palm, she nodded. "Pretty." She placed it back on the table and slid it over to me.

I snatched it up and examined the lustrous gem. "I'm almost afraid to ask what this is leading up to."

McMasters said, "You asked what the test is…well, you're holding it. I want you to steal another one of those. Actually, a very large one."

"How large?" Ryder asked, now holding the gem I'd just passed to him.

"That stone you're holding is about nine carats. The one you will be pilfering is more in the neighborhood of one hundred and twenty carats."

Mr. Phillips did one of his hand-on-heart gestures, while Bosun Johanna Polk actually smiled. Evidently, the woman liked her bling.

McMasters said, "There's a once-in-a-generation spatial anomaly just now starting. Called an ionic swirl, it typically lasts three to four weeks. Spanning a distance of over two hundred thousand miles, picture multiple constantly swirling rainbows upon the black backdrop of deep space. Every prismatic color you can imagine in a dazzling display. It is located within the Gliese binary star system, which is—"

"In the northern constellation of Draco," Porter, Ryker, and I all said at the same time.

"So, this gem of yours is there within that Gliese binary star system?" Viv asked. "Is it on a planet, or maybe a moon?"

"No, my dear Ms. Leigh…it is on board the luxury starliner *Pecunious*. As I mentioned, this is a once-in-a-generation phenomenon. Affluent tourists on board are readying to make the journey to the Gliese binary star system as we speak."

"And why do you need us? This sounds like a job right up your alley. A priceless gem, a seemingly accessible nonmilitary ship; it's a pirate's dream, no?" Vivian asked.

"Normally, yes. But in this case, the Sultan's Fist, the most common name for this one-of-a-kind gem, although there are others, cannot be stolen by any conventional means. Lord knows we've tried, as have a number of other organizations within the quadrant."

"You're saying this Sultan's Fist is un-stealable?" I said.

Porter was holding up a fist while looking at the gem in his other hand.

"It's not un-stealable; nothing is if you have the right resources. The technology."

"Ah…and we have the technology. Our quansporter," I said.

The admiral smiled. He tapped the tip of his nose with his index finger. "Now you're catching on, Captain."

"That doesn't sound so difficult," Ryker said with a shrug.

The admiral held up a palm. "There are a couple of, shall I say, considerations you need to be aware of."

I raised my brows. *Of course there are…why should this be anything but easy?*

"First, no one can know you are there on board the vessel. Second, no one can know you have stolen the Sultan's Fist. At least not until you are far, far away from the Pecunious."

"Like a fist-sized gem going missing won't be noticed?" Viv said.

I said, "We'll be swapping a fake gem with the real one."

McMasters's grin widened. "I knew you were clever, Captain."

Raising a spindly arm and hand, Coogong spoke for the first time. "Why not simply duplicate this Sultan's Fist? That is a possibility with our technology."

I watched for McMasters's response to that as he mulled it over.

He pursed his lips. "No."

"Just no?" Porter said, looking dismayed.

I said, "It makes sense, Craig. What do you think happens to the value of the gem when it's determined it is no longer one of a kind?"

"Correct," the admiral chimed in. "After the theft, perhaps within a few days, or a week, we would inform the owner of the Sultan's Fist that they have, unfortunately, been the victim of a robbery. That, and their priceless, prominently displayed one hundred and twenty-carat Alexandrite gem is a poor fake."

"It's prominently displayed?" I asked with trepidation.

"Of course. The Sultan's Fist is the centerpiece attraction of the starliner. The most prized, most expensive gem in the known galaxy has made the *Pecunious* the one luxury vessel everyone who's anyone wants to book passage on."

"When you say prominently displayed, what exactly does that mean?" I asked.

"Well, it's right there upon the *Pecunious's* promenade deck, where passengers can stroll and gaze upon the stone's translucent beauty," McMasters explained. "It's on a pedestal within a diamond glass display case. It's well lit, of course. That, and it is surrounded by a Stinemark Lattice."

I looked to Coogong to explain what that was.

"That is a specific type of dampening field, not so different from the kind used by starships. Although a Stinemark Lattice has a much, much smaller breadth of influence. That, and it is virtually impregnable."

"Our quansporter couldn't simply lock onto the gem and—"

"No, Captain. I am sorry. As advanced as our transporter technology is, it cannot pierce the energy field of a Stinemark Lattice…nothing, as far as I know, can."

Admiral McMasters sat back in his chair with arms crossed over his chest. "And now you see why the Sultan's Fist remains the most elusive of prizes." He held up a finger, "Oh, and did I mention the ChronoBot?"

"Our ChronoBot…you mean Hardy?"

"No, Captain. Not yours…I'm referring to the ChronoBot that keeps a constant vigil upon that ship's promenade deck. I would dare say the passengers are nearly as enamored at seeing the rare and impressive seven-foot-tall battle bot as they are the gem itself."

Terrific…

Now it was my turn to sit back. I looked at McMasters—holding his stare. "We do this thing…this impossible heist, and we're in. We get our letter of marque, and we keep our Pylor support to go after the Varapin."

He raised his palms as if ready to object.

"No. No hemming and hawing, Admiral. We'll agree to do various, um, jobs for you, but I need your help. I'll be building a fleet over the next few months. We'll be absconding with a number of warships within what you would consider Pylor territories. Although, I have to tell you, established celestial world governments don't recognize those territories as yours. This agreement will only work if there is trust between us."

McMasters considered my words. "Fine. I will agree to those

terms. You'll get your letter. But Captain, my expectations are low in regard to you managing to pilfer the Sultan's Fist. So this conversation may be moot, yes?"

"We'll see."

The admiral stood up. "The clock is ticking. That ionic swirl within the Gliese binary star system will dissipate within two weeks. After that, the *Pecunious* will be gone. We do not have her next port of call destination. So, I suggest you get busy."

Chapter 9

It was well past midnight before I got to bed, but my mind was a tornado of bombarding thoughts. As if my life wasn't complicated enough just trying to keep this starship operational with such a minimal crew, now I had to worry about pulling off the most impossible jewel heist of all time. And then there was Shawlee. I still hadn't reached out to her. *Tomorrow—actually, that's now later today.*

That reminded me, I needed to spend some time with the Symbio-Poths. I then thought about the still not fully functional and still-under-construction bridge, and that much of this ship's operation remained a mystery to my crew and me. And then I thought of Lieutenant Akari James's all too appealing short-shorts and her partially exposed butt cheeks.

Screw it! I got up. There was no way I was going to get any sleep right now. I threw on a pair of gym shorts, a T-shirt, and sneakers. I headed out.

While the ship's bridge, as well as the officers' quarters, were on Deck 23, the vessel's gymnasium was on Deck 8.

Approaching the gym, I was looking forward to clearing my head. Because the Varapin ghouls had had little use for such a facility, the gym had mostly been assembled by Sergeant Max and the rest of the marines on board. There were free weights, several treadmills, stationary bikes, and a universal machine LaSalle's

SWM crew had pieced together from spare parts. There were also two MMA fighting rings, which I frequented regularly to train with Wanda.

I had it all planned out. I'd start out with a nice long run. As part of the reconfiguration of space here on Deck 8, a number of large cargo holds had been opened up for an oval half-mile running track.

Through the long wall of windows fronting the gym's exterior, I saw that it was empty. That was a relief. I needed time for myself. Not to fill my head with any more chatter. Like much of the ship during this third-watch time span, the overhead lights within the passageway had been dimmed to 30 percent illumination—which gave the surroundings a kind of eerie ambience.

It was then, coming up to the gym's entrance, that I saw movement—a reflection in the glass windows. I slowed but didn't look to my left. Whatever had caught my attention had been little more than a dark blur. I studied the irresolute black form. A form that was hovering, not walking. *Shit!* I was, of course, unarmed and in no position to take on a Varapin warrior at this moment. This was one of the fifty or so ghouls still hiding out on board the ship— only coming out from their Ebom-Pods when the ship's passageways were most deserted.

I came to a stop and slowly turned my gaze toward the still-moving, all too creepy Varapin. Fortunately, it was not heading in my direction. It made a left down an intersecting passageway. I thumb tapped three times, then once more onto my Jaadoo ring. That was my direct connection code to Hardy. By the way, I had no idea where he'd been most of the day. His image projected out from the top of the ring. Before he could say something probably loud and obnoxious, I whispered, "Get to my position, fast!"

I rushed across the passageway and made the left at the intersection. I could still see the flowing black robes up ahead. I stayed close to the left-hand bulkhead, following in a fast walk some thirty yards back. I tried to recall what else was down this way. *Damn. The ship is so damn big, I'll never be able to fully explore her.*

Up ahead the ghoul was slowing. Then I remembered there were several science labs down here. My breath caught in my chest as none other than Coogong Sohp calmly strode into view. I wanted to yell out. To warn the Thine scientist to run. To get the hell away from that vile creature. And to do so before the Varapin's Ghan-Tshot would rob him of his very life force.

But wait a minute. Were Coogong and that…thing…conversing?

I moved several yards closer. Yes, most definitely; they were having a conversation. While Coogong, looking far too relaxed, leaned against the nearest bulkhead, the ghoul continued to hover about. Both were making animated hand gestures.

Before now, nothing could have convinced me Coogong could be some kind of traitor or abettor to the enemy. But there they were, the two of them gabbing it up like two old friends.

Suddenly, in a flash of reflective pinkish chrome, Hardy was there—he had sprung forth from a nearby corner farther down the passageway. With wickedly fast reflexes, he grabbed for the Varapin's neck—snatching the now-flailing ghoul within his iron grip.

I ran toward the pandemonium, reaching them with Hardy holding his quarry high up in the air, while Coogong—stick-figure hands held high—yelled for Hardy not to hurt the black-robed being.

"Please, Hardy…you do not understand. Let go. You are killing him!"

I looked at Coogong, trying to make sense of it all. I said, "Hardy, don't kill him. At least not yet anyway."

Hardy lowered the Varapin down several feet and seemed to have relaxed his grip on the thing's neck.

"Talk to me, Coogong. What the hell is going on here?"

"Captain, this is Shout Coke," Coogong said.

"As in things go better with Coke?" Hardy said.

I rolled my eyes; Hardy was most definitely back. *Is that a good thing?*

"Why are you here talking with humanity's biggest enemy?"

Coogong shook his helmeted head. "Look at him. Shout Coke is very old. And frail."

"They are all dangerous…you know that."

"Yes, undoubtedly. But Shout Coke has agreed to help me, to help us."

"Oh really, and at what price?"

It's strange the things one notices in the midst of a charged situation. But I noticed Hardy was no longer wearing his leather vest. In its place was a long strap or throng necklace, supporting a leather pouch. A tiny golden glow emanated from the top. A top that was drawn tight with a knotted string.

Now totally distracted, I said, "Hardy, is that Iris in there?"

He looked at me but said nothing.

"Is that a tied knot? So, what? Are you keeping her a prisoner in there?"

He shook his head. "No…I would never…Okay, yeah, it's a knot. But she's being unreasonable. It's for her own good."

"You can't hold a creature prisoner just because you don't like her attitude."

Hardy turned his head to look at the still-squirming Varapin.

"Not the same thing. You know what I mean. Iris is a friend. She's gentle and cares about you."

"Fine!" With that, he shoved Shout Coke into my chest. "Hold him for a second."

Not knowing how or where to grab the ghoul, I awkwardly got a hand wrapped around the back of its neck area and gripped tight. Hardy in turn began using clumsy, oversized metal fingers in an attempt to loosen the knot.

"Let me," Coogong said in an uncharacteristically irritable tone. He used his nimble little fingers to untie the knot and open the small pouch.

In a dazzling blur of golden light and fairy dust, out shot Iris like a bullet—tiny wings fluttering. She zipped about, circling above us, and I heard her little voice. She was clearly upset. Then again I would be, too, if I'd been held captive in that little pouch.

She lowered down to my shoulder. With a pointed finger, she continued to lambaste Hardy. "I am not thy little toy to lock away! I have a mind, and I am a free person!" She looked up at me. "Is it not true thou hast freed me, hast freed all of the Symbio-Poths, master of this vessel?"

I opened my mouth to speak but held my tongue. *Did I free all the Symbio-Poths?* I supposed I had back on the *Jefferson.* I nodded. "Sure, Iris, you and the other Symbios are free. But I hope you'll stay. There is no excuse for what Hardy has done."

I glared at the ChronoBot. "Do you have something to say to her, Hardy?"

He shook his head.

"Aren't you two friends? Don't you care what happens to her or if she's happy?"

Reluctantly, he nodded.

"Then say it."

The oversized robot looked at Iris, who was now standing with her hands on her little hips, her brows knit together.

"I'm…I'm sorry, Iris. I shouldn't have done that. Will you forgive me?"

"No, never!"

I had no time for this. I had to literally count to five to settle my own irritation. "Iris, you know Hardy would never mean you harm. Maybe you can give him another chance?"

She narrowed her eyes and huffed. "I suppose I can give him another chance." She pointed a finger at him again, "But thou better behave!" And with that she zipped up into the air again and circled twice around Hardy's big head before diving headfirst into the open pouch hanging from his neck.

I let out a breath before turning my attention back to Coogong and the somewhat more settled Varapin—who I shoved back into Hardy's clutches. "Take him. Coogong, tell me why I shouldn't let Hardy snap this ghoul's neck."

"Because he has the answers…he is, for lack of a better explanation, my counterpart."

Chapter 10

"You can let him go, Hardy. Coke will not try to escape," Coogong said.

Hardy looked to me for agreement.

I nodded. "But watch him. If he tries to fly off, grab him." I saw that Iris was peeking out from her pouch, watching the unfolding situation.

"Captain," Coogong said, "Shout Coke is an elder scientist. He was brought on board specifically to make sense of the Gorvian technology."

I looked at the hovering ghoul. The alien was smaller than the others I'd seen. And even uglier, if that was possible. His obsidian black skull of a face with exposed white jaws had no luster—he looked old. Hell, he looked ancient.

"First of all, Coogong, have you divulged any proprietary information, military secrets—"

"Certainly not, Captain," Coogong said. "But what he has told me…the technological information he has divulged is beyond enormous."

For the first time I addressed the alien. "Why would you do that? Why help us?"

When Coke spoke, it was as if his vocal cords were made of sandpaper. "I am a scientist first. That, and I do not abide by my brethren's interminable quest for conquering. I will not provide you with Varapin strategic or battle information. But I can assist you to better understand the Gorvian technologies."

"How are you and the others like you on board staying alive without Ghan-Tshot?"

"Inter-ship power couplings. It is not optimal, but we have found a way to leach minimal amounts of energy. Although this will not sustain us for much longer."

Hardy said, "It makes sense, Cap; the ghouls I've come across late during third shifts have been hanging around the power conduits." He pointed up, "They run along passageway overheads."

"You can help us understand this ship. Bring her full functionality to bear?"

"Oh yes. This vessel is like none other in the quadrant, perhaps the galaxy. I will help you. I will help Coogong. But…I need Ghan-Tshot."

I grimaced. I couldn't believe I was going to say what I was going to say. Looking to Coogong, I said, "Is there something you can do?"

The Thine scientist looked thoughtful within his helmet. "The Symbios do need living—"

In unison, Hardy, Iris, and I all loudly said, "No!"

To be honest, I had thought of Sloppy Joe as a possible good faith offering but immediately doused that notion.

"Okay…Perhaps I can grow a simple bio life-form in the lab. One large enough to provide a life-force adequate for repeated Ghan-Tshot feedings."

"But no consciousness, and certainly not something that is self-aware," I said.

Coogong looked to Coke. "Would that be acceptable?"

"Yes. Better than sucking on power cables night after night."

I wasn't sure if that was intentional sarcasm or not. Something

I didn't think the Varapin were even capable of. "In the meantime, I don't want this…alien having full run of my ship. We'll have Coke's Ebom-Pod brought to this lab area. Hardy, can you take care of that?"

"Those things are bigger than me. Heavy as fu—"

"Then use a hover cart." I looked to Coogong. "Coke will need to be kept locked in a lab compartment. No field trips out to other areas of the ship unless accompanied by Hardy. Is that understood?"

"Yes, Captain. Thank you…I think you will be more than pleased with the results," the Thine scientist said.

"I better be. I'll check in here tomorrow to get a full rundown on what you've learned thus far."

I watched as Coogong, Hardy, and Shout Coke moved off toward the Deck 8 R&D Lab.

Heading back toward the gym, I was no longer in the right state of mind for a workout. And I was far too wound up to sleep. I strode toward the nearest bank of StreamLine lifts. There were two things I'd been avoiding long enough. One was visiting the upper decks, the Symbio decks, and the other was contacting Empress Shawlee Tee.

Stepping into the closest lift, I said aloud, "MORROW, take me to Decks 88/89."

Yes, Captain…that would be my greatest pleasure.

And there you go…that was the reason I so seldom spoke to the onboard AI. He—it—irritated me. Was it possible for an AI to be patronizing? Condescending?

"And I want you to reach out to Empress Shawlee. See if she'll take my call."

Yes, Captain. I'm sure you are aware she is probably asleep. The current time at her Weonan estate is the equivalent time frame of 4:53 a.m.

"MORROW, please just make the connection. I can leave her a message if she's asleep." My tone was harsher than I'd intended.

Yes, Captain…no need to get cross.

A few moments passed before I heard, "Hello…who is this?"

Hearing her voice, I froze. My breath caught in my chest.

"Galvin, is that you?"

I should have known she'd know it was me. Some Pleidians had what was referred to as a scopic sixth sense. Highly emotional beings, they were far more perceptive than humans.

"Um, Shawlee…yes, this is Galvin."

The silence within the lift was thunderous.

I stammered on, "I'm so, so sorry. You must think me a terrible friend. Worse than that."

"Galvin…my love for you is immutable. But, well, yes…I am disappointed."

"And you should be. I won't give you any lame excuses—"

"Oh, be still. I don't need excuses. I know you killed Thunderballs in hand-to-hand combat. That he shot you and you still managed to best him." I heard her let out a breath. "But you have aligned with the Pylors. Perhaps you have your reasons…"

"I'm a wanted criminal now, Shawlee. Probably have half the US Space-Navy is hunting for me at this very moment. But I needed to do this. I needed to fight the Varapin in a different way. My way."

"Normally, I would say one person alone could not make much of a difference. But you're the exception to that rule, Galvin. I've been waiting for you to reach out to me. Hoping that with your—"

"Going AWOL"

"Yes, AWOL, but that you weren't also throwing away our friendship. You have saved my life on multiple occasions. More importantly, you saved my younger sister from Thunderballs's inevitable abuses and violations back on Ironhold Station. Violations

I personally remember as being beyond cruel and painful. "

"Throw away our friendship? That will never happen, Shawlee. You are more family to me than my own."

"Thank you for reaching out to me, Galvin. You have no idea how much that means to me."

I felt relieved. Before I could thank her and cut the connection, she said, "So, how can I help?"

"Help?"

"Yes. Help you. The Alliance is failing. Earth is in jeopardy, as is Weonan. You wouldn't have thrown your career, your life, into such disarray if you didn't think you had a chance of success. So, again, how can I help?"

I thought about that.

"Now, keep in mind, I can't help you openly. I am the empress of the Pleidian Weonan people, after all…but maybe I can be something like an undercover pirate?"

I was both shocked and thrilled to hear her words. "I…I need ships. I need crew members."

"To build your own fleet, yes. Around that new starship of yours, the *Oblivion*, yes?"

"That's right. So I can attack the Varapin using tactics they won't be anticipating."

"I'm sorry, Galvin. I cannot arbitrarily assign Pleidian assets to your cause. Anyway, that sort of thing is handled by the minister of defense. My empress title is more symbolic than substantive. Although I still do have influence. The three ships I gave you… they are a good start?"

I was stymied. I did own goliath dreadnought warships. "Shawlee, the US Space-Navy will not simply hand over valuable war assets to someone they see as an outlaw."

"No, of course not. But I can take three of the ships back. Think of the Pleidians as being kind of cosigners on a loan. Yes, those great ships were given to you as a gift. But we didn't pay cash for them. There were loans taken out, financial institutions involved. The US Space-Navy does not simply get to keep those ships simply because you've gone rogue. It would be considered a default on the loan. They'd come back to the bank. Which in this case, I own."

"You have quite a robust financial prowess, Empress."

"You have no idea. But I most certainly will be getting those vessels back. Immediately. And Galvin…They are yours."

"Um…you mentioned three ships. I only had two, the *Hamilton* and the *Jefferson*."

"Don't be silly. There were three dreadnoughts."

What she was referring to were large and powerful dreadnoughts manufactured by the US Space-Navy more than a half century ago as a set. Until recently, all three had been in terrible shape, ready for the scrapyard. Yes, the *Hamilton* and the *Jefferson* had been brought back to life, but not the *Adams*. Which, by the way, was still in a sorrowful state.

"And you think you can get them back?"

"I do…all three are situated at Halibart. Halibart Shipyards was the US Navy's primary space warship manufacturing hub, situated in high orbit around Earth's moon."

"I'll leave that to you, Shawlee. Thank you again. I'll be in touch."

"I needed to hear your voice, Galvin. Be safe."

***

Reaching Decks 88/89, I tapped the illuminated menu to keep the lift doors closed. I wasn't ready for what must lie on the other side. It'll be mayhem. *It'll be ruckus. Pandemonium.* I chided myself for not coming up here before now. I thumb tapped Hardy.

"What's up, Cap…little busy here."

I heard the strain in his voice. My projected view was from his own face display optics. It took me a second to make sense of what I was seeing. Hardy was lugging a gargantuan Ebom-Pod down a passageway.

"I told you to grab a hover cart."

"Only pussies use hover carts."

"I've used a hover cart."

"I rest my case. I'm almost at the lab…is there something specific you wanted?"

"Just get up to the Symbio decks when you're done. I…may need your help." I cut the connection.

I took in another deep breath, held it, and then slowly let it out. *Here goes nothing.* I tapped the lift menu, and the doors opened.

Chapter 11

It's funny how you wince in preparation for what's coming, as if putting on a grim expression will ease the harsh reality of what is imminent.

In this case, it turned out to be young ensign Plorinne. The slightly blue, glowing Pleidian Weonan was standing there, dressed in his oversized US Space-Navy uniform, his hair cut extra short, and a pasted-on smile that made him look like he was ten years old. He most certainly was dressed for success. And maybe he should be—Plorinne had gotten himself in a bit of trouble back on the *Jefferson*. He had been coerced by the righteous and always meddling chaplain Thomas Trent into disengaging Symbio-Poth safety restraints within Convoke Wyvern.

Convoke Wyvern was a kind of onboard medieval quest game for the crew where there were knights and bandits, peasants and fairies, all played by various Symbio-Poth characters. There were a number of dragons too. Having the game's safety restraints removed was intended to kill the players, namely me. Again, Chaplain Thomas Trent was never really a big fan of mine.

"Welcome, Captain Quintos," Ensign Plorinne said far too loud and then saluted.

"You don't need to do that anymore, Ensign. And you certainly don't need to wear that uniform."

"Yes, sir." He saluted again.

"And if you'll stand aside," I said, "I'll be able to exit this lift."

"Oh, sorry, sir." He scooted to one side.

"I take it you knew I was on my way up? Even at this late hour?"

"Um, yes…I asked MORROW to inform me when you were coming."

We were standing within a narrow vestibule area. To my right was the entrance into the actual Symbio decks. "Is there a reason for such personal attention? I just wanted to check on the status of the Symbios…I should have come by earlier. Much earlier. I'm sorry. I suppose you feel I've been ignoring your work here. You handling the Symbios' programming and all. Trying to keep things, well, organized up here as best you can."

Plorinne nodded nervously.

I continued, "I guess it's pretty bad in there. You are here to what, warn me? Let me know what to expect?"

His dumb, happy expression quickly became one of confusion. "No, no, sir. I think you have it all wrong. I'm here to introduce you to the new crew—"

The lift behind me dinged, and the doors opened. Hardy loomed within. Plorinne and I moved out of the way so Hardy could join us.

Plorinne gave a little wave to Hardy and continued, "I'm here to introduce you to the new crew adventure, Caveman Glory."

"Caveman Glory?" I said, totally confused.

"I have to admit…" Plorinne babbled on nervously, "I didn't have the heart to alter all of the dragons into dinosaurs, and… well, of course, prehistoric humans and dinosaurs didn't inhabit the earth during the same time period…but this is make-believe, right? Meant to be fun. An escape for the crew!"

"Ensign, I did not direct you to—"

Plorinne threw his hands up defensively. "Oh, I know that. Sorry, sir, but the Symbios don't sit by and idle their time. They have to be doing something. They do far more than play characters, you know. Were you aware it was the Symbio-Poths that did most of the set design construction for the town of Clairmont back on the *Hamilton* and Convoke Wyvern on the *Jefferson*? Well, I had to give them a project. That or we'd have a real problem up here. Like total mayhem."

"Can we go in? Can we see?" Hardy said, his face display exhibiting a flock of animated pterodactyls in flight.

Plorinne smiled. "We have some of those in development."

"Well, you have dragons!" Hardy exclaimed. "Can we go in… can we?"

"What are you, five?" I said, still not sure if I should be irritated that Plorinne had taken it upon himself to direct such a large-scale endeavor without getting permission. But, truth be told, I knew I should just be happy I didn't have to be involved. It wasn't as if my plate wasn't full enough with things to do.

Both Plorinne and Hardy were looking at me. Waiting for me to say something.

"Let's go. Let's see what this Caveman Glory thing is all about!"

The hatch door to our right slid open with a *swoosh*. I heard distant nature sounds.

The three of us entered the realm of Caveman Glory. I looked up and all around with what I'm sure was a dumbfounded, drop-jawed expression. It was a vast space. Even knowing much work had been done to represent the illusion of a boundless area of prehistoric Earth, it had to take up a few miles of the two top decks on the ship.

The first thing that caught my attention was the heat and humidity. A thin fog layer wafted just above the ground. And then there was the surrounding thick vegetation—the trees and plants.

We were at the precipice of a dense jungle. There were also the loud noises. Beastly sounds, screeches and wails.

But none of that grabbed my attention as much as what was standing ten paces in front of me. I recognized her immediately, Elsa McDonald. She had been one of the Convoke Wyvern peasant girl characters. A Symbio-Poth. And she just so happened to be Ensign Plorine's, um…significant other. She was also dressed in something akin to what Raquel Welch had worn in the old twentieth-century movie *One Million Years BC*. Basically a bikini put together from a few strips of animal hide.

"I was going for true realism, Captain…the cast, well, they're all in authentic caveman garb."

Hardy tapped at what would have been his chin, if he had a chin, and displayed a complex animation of multiple spinning gears. "Hmm, yes…aside from the word caveman, which is considered overly gender-specific and quasi politically insensitive, I believe you have captured the true essence of the time period. And this Symbio-Poth female shows ample talent. Actually, she has huge capabilities—"

"Okay, okay, enough of that, you big cretin," I said, having also noticed Elsa's not insubstantial, um…physical attributes. "Hello, Elsa. And your role here is…"

"I'm the greeter. Or hostess." She looked to Plorinne with a shrug.

"Greeter works," Plorinne said. "Elsa will take the guests or players to the changing area to select costumes and weapons. She does the equivalent of what Big Gunther did back on the *Jefferson*. I think Elsa is an immense improvement."

Even Plorinne was in on the juvenile act. I ignored his double entendre. "Just hold on a second. What is in there?" I gestured to the all-too-spooky-looking jungle beyond. "Specifically."

Plorinne looked momentarily stymied. "The game. Cavemen

and cavewomen…although I didn't change their looks to anything like Neanderthals or anything like that. And the beasts, of course."

"What beasts? Specifically."

"Well, if you remember, there were a total of seven dragons back on the *Jefferson*."

I remembered seeing three of them during the siege on the *Oblivion*. The largest of the Symbio dragon beasts was called Sadon.

"I didn't have the heart to alter all of them. So Sadon and Trill are still dragons."

"Okay, and the other four?"

"Uh, reconstituted…but I really would rather you discover that for yourself, Captain. It'll ruin the surprise."

"Big surprise!" Elsa parroted.

I was getting irritated. "Ensign, tell me about the dinosaurs! We've all seen the old movie…there was a reason *Jurassic Park* didn't work."

"But those were real dinosaurs…well, I guess not real. But in the story they were real. Our dinosaurs are programmed. Perfectly safe."

I swallowed my urge to yell at the young man. Through gritted teeth, I said, "Really? And wasn't Hardy supposedly impossible to hack into? Why don't you go down and ask Sonya, our guest inmate within the brig, just how easy it is to hack into just about fucking anything!"

"No, she didn't hack the dinosaurs. I promise you that. We're like…friends."

Hardy looked over to Elsa and tilted his head sympathetically.

"Nothing like that!" Plorinne spat. "She's sixteen, just a kid. But she wouldn't have done that to me. She actually helped me with some of the programming…" He caught himself mid-sentence. Now looking concerned and not nearly as confident, he shook his head. "She wouldn't have…"

I intentionally kept my words just above a whisper, "What fucking dinosaurs are here in Caveman Glory?"

He swallowed hard. "There are thirty-three of them. There are the five triceratops, twenty velociraptors, five stegosaurus, two dilophosaurus, and one, um …tyrannosaurus rex."

I just stared at the young ensign, flabbergasted. "There is a tyrannosaurus rex on my ship, and you didn't think it smart to inform me?"

My Jaadoo ring began vibrating. I checked the caller—it was Bosun Polk.

"Go for Captain."

"Captain…we have an issue on the bridge."

"On my way." I cut the connection. I knew Polk wasn't due to start her shift for several more hours. Something really must be up.

I looked to Hardy. "How much of this did you know about? No, forget that question. Nothing happens on this ship without you sticking your big nose into it. Why did you keep this from me?"

"Simple…you expressly told me to."

"What I told you was to not bog me down with interdepartmental minutiae and details until we had an acting XO on board to whom I could delegate much of that stuff. But a tyrannosaurus rex hardly qualifies as minutiae and details."

"Tomatoes, to-mah-toes. Yes, I reviewed the plans for this project. I didn't see any blatant safety issues. I would have brought something like that to your attention."

I headed for the exit, then turned around. "Ensign, no one comes into this part of the ship without my express permission. Make sure Decks 88/89 are locked down like a vault. Hardy, you're with me. We're needed on the bridge."

"Ah yes. They must have detected the Grish fleet currently approaching the asteroid field."

***

I entered the bridge, seeing the day shift crew were already at their respective stations. Apparently, much of the construction had been completed overnight. The new 3D halo display, similar to what I'd been used to, was depicting a large area of the Eta Carinae star system. The big, flickering Eta Carinae star itself was there, as was the nearby asteroid field where the Pylor world of Haven was located—but it was a mere green dot in this expanded view perspective.

I looked to the tactical station and found Bosun Polk seated there.

"Bosun, are you qualified—"

"Yes. Well, sort of. I've been learning. I can go back to my old station…"

I followed her gaze to behind me. It really was amazing how closely the *Oblivion's* bridge layout conformed to that of the *Hamilton* and the *Jefferson*. It was what I'd asked for, and, evidently, what I'd been given.

"So, what's all the hubbub about?" I said, taking a seat within the captain's mount for the first time.

"This, sir," she said. The halo display was now showing a zoomed-in area at one edge of the asteroid field. And there, some two hundred thousand miles' distance out, was a fleet of small warships—perhaps twenty in all.

Chen, perched behind the comms station, said, "Captain, been picking up Grish comms chatter from that location."

Hardy was standing to my left with his head slightly angled to one side as if he was listening to something the rest of us could not hear. "Interesting…seems they have a Pylor informant on board. Not sure if he's a willing informant or more of a hostage."

He raised a mechanical finger, "Ah…most definitely a hostage."

Chen said, "The channel I was eavesdropping on just closed."

Hardy nodded. "Ditto."

Chen said, "We're being hailed. It's Admiral McMasters."

"On display," I said.

The admiral was dressed far more casually than I was used to seeing.

Chapter 12

USS Hercules, Warble 8 Star System
Captain Gail Pristy

Captain Gail Pristy was studying a star chart on Derrota's tablet when the Hercules, along with the rest of the six-warship attack group, emerged from its most recent jump.

Derrota pointed to the small star system. "The star's called Warble 8. A small yellow dwarf. The planetary system consists of three gas giants and two ice giants. There is life on two of the worlds, microbial…"

Derrota's explanation was cut short at the sudden blaring of the overhead klaxon. Then came MATHR's voice:

Enemy targeting lock detected. Multiple missiles inbound.

Both Pristy and Derrota looked up to the halo display. Pushing Derrota's tablet out of her way, Pristy stood and took a step toward the tactical station. Without looking at Lieutenant Darlene Mansfield, the third-watch tactical officer, Pristy said, "Why aren't I seeing them? I need telemetry, Lieutenant…location, speed, time to impact…"

"Working on it, Captain."

"Well, MATHR certainly can see them."

Derrota, still a step behind her and tapping furiously at his tablet, said, "Stealth fusion-tipped. I see thirteen, no eighteen—oh, for fuck's sake, twenty-seven."

Multiple missile impacts in six minutes…

"Got them!" Mansfield exclaimed from Tactical, and with a jab of a finger, the halo display split in two, now showing an icons-based simulation.

Pristy saw blue icons representing the US Space-Navy's attack group, positioned approximately ninety million miles out from the star system. Emerging from the closest gas giant, in red, were ten enemy warship icons. But her eyes were steadfast on the quickly moving yellow icons—the twenty-seven inbound, fusion-tipped missiles. Glancing to the right, to the real-time visuals, she saw there was nothing showing up.

"Highly advanced stealth tech being employed here, Gail," Derrota said.

Without looking over to Gallaher at Comms, Pristy said, "Inform the rest of the group, we're leaving. Emergency jump alpha-nine! Helm, get us the hell out of here!"

An emergency jump alpha-nine order was a prearranged jump command. One that would put them out some twelve light-minutes distance away—based on their current spatial coordinates.

"No can do, Captain," Roper said from the helm station.

Mansfield, her voice anything but calm, said, "We're sitting within a dampening field, sir."

Multiple missile impacts in four minutes…

"Battle stations!" Pristy shouted. "Phazon Pulsars…all guns. Target those nukes!" With a furrowed brow, she shot a look back at Derrota. "Who are they?"

Derrota paused his tapping and looked up. "Varapin. Their stealth algorithms are…well, impressive, to say the least. My guess, we're looking at, or not looking at, four heavy battle cruisers, four Savoy-class destroyers, one space carrier, and one…maybe it's a type of large personnel transport vessel."

Multiple missile impacts in three minutes…

"Captain, I'm not able to target any of those missiles," Mansfield said.

Gallaher at Comms said, "Same goes for the rest of the attack group…ship Phazon Pulsars are ineffective. Ma'am, I have five captains all awaiting orders…"

Derrota was now at Pristy's side. "There'll be no way to get missile locks with their stealth capability, Gail."

"Gallaher, everyone's to employ rail cannons. Constant lateral sweep dispersal patterns." Pristy leaned over Mansfield's right shoulder and whispered, "Come on, Lieutenant. Show me what you can do; remove some of those missiles from the chessboard."

"I'm trying, but…"

Multiple missile impacts in two minutes…

With more force than she'd intended, Pristy physically scooted Mansfield out of her seat and took her place in front of the tactical station. She saw that each of the missiles was bouncing back decoy-targeting information and understood the issue Mansfield was having. But there was…*something*. She'd almost missed it. In the rapid-flashing readout of numbers, there was one consistent string that occurred every four seconds.

Both Mansfield and Derrota had leaned in, watching Pristy's every tap, swipe, and execution strike on the board.

"I'm narrowing lateral sweeps. This will provide a more concentrated rail spike dispersal array specifically where I think the actual missile is."

Gallaher's sudden "Got it!" almost caused Pristy's heart to jump out of her chest.

"You nailed it! One down and—"

She cut the Comms officer off. "Stephan. Hurry. Get on the horn…explain to the other Tactical officers what I just did. Hurry!"

"On it!" he said, already accessing a comms menu via his Jaadoo ring.

Multiple missile impacts in forty-five seconds…

Pristy continued her work at the board. Three more red fusion-tipped missile icons faded from the halo display.

Cheers arose from the surrounding bridge crew.

Mansfield said, "Um, Captain…"

"Hold on, Lieutenant…" Pristy said, not wanting to be distracted. She was getting faster at taking out the missiles. She could see, now with the help from the other five warships, only seven nukes were still viable.

Multiple missile impacts in thirty seconds…

"Captain!" Mansfield shouted. "The Varapin…they're on the move!"

Pristy had gotten so caught up with railgun spike dispersal sweeps, she'd lost track of the proverbial forest for the trees. "Shit!" Sure enough, the ten Varapin warships were on the move.

Multiple missile impacts in ten, nine, eight…All missiles destroyed.

Pristy sat back, letting out an audible exhalation. She felt both exhausted and exhilarated. Now, eyeing the halo display, she watched as the enemy fleet slowly crept forward—closing in on them.

Derrota emerged from the adjacent CIC compartment, eyes glued to his tablet. She hadn't been aware he'd even left the bridge. And she also hadn't been aware of the enemy ships on the move. And there was the problem. She'd jumped at the chance to work her magic at the tactical board. But that wasn't her job anymore. She was the commanding officer of an advanced warship attack group.

Pristy got up and gestured to Mansfield to resume her duties. "You see what I did?"

"Yes, sir."

"Next time ask me to tell, not show."

"Uh…okay, sir."

"Tell me you've figured out how to bring down that dampening field, Stephan," Pristy said, dropping into the cushions of the captain's mount.

"There may be a way."

"Really?"

"Maybe…But first of all, I've been doing some preliminary research on this particular Varapin armada. Our own minimal fleet intel has it pegged as the Vanquishing Shadow Strike Force."

"Okay."

"It was assembled mere weeks ago. Their one purpose is to do exactly what we are intent on doing ourselves."

"Find the *Oblivion*," she said.

"This is Strike Force, Gail. It's the best of the best. These ten asset warships come equipped with the highest level technology they possess."

"Going after the *Oblivion*…not a bad idea." She knew her far smaller attack group was supposedly the US Space-Navy's top technology. But she doubted that. And she knew for sure, they were dramatically outclassed here. "You mentioned maybe you had an idea?"

"We can't power our way out of this dampening field. Not without burning out our propulsion drives."

"Enlighten me, Stephan. That Vanquishing Shadow Strike Force is closing in."

"From what I can determine, the dampening field is being generated by only one of those vessels. The command ship, one of the heavy battle cruisers, is called the *Bow Before Me*."

"So the Bow Before Me is who, what, we go after. But as of right now, this dampening field makes our missile ordinances as stuck in place as we are."

"We have one thing the enemy, with all its superior technology, does not," Derrota said with the beginnings of a smile.

Pristy thought about that. "Our quansporter unit?"

Derrota nodded.

She had had to plead for the fancy old relic. It was the original Sir Louis de Broglie quansporter unit that had been stored on the *Jefferson*. Pristy knew from multiple past experiences just how useful the technology was. With that said, this particular unit was old and temperamental.

"You're not suggesting we use that thing to transport onto one of those warships, are you?"

"No. That would more likely do more harm to our own forces.

Although you may find my suggestion to be just as dangerous."

"Go on."

"I believe there is a way for one ship to escape the dampening field. And with that said, there is no guarantee that that selected ship will even endure the process. I put the odds at an even fifty-fifty."

"Captain. We're being hailed by the Bow Before Me," Gallaher said. "A captain Flinth Shap, I think that's the pronunciation.

"Been expecting that," Pristy said. "We'll let Flinth Shap wait a few minutes. Talk to me, Stephan. Tell me specifically what you have in mind."

***

It was three minutes and twenty seconds before Gallaher opened the channel with the captain of the *Bow Before Me*. His dark-robed form came alive up on the halo display.

"Flinth Shap, I am EUNF US Space-Navy Captain—"

"Gail Pristy," came the grating Varapin voice. "I know who you are, and I know what you are doing here."

Pristy exchanged a quick glance with Derrota. "Why don't you just tell me what it is I can do for you, Captain Shap?"

"Oh no. It is what I can do for you, young human."

Without missing a beat, she said, "Fine then. Release my ships from your dampening field."

"I am not here to destroy you or to harm your crew members."

"We shot down twenty-seven fusion-tipped missiles…that tells a different story, Captain."

He waved a black claw dismissively. "I had little doubt you would dispatch those ordinances with relative ease. I was not disappointed. It shows I am dealing with an intelligent warship officer…one who remained cool under pressure."

"I don't know if you're patronizing me or just blowing smoke up my ass, but knock it off. What do you want?"

"Simple. You and I are after the same thing. I suggest we work together."

"Impossible."

"Nothing is impossible. While you wish to find the *Oblivion* in order to bring Captain Quintos and the rest of his disserting crew members to justice, we merely require the return of the starship to its rightful owners."

"Okay, I'll humor you with this proposition. How exactly would this work? And remember, I have no influence over Captain Quintos. He won't simply turn over his ship to humanity's greatest enemy just because I ask him nicely."

"But he will do exactly that if I have something he wants perhaps even more in return."

Pristy said, "Let me guess. Hostages."

The Varapin captain inclined his head to affirm her assumption. "It would be temporary, of course. I assure you, your crew will not be harmed in any way. You will be treated with the utmost respect. Your attack group warships will remain fully intact."

Mansfield murmured under her breath, "And that's why they brought along that big personnel carrier."

She was right, Pristy acknowledged. The Varapin had been planning this for some time now.

Captain Shap said, "You have few options, Captain. Escape from our dampening field is impossible. But know this: we could have destroyed your little attack group many times over by now if that was our intent. Make the wise decision. Save the thousands of crew members, as well as yourself. Perhaps you and I will fight again another day…but today, you have lost. Know when to capitulate…you have no viable alternatives."

"We could destroy ourselves…self-destruct."

Once again the Varapin captain inclined his head. "That is an option."

Pristy glared at the arrogant ghoul. He knew as well as she did, committing mass suicide was not the way of US Space-Navy officers.

"It's a lot to take in. Will you give me a few minutes to communicate with my fellow officers?"

"You have five minutes…after that, we will destroy your attack group and move on to alternative plans."

The display went black.

She didn't need five minutes. She didn't need five seconds. But she waited three for good measure. "Go ahead, Mr. Gallaher. Get the Varapin captain back online."

"Ah…I see you have come to a quick decision. I have taken the impetus to dispatch our shuttle crafts. They should arrive at each of your—"

"Not so fast, Captain."

The ghoul stared back at her, expressionless.

"Let me ask you. Have you ever dealt directly with humans prior to today? Am I the first human you have ever spoken with directly?"

"That is correct."

"Then you are ignorant of how we, as a people, do business."

"Educate me then."

"You would like me to take your word that the crews of this attack group will remain unharmed. That our assets will be returned to us fully operational."

"I have said as much, yes."

"Then we must meet in person. We must engage in the shaking of hands."

She watched as the Varapin looked to his subordinates off camera. A bewildered look, if that was even possible for a Varapin, pervaded his demeanor.

The ghoul looked at one of his own claws. "This shaking of hands…is it not a mere formality?"

Pristy stood taller in indignation. "It is how humans convey trust for one another. When we make such an agreement, we look each other in the eye and shake hands. It is about trust, Captain. So let me ask you: are you willing to shake my hand right there on your bridge in front of your crew? To establish an honor bond?"

"Uh…an honor bond? Well…"

"Or is honor not a concept the Varapin can relate to?"

Apparently, that had struck a chord. Now it was Captain Flinth Shap's turn to stand, more like hover, taller. "Honor is the core of our civilization, the very basis of our empire."

"Then you agree? I will transport over immediately. Of course, I will come alone. Unless you are afraid of a lone, unarmed human."

The Varapin went quiet, and Pristy was tempted to turn away from his deathly stare. "I accept your offer to come aboard. You will come alone. There will be one more precaution."

"And that is…"

"You will arrive here unclothed."

"You want me to quansport over there naked?"

Someone on the bridge unsuccessfully tried to hold back a laugh.

"Fine. Let's do this right. We will all be naked on your bridge." Pristy shot a serious glance at her bridge crew. This was no laughing matter.

She didn't let the Varapin commander noodle on the point. "I will quansport in exactly," she looked at her TAC-Band, "five minutes. I require a ten-second window."

"Window?"

"Well, yes…as advanced as quansporting is, transporting past defensive shields is dangerous. Would you have me killed while so close to our agreement? No missile will magically arrive within that short window of time. Now please, stop stalling. I must prepare for my departure." Pristy motioned to cut the connection with a cutting gesture across her neck.

She looked over to Derrota and remembered he was gone. He was already situated within the small, makeshift quansporter compartment, doing his best to get the temperamental device operational.

"I'll be in my ready room, um…getting ready." She avoided glancing about the bridge. She knew they were biting through their own lips, trying not to smile.

"Ah, Captain?" Mansfield said. "Are you sure you want to do this?"

She didn't answer. She strode purposely toward the adjoining captain's ready room. She waved the hatch door open and entered.

Pristy leaned against the now sealed door and closed her eyes. How the hell had she gotten herself into this mess? She had to smile to herself. She wasn't the least bit concerned about quansporting, even though that was no sure thing, or even about what she would be doing once she arrived within that enemy ship. No, she was concerned about being totally naked. Being ogled by a bunch of alien ghouls. Well, at least they would be naked too. That was if they kept to their end of the bargain. She abruptly started to laugh and instinctively covered her mouth with her hands, even though there was no way anyone would be able to hear her.

Pristy tapped at her TAC-Band. "Stephan…you have a lock on me?"

"I do. But I still don't like this plan."

"You promise you won't leave me over there, right?" She had slipped out of her uniform and was just now taking off her underwear.

"As long as their shields remain down, I should be able to retrieve you, yes."

She was now standing in the middle of the ready room, naked. Her arms self-consciously wrapped around herself. "How much time before—"

Derrota cut her off. "Their shields just went down. Five seconds, Gail. Get ready."

Pristy willed herself to drop her hands and try to look confident. She caught her own reflection in the mirror on the opposite bulkhead. She took pride in her physical appearance. She was slim, and certainly not curvy, but she had nothing to be self-conscious about. She needed to own this. She straightened her shoulders and raised her chin. *I've got this…*

Chapter 13

Starship Oblivion, High orbit over Haven
Captain Galvin Quintos

"Ah, Captain Quintos. So glad I caught you so early in the morning. An early riser, I see."

I refrained from mentioning the fact that I'd never gotten back to my bunk. "How can I assist you, Admiral?'

"As you've undoubtedly noticed, we have a few nosy passersby at the edge of the asteroid field."

"We've noticed the Grish gunships, yes."

"Then I would appreciate it if you would deal with them expeditiously."

I wanted to tell the Pylor leader that the *Oblivion* was not in any shape to go into battle right now—more accurately, the ship's captain and crew were not in any shape for such actions. But doing so would do little to evoke confidence in our collective battle-readiness capabilities. McMasters needed to value our contributions, or why would he provide me that letter of marque?

He said, "With that ship of yours' impressive competencies, a quick jump, a show of force, and presto…you can jump right back here…resume your preparations for the heist."

And of course, I knew this was just one more test, another hoop to jump through.

"We have an eye on the warships. If they attempt to enter the asteroid field, we'll be on them like white on rice."

"I prefer sooner than later, Captain…but as you wish," the admiral said, then cut the connection.

I scanned the faces of my bridge crew. They looked how I felt—*uncertain.*

"Let's review," I said. "We're not totally daft on the operation of this vessel. We certainly know the basics. Thanks to the Pylors, we jumped to these coordinates here within this asteroid field with little effort."

At the helm station, Grimes scratched at his bearded chin. He said, "Sure, we've got basic jumps down pat. If they're short jumps. And we're good with sub-FTL navigation."

"Weaponry—I'm not even sure what's available on this ship," Bosun Polk said.

Irritated, I stood and headed out of the bridge. Hardy caught up to me in two long strides.

"Where you off to, Captain?" Polk yelled after us. "And the Grish?"

"They'll have to wait. When I get back, I'll have more of a clue as to what I'm doing."

***

We'd arrived at the Deck 8 science lab within five minutes. I'd given Coogong a heads-up that we were coming, telling him to rouse the old Varapin. The science lab's R&D area spanned no less than eight large, adjoining compartments. All were separated by glass walls. Everything was glass or a diamond glass equivalent. The reflective sterile surfaces and sleek-looking equipment provided for an ultra-modern feel to the place.

I spotted both Coogong and the hovering ghoul at the far wall, where Coogong was writing some kind of formula on a virtual-gesture panel—that being our Jaadoo rings' projected equivalent of a whiteboard. And by simply using one's fingertips, one could write characters or symbols and have them magically projected, suspended in the air.

Behind us, more of the crew shuffled in. I wasn't the only one that needed to be brought up to speed on the functionality of this damn ship.

Doc Viv, looking perturbed, hurried in—something orange and slimy splattered onto the front of her scrubs. She flashed me a *What now?* look and took a seat at one of the glass counters. Next to enter was Craig Porter—chief of engineering and propulsion, followed by LaSalle, chief of SWM, followed by Arrow pilots Captain Wallace Ryder and Lieutenant Akari James.

Everyone found a stool and took a seat. It was clear no one wanted to be here, except maybe Hardy; he seemed to be happy just about anywhere these days.

"Thank you all for coming," I said.

"Why is there an enemy ghoul here in this compartment with us?" Ryder asked, staring down the old Varapin.

Before I could answer, one more person sauntered into the lab—accompanied by Wanda.

"Thank you for coming, Sonya."

"You make it sound as if I had a choice."

I said, "Wanda, thanks for bringing her…you can go. Or stay. Up to you."

"I'll stay. If that's all right?"

"It's fine. Look around, people. You are about to learn what makes this ship tick…how she does what she does. And perhaps more importantly, what she can do that we're not even aware of."

Akari James raised a hand. "Uh…did you mean to invite me to this?"

"Yes," I said. "With Captain Ryder's permission, I'm going to borrow you."

Ryder raised his brows, momentarily hesitated, then shrugged. "Sure. Take her. Until I need her in a bird."

"Borrow me for what?" she asked, looking bewildered.

"You'll be sitting on the bridge, front and center. Riding the tactical station."

"Ah…I'm not the kind of person who can sit in one place for very long."

"Then you'll have to learn. You're about as well-versed in space warfare tactics as just about anyone I know. I'm looking for people that can hit the ground running. Akari, I'm not giving you a choice in the matter."

"Will I get a pay raise?"

"Maybe. Now can we move on?"

"You still haven't answered my question. What's that doing here?" Ryder said, still glowering toward the Varapin.

"He's here to teach us about this ship. Think of him as the Varapin version of our Coogong."

"I like his robes. Retro Goth," Sonya said.

"Why is she here?" Akari said. "Didn't she almost get you killed dirt side?"

I had to stop and consider that. "Yeah, but I'm hoping she can be reformed."

"Uh-huh, right," both Akari and Ryder said at the same time.

"Okay, enough side chatter. This is our chance to ask Shout Coke specifics about this ship."

No one said anything. Finally, Porter raised a hand. "Okay… talk to me about the jump spheres."

Coke hovered closer to what was now an impromptu classroom.

"The advanced civilization that developed this ship before the Varapin had it was the Gorvians." He looked to Coogong. "More advanced than the Thine, even more advanced than the Varapin, they had knowledge of an extra-spatial dimension existing in perpendicularity to normal spacetime. This is why I call them the perpendicularity spheres, which is an oxymoron because spheres have no traditional right angles!"

If that was supposed to be a joke, no one got it.

Coke continued, "This is a dimension, let's call it a fourth dimension, not only of space and time, but also of pure electrical energy. Via Gorvian technology, they have managed to travel to this realm and bring back this strange perpendicularity energy. An energy now infused into the *Oblivion's* spheres. This is an electrical energy that does not belong here and is like nothing of our realm.

"By agitating this form of other-dimensional electrical energy with mass surges of power from our fuel system, the spheres are coaxed into taking the whole ship back to their own home, that fourth-dimensional perpendicularity. Once there, controlled micro-electric bursts happening in the blink of the eye jump the vessel through the perpendicularity, much faster than could happen here in our own dimension.

"Needless to say, motion and momentum are hugely amplified there. Then, by removing the electrical agitation, we thus disengage the spheres, and the ship, from the perpendicularity. The ship falls back into 3D space at its new jump location."

Porter spoke up, "We've been able to make jumps, albeit short ones. Anything over several light-years, and those perpendicularity spheres you're talking about crap out—are you telling me you have a fix for that?"

Coke assessed Porter for several long beats. "There is nothing wrong with the perpendicularity spheres. This is a simple matter of output exertion management. Am I correct in assuming you are employing all four spheres in parallel?"

Porter stared back at the robed ghoul. "Well, yeah…"

"That is your problem. The spheres do not play well together. A single perpendicularity sphere will jump the ship up to four light-years' distance."

"The *Jefferson* could jump six," I interjected.

"Ah, but could it jump right away after that?"

"Well, no…"

"The *Oblivion's* perpendicularity spheres are to be used in series, one right after the other. If necessary, the vessel can cumulatively jump sixteen light-years between charge times."

"And how long will that take?" Porter asked.

"Approximately five of your hours, Chief Engineer."

"You good with that, Craig?" I asked.

He nodded. "Yeah…if what he says is true, our problems were mostly operator error."

I said, "Okay, next. Let's talk about onboard weaponry and shields." I looked to Akari James, who today was wearing form-fitting, dark blue, Spandexy athletic wear. "Pay special attention, Akari…the tactical station on the bridge will be the area of responsibility for you, as will instructing the rest of the bridge crew."

"So this is a for-sure thing? I'll be planted at a console hour after hour each day?"

Captain Ryder chimed in, "Come on, it's not the end of the world, Ballbuster…we all have to make sacrifices."

I looked at Coke. "What can you tell us about the onboard weaponry and shields?"

Coogong raised one of his twig-like hands. "I have discussed this extensively with Coke. For communications purposes, I may be able to provide the explanations in a way that will make the most sense. First, we have what I call nullifier missiles. When contact is made with any given target, these interesting smart-missiles remove everything within the blast radius. Remove joined matter from existence."

"No, that's not possible," Akari said, shaking her head. "There's always residual debris…"

"Oh, on the contrary, Lieutenant James…nullifier missiles undo the fields that make up the very molecules within an object."

"So the material does what? Comes undone? How large is the radius of these nullifier missiles?"

Coogong looked to Coke, then back at Akari. "The explosion radius, if that is what we can call it, is relatively small, several meters in diameter. So no, they cannot undo the molecular structure of an entire warship, but the cumulative damage after several missile strikes could be, well…profound."

I said, "During our battle between the *Jefferson* and the *Oblivion*, these nullifiers were not a part of the equation. I think I would remember having parts of my ship…nullified."

Coke stared at me. His sinister, creepy face made me want to turn away. But I didn't. "I had not shared the knowledge of these ordnances, Captain. I alone had that Gorvian knowledge up to that point."

"And you'll be providing the detailed operating instructions for everything you're discussing here with us today? Deployment steps, best usage practices, and so forth?"

Coogong said, "I have taken the liberty of forwarding all the findings provided by Coke into MORROW's databanks. The bridge crew, with your approval, can start familiarizing themselves immediately with the tech discussed here."

Coke hovered closer to Akari James, which made her sit taller on her stool. Not one to ever back down from a fight, her face took on a more serious expression.

Coke's scratchy voice was now little more than a whisper,

"Nullifiers are dangerous. Not to be used indiscriminately. I am talking about quantum probability cancellation…the missiles' AI, at the point of activation, will decide what the various localized probabilities add up to. Taking something that is real, that is whole, and dematerializing it out of existence…that is a great responsibility. One that cannot be undone."

Akari looked at the ghoul with a flat expression. "Got it. Be careful what I shoot at. Been doing that with a good amount of precision for a good while now, Varapin traitor."

I watched the exchange. *Note to self; don't talk down to Akari James.*

Coogong interjected, "All of the information, in addition to being integrated with MORROW, is also available via your Jaadoo rings."

Chapter 14

"Next, let's talk about what I call the 'Baby Pulsars'…Dual Pion Pulsar Beams, or DPPB," Coogong said.

"Good. I like energy weapons; you don't run out of munitions for those," Ryder added.

Coogong continued, "The *Oblivion's* DPPBs will superheat most enemy shields and will burn up anything and everything within their path."

"Don't most conventional shields compensate…have dispersive heat nullifiers?" I said.

"A single hit from the DPPB will typically not bring down a warship's shield, but concentrated hits can disable shields relatively fast. The trick is getting a targeting lock and continuing fire onto singular locations. The DPPB system requires relatively short firing distances, or the beam loses heat to the vacuum of space. So while Dual Pion Pulsar Beams can be quite devastating, it is not a one-stop solution. As a side note, the system takes away valuable fuel, so that must be part of the balance of use."

Porter said, "Fuel. That's another question I had."

"That and the manufacturing of wormholes," I added.

"We'll get back to those, Craig and Galvin." Coogong said, " If you please, we can finish up with onboard weaponry." Without objection, Coogong continued, "Smart ordinances, hydro-missiles, which can be fired from any angle from dozens of stations spread across the surface of the *Oblivion*. They are clean-fusion tech. The only fuel, believe it or not, is concentrated hydrogen. We're talking cold fusion here."

"That's been around for a century," Ryder said, looking skeptical.

Coogong smiled within his environment helmet. "Not like this. Essentially, these missiles contain a mere dewdrop of liquid hydrogen payload, which essentially goes supernova via a cold-stacking fusion reaction. The resulting explosion is, well, devastating, albeit clean. Virtually no lingering radiation.

"I would say the *Oblivion's* vast stockpiles of hydro-missiles lead one to think these were the primary weapons of choice for the Gorvians, aside, of course, for Phazon Pulsar Turrets, which we are already familiar with from our times on board the *Hamilton* and *Jefferson*."

Coke held up two clawed palms. "There are a number of other weapon choices, but those are the ones I believe will be the most effective and utilized. Shall we move on to the *Oblivion's* shields?"

"Are they significantly different from any other conventional shielding?" I asked, wanting to move on to issues I felt were more pressing.

"Quite," Coogong said. "Contemporary shields work on electrostatic barriers; huge electric generators working to establish a massive potential difference, essentially creating a highly charged layer around the ship that acts like a giant battery."

"Okay…"

"As you get more and more attacks, electric shields essentially lose their charge and subsequently won't block incoming attacks. Energy weapons essentially just discharge the shield, whereas ballistic attacks are essentially stopped by 'lightning bolts' upon collision. Still, it is difficult to maintain charge, and it is especially inefficient for such a large vessel as the *Oblivion*."

I let out an audible breath. We really needed to move things along.

Coogong said, "But the *Oblivion's* shields are what you would call zero entropy deterrence shields, or ZEDS. Totally different technology, Captain. The *Oblivion* establishes a micro-entropic force-field band just outside the hull. This band is perfectly organized; think of it as flawless atomic chain mail. This web, if you will, is kept tight by many billions of spider-quantum-nanites—I call them Spidites—which sweep along the surface of the ship, always doing maintenance on the lattice/web with MORROW's oversight. Thus the web is always in a state of repair and rebuilding itself, keeping itself in the zero entropy state."

"Back to what you said…so, you're saying there are actual spiders crawling around on the outside of this ship?" Doc Viv asked with a less than thrilled expression.

"These nanites are not so different from the medical nanites, or Medites, you utilize within HealthBay every day," Coogong said.

Doc Viv nodded but still looked disgusted.

"So what actually happens when the ship is struck, say by a fusion warhead missile?" I asked.

"Whenever the ship is fired upon, the attack touches what is called a zero entropy point and is simply dispersed."

"That seems a little overly simplistic. Like a magic show, one second it's there, the next it's not?"

"The trade-off for the web's order, for that perfect latticework, is that the nanites have an excess of chaos stored up. The moment any attack hits the zero-entropy lattice, the lattice first deflects the attack, then the nanites flock to that point and release their pent-up chaos on the attack; energy pulses just flatten out to nothing, while ballistic attacks turn into space dust. In short, the perfectly ordered armor of the web deflects initially, then the stored-up chaos disperses any aftereffects. The nanites then take the new debris and weave it into the shields. Of course, they cannot work infinitely fast, but leave it to say, the *Oblivion's* ZEDs are far superior to anything the Alliance, or the Varapin for that matter, can touch."

I jumped in, "Manufactured wormholes. Operationally, how do they differ from those on the Jefferson?"

Coogong differed that question back to Coke.

"As you know, manufactured wormholes require the bending of the local space/time continuum. MORROW handles the complex computations. The perpendicularity spheres come into play here on the *Oblivion* to support that function. The main difference to what you would be used to with, say, Space-Navy vessels, is that the technology on this vessel leaves behind virtually no radiation trails in its wake. But mind you, the manufacturing of long-distance wormholes requires much in the way of fuel resources."

"That's what we need to talk about," Porter said, exasperated. "I think we're running low…"

That got my attention.

Coogong let Coke address this.

"We cannot talk about the fuel system without talking about the ship's internal energy-generation mechanics…a complex system."

Porter waved a dismissive hand. "I think I can follow along."

"The generators extract energy from dual streams of plus and minus Pions. Normally $+/-$pi-mesons are unstable quark pairs, are anti-particles to each other, and would tend to react as our old anti-matter fuel would. But by storing the two types of Pions separately and at extremely low temperatures, we can stabilize and confine them into an incredibly dense but quickly flowing superfluid."

Porter nodded appreciatively. "How do we combine them then?"

"In order to combine them in a way that isn't just the highly radioactive matter/antimatter combination of conventional fuel, each fuel stream has to go through its own Krystalization chamber, which is nothing but a section of the generator where each super-fluid is streamed toward a kind of tuning fork, one which is tuned for a perfect vibrational frequency such that the fuel is effectively reshuffled on the quark level, creating a crystalline beam."

Coogong added, "But it's not solid, mind you, Chief. It is a flexible chain crystal; think of it as somewhere between a stream of water and a whip; a Pion whip if you will. This process, known collectively as quark confinement Krystalization, or QuaCK, stabilizes the fuel and prepares it for combination and burn. The whips can combine in one of two ways and are shunted toward different areas of the ship for each; one for jump tech, one for propulsion tech."

"Shunted to different parts of the ship?" I asked.

Coogong took this one. "From the generators, the streams travel to all the different propulsion drives across the ship in twin conduits, as they still need to be separate. There are hundreds of tiny ones for fine maneuvers, and the fuel channels are more like wires than conduits. But if you look for them, you start to see them embedded in the bulkheads and along the overheads, especially in the more mechanical areas of the ship."

Porter looked thoughtful. A lot to digest.

"As you know, Chief, there are four primary plasma drives at the rear of the ship. These propulsion drives work by beaming the dual fuel streams at each other, essentially causing a recreation of the universe's originating big bang in a micro-fashion. This is why DPPBs are the perfect means of propulsion. For the many smaller, positioning thrusters along the *Oblivion's* sides, this yields immediate turns/rotations in open space. And when throttled up and directed into the main drives, well…you get your directed FTL thrust."

"So the fuel is Pion pairs. Got that. Where can we fill up the *Oblivion's* tanks with that substance?"

"You would need a specific type of collider space station," Coke said. He continued, "Once they knew what to look for, Varapin high command on board the *Oblivion* eventually located three separate Gorvian refinery outposts here within this quadrant of the galaxy. Each of the three, we'll call them helix colliders, are located light-years from the nearest star or star system and away from even minimally traversed shipping lanes. Clearly, total obscurity was the objective."

"So all we have to do is pull up to one of these three outposts, open our tanks, and initiate fueling—"

Coke looked to be getting annoyed. Something I found more than a little amusing.

"You cannot simply pull up and commence fueling, arrogant human!"

That brought the lab to a full stop.

"First of all, these helix collider outposts are old, very old. All three are well protected, having defensive capabilities you'd expect from a superior race. Only one of the refineries is operational, and minimally at that. The *Oblivion* has refueled there twice before while within Varapin control, that I know of."

"So, the *Oblivion* is an already known Gorvian asset. Won't it be accepted by the outpost, as it had been by the Varapin?" I asked.

"Your ship's AI, MORROW, is an abomination. It no longer resembles what the Gorvians utilized. Our Varapin coders knew enough to make only subtle alterations."

Sonya nodded. "He's not wrong about that. MORROW is a total shitshow."

I sent Sonya as close to a parental glare as I imagined one would look like. She chuckled and rolled her eyes.

Coogong said, "I apologize. My attempts to modify MOR-

ROW have been fraught with setbacks."

"News flash…I've offered to help."

"That's coming from the same person who tried to get us all killed," Akari chimed back.

"Get real. I never wanted to kill everyone on board this big tub, well…maybe you, Lady James. You're starting to bother me."

"Lady James?" Akari said.

"Enough!" I said. "The two of you are acting like children."

"She started it," Sonya said.

"Sonya, you need to decide what you want," I said. "Maybe this isn't the best time to deal with this, but when would be? You certainly wouldn't fit in down on Haven."

"Yeah, I can just see her wearing long gowns and petticoats," Akari said with a sneer.

"So do we send you back to your Briggan clan? You were working for them, right?"

She suddenly looked uncomfortable and shifted on her stool. She pursed her lips. "I wouldn't say I worked for them, per se. More like took it upon myself to try to, um, impress certain high-er-ups within the clan that I would be a worthwhile addition."

"So you're not an actual Briggan?" Doc Viv asked, her voice nonthreatening.

"I should have been!" the teenager shot back. She blinked away tears. "My father, my now-dead father, was a kind of traitor to the organization. I don't know the whole stupid story. It was a total clusterfuck…and I don't want to talk about it. I thought I could, I don't know, prove myself worthy."

"So again, I'm asking you…do you want me to return you to—"

"No! I have no place, no one to be returned to!"

"Your mother?" Viv asked.

Sonya shot angry energy beams from her eyes. "Lady, how

many ways do I need to say it? I HAVE NO ONE!"

Even Akari looked saddened by her words. Then she said, "Well, if you weren't such a self-absorbed brat, maybe you could have someone and have a place somewhere."

Sonya, her skinny arms wrapped around herself, just stared down at the deck. She was no longer engaging in this conversation

"Let's move on. Coke, can you help us with the outpost? The refinery?"

"I can try…it means breaching what is called a labyrinth network screen—"

"I'll get us past the LNS," Sonya quietly murmured, eyes still steadfast on the deck.

"What was that, Ms. Winters? Did you say something?" I asked.

Head still lowered, her eyes looked up to me. "You heard me."

And there it was. I had a choice to make. Trust the irreverent teenager genius or not. Make her a part of this crew, or send her back to her below decks cell.

Chapter 15

On the way back to the bridge with both Hardy and Lieutenant Akari James, I'd gone quiet, ruminating over the information provided by Coogong and Coke.

Hardy said something, and Akari agreed with him.

I stopped. "What was that? What did you say?"

"We need to purge this ship of the Varapin stowaways," Hardy said.

"I couldn't agree more…creepy fuckers lurking around at night. What's to keep them from making a united stand and trying to take the ship?" Akari said.

"From what I've gathered, the stowaways, as you put it, aren't exactly the cream of the crop Varapin warriors," I said. "They're mostly hiding and trying not to be noticed. Yes, we need to deal with them…and Bosun Polk is putting together a kind of neighborhood watch thing—"

"We have fifty murderous ghouls floating around this ship, and all you've come up with is a neighborhood watch?" Akari said, looking flabbergasted.

"Actually, the bosun came up with that idea. I don't have a clue what can be done." I looked to Hardy. "You have any ideas? You said your sensors can't detect the Varapin when they're in their Ebom-Pods."

We entered the bridge together.

"Ah, Captain, I was just going to contact you. We have those Grish gunships slowly moving into the asteroid field. They seem to be following a prescribed course," Bosun Polk said.

"No doubt they've motivated their Pylor hostage to provide that information," I said.

"At least he or she hasn't given the jump coordinates," Grimes added from the helm station.

I took the captain's mount and gestured to Polk. "Lieutenant Akari James will be sharing the tactical station with you for the foreseeable future. Please help her get familiarized with the board."

"Um, okay…so I've been replaced?" Polk said.

I tore my eyes away from the halo display. "Bosun Polk, a ship this size, hell, any starship, requires multiple day/night shifts. We can ill afford to have just one still untrained tactical officer on the bridge. The lieutenant brings with her a wealth of combat expertise, while you can share with her the various bridge functions and operations. Work together; we're a team here…or at least we're supposed to be."

I put my attention back on the display. One after another, the Grish gunships were making their way through the maze of spinning rocks. Even now, it would have been impossible for the squadron to have made it as far as it had without having lost several vessels due to asteroid impacts.

Grimes said, "At this rate, it'll take them weeks to reach Haven."

Chen shook his head. "The problem is bigger than that though. This course they are following can be relayed back to Grish command, providing a road map to Haven itself. Hell, that would be—"

"That would be the end of the Pylors' top-secret hideout," I said.

"Can't we quansport Hardy onto that lead gunship, have him

grab the hostage, and quansport back?" Akari asked with a look at me over her shoulder.

Hardy teetered his head one way and then the other. "Probably not from this distance. Between Eta Carinae's fluctuating radiation, the innumerable tumbling asteroids, and the simple fact the device is so unstable, it wouldn't be a mission I'd jump to volunteer for, if you'll excuse the pun."

I couldn't think of any other means of stopping that attack group. Unless…"Look, clearly they're following a road map, yes? A tried and true pathway to navigate through the field."

Hardy said, "Correctamundo."

"So, can we change that aspect? Switch up some of the obstacles they'll be approaching? Put an asteroid in their path?"

"It would have to be large enough that simple weapons fire couldn't pulverize that asteroid or multiple asteroids," Akari said.

Hardy said, "If you're going to suggest we attempt using the quansporter to transport those asteroids, just know it won't work."

"Why not?"

"Too much interference, and the sheer mass would be a problem," Hardy said.

I leaned back and concentrated. There had to be a way. "Hardy, can you scan the asteroid field?"

"No problem."

"I mean really scan the asteroid field, all the objects, including their magnetic fields. Their individual trajectories. All of it?"

A complex spinning of animated gears came alive on his face display. "Done and…done."

I stood and stepped down from the slightly raised captain's mount. I felt the eyes of the bridge crew on me as I started to pace.

"How's your game of billiards, Hardy?"

It didn't take long for the ChronoBot or the rest of the bridge crew to catch my meaning.

"What I'm proposing is that with your expert detailed scans of the field, you can calculate which of the nearest asteroids can be propelled into an adjacent asteroid, then another, and then another... "

"A chain reaction that will alter the known pathway toward Haven," Chen said.

I nodded.

Akari smiled. "I like it. But it'll certainly throw a wrench into the works for the hundreds of Pylor ships that don't have jump capability."

"Your new admiral friend won't be very happy about that," Polk murmured under her breath.

I nodded. But the admiral was not a friend. "I'm sure he'd prefer that over having Haven's whereabouts broadcast out into the four corners of the galaxy."

I looked to Hardy. He still hadn't answered my question.

"Moving an asteroid large enough to bring about the cascading effect you're looking for would require an immense amount of mass displacement. The physics, the kinetic energy of an object, in this case a nearby asteroid, is defined as the work needed to accelerate that rock's mass from rest to its required impact velocity."

"So? Can it be done?"

"Let me do some modeling."

The visuals on the halo display changed to a 3D animation with Haven at the middle of all the moving and spinning individual asteroids. The detail Hardy was displaying was phenomenal. He then added two more elements into the artistry—the Grish attack group and the *Oblivion*.

Immediately, the mock *Oblivion* fired a missile at one of the nearest and largest asteroids to the ship. The result was an impressive blast. Sure, the asteroid was propelled away and initiated the necessary cascading effect, but the magically held at bay asteroids nearest to Haven became unstable. Soon they were tearing into the Haven like fired buckshot into a melon.

The simulated modeling continued, a different nearby asteroid being targeted each time. Although the results varied, each time Haven was if not destroyed, so battered no one would have survived the resulting catastrophe.

After thirteen simulated models, Hardy said, "This was a good idea, but a dangerous proposition, Cap. Any other ideas up your sleeve?"

Akari spun around. "Why are you only targeting the local asteroids? Didn't you watch the ghoul's boring presentation? The *Oblivion's* hydro-missiles provide for substantial explosive yields, but they're also smart-missiles. You don't need to concentrate fire on any of the nearby asteroids; you can guide them far into the field and pick your target somewhere deeper in there."

Hardy recommenced his simulations using Akari's suggestion. We watched as a dispatched hydro-missile wound its way through thousands of miles of spinning rocks before finding its target. The explosion was enough to propel the asteroid into another asteroid, but the cascading effect worked in the wrong direction, ultimately causing the destruction of Haven—again.

"Keep trying," Akari said, now standing with her hands on her hips.

Hardy kept the simulations going, which were now taking place at an ever-accelerating pace. One after another, the results varied, none affecting the intricate pathway being utilized by the progressing Grish gunships.

When I was about to call a halt to the seemingly futile exercise, the simulations suddenly froze up on the halo display.

"What happened?" I said.

Akari, smiling with an ear to ear grin, said, "That one worked. That's what happened, Galvin!"

I didn't like that she'd used my first name here on the bridge. I turned to Hardy. "Really? That one worked? It caused the necessary cascading effect to alter the—"

"Yes, well…I would have tried that scenario on my own… eventually," Hardy said defensively.

"Uh-huh. And we can deploy one of these hydro-missiles?"

"MORROW handles the missile programming, of course," Akari said. "Now that Hardy did all the heavy lifting," she said, looking up to the ChronoBot.

Hardy didn't respond to the lieutenant's praise. "Captain, the asteroid field is a dynamic, always-moving thing; this last successful model will not stay accurate for targeting long."

"So we need to do this like now? Even though we've never fired a damn missile, or anything, from this ship? A missile that may in fact destroy Haven or even us if your calculations are off?"

"My calculations were correct three minutes and thirteen seconds ago."

I eyed the continuing snake-like progression of the Grish gunships, slowly moving farther and farther into the asteroid field.

Bosun Polk said, "Captain, this is a big decision. Protocol dictates we contact Admiral McMasters. This greatly affects his world. Navigating his fleets through the field."

"And what if that last simulation was the only means to stop the Grish?"

The bosun had no answer to that.

"Tactical…have MORROW target that asteroid using Hardy's analyses…fire one hydro-missile."

Chapter 16

Captain Gail Pristy

She felt the familiar unsettling sensation throughout her body as the quansporting process initiated. Pristy had a split-second of reservations—*what the hell am I doing?*

All too soon, she was rematerializing, stark naked, within the bridge of the *Bow Before Me*.

Immediately, she was on guard for an attack of some kind. The ship's command center was smaller than she'd expected, but all her attention was on the one hovering a foot off the deck in front of her. *Oh God, he's…naked too.* She wanted to tell Captain Flinth Shap to put his robes back on, screw what she'd said before. The stripped-down alien was a disgusting sight, a rack of skeletal bones covered by thin, sagging skin just as black as his skull-like head. A quick glance about the space told her there were no less than ten others, all naked, situated around the bridge.

The seconds ticked by, and she'd already wasted three. How long before they would apprehend her? She had mere moments to act—her window of time was closing.

Captain Flinth Shap was already moving, hovering forward with his disgusting clawed hand rising—eager to get this human honor tradition over with. Pristy thought it interesting he was actually going through with it. The plan she and Derrota had come up with cycled through her mind. The depiction of MORROW's surprisingly accurate standard Varapin ship schematics had told her precisely where she needed to go. She'd studied what each and every control interface did within this compartment. Three consoles over to her right was the *Bow Before Me's* tactical station. If her and Derrota's calculations were correct, Pristy had a mere eight to ten seconds to do what needed to be done here. After that, she would be killed—probably shot.

Raising her own hand, as if to shake the approaching rack of bone's claw, she suddenly leaped. With four years of high school gymnastics under her belt, the ensuing flip, called a standing front tuck, had her vaulting over the nearest console and landing atop the second-row console.

The ghoul at that station moved fast and reached for her. That prompted Pristy's next maneuver, named for the infamous gymnast Mitsuo Tsukahara. She vaulted backward with a half turn to her left, tucking her legs in tight while praying her acrobatic abilities hadn't dissipated over the last ten years or so. They hadn't, and she stuck the landing true to form. That, and she was now standing directly in front of the tactical board.

Without hesitation, she went to work. First, she ensured the ship's shields were in fact still down. Second, she locked them into that setting by entering in a new seven-digit passcode. Six seconds had elapsed. Captain Flinth Shap was screeching out commands while naked ghouls were nearly upon Pristy. She had mere seconds to do the impossible. Her fingers flew over the board, twice making the same mistake using a double tap instead of a triple tap. She needed to not only bring down the dampening field but lock in those settings as well.

A bony claw was upon her shoulder, hard, sharp digits penetrating, ripping at her flesh. Another claw grabbed a fistful of her hair and was trying to pull her head backward. Pristy had three more input strokes to make, just three tiny movements of her forefinger—but she was being pulled away. The tactical board was now beyond her reach. Forced to take a step backward, tears filled her eyes—*I was so close.*

Thinking it was the accumulated moisture that was disrupting her vision, she blinked and went slack-jawed. Segment block by segment block, someone was quansporting onto the bridge on the opposite side of the tactical station.

Lieutenant Darlene Mansfield, now the only one fully dressed on the bridge, looked about the space with eyes as wide as dinner plates.

Head still being forced back, Pristy yelled, "Tactical's right in front of you. Enter the last three keystrokes and then set the new passcode!"

By the time she'd barked off the orders, Pristy was being thrown to the deck, unable to see what was happening.

Mansfield's high-pitched scream was an all too clear revelation that their plan had failed. The Varapin had achieved exactly what they'd come for. Hostages. Pristy…a bargaining chip that Galvin could not turn a blind eye to. The pain in her upper back and shoulders was excruciating. Blood seeped from her numerous stabs, slashes, and gashes. Consciousness was fading. And then she felt that familiar feeling in the pit of her stomach. *I'm being quansported …*

As previously planned, Derrota quansported Pristy, and apparently Mansfield, back onto the *Hercules's* bridge. Lightheaded, she staggered, almost losing her balance. Someone draped a cover over her back, which made her yelp in pain. She lowered it off her shoulders while wrapping it around herself like a large bath towel. She saw the ship's doctor was working on Mansfield's prone form, lying upon the deck.

Pristy moved toward the captain's mount with her eyes pinned to the halo display. There was nothing but black space and the twinkle of a million distant stars.

She heard running footsteps from behind and turned to see Derrota entering the bridge.

She took her seat, careful not to sit back. "Somebody give me a sitrep."

Derrota, out of breath, used the captain's mount armrest for support while he caught his breath.

"We made it…we all jumped?" Pristy said, looking about the bridge for some

indication things had turned out as planned.

"We watched your, um, well, performance on the halo display."

"Wait, they broadcast me—" She cut herself short. Her naked acrobatics should be the least of her worries.

"The *Hercules* alone was able to jump away. And prior to doing so, it sustained extensive damage to the propulsion system."

It was only then that Pristy became aware of the lack of drive vibration coming up from the deck.

"No sooner had you arrived on the Varapin ship's bridge than it occurred to me you might need some help. I gambled that it was the right thing to do. We hadn't talked about it. I transported Lieutenant Mansfield right from her location on the bridge and put her there with you on that ship. She had observed our basic plan and would be somewhat familiar with their tactical board."

Taking in Derrota's unsure expression, Pristy offered up an assuring smile. "Your quick actions saved my life, Stephan. Thank you. Mansfield was amazing." She glanced over to where the lieutenant was still being worked on. At least now she was sitting up.

"Talk to me about the rest of the attack group. What happened?"

Derrota scratched at the scruff on his chin and let out a resigned breath. "The Varapin must have been anticipating us pulling something. While sure, you and Mansfield had nullified the dampening field, the other Varapin warships began firing on us almost immediately. And yes, we all had the same orders, to jump the instant you were on board the *Bow Before Me*."

"So what happened? Why, for the love of God, didn't they jump?"

"I'm not sure. We may have been the first to beat the enemy to the punch. Any other of those Varapin vessels could have initiated a new dampening field."

"So, if not outright killed or performed Ghan-Tshot upon, they'll be taken hostage. Used to coerce Captain Quintos to give up the *Oblivion*."

Two med-techs were now ushering Mansfield out of the bridge. She straightened her back, probably feeling the cold spray of an active flesh regrowth compound.

"Sorry, Captain. I forget how cold this stuff is," Dr. Pillbon said from behind her.

Derrota continued, "The *Hercules* was hit hundreds of times by enemy fire. Phazon Pulsars. Our shields fell right before we jumped."

"And the damage?" The doctor was still futzing around with the wounds on the lieutenant's shoulders and upper back. "Doc… Can you finish this up in HealthBay? I'll be down as soon as things settle down here."

The doctor took the hint and hurried off. Doc Viv, Pristy knew, would have told her to stuff it and just continued doing her work.

"We're basically dead in open space, Gail. FTL nav is off-line and our shields are down, along with multiple other ship-wide systems. Fortunately, life-support functions are operational. So, we're not going anywhere anytime soon."

Pristy thought about that. "Comms?"

Derrota shook his head. "Working on it, but it could be weeks before we're able to send for help. Then again, it may be too shot to shit to be repaired."

"That means we could be drifting in space for…possibly a very long time."

"There is one bit of good news coming out of Engineering. Our maneuvering thrusters are operational…won't give us any-where close to light speed. And we have one charged jump spring."

"So we can jump!" Pristy said with a glimmer of hope in her voice.

"Once. We can jump once, maybe…" Derrota said.

"So we'd need to make it count. We'd need to put ourselves where we could—"

Derrota cut in, "Increase our chances of being rescued."

She shook her head. "No. Jump to a location that would have the highest odds of finding the *Oblivion*."

Chapter 17

Starship *Oblivion*, High orbit over Haven
Captain Galvin Quintos

We watched as the lone missile headed off toward an opening between a cluster of spinning/twirling asteroids. It was then, with the quiet background hum of countless bridge components, that weariness set in. I needed sleep. MORROW'S voice came over the Bridge PA.

Based on the current hydro-missile trajectory, target impact will occur in three hours and twenty-seven minutes…

Without making it obvious, I glanced about the bridge and looked at the faces of my fellow crew members. Who among them could fill the position of XO? Who would I be able to rely on, even in times of chaos and stress? The short answer was none of them for one reason or another.

"Hardy, you have the conn…stay vigilant. I'll be back in a few hours." I raised my ring finger. "Call me if anything changes."

Once out of the bridge, I headed toward the row of officers' quarters farther down the expansive corridor. As tired as I was, and God, was I tired, my mind was racing—there was so much to do, and it felt like my feet were stuck in cement. How much more of Alliance territory had fallen to the Varapin in just the last day? And what was I doing to change that other than plotting refueling missions and priceless gem capers…not to mention, I needed to address the fact that there were dozens of fucking dinosaurs on my ship.

Approaching the hatch door to my quarters, I motioned with a swipe of one hand, and it quietly slid open. I took a step, then stopped at the threshold and peered into the softly lit, well-appointed compartment. The bed, which a domestic bot had made for me, looked more foreboding than restful. There was no way I would be able to turn off the mental noise in my head here. I took a step back and gestured for the hatch door to close.

I continued on down the corridor. I walked in relative silence, not knowing where I was going, but walking felt good. Ten minutes later, I stood at another hatch door, this one most definitely not leading into an officer's quarters. I'd been here before.

I swiped my hand and stepped inside. It was dark, but not so dark I couldn't make out the Ebom-Pod at the center of the compartment. The lid to the thing was open. I took another three steps and peered down into the dark, heavily padded cavity. I lowered myself down, taking a seat upon the crypt's rim. I looked about the compartment, Nothing was on the walls. There was no sound in here.

Fuck it.

I half crawled, half fell into the thankfully empty Ebom-Pod. I repositioned myself so I was on my back. The thing was comfortable; I had to give that to the ghouls. A sudden sound jarred my senses. The lid was closing—I could both hear and see it enclosing me within the crypt. I nervously felt around with both palms for a switch or something, a control of some kind, but found nothing.

Then it occurred to me.

"MORROW, can you stop this thing from closing on me?"

Ebom-Pod canopy cycling discontinued.

As my heart rate settled back down, I peered down to my feet; an eight- or nine-inch gap remained open above. I let my head fall back upon the cushions. I said, "MORROW, wake me in two hours and fifteen minutes."

Yes, Captain…I count the moments until then…

I slept.

***

I entered the bridge feeling more rested than I could remember. Everything and everyone was right where I'd left them two and three-quarters of an hour earlier. All except one thing—up on the halo display, the smart hydro-missile had progressed significantly farther into the asteroid field. That, and now all of the Grish gunships were weaving their way farther through the maze of tumbling rocks.

MORROW provided an update:

Based on the current hydro-missile trajectory, target impact will occur in forty-two minutes…

I said, "Anything to report…anyone?" I glanced over to Hardy. "Not so much. Been like watching paint dry."

Lieutenant Akari James turned around. "With the bosun's help, I've been acquainting myself with the tactical board. Shared the

Varapin tech I picked up from Coogong and Coke. It's a lot, and not all of it belongs on the tactical console. I think we'll need to offhand some things to the CIC," she said, gesturing to the newly configured adjacent compartment.

Since virtually all bridge and CIC consoles could be reconfigured on demand, that sounded like a good suggestion. Although there was one problem with that idea: we didn't have the necessary crew members to support manning several bridge shifts as well as the CIC.

Up until now, I had been reluctant to give any of the pirates on board. Thunderballs's Pylors, key responsibility positions. Oh, they were still on board the *Oblivion*, probably several hundred of them, but they weren't doing much of anything. A good many of them had opted to return to other Thunderballs's fleet assets, probably out of boredom. I really needed to stop thinking of the ships and those Pylors in those terms. Thunderballs was now long dead. Those men and women were now my responsibility. And hadn't they proven their loyalty by bucking McMasters's orders?

"Bosun Polk, let's take a walk. Hardy, you too."

The three of us headed out of the bridge. I said, "Crew Member Grimes, you have the conn."

I didn't need to look at the young helmsman to know that this was a big deal for him. Moving out to the Deck 23 corridor, the three of us strolled.

"Bosun, I've decided to bring key Pylors, let's call them the *Oblivion's* Pylors, onto the bridge and CIC to fill certain still-unmanned positions. I need your organizational skills to make that happen. Make a list of the most qualified candidates. Oh, and while uniforms are not necessary on board this ship, bathing is. Come up with a minimum level of hygiene everyone on board, namely the Pylors, must adhere to."

"I'm on it…shall I go do that now? I can do much of that

from my station."

"Sure, head back on in."

We watched her hustle off before I said, "Hardy, I need you to take a more active role on board this ship. To take on more responsibility."

A small glow emanated from the top of his leather pouch. Iris had come awake in there.

"What did you have in mind? I'm already busier than I'd prefer."

"Doing what? Not to be overly blunt, but I have no idea where you go for hours on end each day. I appreciate you're around when you feel I'm in danger or the ship is in danger, but I'm not really sure you have any real sense of commitment here."

We walked in silence for a few more moments. I knew I had to get back to the bridge. I didn't want to miss the hydro-missile hitting its target.

"Look, Cap…I'm a ChronoBot. Basically a war machine, a battle bot—"

"No."

"No? I'm not a battle bot?"

"Sure, you're that. But you're so much more than that. You're a person. As much a human as the rest of us on this ship. And it's time you had, well, some well-defined duties."

His face display stayed uncharacteristically blank. "That sounds absolutely dreadful."

I almost laughed. "I'm serious about this, Hardy."

"What kinds of duties did you have in mind?"

"A crew member position. Actually, I was thinking you could fill two positions."

"That doesn't seem fair. I think the union would have a real issue with that level of abuse."

"And what union is that?"

"The pirates' union. There has to be something like that with all the pirate clans about."

"Yeah, I don't imagine that's a real thing, Hardy. So what do you think? You are two, um, individuals in one. LuMan and Hardy, right? And you don't need to sleep."

"So you want me to have this responsibility, to do these jobs, what? Like twenty-four-seven?"

"No. I'm sure we can work out the time frames."

"This is really starting to sound awful."

"We're understaffed. You can see that, right? And come on… you are qualified, more qualified, for any number of posts."

"Fine. What posts did you have in mind?"

"I was thinking chief science officer, like what Stephan Derrota does."

"Okay. Maybe I could do that. Is that it?"

"No. That and temporarily fill the job that Alistair Mattis filled on the Jefferson."

"That was chief of security."

"That it was," I said, turning us back, walking in the direction toward the bridge.

Hardy seemed to be contemplating it all.

"You'd need to do the jobs concurrently. Not so much as in different shift periods."

An animation came alive of a circus clown spinning plates on long sticks.

"I can't argue with that depiction," I said. "You know as well as I do, the whole Varapin stowaways issue has to be dealt with. Work with Bosun Polk; she's already organizing nightly search teams."

Chapter 18

When the smart hydro-missile found its target, I was seated back within the captain's mount. My expectations were low that much would be changed by this single ordinance strike. But I was wrong. When that little, relatively speaking, missile exploded on the surface of the house-sized rock, it fractured into three smaller-sized rocks—each then being propelled into neighboring asteroids. The domino effect had begun. And like a pool game scenario, the shot-forward cue ball was now triggering a wild disruption within the table. Where we had been anticipating a minor, localized disruption within the field, there was now an ongoing chain reaction that just wouldn't fucking end.

I rubbed at my right temple, feeling a headache coming on. Or maybe I was just subconsciously anticipating Admiral McMasters's shredder bolt being shot into my head.

"That…I did not anticipate," Hardy said

I was speechless as the cataclysmic spatial event continued. Like a pebble thrown into a placid pond, now ever-larger concentric rings of destruction were expanding outward in every direction.

Akari stood and pointed. "The Grish vessels…they're about to be—"

It happened before she could get the words out. As if caught within a giant blender, the enemy warships were shredded.

"I almost feel sorry for them," she said, plopping back down into her seat.

But I was watching those concentric circles of mass destruction getting closer and closer to Haven, not to mention the *Oblivion*.

"Helm, prepare to jump the ship," I said.

Grimes said, "Perpendicularity spheres are charged and ready. We can jump on your command, sir."

And what about the entire population of Haven? What about those Pylor vessels in orbit that don't have jump capabilities…

Three-quarters of the asteroid field was in a state of agitation—virtually every asteroid was moving.

"I think it's slowing," Grimes said.

"Yeah, seems to be quieting down," Akari said. "And just in time."

"Captain, we're being hailed," Chen said.

"Let me guess. The admiral?"

Chen didn't need to answer.

"Put him through. On display. May as well get this over with…"

Admiral McMasters's panicked face practically filled the entire halo display. Eyes wide and constantly blinking, he audibly gasped as the channel went live. "Quintos, there's been a…tremendous disruption within the asteroid field." He shook his head. "Obviously you already know that. You have far more superior sensors there on the Oblivion."

I nodded. "About that, um—"

"The fucking Grish. Oh, we saw them all right…as soon as they entered our system, they were being monitored. Four different Pylor scout ships were tracking them. Then they were sneaking their way into the asteroid field…were they crazy, or just stupid? Fucking piglets. It was bound to happen…A ship miscalculates, strikes an asteroid. Boom! The explosion causes…well, you saw it.

We're all just lucky the field has stabilized."

I was well aware everyone on the bridge was now looking at me. I said, "Yeah, fucking Grish. Can't add much to that, Admiral."

"You can say they got what they deserved. But it nearly cost us all our lives." He let out a breath and seemed to have calmed down some. He dragged two palms down his face. "We'll need to remap the entire system; that won't be easy. Could take months; hell, years, even."

"May I make a suggestion, Admiral?"

"Sure. Go ahead, Captain."

"Uh…Hardy here, our ChronoBot, I believe, has prior experience mapping fields not so different from this one. His long-range sensors are quite accurate. If I get him going on this, he may have something for you later today." I looked to Hardy. "What do you think, Hardy…you think you can help the admiral out?"

"I'm already working on it as we speak. It won't be the first time I've had to clean up after the Grish."

I avoided rolling my eyes. Attempting a smile, I said, "We'll be in touch, Admiral.."

Chen cut the connection. Everyone was still looking at me.

"Hey, I'm a pirate now…get used to it."

***

Seven hours later, the grateful Admiral McMasters had his Eta Carinae star system asteroid field completely cataloged and mapped. In addition, Hardy had provided three viable commerce routes within the system for the Pylors to utilize once it was verified things had truly settled down.

And with that, I gave the order to jump the ship 1.2 light-years out of the Eta Carinae star system. Our tanks were low, and we needed fuel.

"Captain, MORROW has provided me the necessary wormhole manufacture calculations," Grimes announced from the helm station. "Chief Porter has reiterated that a distance of 21.4621 parsecs will almost completely drain all our fuel reserves."

I mentally converted parsecs to light-years. We'd be manufacturing a gargantuan wormhole, one spanning a distance of close to seventy light-years. We had few other choices, and time was an ever-present issue. It was time to shit or get off the damn pot.

"We're go for wormhole manufacture, Helm."

It didn't take long. And no matter how many times I witness this phenomenon, it is always beautiful and awe-inspiring. I watched as the confluence of brightly colored prismatic spatial distortions formed into a yawning wormhole mouth. A slightly narrower throat beyond was taking shape—and deeper still, the circular black event horizon. I knew another mouth had already formed at the opposite end.

Now, seeing the fully formed jump wormhole, without a reference to compare it to within the vastness here in open space, it was hard to tell just how large the thing really was. But taking into account the size and mass of the *Oblivion*, I knew the wormhole was enormous. And it took immense amounts of energy, of fuel, to both form the thing as well as keep it open.

"Helm…take us in." Next stop would be a collider space station in the middle of nowhere.

***

Three hours and six minutes later we emerged from the wormhole. And in accordance with Coke's description, there was nothing here but black, empty space. Playing things on the safe side, we'd had MORROW put us two light-minutes out from the Gorvian refinery outpost.

Hardy said, "I'm not picking up any vessel resonance, Cap. It's as quiet as, well, as what you'd expect from somewhere out in the farthest reaches of deep space."

"And the outpost?"

"Nothing."

I continued to stare at the ChronoBot. Call it a captain's intuition, or just a hunch, but for some reason I was certain someone or something would be waiting for us here. It wasn't a great leap in strategic thinking. Those that were looking for the Oblivion would figure we'd need to fuel up, and this was the most logical location to do just that.

"Can you check again?" I asked.

He turned his big head in my direction. "It's not like I flip a switch and then switch it off; I'm always checking. There's nothing going on within this area of space. No residual radiation trails from recent spacecraft activity; even the outpost's ambient operating temperature is normal."

I nodded, then said, "Why would the outpost's ambient operating temperature be normal?"

"Let me explain just how cold deep space gets without a nearby star around to provide radiant heat…so, it's real chilly. Like -454.67°F chilly. That's insanely close to absolute zero. Would you want to work inside of a helix collider outpost at that temperature?"

"I know how cold deep space gets, Professor Obvious. What I'm saying is, isn't the outpost supposed to be completely shut down? Getting the power grid up and running again was going to be one of our first tasks."

Hardy's face display was of John Hardy's face some sixty years back in time. A face now going pink with faux embarrassment. "I see your point. I cannot explain why the outpost is powered on."

"Can you do a more thorough scan of the facility?"

"Not at this distance…I'd need to be within three light-sec-onds."

I figured that was close to around five hundred thousand miles.

"Make it one light-second, to be safe," Hardy said. "Yup, one hundred and eighty-six thousand miles. Should do it."

I nodded to Grimes.

"Jumping now," the helmsman said.

I didn't bother looking at the halo display; it would still be black. So I stared at Hardy. "Maybe MORROW can determine—"

"Got it. Very clever. Very, very clever."

"Is he always like this?" Akari said, looking at the ChronoBot with a pained expression.

"He has a flair for the dramatic," Chen said.

"Whoever is occupying that outpost is utilizing a restrictive dampening field. Quite shrewd I must say…and in so doing, they are blocking my—anyone's—sensor scans from penetrating inside that structure."

When I was about to ask another question, Hardy held up a mechanical finger. "Hold on…" he nodded as if receiving more intel. "Ah, very clever indeed."

I rolled my eyes. "Enlighten us, oh wise one."

"They, and I have a good idea who they are, have made one crucial error with their clandestine concealment."

From above, MORROW's voice announced:

I got it, I got it…it's random vibrations!

Hardy's teardrop-shaped head slowly looked upward. "If you don't mind, MORROW, best if you leave the fundamentals of me-chanical vibrations to an expert."

"At least MORROW was getting to it," Akari said.

Hardy continued, "Vibrations can be either harmonic, as in

continuous, or random.

And as MORROW so rudely interrupted, the outpost is generating a substantial amount of random vibrations, which are making their way onto the outer skin of the facility. They are, of course, nearly undetectable, but they are there just the same."

"Maybe the facility has a rodent problem or a loose ventilation panel," I said.

This outpost has only recently been reactivated. Vermin do not typically reanimate, and as for the panel…that's just nonsense.

Now I was looking up, although I was well aware MORROW's actual electronics were cloistered away within the CIC compartment. "MORROW, please refrain from randomly joining in on, um, human conversations."

The ChronoBot believes he is the only one around with advanced long- and short-range sensors.

My patience was being tested. "Hardy, what are the vibrations being caused by?"

"Don't you want to first check in with your cocksure ship's AI?"

"I don't even know what cocksure means—"

"It means assertive, I think," Akari said.

"Just tell us, Hardy."

"The vibrations are consistent with multiple sets of footfalls. Organic beings hustling about within the structure."

"So, not vermin?"

"No, heavier. My guess…more like the Grish."

Concur.

"Any way to determine how many piglets are running around in there?"

"More than three hundred. Less than five hundred."

"Well, they have to have gotten onto that refueling outpost somehow," Akari said. "There has to be a ship or multiple ships keeping their distance."

True that.

"MORROW, stop with the commentary," I said

Something new occurred to me. "MORROW does the Oblivion have scout droids available?" I waited longer than would be normal, but eventually the AI spoke up.

There is a stockpile of scout droids with full sensor capabilities eager to do your bidding…

"Do all the machines on this ship have…contrary personalities?" Akari asked.

I said, "MORROW, go ahead and deploy twenty-five scout droids in an omnidirectional dispersal. Once any of them detect a ship, report back."

Deploying now…

We waited.

"I don't think I have a contrary personality," Hardy said.

"Drop it, Hardy. Tell me something else you've figured out about that outpost."

"Well, it's more of an observation and conclusion. With our

minimum numbers of military personnel, even with my contribu-tion—"

"There's no way we're taking that outpost."

The robot nodded.

"Chen, you have the conn."

***

I arrived at Decks 88/89, the Symbio decks, eight minutes lat-er. The StreamLine lift's doors opened, and I shouldn't have been surprised; there was Ensign Plorinne standing there—waiting for me.

"You know that's creepy. You being there like that."

"Just exhibiting outstanding dedication to the job, sir.'

"Let's go inside."

"Your Caveman Glory area."

"Inside? You want to go in?"

"Yes. I didn't come here to stand in a hallway."

"Well, we can speak here. I'll answer any of your questions—"

"Ensign, is there a reason you don't want me going beyond that hatch door?"

Pfft. "No! Of course not. It's just that—"

"Open that hatch now."

Reluctantly the young ensign entered the necessary code, and the hatch doors slid open.

It was the deafening noise that hit me first. And then the swamp-like smells, and then the rowdy cheers.

There were too many of the, uh…cavemen and cavewomen to count. All were minimally dressed in various forms of primi-tive attire. Animal pelts, skimpy loincloths and so forth. All were mangy-looking, and many of the males were lugging a stereotypi-cal caveman-style club.

139

Speechless, the raucous crowd encircled something I honestly never imagined seeing. There before me was the largest creature I'd ever laid eyes on. A tyrannosaurus rex. But that wasn't the most strange aspect of what I was trying to comprehend, because there, some twenty yards distance away, and also there within the ring of encircling cavemen, cavepeople…was Sadon. Head raised and wings spread, he was almost as tall as the towering dinosaur. The dragon screeched and spewed fire, causing the T. rex to take a step backward. The two immense beasts began to circle one another, the T. rex showing its teeth and Sadon doing the same.

A drumbeat began as the cavemen began pounding their clubs in unison onto the ground. "Fight, fight, fight, fight…"

"They don't really fight, Captain. More like…horse around. You know, like wrestle."

"You have a full-grown T. rex and a killer fire-breathing dragon fighting each other on my ship!?"

Ensign Plorinne opened his mouth to talk, but no words came out.

"You will put a stop to this now. Is that understood?"

"Y-Y-Yes, sir. Right away."

Plorinne sprinted into the crowd of barbaric Symbios and, to my surprise, the makeshift fighting ring. Waving his hands over his head, he yelled, "Stop! Sadon, stop with the fire. Reggie, enough with the teeth!"

The two goliath creatures looked down at the puny human like two crestfallen puppies being reprimanded.

But then the twenty-five-foot-tall dinosaur spoke. "Pray thee… thou just got us started! Can we not continue for just a while?"

"Yeah, they still talk like medieval peasants."

At some point Sonya had joined me at my side. She laughed, something I hadn't seen her do before, and for that moment, she looked her age of fifteen. It was a good look on her. She covered her mouth with one hand. "Seeing your surprise at seeing a full-grown T. rex talking like a totty medieval Brit is priceless."

Her laugh was contagious, and I couldn't help laughing at the ridiculousness of it all. "Among other things…several hundred cavemen—"

"And cavewomen."

"And cavewomen clamoring to watch a dragon and T. rex duke it out isn't exactly an everyday circumstance."

Sonya chuckled and then, becoming more serious, pointed ahead. "I think you have their attention."

Two hundred pairs of eyes were upon me. Not to mention those of Reggie and Sadon. As a hush came over the crowd, Ensign Plorinne emerged and strode toward us. "Sorry, sir. Again. It's just that they get a little pent-up. No one's come up here to visit the game. I have to tell you; they've all put a lot of work into playing their parts."

A good many of the Symbios were nodding their heads. As did Reggie. Sometimes I forgot, all of the Symbios were highly intelligent beings.

I had planned on just talking to Plorinne about this. But why should he speak for all of them? I cleared my throat. "Hello, everyone. You know who I am, obviously. Um, first of all, I'd like to thank you for your, uh, well, your dedication—"

"Wherefore don't thou just say what thou want to say, Galvin?"

It was a thirty-something cavewoman with messy dark hair, who also happened to be holding a large club. There was a dark smudge of dirt on one cheek, and she was smiling. That, and she was my mother.

Chapter 19

I smiled back at the Symbio-Poth female—the same Symbio that had played the part of my mother on board the USS *Hamilton*, within the faux town of Clairmont and later, on board the *Jefferson*, enacting the part of a medieval peasant woman. Was she more than a Lori Quintos replica? More than a simple biologically constructed artificial entity? I didn't know. And now wasn't the time to contemplate such esoteric concepts.

I said, "Thank you, Mo—Lori. What I'm here to ask you, all of you, is if you are open to going into battle as you did fighting the Varapin on the *Jefferson*. To do so along with the rest of us here on board the *Oblivion*."

"Isn't that what we were programmed to dost? To fight?" one unnaturally tall Symbio caveman queried back.

Clearly he and the others had maintained their cockney Convoke Wyvern game dialects.

"I think we have already proven ourselves, nay?" Sadon, the towering dragon, asked.

"I'm still not used to that," Sonya said under her breath. "Talking dragons."

I said, "Look, I'm not here to order you into battle. I'm here to ask for your help. Volunteer or don't; there won't be any repercussions, I promise."

The crowd began to murmur between themselves. An uneasiness befell the Symbio-Poths. This time it was the T. rex that spoke up—his voice so deep and forceful I felt the air vibrate around me. "We art ready to do thy bidding…just, we wonder…Wilt we ever get to play Caveman Glory? We have practiced our parts—"

"I promise, once things settle down, the crew, and I personally, will be lining up, excited to play."

***

By the time I returned to the bridge, there were six new crew members seated at previously unmanned stations. Both Vince and Sloppy Joe were present, as well as, surprisingly, Mr. Phillips. I thought he'd quansported down to Haven along with McMasters.

Up ahead, Bosun Polk, looking nervous to the point she was wringing her hands, waited for me at the captain's mount. "Sir, as instructed, I've spoken to all the Pylors still on board. All one hundred and thirty. All but a few are willing to take a more active role among the crew. I have determined these men here have extensive prior bridge duty experience."

"Well done, Bosun. And the other aspect?"

She looked unsure and then nodded. "Oh, their hygiene," she whispered as if somehow everyone else wouldn't be able to hear her.

I nodded.

"They've all bathed and, as you can see, are wearing US Space-Navy uniforms."

"I don't require anyone to wear a uniform."

"They didn't have any other clothes…well, except Mr. Phillips."

I glanced toward the small man, who was wearing a white satin frilly shirt with beige leggings with a paisley pattern. He looked, well…smartly dressed.

"And they're all well suited for their particular station duties?"

"Yes, sir. I put them all through a rigorous amount of testing."

"Thank you. Well, they look to be on their best behavior."

"I've given them the riot act. But Captain, I have to warn you… Vince is quite vocal. You may have noticed that in the past?"

"Oh, I have. Again, let's just see how things progress." As I took my seat, Hardy emerged from the adjoining CIC compartment. He was now acting chief science officer, and I was glad to see he was keeping to his commitments.

"Cap, we're just now starting to hear back from our deployed scout drones."

"And…"

"And it's mostly what we expected. Grish warships are lying in wait some eight light-seconds out from the refueling outpost. Some seven warships…all are cloaked and have gone dark."

"So they're not taking any chances at being discovered," I said. "You said mostly what we expected. What's the unexpected aspect?"

"One vessel out there that is not Grish or Varapin…it's a US Space-Navy heavy battleship. And it's damaged."

"Scans pick up signs of life?"

He nodded. "Full crew complement."

"Do the Grish know the ship is there?"

Akari interjected, "No way…that ship is really well cloaked. And her propulsion system is totally off-line. Our drones would have missed it completely if one of them hadn't almost plowed right into it."

Before I could say anything, Vince was standing at my side. "The Grish scallywags are here for you or the *Oblivion*…or maybe both. Did you think no one would figure out that this big tub would need fuel at some point?"

Bosun Polk stood back up. "Vince, return to your station."

"Blow it out your blowhole, lady. This is important information I'm conveying to the good captain here."

"Yeah, he needs to hear it," Sloppy Joe added from the back row of consoles.

I waved a dismissive hand. "It's fine, Bosun. And he happens to be right. The question is, what does a heavily damaged US Space-Navy warship expect to accomplish going up alone against a ship like the *Oblivion*?"

No one had an answer to that.

Then Akari said, "You could ask them."

Hardy said, "MORROW has passed along an interesting tidbit."

All eyes went to the ChronoBot. "That heavy, the USS *Hercules*, was recently deployed from Earth as part of a specialized attack group of six warships. Their mission was indeed to find the *Oblivion* and to bring back her crew to face charges of desertion."

I nodded. I'd expect nothing less from my previous employers.

"But that's not the most interesting part."

I noticed Iris was now standing on Hardy's left shoulder. Excited, she was clapping her little hands. "Tell him! Tell him the rest of it!"

Hardy said, "The captain of that vessel, Cap, is none other than—"

"Captain Gail Pristy," I blurted out. I'm not sure how I knew, but I did.

"You really know how to steal someone's thunder," Hardy said.

"Sorry."

Vince said, "Even more reason to reach out to them sooner than later. If the Grish do detect that heavy just sitting out there…"

I nodded.

Chen said, "Shall I hail the *Hercules*, sir?"

"Yes…but I'll take it in my ready room."

***

Sitting at my desk, I was surprised at my own nervousness to see Pristy again. We hadn't left things on the best of terms. My decision to leave the US Space-Navy had not included an invitation for her to join me for a pirate's life. Young, and just making a name for herself as a fine starship officer, she had far too much to lose. Perhaps I should have let her make her own decision at the time. But it was too late now to be second-guessing myself.

The smaller version of a halo display above my desk blinked and came to life. And there she was. She, too, was seated at her desk within the *Hercules's* ready room. She looked tired, stressed, and just as pretty as I remembered.

"Captain Pristy…welcome to the middle of nowhere," I said.

"I think you can call me Gail, Galvin…after all we've been through together."

"Okay, Gail. Talk to me."

"You obviously found us. Clever move with the scout droids."

"Where's the rest of your attack group…and what happened to the *Hercules*?"

"Getting right down to business, huh? No, 'how have you been, Gail?' No 'sorry for quitting the Space-Navy'? No…nothing!"

"You know why I did what I did."

"Maybe. But it's how you did it, Galvin."

We held each other's eyes for a long moment.

"I wasn't going to drag you down into the gutter along with me, Gail."

"That wasn't your choice to make."

"Would you have come with me?"

"No! You don't get to ask me that now. It's too late. Now I'm here to bring you back to face charges. And to take that bloated tub back to Earth. If you haven't noticed, the Alliance is in need of replacement warship assets right now."

"Gail…listen to me. I can do this. I know you don't get what I did. Why I did it. But continuing to take my orders from Fleet Command wasn't going to win this war."

"How much of an arrogant ass are you? You think one person, one man, is going to alter the facts of interstellar war?"

I didn't answer her right away. Then I shrugged. "Maybe."

She let out a frustrated breath. "I think you broke Admiral Block's heart. He's been like a father to you, Galvin."

She got me with that one, and it stung. "I know."

"So what now?" she asked. "You've got seven capable Grish warships hiding in wait nearby. You've also got an even more dangerous problem…powerful next-generation Varapin warships under the command of one captain Flinth Shap. You asked what happened to the rest of my attack group and the thousands of ship's crew? Well, right now, if they are still alive, they're all being held on a Varapin personnel carrier. Captain Shap would like to trade these prisoners, my crew members, for the *Oblivion*."

I took a moment to digest that.

"And you do know that that refueling station is jam-packed with armed warrior piglets, right?"

I nodded. "We have a well-thought-out plan," I lied.

"Uh-huh. Which means you're doing what you always do… flying by the seat of your pants."

I didn't dispute her accusation. "Stay cloaked and run quiet. The Grish won't discover the *Hercules* once the *Oblivion* grabs their attention. This is my mess."

"Like hell it is. Like it or not, I'm here, and I'm not sitting this one out."

I laughed at that. "Okay, Gail, how exactly do you plan to make an effective contribution with a ship that can't even get into first gear?"

"Hey, this is a fine ship and don't disrespect her!"

"Whatever."

"You're going to jump in alongside us. Then we'll…nest abeam."

I raised my brows in surprise. That was an old sea navy term for two ships cozying up to one another hull to hull.

"So, do you want to do that with me…nest abeam, Galvin?" Her face was perfectly professional and all too innocent-looking.

But oh, I got the double entendre. Damn, I hated that she could fluster me. "Stop that."

"Stop what?"

"You know what."

"No, I have no idea what you're talking about."

"Can we get back to your nest abeam idea?"

"Isn't that what we're already talking about?" she said, but a slight upward curl to her lips gave her away.

"Fine. There's no reason for you to jeopardize ship and crew… this is my battle. My problem."

"Let's just say, for the time being, we're in this together. The *Hercules* will likely be discovered at any moment. The *Oblivion's* shields could go a long way toward giving us protection. And, I imagine you could use a little extra firepower when the shit hits the fan."

She might be right.

"Can I ask you something?" she said.

It was a rhetorical question, so I waited.

"Why did you opt to make this call in your ready room?"

I shook my head and looked bewildered. "I don't know. It's inconsequential."

"Liar."

"You can expect my answer concerning your, um, nest abeam suggestion within the hour." I cut the connection.

Chapter 20

It would be near impossible to take the refueling outpost while fighting the Grish both within the complex itself, as well as those seven warships currently hiding in wait. So what do you do when the game is stacked against you? You alter the playing field, of course. I had a rough idea how to do just that, but didn't know for sure if it was actually feasible. Moving forward, I would need Pristy's help—more importantly, her trust.

This time when I opened a channel to the *Hamilton*, it was from the bridge.

She appeared up on the halo display with a bemused expression. "Calling back so soon, Galvin?" Only now did she realize I was sitting amid the *Oblivion's* bridge crew, whereupon she sat up straighter and took on a more professional demeanor. "What have you decided, Captain?"

"I've decided your idea won't work. But I have a better solution."

"I'm here to help."

"You may not be so willing once you've heard me out."

"I'm listening."

"First of all, can you fetch Stephan?"

She looked more dubious now, but nodded. A minute later, I saw Stephan Derrota standing at her side. Rumpled and unshaven, it sure was good to see my old friend again. Just hearing his jovial Mumbai-accented voice made me smile.

"Galvin, how good it is to see you again. Just like old times!"

"Back at you, Stephan. But right now, I'm in need of your scientific expertise when it comes to manufactured wormholes. Hardy has given me his best-guess analysis, but I wanted to get your input, if Captain Pristy will allow it."

Derrota looked to Pristy, who reluctantly nodded.

"Okay, what do you need to know?"

"I'm sorry, I'll need you here on board the *Oblivion* for this."

"Oh no. No way are you stealing my chief science officer." Pristy crossed her arms over her chest and shook her head defiantly.

I'd expected that response and was ready for it. "Gail, you do have a capable XO, I presume…"

"Of course, the best. Commander Wringer has a distinguished—"

"That's perfect. Then you'll be coming over as well, Captain Pristy. That is if you want to get out of this mess while saving your ship and crew in the process."

***

We'd had to jump in closer to the *Hercules*, while still maintaining enough distance from the Grish warships that we'd remain undetected from long-range sensors. Both Derrota and Pristy had balked at the idea of quansporting over, but there really wasn't much choice in the matter. Hardy, Coogong, and I were waiting for them when, within the time span of a second or two, block by block, their forms took shape upon the raised transporter device's pedestal.

Both were dressed in dark gray official US Space-Navy uniforms. They both did a cursory look at themselves, making sure all their limbs were still properly attached—something I still did myself to this day after quansporting anywhere.

I put my hand out to shake hands with Derrota, the first to step down. He ignored it, enfolding me into a bear hug instead. "Oh, it's so good to see you again, Galvin."

He stepped away, looking momentarily awkward at his exuberant show of affection.

Gail stepped down, and to my surprise, also embraced me—although her hug had far less veracity than Derrota's.

After the two greeted Hardy and Coogong, I escorted our two visitors over to the captain's conference room. Waiting for us there were Captain Ryder, Chief Porter, and Sergeant Max.

After more warm greetings, I prompted the group to take a seat. Time was ticking by, and there was a lot to accomplish.

"You are all aware of the sticky situation facing us. The enemy is hiding and waiting for us to arrive to refill our fuel tanks."

"Can we skip to the part where you tell us why Stephan and I needed to be here?" Pristy said with impatience.

"Stephan, with all you know about manufactured wormhole physics, what would keep us from propelling that hyper collider refueling outpost into its mouth and delivering it somewhere else, preferably several parsecs distance from here?"

I turned to the room's halo display, where there was a live view of the immense refueling complex.

"You do know, Galvin, that that outpost is gargantuan…it even dwarfs the Oblivion."

"Yes, I know that."

"And you want to create a jump wormhole large enough to transport that entire construct?"

"Yes. I've seen what this ship can do. The wormhole that brought us here was at least twice the size of anything the *Jefferson* would have been able to manufacture."

Pristy moved to stand up. "You're out of your mind, Galvin. Stephan, let's go. This has been a waste of time."

"Hold on, everyone," Hardy interjected, striding over to the display with Coogong hurrying to catch up. "Yeah, we thought the cap had lost his marbles too. A colossally stupid idea. But, well, just maybe he's onto something." Hardy gestured for Coogong to take over.

"Thank you, Hardy. Gail, Stephan…it is not so much a problem of creating an adequately sized wormhole, as the captain suggested. It is more a problem of achieving an adequate velocity while entering the mouth of the wormhole. The outpost is just that, an outpost, one that was constructed here in deep space. It is not a spacecraft."

"So how do we make it into a spacecraft?" Ryder asked, for the first time looking somewhat more interested.

"That's the tricky part," I said. "It's moving the mass of an incredibly heavy object not designed to go anywhere, especially forward from a dead standstill."

Hardy pretended to scratch his nonexistent chin. "Okay…getting something that big moving that fast," he began to murmur, "Hmm…momentum equals mass times velocity equals force times time…that means we'd have to apply a huge external force…but for how long?"

I knew this was all for show—actually more like showing off. Hardy's AI brain needed zero time to make calculations such as these. But I allowed his antics to continue.

"With the refueling outpost weighing in in the neighborhood of one hundred million tons, and the speed at which the outpost must be traveling when it enters the mouth of the wormhole being ten thousand miles per hour…Hmmm." He bobbled his head. "Well…to get that much change in momentum, we'll have to generate about two hundred and ninety-two quadrillion pound-seconds of impulse in order to get that outpost moving at the necessary pound-seconds of force." He raised a mechanical index finger. "Unfortunately, that's more impulse than the *Oblivion* alone will be able to generate. Especially with the limited time she'd have. Yes, she's an amazing vessel, but she's not capable of doing that kind of heavy lifting, or pushing, in this case."

"So she'd need some help?" I said.

"Problem is, the *Hercules* is dead in space," Pristy said. She pursed her lips, "She does have an integrated tractor beam though…could that help?"

"Maybe. But there'll be nothing for the *Hercules* to latch on to," I said.

"Hold on," Derrota interjected, "We could direct the *Hercules's* tractor directly into the mouth of the wormhole, shoot it right toward the distant event horizon, which is in actuality a black hole. One with immense gravitational pull. We will need to crunch the numbers. Maybe the Oblivion can generate say two hundred to two hundred and fifty quadrillion pound-seconds of impulse, as Hardy mentioned. But with the *Hercules's* implemented tractor beam, just maybe it could offer up a major secondary pull…and do so at just the right moment."

"Hate to throw a wet blanket over your clever brainstorming, but there's one big issue you're not considering," Chief Porter said. He waited until he had everyone's attention. "The amount of power necessary to generate such a gargantuan wormhole will be limited by the *Oblivion's* current lack of fuel reserves."

"Well…the *Hercules* has nearly a full tank," Pristy volunteered. "Would it be possible for the *Oblivion* and the *Hercules* to manufacture a wormhole together? To combine their efforts?"

"The fuel supplies are not compatible in the slightest," Porter said dismissively.

Coogong raised a spindly hand. "Actually, that is an ingenious suggestion, Gail. I believe it is still possible. Know that the actual wormhole manufacturing aspect must be generated from the Oblivion, but we could use a directed micro-wormhole energy coupling between the two vessels, whereby the *Hercules* will be providing the raw power to infuse the Oblivion's more advanced wormhole projection technology."

Derrota said, "But understand, Galvin…this wormhole of yours will allow for only the shortest of jumps. Perhaps several light-seconds distance. The enemy's sensors will, in time, pick up the radiation signatures. They will find us. In the end, this buys us some time, maybe four or five hours…that's all."

I nodded. "Look, the whole purpose of this exercise is to allow us to fight the enemy forces one at a time. Once we're away from here, we deal with the piglets inside the outpost, and then we can deal with those seven warships."

"Let me make something perfectly clear," Pristy said. "My ship and crew remain my priority. The US Space-Navy's interests only go so far. Jeopardizing any of my onboard marine forces to assist with taking the refueling outpost is out of the question."

Chapter 21

While Pristy headed back to the Hercules, Derrota stayed behind—his wormhole-generating technology expertise would be needed on the *Oblivion*.

With Hardy standing on one side of the captain's mount, and Derrota on the other, things really did feel like old times again. The only difference was that Pristy was sitting on the bridge of the Hercules, which I could see on a split segment up on the halo display. Both Coogong and Chief Porter were standing ready within Engineering and Propulsion.

Pristy said, "This has to happen fast, Galvin. Sure, we may be catching the Grish by surprise, but they're not going to sit around with their thumbs up their little piglet asses for long."

I nodded. "You're right…so, let me ask you, Captain Pristy… are you ready to nest abeam with me?" I couldn't resist throwing that back at her.

But before she could answer, Derrota said, "We all know it's more than about time for that to happen between you two…"

Amid chuckles from both bridges, I said, "Helm, go ahead and jump us in alongside the *Hercules*."

Grimes jumped the *Oblivion*. He said, "And…we are two thousand feet off the Hercules's portside bow, sir. Firing maneuvering thrusters now."

Hardy said, "We've been pinged...Piglets have detected our presence here in local space."

"As well as that of the *Hercules*," Derrota said, tapping at his tablet.

"Seven hundred feet distance and closing," Grimes said.

"Piglet propulsion drives are powering on for five, six, now all seven warships."

"Three hundred feet distance and closing," Grimes said.

"We've got incoming!" Akari James announced from Tactical. "Oh crap...smart-missiles...twenty-two, all nuclear-tipped."

"ETA?" I asked.

"The first will make contact in four minutes thirty-three seconds."

"We'll be taking those hits," Derrota said.

"*Oblivion* shields should hold," I assured him.

"They better," came Pristy's voice from the halo display.

"Fifty feet distance and closing. Maneuvering and...reversing firing thrusters now," Grimes said.

The *Oblivion* shook.

Grimes said, "We are nest abeam with the Hercules; activating securing clamps."

Pristy said, "Shit...a second wave of nukes is inbound! I don't know about your ship, Galvin, but the *Hercules's* shields won't be able to stand up to that kind of bombardment."

Derrota said, "Gail...the Oblivion's shields are blanketing both ships."

But my attention was on the other halo display segment, where Coogong and Craig Porter were working frantically to establish that micro-wormhole energy conduit between the two vessels. "Craig, I don't mean to rush you, but—"

He glanced up with a scowl. "You're not helping."

Hardy said, "And a third wave of twenty-two nukes just deployed from the Grish warships."

Sixty-six inbound missiles, and we couldn't do anything to avert them. Apparently, implementing a micro-wormhole energy conduit was an intricate process. One where even the vibrations caused by Phazon Pulsars, or railgun fire, could jeopardize the tenuous connection.

"Craig," I said, "first wave of missiles will be striking us in thirty seconds."

Both Porter and Coogong were now tapping furiously at two different engineering stations. Coogong said, "*Hercules's* micro-wormhole generator is now online."

Porter said, "*Oblivion's* micro-wormhole receiver...is...online!"

I looked at the countdown timer on the display. He'd made it by three seconds. The first wave of nuclear-tipped smart-missiles was now striking the *Oblivion's* shields.

"Grimes, get us moving!"

I watched on the display as the two conjoined ships, slowly at first, began to move, making a gradual arc in space in the direction of the refueling outpost. With every second that passed, I knew we were burning through valuable fuel reserves. It took an excruciatingly long three and a half minutes to reach the massive, dark, and seemingly off-line outpost. With the *Hercules* secured to the *Oblivion's* starboard side, her portside was now cozying up to the starboard side of the imposing, massive outpost.

"Activating securing clamps," Grimes said. "And...three become one."

"Let's get that wormhole—"

Grimes cut me off, "Already on it, sir."

Akari spun around in her chair. "Captain...did we factor in the missile impacts, the explosions, to the wormhole's overall stability?"

"No, Lieutenant. We didn't."

She nodded. "Then let's cross our fingers and toes and hope this plan of yours still comes together."

Tracking our trek across local space, the smart-missiles continued to bombard our two adjoined starships, while avoiding any strikes to the outpost. The bridge continued to shake as the second wave of missiles impacted the shields.

"Zero entropy deterrence shields. ZEDs, baby, wow…they're holding!" Akari yelled.

The halo display was now coming alive with a dazzling display of prismatic colors as the mouth of a wormhole began to take shape some twenty thousand miles off the forward bow.

Hardy said, "Cap, it's time."

I said, "Helm, gun it! Pedal to the metal!"

Even with the *Oblivion's* inertia dampeners, we were all thrown backward into our seats, while Derrota was flung onto the deck. Hardy managed to stay upright, but just barely.

"Third wave of missiles impacting in ten seconds," Akari announced.

Grimes said, "We're at eight thousand miles per hour…and topping out. Can't get that big turd moving any faster than this."

"Wormhole is now viable," Derrota said. "Event horizon established."

"Captain Pristy, how about you give us a little help?"

She smiled. "On it." She signaled to her tactical officer.

Hardy said, "You don't see it, but I do. Tractor beam has been established and is reaching into the wormhole's gravity well."

"We've got 9,000 MPH," Grimes said, his face contorted as if he was pushing the three vessels into the wormhole all by himself.

Up on the halo display I saw we were approaching the spatial anomaly's yawning mouth, but if our speed remained insufficient, we would not have the necessary velocity to catapult us forward across virtual space and time. All we could do was wait and hope.

Akari said, "Entering the mouth in four, three, two—"

"We have 10,000 MPH!" Grimes yelled.

And with that, the three vessels, the starship *Oblivion*, the USS *Hercules*, and the refueling outpost, together left the seven Grish warships behind, along with any remaining smart-missiles.

Chapter 22

We'd entered an area of space that was just as dark and desolate as the one we'd left—although this one didn't have incoming Grish smart-missiles homing in on us. I got up from the captain's mount and headed for the exit. Stopping mid-stride, I turned toward the halo display. "Captain Pristy…would you mind keeping an eye on your ship and mine for the time being?"

"You're really going to do this? Join in on the battle?" she asked, incredulous.

I nodded. "If I want to maintain any semblance of Pylor respect, as well as motivate our Symbio-Poth forces, yeah…I have to be there."

While Vince and Sloppy Joe had already hurried off, Hardy was waiting for me out in the passageway. Together we headed toward the quansporter compartment.

With the exception of a few tweaks from me and Hardy, the plan of attack for taking the outpost had been developed by Max and his team. Hardy had zeroed in on the actual number of Grish warriors we'd be contending with as being four hundred and fifty-three. And he knew where they were located.

To the piglets' advantage, they'd had time to hide and set booby traps. That, and they had a superior number of combatants. On their side were four hundred and fifty-three piglet warriors to our one hundred and twenty Symbios and one hundred five Pylors—add to that Max's team of five, Hardy, and myself, and it put us at two hundred and thirty-two combatants. It was imperative that I leave some Pylors and Symbios on board the *Oblivion*, in case the Grish got the better of us and stormed the ship. So, we would be going into this battle with almost half as many forces as the enemy, but still, I did have a few surprises up my sleeve.

There was a throng of activity up ahead in the passageway outside the quansporter compartment. Both Vince and Sloppy Joe were there, barking off commands as they proceeded to assign Pylors into smaller squads of ten. I grimaced at the sight of the Pylors' combat suits. They were obviously old and utilized dated technology. Each looked to be hand painted with myriad warrior phrases and symbols. They'd made the age-old mistake of getting overly attached to any one piece of equipment.

Entering the quansporter compartment, I found Coogong inputting the last-minute configurations changes I'd ordered. Max, Wanda, Grip, Ham, and Hock were already in there—each outfitted for battle. Each wore a full cutting-edge combat suit with a tagger pistol holstered to one thigh and held a shredder assault weapon angled down toward the deck. I saw my own combat suit open and standing empty, and matching weaponry was already there, waiting for me. As Wanda helped get me properly outfitted, I said, "Please tell me this transporter device is fully operational, Coogong."

The helmeted Thine scientist looked over to me while his fingers continued to tap at his control board. "Everything is a go, Captain. Checksums are comparative…remote lock-targeting is online."

"Good, then do me a favor. Lock-target onto the six of us and quansport us up to the Symbio deck. There's no time for us to hop onto a StreamLine lift."

***

Arriving on Decks 88/89, the scene there was similar to that down on Deck 23. Bosun Polk's authoritative voice bellowed over the chatter of the one hundred and twenty milling-about Symbios.

We'd quansported into the open area adjacent to the dark and looming Jurassic jungle beyond. The moist, humid air was already starting to adhere to our faceplates.

I surveyed the spectacle of the readying Symbio-Poths and wished they would wear combat suits. But they had insisted on going into battle as they saw fit. I'd been assured their physiology was far more resilient than that of any human. No, they would go into battle as they would have within the high-stakes game of Convoke Wyvern.

Putting my foot down, I insisted that everyone, Pylors and Symbios alike, be properly armed with taggers and shredders.

Ensign Plorinne, who was wearing a full combat suit, emerged from the fray of Symbios. "Captain, I know it doesn't look like it, but we're ready. Just some last-minute shuffling within teams."

I glanced away from the melee, not wanting to catch a glance of the Lori Quintos Symbio-Poth. I was well aware of my own instinctive tendency—wanting to protect her from the brutality of battle. But she was not my mother; she was not human.

I reviewed my HUD indicators and readouts. The various comms channels were showing green and active. I reached out to the quansporter compartment. "Coogong, it's just about time for you to start doing your magic."

"Yes, Captain. I am ready to begin quansporting teams into the outpost on your command."

I looked up and found Max and his team huddled together. Their mission would be that of a drop-in assault group. When

Pylors or Symbios ran into overwhelming opposition, Max's team would jump in to lend a hand.

Next I checked in on Sonya, who would be behind the scenes monitoring and updating the Symbios' programming. As autonomous as they were—they were not fully organic, self-actualized individuals. Not yet, anyway.

Sonya's face, her brow furrowed in concentration, came up on my HUD display. She was sitting within the little server alcove some thirty feet behind me. "Sonya, any last words before we head out?"

"Yeah. I like these Symbios. They're not like us. Maybe they're what's best about us. So bring them back. All of them…even if they're not…um, operational anymore."

"I'll do my best."

I gave Coogong the go-ahead to start quansporting teams over to the outpost. Immediately, clusters of ten Symbios began to disappear. Ensign Plorinne was the communications conduit for the Symbios, and it would be up to him to provide me with sitreps on the quarter hour.

Within a few minutes it was just Max and his team, Hardy, and Ensign Plorinne standing with me. I looked to my right—there in the dense jungle beyond, I thought I saw movement. The shifting of dark elongated shadows established *something* was there—and was watching us.

Ensign Plorinne held up a finger—he looked to be listening to an incoming message. "Trouble, Captain. Team 8 of the Symbios is being overtaken by Grish combatants near the Level 3 mess hall. They need the marines, sir."

Max said, "On it. Got the QDL on my HUD. Coogong, get us over there." And with that, the five marines were gone.

Ensign Plorinne said, "QDL?"

"Quansport drop location," Hardy said.

The young Pleidian nodded.

"Unless absolutely necessary, I want you here coordinating with the Symbios."

"Where will you be, sir?"

"Hardy and I have our own mission of sorts." Before he could ask, I said, "We're heading over to get the lights turned back on… if we can't get that refueling outpost operational again, this whole operation will be one big waste of time."

I gave Coogong the go-ahead to put us at the necessary outpost QDL.

Chapter 23

Gorvian Helix Collider Outpost — Level 3 Mess Hall
Wanda

They'd quansported into a kind of vestibule outside the outpost's mess hall. As the five of them cleared the space, Wanda briefly wondered what kind of food the Gorvians would have eaten here. She didn't suppose it was mac and cheese or spaghetti and meatballs—but maybe Grish-bacon BLTs. She smiled at her own humor. But something was off. Where was the ensuing Symbio-Grish battle they'd been dispatched to intervene in? No bodies lay dead upon the deck. There were no plasma weapon scorch marks on the bulkheads.

At the moment, Wanda was bringing up the rear as they proceeded forward down a narrow, too-dark passageway. Even with their advanced night-vision enhanced tech, it was hard to see what was what. And thus far, helmet heat sensors weren't picking up active life-forms—no one hiding within the many alcoves or behind support girders.

As the lone woman among the five marines, Wanda had never been treated as anything but the badass warrior she was. And she was well aware that those within Max's small squad were considered deviant recluses that didn't play well with others—she was fine with that. Hell, it was true. Until that day when Sergeant Max showed up at her jail cell, Wanda had been facing charges of accosting an officer, disobeying a superior officer's orders, and a slew of somewhat more minor offenses. All told, she had been up against a sixteen-month stay in an off-world penal stockade somewhere near Jupiter.

Since she was muscular and close to six and a half feet tall, those outside of their small tribe had labeled Wanda an assortment of titles. Lezbo-Joe seemed to be a favorite. The fact that she was not a lesbian hadn't made a difference. On those occasions where she was interested in a certain man, he'd have to deal with the fact she was undoubtedly stronger and far more lethal than he was. Some dealt with that just fine, others not so much.

To say that Wanda had found the perfect home within this band of softhearted albeit ruthless killers (when they had to be) would be an understatement. She'd willingly die for any one of them, and she knew they would do so for her as well.

Wanda let out a resigned breath. Today was her birthday. She didn't expect anyone to remember. The guys had a hard time remembering to zip up their flies after taking a piss, let alone remembering a chick's birthday. But the day still felt different to her. Not so much special, but, well, just different. She wasn't nostalgic or particularly sentimental. Her tumultuous childhood upbringing in that overcrowded group home in urban Cleveland had cured her of that.

Max's voice came over her comms. "Look alive, Marines. We have motion up ahead."

She'd seen the same warning indicators displayed on her own HUD. Shredders raised, Wanda and Grip separated, both keeping close to opposite bulkheads as they progressed forward with more caution. While Max was taking point, Ham and Hock flanked him a half step behind.

Grip's deep voice crackled to life. "When the hell is someone going to turn the lights on? It's fucking creepy in here. I don't like the dark."

Max said, "Captain's working on it…in the meantime, grow a set of balls and keep quiet. We've got signs of life up ahead. And remember, everyone's got a plan till they're punched in the face. Be ready."

Bright blue plasma fire flared to life up ahead.

"Shit! Shit! Shit!" Max yelled. "They're up above us! Lying on top of those cooling ducts. Get your helmet lights on!"

Wanda did as told and immediately saw, ten feet above her, the large metal environmental cooling ducts running the length of the passageway. Startled, she saw him there, peering down at her from directly above—a Grish combatant; his light blue and oddly rounded helmet was a dead giveaway he was of the piglet persuasion. She took three energy bolts to her chest before diving forward, rolling on the deck, and coming up firing herself. "Shit, that hurts," she said to no one in particular. Her return fire did little more than sear holes through the underside of the metal ducting.

Three more energy bolts tagged Wanda, this time in the back. Even with the protective armor provided by her combat suit, taking three shots to nearly the same point was beyond painful. Like repeatedly getting jabbed by a hot iron. Now, forced down to one knee, she tried to clear her mind of the pain and the realization that her team was immobilized and totally ineffective at thwarting this continuing attack.

She could see that Grip was down, as was Ham, or maybe it was Hock. Wanda leaped over the all-too-still body while attempting to fire upward. But it was impossible to aim. Aim at what? The little fuckers were now skittering around up there like crazed rats.

She was approaching Max, who was holding his ground, shredder up and firing nonstop. Two, then three Grish tumbled down from above, each hitting the deck with a heavy thump. Wanda joined Max at his side, and the two of them continued firing. Like hot lightning bolts, she endured the ensuing energy strikes. That was until first Max's and then her own shredder weapon overheated, seized up, and died. In unison they pulled their taggers and continued firing. Several more Grish fell from their overhead perch.

Max shrieked out in pain and dropped his tagger while reaching two hands up to his faceplate. Seeing him stagger, Wanda did her best to get in front and shield him from any further energy strikes. "Talk to me, Sarge! What is it…you get hit in the face?"

His between-clenched-teeth answer sounded furious. "Yes. No…can't see for shit. Blinded by that last energy bolt."

Wanda continued to fire. Her tagger was now getting too hot to grasp. She knew she had mere moments before the weapon, like her shredder, would also be giving up the ghost. *Fine…maybe today's a good day to die…good as any. I was born on this day, and I'll die on this day. So be it.*

The lights came on, and for a moment, all weapons fire ceased. But that wasn't the only thing that had Wanda catching her breath.

There's something that happens within a surrounding space the moment before a quansport takes place—debris and any dust within close proximity suddenly become perfectly still.

The ChronoBot was suddenly right there no less than fifteen feet in front of Wanda—a shining god—big and pink and oh-so-beautiful. And if that wasn't enough of a surprise, there on his face display was a beautiful white frosted cupcake—a lone candle with a flickering flame atop completing the acknowledgment that, yes, somebody indeed had remembered Wanda's birthday.

Hardy's concealed energy cannons snapped into position, small turrets tracking then locking onto targets; then he was firing in multiple directions at once. Wanda ducked down and prayed she wouldn't catch a stray energy bolt.

Grish combatants thumped down onto the deck from above—it was literally raining piglets. Within ten seconds there was stillness and quiet once again.

Someone else was quansporting in—then there he was. Captain Quintos looked about his surroundings. He looked to Hardy with his still-smoking energy cannons. Wanda saw the captain take in the carnage upon the deck, and then he looked to her.

She was about to say something, but the captain's voice was already barking off orders over the open channel. "Coogong, get a medical detail to my location…now!"

Obviously they had been standing by. Within seconds, Doc Viv and two MediBots were quansporting into view.

Wanda tried to stand, to find the strength to help her fallen team, but she couldn't. Only now did the pain register. She looked down at herself—at her pocked and blackened combat suit. *How many times have I been shot?* Feeling lightheaded and finding it difficult to breathe, she wavered. *So tired.* Then strong hands were holding her upright. She opened her eyes to see the captain was there and working her helmet off.

"Hurry, get her helmet off!" came Doc Viv's voice.

"What do you think I'm doing here, playing dominos?" the captain snapped back.

As soon as her helmet's seal separated from the suit's neck cowling, fresh air rushed in around her face. Wanda gasped in a breath.

Viv was now next to her, looking into her eyes. "Uh-huh, hypercapnia. It's when you have too much carbon dioxide in your bloodstream. Simply put, your suit crapped out on you, and you were breathing in your own expelled air."

Wanda tried to talk but couldn't get her tongue to work. Viv put a straw to her lips, and she sipped down several burning gulps of water. She croaked out, "My team…Max?"

"I'm fine, Wanda," croaked the sergeant's voice nearby. "We're all still alive, although Ham's the worst off. Still unconscious."

"We're getting you all back to the Oblivion's HealthBay," Viv said, getting to her feet.

Wanda shook her head. "No. I'm staying in the fight."

"Yeah, me too," Max said. "But we'll both need new gear, suits…weapons. Can that be arranged?"

For the first time, Wanda got a good look at Max. Her own reaction took her by surprise—she laughed out loud. Not only was his suit blackened and full of too many encrusted craters to count; his faceplate had melted into a grotesque sagging mess. A kid's Halloween mask that would be all the rage back home.

"Go ahead; laugh it up. I'll just take back your birthday gift."

"You got me something?"

Chapter 24

Gorvian Helix Collider Outpost
Captain Galvin Quintos

As I watched the MediBots move about the passageway, I wondered how such a spindly, unsteady design had ever been approved for production. They might be fine for surgery procedures, making delicate scalpel incisions, but the simple act of walking seemed to overtax the awkward robots.

Viv must have read my expression. "I know, in HealthBay we sometimes call them GeekBots behind their backs."

Grip was the last of the injured marines being readied for quansporting. He was griping about leaving, saying he was fine to stay, but he was clearly in need of some serious medical attention.

Before Viv could turn away, I said, "This is going to get worse…a lot worse. Talk to LaSalle. He has SWM bots that can assist you with this sort of thing."

She nodded, offered up a half smile, and quansported away.

While Hardy helped Max with his replacement combat suit, I did the same for Wanda. Her body had indeed taken a vicious beating, but there was no persuading her to return to the *Oblivion*. It was now the four of us—Max, Wanda, Hardy, and myself. We were now the on-call reinforcement team.

Hardy said, "I believe the Grish are using jamming tech to hide their own bio-signatures from your suit's sensors."

"Cap…we never found the Symbio team we were sent in to assist with," Max said.

I looked back to Hardy with raised brows. "Any ideas on that?"

The ChronoBot, in an all-too-human pose, stood with hands on hips while looking about the passageway. "Once deactivated, the Symbios are near impossible to detect. What you would call a cold-blooded organism, whereby infrared scans come up negative. Then again…sometimes I can lock onto residual neurological activity, if there is any."

"And?" Wanda said.

Instead of answering her, Hardy bent down, took hold of one of the four-foot-by-six-foot decking panels with both hands, yanked it up in the air, and tossed the thing aside as if it weighed nothing. We all looked down into the sublevel space. And there, stacked like cords of firewood, were several Symbio-Poth bodies.

I tried unsuccessfully to lift a decking panel myself. With Wanda's help we were able to lift it up and topple it out of the way. More lifeless Symbios. "They must be laid out all along this stretch of the passageway," I said.

Hardy and the rest of us moved faster now—removing deck panels one after another. By the time we were done, thirty panels had been removed. Talking to Ensign Plorinne, he wanted them quansported onto the *Oblivion's* Symbio deck, where he'd ensure they'd be properly cared for and reanimated if possible.

I said, "From now on, any Symbio who wants to join back in the fight gets fitted with a combat suit first."

"Copy that, sir."

By now, all of the teams had been warned of one, the Grish jamming tech, and two, the possibility of overhead Grish assaults.

At this point, fighting was breaking out all over the outpost. Currently, five Pylor teams were exchanging weapons fire with the enemy and not making much leeway against the piglets. Injuries were mounting—and where I wanted to say *I told you so* in regards to their crappy old combat suits, I figured they'd already learned that lesson perfectly well on their own.

Doc Viv, now staying within HealthBay, was receiving the quansported injured Pylors one after another. MediBots and SWM bots were deployed as needed for off-ship pickups. The last time I'd touched base with Viv, she'd informed me of thirteen Pylor deaths while Ensign Plorinne let me know seventeen Symbios were too badly damaged to be reanimated. I didn't want to think too long on exactly who any of those unrepairable Symbios might be.

Quansporting in, the four of us were getting better at dispatching the lying-in-wait Grish assault teams. With that said, we were still not winning. Hardy could not be at all battlefronts at the same time. And at current attrition rates, we would not prevail over the enemy. We were currently at a major enemy stronghold of close to two hundred Grish. Apparently the piglets were making a midship stand—and doing so quite effectively.

I knew Plorinne was monitoring the open channel. I said, "Ensign, it's time now."

"Sir, I still don't think that is a good idea. They're not designed for off-ship battles… especially against live-fire situations."

I felt for the young ensign. He was more than just fond of the Symbios—they had become as close as family. "I'm sorry, Ensign; the situation here is quickly going critical. How about this. Let me talk to them…if they don't want to join the fight, so be it. We'll think of something else."

"Talk to them?"

"Yes, patch my comms into the Symbio deck's video PA system. Do it now."

It took a full minute before I could hear the familiar ambient jungle sounds filling my helmet. Then I saw them, four medium-sized Symbio dragons, along with the very large dragon named Sadon. And there, standing next to Sadon, was Reggie, the all-too-frightening Symbio T. rex.

Plorinne said, "You're patched through, sir."

I was thinking how best to ask for their help when Reggie spoke, "We art ready to serve, my lord."

A burst of fire belched from Sadon's elongated snout, "Hither we do nay good. Send us forth into battle, whither we can bring honor to all Symbios."

I said, "Sonya, you're listening in?"

"Of course."

"What do you think?"

"Well, from a code or programming perspective, I think they'll have no problem with the mission directives as they stand…"

"What other perspectives are you concerned with?"

"Um…the bigger Symbios…well, they are…how do I put this without getting them upset? They are emotional beings."

Both Sadon and Reggie looked to be getting agitated. Reggie said, "We art not emotional. We art strong. We art powerful!"

I briefly wondered if Sonya could program out those annoying medieval speech attributes but let that go for now.

She yelled back at Reggie, "Stop with the tough talk, you big dumb lizard! You know as well as I do that if you lost, say, Sadon or one of the other dragons in battle, in a real battle, you'd crumble…curl up into a ball and cry for…well, like forever!"

Now the three smaller dragons were getting into the conversation, bickering with one another, each expounding on how unemotional they were compared to the others.

Sonya said, "Captain, I need to work with them some more. Eventually they will be ready, I promise."

"We don't have time to wait. I'm sorry."

Plorinne said, "I have an idea, Captain. Let me send over the raptors."

"Raptors?"

"They have far less of an emotional AI component. They're far more like an actual Jurassic period predator. They're killers. There'll be only one minor drawback; sending the raptors…"

"I'm almost afraid to ask."

"They sometimes, very rarely…okay, occasionally, they will get into a kind of feeding frenzy. When that happens, they have a hard time determining friend or foe. Here on the Symbio deck we can quickly put a stop to things, even turn them off. But over there… the delay could have devastating results."

"I'm open to trying it. How many of the raptors are we talking about?"

"There are twenty velociraptors…perhaps leave five on board the *Oblivion*. Just in case?"

"How long before they can be ready to quansport?"

I could hear Sonya attacking her keyboard. "I'm just now up-dating their common attack parameters. Mainly to sniff out ba-con."

"Funny girl. How long specifically?"

"God, you're impatient." I heard another flurry of key taps, then one finishing loud one. "Done. They are ready to hunt. We want them ALL back alive, dude."

Dude?

***

After leaving several small teams scattered around the outpost, we had a total of ninety-two combatants, Pylors and Symbios, assembled there for what I assumed would be the pivotal battle of the campaign. We were dramatically outnumbered, and a good portion of our warriors weren't wearing proper combat suits. This wasn't the first time where I inwardly acknowledged the advantages of a true military hierarchy. There really wasn't much room in battle situations for personal choice. But those were thoughts for another time.

We were hunkered down approximately midship within the widest region of the outpost we'd just started to call the potbelly. This section was, for the most part, an open expanse. We figured at one time this had been a kind of recreational area—one that was easily a mile in circumference. So this had been like a park for the Gorvian crew. But now, the outpost being deserted for who knew how long, what had once been rolling hills of grass or turf covering was little more than dried-out chaff.

We'd scrounged various-sized makeshift barricades from nearby compartments and positioned them as far out into the potbelly as we dared. Grish weapons fire had made it perfectly clear just how far we would be allowed to move out into the open space before facing repercussions.

Standing with Hardy and Max, we looked out across the open divide.

"This seems like an archaic means to conduct a proper battle," Max said.

I couldn't disagree. If it wasn't for the fact we needed this outpost probably long term for providing the lifeblood for the *Oblivion*—we couldn't simply fire off limited-yield missile ordinances or the like. We just couldn't chance causing catastrophic damage. And since the Grish were hoping to come away from all this by absconding with the *Oblivion*, they, too, would need to keep this big outpost in one piece. So archaic warfare was mutually advantageous to both sides.

To make things worse, we'd already attempted several times to deploy small scouting drones into enemy territory—each had been destroyed within seconds.

"What are your sensors telling you, Hardy?"

The ChronoBot scratched at an imaginary chin. "They have seven fortified strongholds placed along the opposite side over there. Sure, I can determine numbers of piglets, but I'd like to have more intel. They were smart, destroying the outpost's security surveillance system…ensuring there'd be no hacking into overhead cameras or the like."

It was then that I noticed a soft golden glow emanating from the leather pouch hanging from Hardy's mechanical neck.

Max, pointing, said, "What about her?"

Hardy made an almost comical attempt to angle his head down in such a way to see the pouch.

"Could Iris do a little sleuthing for us, big guy?" I asked, already knowing how protective Hardy had become of his tiny Symbio-Poth fairy.

He was already shaking his head. "Not an option. No way, José. Ain't going to hap—"

But Iris had already shot out from the top of the pouch like a bullet. Glittering fairy dust followed in her wake. Tiny wings fluttering, she circled around the three of us twice, then around and around Hardy's head.

"Thou does not get to determine what I dost…and what I dost not dost!"

Hardy's shoulders slouched. "It is unsafe…did you not see what happened to the drones—"

"I am not a drone. I am intelligent. I am clever. More clever than thou. I will be right back."

And with that, Iris was gone, a tiny spark of light dodging and weaving her way across the open divide.

After ten minutes we were starting to get worried. I knew Hardy would blame me if anything happened to his strange, special friend. And as close as Hardy and I were, I doubted our relationship would survive him losing Iris.

Max, who had been staying busy readying his team, returned with a questioning expression. "No word from the…fairy?" He seemed uncomfortable having to say the word.

"No," Hardy said.

"Can't you scan for her presence over there?"

"No."

Max looked at me.

"I asked him the same thing. Apparently she's not showing up through the Grish bio-signatures' jamming tech."

Max blew a resigned breath out through puffed-out cheeks. "Ten minutes is a long time. Maybe—"

His reaction was swift, and before my eyes had registered the movement, I saw Hardy had a fist wrapped around Max's neck. All the ChronoBot had to do was tighten his grip, and Max's neck would be snapped like a dried twig.

"Hey, hey, hey, let's take a breath here. Hardy, remove your hand from your friend Max's neck. Do it now."

Hardy did as he was told.

"Now, tell Max you're sorry. Do it."

"I'm sorry, Max. I don't know what came over me."

Max was still rubbing the life back into his neck muscles. He nodded. "No worries."

I gave Hardy a sideways, narrowed-eyed glance that said, *Don't pull that shit again.*

Max said, "Anyway…your little friend's back."

The Symbio-Poth fairy made a beeline for Hardy, landing on his shoulder. Excited, she started speaking so fast, it was hard to make sense of what she was saying.

"They art clever, these chubby piglets. Well-hidden they art, standing in ditches…is that the word? Mayhap trenches is a better word, nay? They art waiting for thou to attack. And they have many robots that fly. Dronebots? Is dronebots a word? If not, it should be. They expect an attack from the front and not the back…not a one is looking over its shoulder."

Chapter 25

Iris's enemy assessment was both informative and worrying. With her dronebot description, although she wasn't able to express their actual quantity or numbers, it was clear there were a hell of a lot of them. Add to the fact we were already outnumbered nearly two to one, and the addition of the weaponized drones only made for a more discouraging situation.

The awaiting Pylor and Symbio combatants that were crowded in behind us were getting impatient. Constant squabbles were breaking out between and within the two groups. Truth was, my own patience with the whole situation was running thin.

"Look, the dronebots are an unknown factor, Hardy," I said. "So, they will be your prime targets once the fighting gets started. Max, the rest of your team will be quansporting back here onto the outpost anytime now. You'll need to separate, each of you taking charge of an assault team. Captain Pristy has agreed to provide us with several crates of low-yield bio-concussion grenades…ones that will, hopefully, only damage organic material while preserving surrounding structures."

As if on cue, Sloppy Joe said, "Incoming!"

The individual that was quansporting in looked to be small. Now, seeing who it was, I was right—it was Mr. Phillips. He was outfitted in a combat suit—his face visible behind his helmet's faceplate.

Immediately other items and people were being quansported in all around us.

"Mr. Phillips, why are you here?"

The little man was taking in his surroundings. Making a disgusted face, he said, "How revoltingly drab…"

"As you can see, we're pretty busy. Is there a reason you are here?"

"Obviously I've come to join the fight."

Max snickered.

"Uh-huh. You don't need to prove anything here. Maybe you should head on back—"

But Mr. Phillips was already shaking his head. He waggled an angry finger at me. "Ask any of the Pylors standing there behind you. Ask if I'm just as capable as any of them are in a brawl."

I looked to Vince and then to Sloppy Joe.

"Sure, he's one tiny buccaneer," Vince said, smiling and exposing brown teeth, "But yeah, he can hold his own. Mind you, best you don't judge that little book by its cover…if you know what I mean."

The other missing marines had just quansported into view.

"Fine, Mr. Phillips. You'll be joining Ham's team. Go on, skedaddle."

He shot me a threatening look before heading off.

"Wait, I have a team?" the newly arrived Ham said, looking confused.

Hardy said, "Cap, the dronebots are on the move…and they're coming this way."

"Looks like it's time to get this party started," Wanda said, looking far too enthusiastic.

I got back on the horn to Sonya and Ensign Plorinne. "Tell me you have the raptors ready for action, Ensign."

"Affirmative, Captain…Fifteen of them are here and—"

I cut him off. "They'll be entering the fight at the rear of the enemy stronghold."

Sonya said, "We've configured five of the raptors with a comms collar. You should be able to see and hear what they see and hear." I heard Sonya frantically tapping at her input device. "And I'm adding their respective avatars to your HUD now."

Over the open channel, I said, "Coogong…start quansporting the raptors." I turned my attention to Hardy. "Get moving, big guy."

As the ChronoBot strode away, his previously hidden energy cannons snapped out into view.

"Max, team leaders, head on out. And do me a favor. Try not to shoot Hardy or the raptors."

"Just as long as any of those dinosaur lizards don't try to eat me," Sloppy Joe said, passing by.

I heard the first of the screams, more like a loud squeal, emanating from the far side of the divide. It took me a moment to learn how to access the raptor avatars via my HUD. Figuring it out, I gasped in surprise. The comms collar provided a strangely intimate view from one beast's perspective. At the moment, I was looking at the decapitated, still-spasming body of an unfortunate Grish warrior. I could just make out the piglet's helmeted head— still captured within the jaws of Tammy. Tammy being the name Sonya had designated for that particular raptor.

One by one, I opened the remaining four avatars for Bonnie, Stanley, Gary, and Johnny. This allowed me a clear view of their respective rampages into the piglets' ranks. I was also seeing some of the other raptors not fitted with a collar. What I was witnessing was pure unbridled mayhem. A bloodbath. But with over two hundred Grish to contend with, I was skeptical the raptors would be enough to turn the tide of this battle. One of the raptor feeds suddenly blinked out—then another. *Crap. Sonya is going to have my hide.*

I was eager to join in on the fight but stayed put anyway. My plan was to hole up here. Use my position behind this barricade as a central command post to keep a vigil on the attacking raptors, the Pylor and Symbio-Poth combatants, as well as keep in contact with the *Oblivion* and the *Hercules.*

Currently, I was taking in the spectacle from Hardy's POV, watching as all five of his Phazon Pulsar energy cannons targeted the darting-about dronebots—which were white orbs, about the size of a basketball, each capable of firing off energy bolts simultaneously in any direction.

Already bodies lay still on the ground; too many Pylors were being taken down, as were the Symbio-Poths. I caught a quick glimpse of Hardy from a passing raptor. His beautiful new chrome was already a scorched and blackened mess. This wasn't working—what I was witnessing was quickly becoming a massacre.

"Ensign…we need to send in the big Symbios. Coogong, quansport them over…the sooner the better."

"Captain, I still—"

"This is not an open discussion, Ensign. For any of us to get out of this alive, we need to change the dynamics of this battle, fast! Coogong, send in the big Symbios. And one more thing. I want Bosun Johanna Polk here next to me within thirty seconds."

Thirty seconds seemed more like thirty minutes. She arrived, looking bewildered and in a sitting position. Clearly, she'd had no notice as to what was about to happen to her. Ten seconds later an empty combat suit and shredder arrived.

Mouth agape, she looked up at me.

"Get up, Bosun…you're taking over as field operations coordinator. You'll be the central conduit between…well everyone."

"What about you, sir?"

Helping her get situated into her combat suit, I said, "I'm going in. This is an all-hands fight, and I can do a hell of a lot more good out there than standing here barking off orders."

"Um…okay."

I said, "Sonya, let's get Bosun Polk's HUD configured like mine with full command authorization."

"Did that already," she said. I heard a loud snapping sound. She chewed bubble gum when she was nervous.

I checked the charge on my shredder, gave Polk a pat on her shoulder, and was off and heading toward the raging battle.

I ran for no less than a quarter mile before I reached the engagement. Green and red energy bolts flashed by from every direction. Hardy was up ahead, and as instructed, he was putting most of his efforts into the dronebots. Discouraged, I watched. Even after multiple direct hits, the drones remained active and all too lethal in the air.

Piglets were everywhere, short, pudgy-looking, and vicious. Their shredder weapon equivalents were spewing off thick and devastating energy bolts. Bodies lay everywhere. Many had lost their heads thanks to the raptors, of which I saw only two remained active. Sloppy Joe and Mr. Phillips were there in front of me, taking on five piglets, neither side having a safe harbor or any kind of barricade to take shelter behind. I barreled forward, shredder blazing.

Hardy's voice came over comms. "Aim for the piglet suits' shoulder joints. Damn suits are nearly impregnable to shredder fire. It's the only weak point."

Mr. Phillips was now down on one knee. I wasn't sure how badly he'd been hurt.

Now, standing shoulder to shoulder with Sloppy Joe, we continued blasting away at the enemy to no avail. "Give me your dagger."

Sloppy, too occupied to look at me, said, "You mean my dirk?"

"Whatever! Give it to me!" I yelled over the battle noise.

He did as told.

The double-sided blade was about a foot long. The weapon had a nice heft to it. I rushed forward, taking two blasts to the chest, but kept going. Their faces partially visible behind round helmeted faceplates, all five of the piglets looked astonished at my brazen, unexpected approach. Remembering Hardy's words, I darted left, then right, then jabbed the blade into the closest piglet suit's shoulder joint. The blade slid in like a hot knife through butter. Even before the Grish warrior began to topple, I was onto the next—a quick jab again, and down went piglet number two.

All three remaining piglets turned their full attention to me. But I was moving fast. Real fast. I'd forgotten about Doc Viv's glowing green elixir. I was moving as fast as my thoughts—or, strangely, faster than that. Within three seconds, all three piglets were down and gushing blood into their suits.

Off in the distance, I saw Wanda. Four piglets, two on each side, had her secured by her arms while a fifth piglet used the butt end of his energy weapon to pound away at her helmet. I felt sick at the sight. Taking five strides, which I'm sure looked more like a blur of motion, I reached Wanda in time to take the next blow to my chest instead of her head.

Sloppy's dirk seemed to move of its own accord. With a jabbing uppercut motion, the blade slipped in between helmet and cowling seal. I caught a glimpse of crimson rising up inside the piglet's helmet, but I was already dispatching the other four dumbfounded-looking Grish assholes who had a hold of the unconscious, or maybe dead, Wanda.

I stabbed each of them once and then again for good measure. As gently as I could, I laid Wanda down. I saw her eyes flutter behind her faceplate. Relief flooded over me—she was still alive. I barked off the command for Coogong to quansport her directly into HealthBay.

Looking up and around, I saw that this shitshow of an offensive was quickly going from bad to worse. *"Where are those damn—"*

The all-too-loud and unmistakable roar of a tyrannosaurus rex stymied my question. Better late than never. Two, then three, then all four Symbio dragons quansported into view. Great plumes of fire swept overhead. And while those marines, Symbios, and Pylors that were still standing watched, transfixed in nervous amazement, the piglets did the opposite—they ran.

Chapter 26

While the Grish piglets ran as if their pants were on fire, the seemingly fearless dronebots did not. They attacked with a well-coordinated aerial onslaught. Obviously knowing that a cumulative effort would be most effective, they united and concentrated their weapons fire onto one of the smaller dragons. I remembered his name was Vandom.

Although putting up a valiant fight, spewing large beach-ball-sized fireballs and eviscerating the closest of the dronebots, Vandom was already struggling under the intense enemy weapons fire. Sadon was the first to abandon his own pursuits and come to Vandom's rescue. But with the smaller dragon there at the center of the surrounding dronebots, Sadon couldn't unleash a burst of fire without taking out Vandom in the process.

Now, pacing back and forth in growing frustration, Sadon fluttered his massive wings, rising up and swiping claws at several of the drones—but it was too little, too late. Vandom toppled over, his body smoldering from countless energy strikes.

Oblivious to the fact that the dronebots were now turning their attention to Sadon, the great dragon stormed forward to where Vandom lay dead.

"Sadon!" I yelled. "Behind you!"

But just as Ensign Plorinne had warned, the great dragon's

emotional component was completely eclipsing good judgment. Sadon used his long snout to push and prod at the smaller, lifeless dragon. Making sobbing, and then loud wailing sounds, Sadon now looked more like a distraught puppy than the threatening and powerful beast he'd been just moments before.

Hardy, Sloppy Joe, Mr. Phillips, and I concentrated our combined weapons fire up toward the dragon-encircling dronebots. Soon Max was at our side, joining in on the firefight.

I heard both Ensign Plorinne and Sonya yelling into their comms for me to do something. To save Sadon, to get him out of there. But the big docile-looking beast just took one devastating bolt of hot plasma after another.

Max said, "He won't survive much more of this. Already starting to teeter."

I continued to fire then stopped. *Shit! Why didn't I think of it earlier!*

Over the open channel, I said, "Coogong! Are you able to get a lock on these dronebots?"

"Affirmative, Captain."

"Can you quansport them, either all at once or individually out into space?"

"I'm sorry, no, Captain. That was already suggested by Captain Pristy just moments ago. There are certain elemental properties within each of those dronebots that interfere with completing the full quantum entanglement process. I suspect each dronebot has an internal self-destruct mechanism. A capture avoidance trigger. A small nuclear bomb constituent. As I've mentioned to you before, this is the reason we cannot simply quansport nuclear bombs onto enemy ships."

My own frustration was mounting by the second. Looking around, I saw the battle raging on. Reggie, with two lifeless Grish legs hanging from one side of his mouth, was trying to stomp down on his many attackers. A raptor in the distance was chasing several fleeing piglets, and a small cluster of Pylors was fending off a larger group of Grish warriors.

I flinched as a young Symbio woman was shot down not ten feet from where I stood. The situation had gone from bad to worse. It was time to pull the plug on this fiasco and have Coogong start transporting those of us still alive back to the *Oblivion*.

I heard Pristy's voice coming over the comms, "I'll send in my troops."

As relieved as I was to hear her voice, not to mention her offer, I said, "You do that, and you can kiss your command, your career, goodbye. Fighting side by side with me, the one you've come to apprehend? That's called aiding and abetting the enemy, Gail. You sure you want to do that?"

"I'm not going to let this massacre continue on any longer! You never did have the necessary boots on the deck to go up against this enemy. And don't forget, the Grish are both our enemy, so yeah, I'm mobilizing my troops."

I could hear the resignation in her voice. This was not how I wanted her to join me. Not if it wasn't of her own free will.

I instinctively ducked as a dark shape suddenly swooped by my head. It took a second for my brain to catch up with what my eyes were seeing. With flowing black robes, a hooded Varapin ghoul had just swooshed past me. *What the…*

Three more zoomed past Hardy—five, no seven, more were approaching from the opposite side of the battlefield. Then I saw several more just as they were being quansported into view. *Coogong!* He'd let his trust in the stowaway ghouls get the better of him.

Pristy said, "Galvin…what is it? What's happening?"

"I think things just went from bad to worse…"

"I'm sending in a company of marines."

I said, "Wait!"

There must have been close to fifty Varapin now; they were circling around above us, but not one had attacked. I said, "Hardy… talk to me."

The ChronoBot had stopped firing, looking as dumbfounded as the rest of us. "They're not carrying weapons, Cap."

"Well, they're each carrying something…I can see it in their hands, claws, whatever."

Max said, "Um…I think those are power drivers…you know, screwdrivers."

As if on cue, one of the ghouls approached, twenty feet in the air, and then climbed atop one of the dronebots. Only then did the mechanical orb stop firing on Reggie and start spinning one way and then the other.

Hardy said, "Oh, I get it. Dronebots either can't detect the ghouls' presence or have been instructed not to fire upon them… since the Grish and the Varapin are allies."

I was only half listening to Hardy's ramblings—the Varapin was being flung this way and that as if riding a bucking bull. I watched intently as the robed alien began using his power driver to systematically remove a series of screws and then flip open a small access panel. He reached an obsidian claw inside. The orb's little flashing lights suddenly blinked out, and energy weapon muzzles retracted. Then the dronebot dropped like a lead balloon. It hit the faux ground with a resounding, loud *clang*! It rolled toward Hardy, who casually stomped a heavy ChronoBot foot down onto it.

I thought of reminding the numbskull robot that there was still a nuclear device somewhere inside of that thing, but let it go. My attention was on the other Varapin ghouls, who were duplicating the actions of the first one. Soon, one by one, inert dronebots were falling like oversized metal bowling balls. *Clang! Clang! Clang!*

I took a moment to scan my surroundings. Everyone, including the enemy Grish, had stopped to watch in astonished silence.

Taking a dozen steps closer to Sadon, I opened my helmet's face-plate and looked up to him. I said, "You okay, Sadon?"

The big dragon growled and then nodded.

"Think you might want some payback for what they did to Vandom here?"

Slowly, Sadon's head rose up, and eyes as black as death itself began to peer around the vast, oversized compartment. With each breath, fire leaped from flaring nostrils. The dragon nodded, then looked at me. "I like my bacon extra crispy."

Chapter 27

With the dronebots deactivated, the remaining Grish combatants were soon either killed outright or taken into custody. As it turned out, the outpost's sizable brig had ample room for close to one hundred squealing and complaining piglets. Our Varapin saviors had disappeared as quickly as they had appeared. That would be a discussion for another day. As for right now, we had a colossal helix collider refueling outpost to get up and running.

Deep within the bowels of the outpost, I stood off to the side, feeling more than useless. My chief of engineering, Craig Porter, along with Coogong and Hardy, was immersed in getting the outpost operational again. And because some of the issues with restarting the collider were of the software variety, Sonya was here too—sitting at a nearby console, incessantly chewing and snapping bubblegum bubbles.

There was a familiar voice from behind me, and I started.

"Galvin?"

I turned to see my old rumpled-looking friend, Stephan Derrota. He saw the surprise on my face and smiled. Forgoing military protocol—I was, after all, no longer in the military—we hugged while giving each other big manly pats on the back.

I said, "I was wondering when you'd make your way over here." I'd put the invite out there to both Pristy and Derrota earlier. Pristy had declined outright but said Derrota was free to quansport over.

"I hope you don't mind, but I've taken the liberty of looking around some. This is quite an impressive complex."

"Find anything…useful?"

Derrota rubbed the stubble on his chin and nodded. "The stockpiles of equipment here…highly advanced equipment…well. It's staggering. I won't lie to you, Galvin…there's an adherent-coated reactor housing the size of a New York City bus that would be a near-perfect replacement for our own damaged reactor housing. It's below, in Hold #839. It could get the *Hercules's* propulsion system fully operational again. And without all that much effort, to boot."

Now it was my turn to rub my stubbled chin. "Hmm…Yeah, my friend, I'd love to offer you that…what did you call it? Some kind of reactor housing?"

"Adherent-coated reactor housing." Derrota narrowed his eyes. "What do you want in exchange?"

Playing it up, I let out a defeated breath. "Nah…it's not possible."

Derrota's expression told me he wasn't buying my act. "Fine. I need your help thinking out of the box. You're good at that." He waited with brows slightly raised.

"I need to make this outpost, um…mobile."

A sharp crease formed between his eyes. "As in making this outpost into what? A kind of vessel?"

"Exactly. If it stays here, I'll never get access to it again. That or it'll be destroyed by our enemies. The *Oblivion* needs fuel…"

But he was shaking his head.

"Hey, the outpost won't need extravagant maneuverability… no barrel rolls, no loop de loops!"

Derrota pursed his lips.

"I just need to be able to maneuver this big complex into and out of a manufactured wormhole."

Finally, Derrota nodded his head. "That…I think, may be possible."

"Okay, so what would it take?"

"How long is this outpost?"

"I'm not exactly sure. Hardy could say for certain, but maybe fifteen miles in length. Three or four miles in width."

Derrota was pacing now, eyes fixed on the deck before him. "Well, you won't find what you need here on board the outpost."

"No? Why not? You just said—"

"Because what you need are fully intact ship propulsion systems. No, scrap that; what you need are actual operational starships. Let's start with five of them…one astern for primary propulsion and two portside and two starboard-side vessels. Best if the ships are all from the same manufacturer, such as those from a near-by Grish attack group." Derrota waved a hand toward the distant bulkhead. "They're out there; it's your problem to capture several of them…"

I was well aware of the nearby enemy fleet, no doubt ready to pounce at any moment. I was also more than a little surprised that that hadn't happened already. No doubt they'd come to terms with the fact their lying-in-wait ambush had failed. I said, "We're sitting ducks here…especially with the Oblivion saddled up to the outpost as it is. Our defenses are pretty much useless."

Derrota looked confused.

"What?"

"Well…the *Oblivion* and the *Hercules's* weaponry are both stymied. But this outpost's defenses are…well, impressive."

I just stared at my Mumbai friend. "Defenses?"

"Sure. Wait, you didn't know?"

"Know what? There are no onboard defenses—"

"That's not true, Cap," Hardy said, clomping his way toward us upon a nearby metal catwalk. "I was meaning to mention it earlier, but with the battle with the piglets and getting the collider up and running…"

Derrota chuckled. "And now you know why the Grish fleet out there hasn't orchestrated an attack. Sure, the guns are well hidden. The outposts shields are currently down, but this outpost is fully fortified. What was needed was the power fully turned back on and the collider energized."

By now, Hardy had reached us. His face display was back to his 3D vintage John Hardy look. "And as of four and a half minutes ago, this big tub will be generating three hundred thousand megawatt-hours of electricity each and every day. And of course, that doesn't include the fuel it's now producing." He pointed up, first left and then right. "See those twin helix tubes? They run aft, aimed at opposite sides of the central beam splitter, which in turn spits out dual Pion beams to their two respective condensers. Those stack the separated Pions into those," he now gestured aft, "twin, at nearly absolute zero, superfluid tanks. Within those babies, it's about as dense as a dwarf star."

"So…we can begin the *Oblivion's* refueling process?" I asked

"Soon. It'll be as simple as connecting an anti-decay hose and letting the superfluids flow." Then the John Hardy face looked up with a scowl. "Thing is…if any of the connection valves are worn, maybe broken, that could be a problem. We'd risk the Pions heating up and having a matter-antimatter decay reaction…right on the spot. Which, in a word, would not be good."

"Maybe you should check on those," I said.

He nodded but didn't move.

Derrota said, "Well?"

"Oh yeah…I just checked all of the anti-decay hoses and connection valves…they're fine. All sensors showing nominal operation. You didn't think I was going to manually check each connection, did you?"

"Back to the outpost's defenses, Hardy," I said.

"Like the *Oblivion*, this outpost is comprised of Gorvian tech, so you have your nullifier missiles, 'Baby Pulsars'…DPPBs, your hydro-missiles—those are plentiful all around the outpost—your standard Phazon Pulsar cannons, and let's not forget the ZEDs."

Coming up through the soles of my boots, I felt a steady vibration. This outpost was truly operational again. And the air around us had a different ozone smell to it.

Coogong, Porter, and Sonya were making their way over to us. I introduced Derrota to Sonya.

My mind was still swirling with possibilities. Possibilities presented by Derrota—that we'd need five intact and fully operational starships to make this magnificent construct mobile. I put my attention onto the Thine scientist. "Coogong, let me ask you a hypothetical question."

"Of course, Captain."

"Let's say we—you—employed our quansporting technology to transport certain individuals, small teams, onto, say…several of the enemy ships."

Coogong's emblematic smile didn't falter. "Go on…"

"How long before the Grish would be able to counteract such tactics?"

Sonya snapped a chewing gum bubble and ignored my annoyed glance her way.

Coogong said, "It is no secret among our enemies that the US Space-Navy, and you specifically, Captain, have this capability. Varapin ship commanders, I suspect, have been instructed on how to best this exact tactic…that tactic being the adjustment of defensive shields to produce a parallel high-radiation belt around a particular ship. As you well know, quansporter technology, quantum attachment, does not play well with radiation potentiality."

"Do we need to dumb that down for you, Captain?" Sonya said.

"No, I think my tiny brain is capable of tracking what Coogong is saying."

Coogong continued, "Then again, if the Grish have yet to implement such a defensive approach, I would say you have mere minutes. Ten, fifteen at the most."

I looked to Hardy. "You concur?"

But Hardy was talking to Iris, who was sitting on his shoulder.

"Hardy. Are you listening to me?"

"Yes, I concur, Cap. But Iris brings up an important point.'

"Which is?"

"With quansported away teams, you may run into more of those killer dronebots. I'm sure you remember; they had pretty much bested us until we had a little help."

Chapter 28

Over the course of the next four days, everyone was busy. As it turned out, refueling the *Oblivion* had not been as simple a process as expected. No one had ever refueled a Gorvian starship before, so there was a bit of trial and error before the newly formulated Pions' superfluids were flowing.

Derrota, Coogong, and Porter worked pretty much nonstop, first to have the adherent-coated reactor housing quansported out of Hold #839 on over to the *Hercules's* engineering and propulsion section.

There was a lot of interaction going on between the crews of the *Hercules* and the *Oblivion*, but it didn't take a genius to notice Pristy was going out of her way to keep her distance from yours truly. Sure, I could understand her situation—after all, she'd been sent here to arrest me, to bring me back to Earth to face charges of desertion. But, there was something else going on, and I was determined to find out what it was. Now, simply showing up on the bridge of the *Hercules* could get me arrested, so, embracing my recently acquired pirate status, I decided to do something a little more unorthodox. I waited until Pristy's end of shift—and after years of working with her, I had a fairly good idea what time she tended to head off the bridge.

When I quansported into her quarters, she was just finishing up brushing her teeth in the adjoining head. Stunned, she watched me take form in the mirror. Momentarily frozen there—toothbrush captured between frothy white lips—she quickly regained her composure. Finishing up, she spat into the sink, wiped her mouth with a small towel, and turned to face me.

That's unexpected. She was wearing a full-length nightgown. *Does anyone even wear nightgowns anymore?* It was cream-colored and made of a thin, sheer fabric; cotton would be my guess. And did I mention it was sheer? In that moment I was seeing more of Gail Pristy's naked body than in any of the four years I'd known her.

Several moments passed in silence between us before she must have registered my roving eyes. Immediately, she crossed her arms over her chest and turned sideways. "So not only have you become a criminal, a space pirate, but you sneak into an unsuspecting woman's quarters!"

It was more of an accusation than a question. I shrugged. "You've been avoiding me."

Her cheeks colored at that. "You're imagining things. I'm the captain of a US Space-Navy warship...did you consider that I may be busy?"

"Busy doing what? Your ship is disabled and it's, for lack of a better word, trapped here along with the *Oblivion* and *Sanctuary*."

"*Sanctuary?*"

I took a step forward. "Uh-huh. I gave the outpost a proper name. What do you think...it has a nice ring to it, doesn't it? *Sanctuary*." I took another step closer to her.

She rolled her eyes. "A better name would be the *Shanghaied*... just like what you did with the Oblivion. You're a marauder now... you're one of the bad guys."

I took another step forward—I breathed in Ivory soap and Crest. "That I am. And I own who I am. I'm a marauder and a bad guy who's going to make a difference by doing things my way."

"And you're going to get yourself killed…either by the enemy or by Earth's forces."

"So you're afraid *for* me? Or maybe more like afraid of losing me?"

I took one last step forward—bringing us to mere inches apart. Her eyes stayed level on my chest, refusing to look up at me. "You need a shave. And a haircut."

"Uh-huh…"

Slowly, her arms relaxed and dropped away. She placed a tentative palm on my chest. "You really shouldn't be here, Galvin."

"Well…I'm a marauder …a bad guy."

The corners of her lips turned upward. Her eyes lifted, and she finally looked at me. "So…what exactly do marauders do…in situations like this?"

I slid an arm around her lower back and pulled her in close. With our lips almost touching, I said, "This is where the ruggedly handsome pirate—"

"Marauder," she corrected.

"Marauder utterly and completely corrupts the innocent young maiden."

She kissed me then—gently at first and then with far more passion. Briefly separating, she said, "I got news for you, Black Beard. I'm not all that innocent."

Captain Pristy, your presence is required on the bridge…
Captain Pristy, your presence is required on the bridge…

"MATHR, stop! I heard you," she said, replacing her palm on my chest and looking upward. "Report. What exactly is the issue?"

"Incoming! Incoming! Incoming!"

I had Coogong quansport me back to the *Oblivion*. I could hear Lieutenant Akari James's voice from out in the corridor. Hurrying in, I saw she was standing at Tactical and issuing orders like a seasoned bridge officer.

"Sitrep, Lieutenant," I said, taking in the myriad colored icons up on the halo display.

"The short answer…we're under attack."

"I assumed as much."

She checked her board. "We have multiple incoming smart-missiles. All seven Grish warships have fired off no less than ten nukes each. I would surmise they have decided waiting any longer to make their move would be futile."

Chen said, "Captain, the *Hercules* is requesting separation from the *Oblivion* and the outpost…um, *Sanctuary*."

I looked over to Grimes and nodded. "Set them free, Helm. But let's keep an eye on that warship…her propulsion repairs have yet to be tested."

"Are we also leaving the outpost?"

I didn't answer right away.

Akari said, "First missile impact will be in four minutes and thirty seconds."

I looked about the bridge. "Can someone tell me where Hardy's run off to?"

"He's still on *Sanctuary*," Chen said.

"Hail him."

Hardy appeared on the halo display; apparently he was still hanging around the helix collider. He said, "I know, I know; we're under attack. On my way back—"

"No, stay on board *Sanctuary*. There's a command center, or some kind of operations center, on board that outpost, correct?"

"That would be a big yes. Gorvian translation, the resource directorate hub."

"Fine, the RDH it is. Get Coogong to quansport—"

"I don't need Coogong to do that…none of us do. It's an integrated function within our respective comms packages via the crew's Jadoo rings and my operating software."

I knew that, but hadn't taken the time yet to figure out how. "Fine. Get yourself up to the RDH and—"

The scene up on the halo display suddenly changed. It took me a moment to realize Hardy had quansported into another area of *Sanctuary*.

"He must have jumped into that RDH compartment," Akari said.

The compartment was almost as large as the *Oblivion's* bridge. Hardy was on the move, first flipping on what looked like power-breaker switches and then rushing about from one console to another. One by one, colorful holographic displays were being projected up over individual stations. While Hardy continued to work, he said, "I am assuming you want *Sanctuary's* ZEDs initialized?" The ChronoBot hadn't waited for my response because up on the *Oblivion's* display, blue, glowing, all-encompassing ZEDS were now surrounding both the *Sanctuary* and the *Oblivion*.

Hardy came to a stop and faced the RDH's camera. His vintage John Hardy face display was that of a man gasping—now making huffing and puffing sounds as if he was out of breath. Raising an overdramatic finger, as if he needed a moment to breathe, he said, "I take it you wanted me to employ *Sanctuary's* missile defense systems?"

"Yes, and thank you for that. One more thing. What does *Sanctuary* have in the way of a dampening field generator?"

Hardy looked over one shoulder and then back again. "I think it might be that inactive station behind me. I have no idea what that board does." He strode over to the station and began tapping.

In the meantime, I watched as at least seventy, if not more,

Grish nuclear smart-missiles drew ever closer. The *Hercules* was on the move, going through what looked to be various tests of her propulsion system.

Hardy was back in front of the RDH camera. "Yes."

"Yes, what?"

"Yes, that station provides for dampening field generation. It's called the Omphalos Station…FYI, you have a similar console there on the *Oblivion*."

"Fine. We'll figure it out another time. Can you use the RDH's, um…"

"Omphalos Station."

"Yes, that…to generate a dampening field around that Grish attack group?"

"Can I…or have I?"

I just stared at the big robot. God, he was exhausting sometimes. "Hardy…"

"Okay, okay…as of one minute and five seconds ago, all seven Grish warships are as immobilized as flies to flypaper."

I looked to the halo display; all of the missiles were still inbound. I briefly wondered if I should be more worried about those.

Hardy continued, "Yeah…because of the extended distance between Sanctuary and Grish warships, there was little I could do about the missiles. As it is, the generated dampening field is being pushed to its power limits."

I said, "Lieutenant James, you have a weapon's lock on each of those missiles?"

"I do, sir."

"Employ the *Oblivion's* hydro-missiles. Fire at will."

"Aye, sir. Firing hydro-missiles now."

The Oblivion shook with the dispatch of each wave of missiles. Soon the halo display was filled with multicolored, converging icons.

"Captain?" Akari said. "Shall I go ahead and target the enemy ships? Now that they're pretty much sitting ducks."

"No. We'll be needing them most of them fully intact."

Chapter 29

I headed to the Symbio deck, not knowing what I'd find. We'd quansported all of the damaged, dare I say killed, Symbios, from *Sanctuary* back to the *Oblivion* after combating the Grish. At least to me, a good number of them had looked beyond repair—heads missing, obliterated arm and leg appendages, severe energy weapons burns.

The open space adjacent to the jungle was dark, and there was no sign of activity. I did a quick check-in with the bridge. All incoming missiles had been taken out by our hydro-missiles. I wasn't surprised—In that regard, Gorvian technology was no match for the Grish.

Caveman Glory was shut down. As I stood there, mind wandering, I heard the distant sound of rapid tapping. I found Sonya sitting within her little cubicle. No less than eight 3D hologram projections hovered over her wraparound control board. Two of them were raptors, another two were smaller dragons, and four of them were Symbio-Poth people.

She didn't look up as I entered her private space. I took a seat in an empty chair and watched her work. She was in a heated conversation with someone else—then I heard Ensign Plorinne's voice.

"I think you're using the same patch routine that failed last time!"

Sonya shook her head. "Don't worry about my code; it's right. You do your job…you still need to completely replace that optical subsystem."

For the first time, her eyes flicked in my direction. "Raptor eye took a direct hit from piglet weapons fire." Turning her attention to the hologram, her thin brows bunched together. "No, what, are you stupid? That's a caveman character eye unit…they don't look anything like dinosaurs, Plori!"

I hadn't realized Ensign Plorinne had a nickname, or maybe it was just her pet name for him.

Sonya turned in her chair to put her full attention on me. Her expression was devoid of humor. "This cannot happen again."

I nodded. She was right. "I'm sorry."

"Sorry's not good enough."

"Look, Sonya…Everyone has a choice here. The Symbios weren't ordered to fight. It's what they—"

"Don't you dare! These beings are not human. They do not have free will…they have reactionary artificial intelligence that is based on programming algorithms. Their response to the question "Do you want to fight?" will always be fucking yes."

I sat back and held my tongue. Her eyes had started to brim with tears. Attempting to blink them away, then angrily wiping at them with quick swipes, she raised both palms as if in an attempt to stop time. "I'm just saying, Captain, that sending these beings into battle without so much as a protective combat vest, well, it's cruel."

"Then we—you—need to alter their programming to accept my orders. They were programmed to be cavemen, cave people, whatever, for the game. They wouldn't accept using combat suits."

She looked at me, chewing at the inside of her cheek. "That's dangerous."

"What's dangerous?"

"Programming in that kind of code. To accept orders unconditionally from one human."

"They don't do that now? Like from you or Plori?"

That caused a twitch of a quick smile. "Only I call him that." She shifted in her seat. "No, actually. Symbios can say no. They can make assessments based on their available inputs…the information within their databanks…based on historical outcomes."

I took that in. This young lady was smart. And clearly she had deep feelings for the Symbio-Poths. "How are you doing with repairs? Are there any, um…casualties?"

"Yes. And I'm not happy about that. Ten Symbios will need to be recycled."

Lori Quintos came to mind, but I let it go. "I'm sorry. I really am."

Sonya somewhat overdramatically looked up to the overhead and groaned. "I'm going to do it. I'll program in a statement script that will override all other code within any augmented reality. A code that their neural networks cannot override." Looking at me now, she narrowed her eyes, "They'll wear battle suits if you tell them to. They'll also walk on their hands while singing nursery rhymes. The abuse you could inflict…"

"I won't."

"You better not."

***

Sonya walked me back to the behind the scenes area of Caveman Glory to an area she referred to as the reconditioning zone. This was where the proverbial sausage was made. As quiet and still as the park out front was, this was the opposite. It reminded me of the behind the scenes area of a commercial airport or spaceport. Hover carts whizzed by, some occupied, others not. An overhead crane arm swung while a suspended, almost pathetic-looking Reggie was positioned over an immense metal vat of some kind. I watched as the big T. rex was then gently lowered until the top of his head disappeared from view. There were a series of large platforms—I supposed they were more of a form of operating table—each occupied by one form of Symbio-Poth creature or another.

The table closest to me supported the girth of a smaller dragon. Lying on its back, its wings were spread out wide and clamped down—reminiscent of some archaic form of torture. The dragon's middle section was opened up, and I could see the various wet and slimy-looking organs, if that's what they were called, inside. If this was an animal back on Earth, its innards, its guts, would be red—but with Symbios, there was no blood. Just various shades of white organs and glistening blood-equivalent clear moisture.

Each table had its own small team of multi-armed hover-bots—part mechanics, part surgeons, all busy repairing the recent battle damage. As if I hadn't felt guilty enough as it was, now I felt downright reprehensible.

We moved deeper into the sausage factory until we found Ensign Plorinne headed our way, lugging something heavy over one shoulder. Once close enough, I saw that it was a raptor's leg assembly.

"Ah, Captain. Um…are you sure you want to be back here?" He shot Sonya a reprimanding glance.

"It's fine. And I need to know everything that goes on…even behind the scenes."

"Yes, sir."

Only now did I see, off to my left, an area that was dedicated to the repairs of the human-looking Symbios. Many smaller tables were occupied by nonfunctioning Symbios. *Shit!* And to think I'd come here to see if there were a few operational Symbios I could appropriate for an upcoming mission.

"Hey, Captain…do you want to see where the Symbios, um, hang out when not in use?" Plorinne asked, seeing my concern.

"Yes, Ensign. I'd like that."

As the three of us strode forward through the reconditioning zone, I forced myself to take in the reality of what was taking place here. Just as I made it a function of my job to visit HealthBay to check on members of my crew after a battle, I would now do the same here when Symbios were involved.

Next, we came to a series of three large thirty- or forty-foot-high roll-up doors. Between the first and second was a standard hatch door, which swooshed open at our approach. We moved from the blaring bright lights and loudly echoing noises of the reconditioning zone to softly muted lights and near-total quiet. Although, now that I heard it, there was sound. Soft music—no, it was more like the harmonizing song of monks chanting—emanating from somewhere. It was as if we'd journeyed back in time into the serenity of an ancient monastery.

Sonya, just above a whisper, said, "Welcome to Palitine. We talk softly in here, but to be honest, there's no need to."

We came to a stop, and Sonya gestured to a nearby bulkhead. I'd noticed that there were imprints or contours upon the walls, but in the muted darkness, I hadn't really observed much detail. Until now. "Oh my…" Not three feet from where I stood was a human form. Standing vertical and nestled into a kind of opened pericarp, arms crossed over her chest as if in a death pose, was none other than Lori Quintos. Her eyes were closed, and she looked peaceful.

"Is she…"

"Dead?" Plorinne said. "No. She wasn't over there. Not part of the battle. She's in *re-gen* mode. Kind of like sleeping. We actually give them dream scenarios they can interact with autonomously. I think it…well, helps them to become more…evolved."

I continued to look at the sleeping Symbio-Poth woman.

"I knew she was your mom, you know…from Clairmont. Thought you'd like to see she's all right," Sonya said.

I fought the rise of inner emotions and smiled. "I appreciate that. But this is simply an advanced robot. She is not my mother."

Sonya looked at me for several beats. "You're right about her not being your mother. But simply an advanced robot, you're wrong. They are so much more than that."

I walked through Palitine's corridors, stopping every once in a while to regard a sleeping Symbio. There were hundreds of them here. "They look content, even happy."

"They are. They're not like humans in that way. They seem to love their existence, their small carved-out purpose within the cosmos," Sonya said.

I looked at her, once again impressed by the teenager's mature perspective. And then she snapped a bubblegum bubble.

Chapter 30

My next stop was HealthBay, where Doc Viv had only a few moments for me, as she had surgeries lined up back to back for the next four hours. A quarter of the space was filled by Pylors. The injuries ran the full spectrum, from relatively simple broken bone repairs to a spinal cord fusion to a total lower jaw regrow. As I was stopping to talk to each patient, about halfway through my circuit around the compartment, my Jaadoo ring began to vibrate.

"Go for Captain," I said to the projected Akari James hologram over my hand.

"We have a problem, Captain."

"Give me a sitrep."

"It's the *Hercules*."

"What's happened to her…has she been attacked?" I thought of Pristy and inwardly prayed she hadn't been injured or worse, killed.

"Just the opposite, sir. Looks like Captain Pristy is taking full advantage of the situation with the Grish. Their assets are held in our dampening field. *Hercules* has come abreast of one of their warships and is pummeling it with weapons fire."

Dammit, I need those assets! But I had to smile—Pristy was not a pirate; she was a US Space-Navy captain, and she was doing her job.

"Captain, the Grish warship just blew up. *Hercules* is moving on to the next quarry. What shall I do…I'm guessing you wouldn't want to fire on—"

"No, Lieutenant, I wouldn't," I snapped back and instantly regretted it. "Sorry, Akari…I'm operating on too little sleep. Can you track down Hardy? I'm on my way. Have him meet me there."

***

I arrived in time to see the second Grish warship explode into a magnificent fireball up on the halo display. Hardy was standing next to the captain's mount. As I approached, he said, "Clever on her part…taking advantage of the situation like that."

"Yeah, irritatingly clever," I said. "*Sanctuary's* dampening field. Any way it can be extended to grab onto the *Hercules*?"

"Not a chance in hell. Already being stressed to the limits."

"You mentioned the *Oblivion* has the same tech." I gestured to several of the unmanned consoles.

Hardy did his irritating scratching at his nonexistent chin thing, portraying deep thought. "*Oblivion's* dampening field generator is not in the same league as that on the *Sanctuary*, but taking hold of one ship shouldn't be a problem, even at that extended distance." He strode over to an empty console, tapped at its board for several seconds, then looked over to Akari James. "*Functions mirrored* onto Tactical."

Akari turned to her own board and began tapping. She said, "That's a stupid phrase, functions mirrored; a mirror image is the opposite of the original. It should be functions copied or functions duplicated." She spun around to look at me. "You sure you want to do this? There'll be hell to pay next time you jump in for a quick visit."

I felt my cheeks redden. I should have guessed the too-smart-

213

for-her-own-good lieutenant would have known about my secret quansporting into Pristy's quarters. I let her comment go.

Smiling, she said, "Then again, all's fair in love and war. Right?" She initiated the dampening field without further comment.

The halo display was already zoomed in on the *Hercules*. Clearly now immobilized, the *Hercules* was also caught in the dampening field, where two missiles were visible, just leaving their respective firing tubes.

Hardy said, "Unfortunately, that Grish battleship under attack…it's pretty much fucktipated. Aft section hull breach. Atmosphere venting."

"All I care about for the time being is if its propulsion system is still intact."

Chen said, "We're being hailed, Captain."

I nodded, "Let me guess. Captain Pristy wants to discuss her current situation."

"She sounds a little peeved."

"On display. Put her through."

No sooner had the *Hercules's* bridge appeared than Pristy was yelling, "How dare you! You don't want to go to war with the US Space-Navy, Galvin! Who do you think you are, throwing a dampening field over my ship…lumping us in with the fucking piglets?"

I waited a full five seconds before answering, making sure she was done. "You know I need those vessels—"

She wasn't done. "I don't work for you anymore! You're a criminal. You're all criminals! And if you had any humanity left in your soul, you'd be helping me. Or have you forgotten that the crews of five US Space-Navy warships are currently being imprisoned by the Varapin?"

"No one has stopped you from jumping away…from heading back to Earth and bringing back reinforcements."

"I don't need to head back to Earth to do that…or haven't you heard? There's this new thing; it's called a micro-wormhole comms link. The cavalry is already on its way."

Realization set in, and I watched her expression change in the time it would take me to snap my fingers. She'd blurted out highly classified information to the enemy. Granted, I wasn't exactly the enemy, but she'd just made an epic strategic blunder, and she knew it. Another thought struck me. I knew that the *Oblivion*, along with my pirate crew and me, was potentially her bargaining chip to get her ships and crew back. If all else failed with her arriving cavalry, I wondered—would she trade our lives if it came down to it? I doubted it.

"Release my ship, Galvin."

"I will…in time. You'll just have to sit tight for a spell." I signaled for Chen to cut the connection.

As I stood there thinking, the bridge crew busied themselves. All except Hardy; he was watching Iris doing loop de loops and other aerial acrobatics performed for his entertainment. I had a question, but Hardy wasn't really the one to ask. I said, "MOR-ROW, where is Coogong?"

Scientist Coogong Sohp is futzing around with something in the quansporter compartment.

I was about to reprimand the ship's AI when Bosun Polk said, "Don't bother, Captain…the thing won't change its snarky ways. Lord knows we've tried talking to it."

"Derrota could fix it," I said, heading out of the bridge. I said, "Lieutenant James, you have the conn. Hardy, if you can break away from playtime, you're with me."

We arrived at the quansporter compartment and found Coogong pretty much doing what MORROW said he was doing—futzing.

"I hope you're not making any major repairs, Coogong," I said to his spindly legs, sticking out from beneath the central control console.

The Thine scientist slid out and looked up at Hardy and me. "Ah, Captain! Hello, Hardy." He got to his feet, "No, no…not repairs. Just checking on something. All is well. The quansporter is right as rain…is that the correct Earth expression?"

"It's fine, Coogong. Listen, I've been meaning to talk to you."

He was already nodding his helmeted head. "The Varapin. My quansporting them over to *Sanctuary* without permission. I am very sorry, Captain. I do not usually breach protocol like that. Quite out of character for me. Do you think this whole space pirate attitude has affected me?"

It was impossible not to like Coogong, and being mad at him would be virtually impossible. I said, "As it turns out, as you well know, the ghouls saved the day. Without their help, those drone-bots would have given the Grish a victory. So, thank you. Can you tell me how you convinced them to do what they did? We humans are their enemy…"

Coogong teetered his head from side to side. "I do not believe these particular Varapin warriors see it that way. Those that remain here, within this ship, have chosen a different life. One where they are free to spend time within Veilhall."

I shrugged. "What the hell is that?"

Hardy interjected, "Veilhall is a kind of ethereal realm. Only through deep contemplation can one achieve the level of con-sciousness to go there."

"This Veilhall, is it like a dream state?"

"No, Captain," Coogong said. "It is an actual place. Not here on the physical realm, but another. A place where one takes on a totally different form."

I was getting more confused, and I didn't have time for any

kind of deep theological or spiritual conversation.

Hardy continued for Coogong, "Cap, traveling to Veilhall is prohibited by the Council of Nine. A millennium ago, the Varapin as a race were almost wiped out by their enemies because too many of them were lazing about all day within their Ebom-Pods. The ghouls preferred an existence in that never-neverland they go to over being here in the real world."

I looked to Coogong for corroboration. He nodded. "That is basically true."

"So they want to stay on board *Sanctuary* and—"

"Laze about in their Ebom-Pods all day," Hardy said, completing my sentence.

"And they helped us why? As a kind of thank you?'

"Yes, exactly. These…let's call them Veilhall Varapin…wish to be left alone, and as long as Coogong provides them with that home-grown sustenance concoction of his, a way for them to exercise Ghan-Tshot, well…they're happy little ghouls."

So we'd gotten to the reason for my visit. I stared down at Coogong, still on the deck and probably biding his time so he could get back to whatever he was doing to the quansporter. "You have a way of contacting them. Their arrival onto Sanctuary was well orchestrated."

The Thine scientist hesitated for only a second, "Yes."

"I won't ask you how, at least not right now. But I need you to contact them. If they want to keep hanging out here and floating off to fantasy land, they'll need to help out with a little mission I'm planning."

Hardy said, "You can put it to them that next month's rent has come due."

Chapter 31

With Hardy and Sergeant Max's help, I organized five capable marauder teams. Each was made up of the best of the best we could muster from our limited resources. Our five marines, once again, would be broken up to lead the onboard assaults. So we had Team Max, Team Wanda, Team Grip, Team Ham, and Team Hock. Assigned to each of them would be someone capable of piloting a Grish warship, and that aspect was a tough one. There were only a select few on board the *Oblivion* with such a capability. We decided on crew members Chen and Grimes, Captain Ryder, Little Vince—he was a tough call with his loyalties somewhat in question—and myself.

The five teams' boots on the deck combatants were an assortment of five Pylors and five Symbios each. And finally, each team was assigned ten Veilhall Varapin. Basically, each assault team consisted of a mix of twenty-two individuals. Lieutenant Akari James would stay behind and man the *Oblivion's* bridge, while Hardy, who was capable of performing anyone's job, would be our roving, on-call ChronoBot, if and when reinforcements were needed.

For this mission, humans and Symbios alike all wore combat suits. That was no longer an option. As for the Varapin, although offered, they declined—stating their hovering ability relied on being light as a feather in the air.

Between the actual drop-in assault teams and support personnel along the outskirts, the expansive Deck 23 corridor outside of the quansporter compartment was packed. There were more than one hundred of us in all, some standing at the ready, others dark and hooded, circling overhead reminiscent of a brood of Halloween witches on broomsticks.

"Listen up, everyone!" I said, standing upon a three-foot-tall storage crate. Mine, as well as everyone else's helmet faceplate, was open. "By now you've all been through the mission directives… what will be required from each of you. We have the element of surprise. But for us to take command of all five Grish warships, we must get in fast and effectively and efficiently dispatch piglet bridge crews, all the while holding off the potential assault mustered to take back those ships. By the time you are on board, Coogong will have already quansported over sleep-agent gas canisters directly into each of the ship's atmospheric recycling terminals. Remember, we can't assume every piglet will have flopped over to take a nap; some may have time to crawl into an environment or combat suit. Any last questions before we go?"

Sloppy Joe, who was on Wanda's team, as well as my own, said, "What's the story with the bridge compartment's air supply?"

Wanda rolled her eyes and said, "Weren't you listening when I explained this to you half an hour ago? Grish ships have a safeguard system. Once the sleep agent is detected, the bridge will be closed off to the rest of the ship, and a backup air supply will be triggered."

Another hand was waving, which I'd almost missed. Mr. Phillips was a foot shorter than anyone—well, maybe not Vince—within the corridor.

"Mr. Phillips?"

The Pylor man pointed overhead. "Aren't we putting a lot of faith in these ghouls?"

The circling Varapin closest to Mr. Phillips slowed and looked down at the small Pylor man.

I said, "Keep in mind, you wouldn't be alive today if it wasn't for these Varapin warriors. Look, we'll have to have each other's backs for this mission today. How about we leave our animosities and prejudices behind and just do our jobs?"

Looking up, and totally ignoring what I'd just said, Mr. Phillips raised a hand and flipped the robed ghoul the bird.

Laughter broke out from at least half the crowd. I reminded myself for the hundredth time, *We're pirates now…this kind of shit comes with the territory.*

Before jumping down off my makeshift pedestal, I gave the go-ahead for Coogong to start quansporting over the sleep-agent canisters. Hardy had assured me it wouldn't take long for the gas to permeate the entirety of each ship. Like a steady breeze, ventilation was triple of that on a human ship since Grish crew members did not utilize any kind of bathroom or head facilities—basically, they crapped wherever they happened to be standing at the moment— while below the deck grates, there were actuators and scrapers busy collecting refuse. Periodically, the mess would be vented out into space.

I looked to my marine team leaders, making eye contact with each of them. A confident head nod was all I needed to know they were not only ready but wanting to get underway. I powered down my faceplate—everyone else followed suit. My HUD came alive with multiple readouts, tiny vid feeds and avatars. The quansporter compartment feed showed both Coogong and Bosun Polk standing ready at the central console. It was go time.

***

Team Wanda quansported onto the bridge of what was referred to as an SM (small engagement) battleship. Sure, a step above a destroyer, but still not as powerful as, for instance, the US Space-Navy's *Hercules* or any of the Varapin heavy battleships.

Even with having quansported into various locations many dozens of times, I still found it fascinating to watch the startled, bewildered faces of anyone who happened to be nearby. While, segment block by segment block, my form took shape before them, both they and I were paralyzed—I because of the transporting process, they from the sheer shock at seeing such a strange sight. In this case, there were twenty-two of us arriving on the relatively small bridge. But what was most surprising was finding the awaiting bridge crew still standing. Each enemy piglet was armed and wearing a combat suit—obviously they had anticipated this kind of assault.

Over the open channel, Wanda's voice motivated us into action. "Move it! Let's go to work!" She was the first to raise her shredder and start firing.

My job was to make my way over to the helm controls and get this old shit bucket moving. While plasma bolts were soon crisscrossing all around me, I spotted the primary navigation console. Two Grish combatants were there, waiting for me, and both let loose with weapons fire. Fortunately, my Gorvian-enhanced synapses already had me moving—fast. Sure, I took several glancing bolts across my suit's chest, but it was as if I had anticipated that.

Without conscious thought, I dove, rolled, and came up behind the two of them. At some point I'd pulled and unsheathed my combat knife. In a blur of motion, it slid into the narrow seam beneath one of the piglets' helmets. And in a second blur of motion, I repeated the same death stab to the other. I watched as both Grish staggered, eyes wide in terror as blood rose up within their respective helmets. I pushed past them, knowing they were dead where they stood.

Taking a seat at the helm station, I went to work. While, sure, I was manipulating the controls, like all modern spacefaring craft, it would be the SM battleship's AI that would interpret my commands and do the actual, highly complex ship navigations. *So why isn't the ship moving?*

I stole a quick second to scan my surroundings. The battle was still raging. No big surprise; dronebots had been deployed and were firing down on all of us. The Varapin were swooping and dodging while trying to climb onto the tops of those vicious little orbs. I heard Wanda yelling for someone to get the bridge hatch door closed. There were a number of Grish, along with *Oblivion* combatants lying still on the deck.

Just do your job! I reminded myself. Again, I worked the controls, prompting the ship to get moving. Nothing. Then it hit me. This vessel, as well as all of the other Grish warships, wouldn't be going anywhere until that dampening field was turned off. *How could I be so stupid?!*

Into the open channel, I yelled, "Hardy, we need that dampening field turned off!"

I wasn't exactly sure where the ChronoBot was at that particular moment. I checked my HUD, figuring he might already be engaged with his own roving on-call duties on another ship. I called up my HUD's mission logistic map. I spotted him. *There he is…*He was, in fact, already on board *Sanctuary.*

His voice crackled to life. "No worries, Cap…You may have forgotten about the dampening field, but I didn't. But just shutting the whole thing down won't be an option. Only those enemy ships we've actually taken control of, specifically their bridge compartments, can be set free. That or we'd have an all-out attack on our hands…not to mention, we'd have the *Hercules* back in the fight."

Chapter 32

A Grish warrior tumbled across the helm station in front of me. I heard him grunt through his closed helmet as he slammed hard onto the deck on the other side. I leaned back in time for Wanda to leap over after him, wielding her own combat knife. Above me, a Varapin was riding atop a dronebot, being jerked around like a rider on a bucking bronco. Plasma bolts continued to streak the air, and everyone, friendlies and foes alike, was fighting.

It would be so easy to jump into the fray—to join this circus. But I had one very important job to do: pilot this vessel over to the *Oblivion*. My comms crackled.

"Cap, you ready for me to release that ship from the dampening field?"

"Hold on, Hardy." I gave the three-ring revelry another assessment. It seemed as though our side was coming out on top. That and the hatch door to the bridge was now closed. "Go ahead; set this bird free."

Immediately, the Grish warship's controls became responsive, and I was able to power the battleship away from the other ships. A nearby display showed two other Grish warships had already broken free and were on their way toward the *Oblivion*.

"Hardy, what's going on with the two remaining warships?"

"That would be Ham and Hock's teams…need I say more?"

Clang! Clang!

Two dronebots crashed to the floor. *Clang!* Then a third.

I caught sight of Wanda stretching her back and rolling her neck. Obviously, she was done killing.

"Have anything left in the tank to help out Ham or Hock's team?"

She didn't answer right away. "Make it Ham's. I'm betting he'll need my help more."

I saw that Coogong's HUD avatar was active. "You heard that, Coogong?"

"Yes, Captain…Quansporting Wanda over now. Both Max and Grip have also indicated they are freed up to assist."

"Roger that…send them over," I said.

I saw that Akari James was hailing me on a dedicated channel. "Go for Captain."

"I have Captain Pristy for you. She's been hailing the Oblivion pretty much nonstop. You want her…or should I say, do you want me to put her through?"

I let her sarcastic comment go. "Yes, put her through."

"Oh, and Captain…two of the Grish ships have come alongside abeam…port and starboard."

"Roger that, Lieutenant. I'm a little late, but as you can see, I'm just now pulling in behind *Oblivion's* starboard side."

Captain Pristy's feed came alive and expanded. "Gail, how can I be of assistance today?"

"Fuck you! Just give the order to release my ship!"

"Now, now, that is language unbefitting a US Space-Navy officer."

"Smug doesn't suit you. Release my ship."

"So you can throw a wrench in my plans? Nah, I don't think so. I need all five of these vessels. Thanks to your most recent attacks on the other two, there are no spares."

"How about if I promise not to do that…um…again."

"Just sit tight, Gail. Once we're ready to skedaddle from this no man's area of space, I'll give the order to set you free. You shouldn't have long to wait for that cavalry you talked about to arrive."

"Galvin, wait!"

"What is it?"

"What are you going to do with the prisoners?"

"That's not your concern."

"The ones you've already taken prisoners…add in five fully manned warships. By my guess, there are seven to eight thousand piglets you're stuck with now. You're just ushering them out an airlock into deep space—"

"Hey, who said anything about killing them?" I said, surprised she thought I was capable of such a thing.

"Well…you are a space pirate now. Isn't that the type of thing that pirates do?"

"Not this pirate." But I had to admit, she'd brought up a good point.

"I'd like to think the rules of the Geneva Convention still play a part in your thinking."

"Of course they do," I said, sounding more indignant than I felt. If things were reversed, the Grish would have no problem marching humans into an airlock and out to their deaths. "There has to be an M-Class world somewhere in the vicinity we can drop them off on…so don't worry your pretty little head over it." I said that last part just to irritate her.

"I'm not going to let you push my buttons. But you can't leave, Galvin. The Varapin…they have my ships…my crews."

"Well, I'm certainly not offering my ship or myself up for any kind of hostage exchange. I can do a hell of a lot more good while not in a Varapin brig, or worse, dead."

"The least you could do is wait."

"Wait for what?"

"For the Third Fleet to arrive. The *Hercules* on her own is no match for that advanced Varapin attack group. And I have zero doubt they're coming."

She was probably right. If Pristy had figured out where the *Oblivion* needed to go to refuel, certainly the Varapin could do the same. "Look, that heavy battleship of yours has state-of-the-art cloaking capabilities…just stay hidden until that Third Fleet arrives." Ready to cut the connection, I offered up a sympathetic smile.

"Damn you, wait!"

"Gail…"

"Okay…I have to tell you something I shouldn't."

I let out a resigned breath and waited.

"I lied," she said.

"Lied?"

"There is no Third Fleet. A delayed distress call came in less than an hour ago…the fleet was destroyed en route. A combined Varapin-Grish armada. There's no one coming to save us…to rescue us."

I let that sink in. The losses being accrued by the Alliance were staggering. And things were far worse than I'd even imagined. Which only bolstered my belief that winning this war by conventional means was a losing battle.

"So, what do you propose, Gail?"

She stared back at me but didn't talk.

"Time's ticking. You said it yourself…the Varapin could show up here—"

"Fine! I'll join your pirate fleet."

She'd offered that last part in a voice so faint I could barely make out what she'd said. "I'm sorry. I didn't hear you…Can you repeat—"

"I said I'll join your stupid pirate gang! You win, okay? You've gotten what you wanted."

I shook my head. "No."

"What do you mean no? You can't say no to me."

"I can, and I do."

"What? You want me to beg and plead? Oh, Galvin…please let me join your little band of marauders so I, too, can play swash-buckling pirate." She was unable to keep a straight face and laughed out loud.

"See? There you go. That's the reason I won't let you join me…us."

"Suppose I had an idea of how we can win this war? By the way, you should have made a better attempt to encrypt your inter-ship comms channels."

"You've been listening to our communications?"

"You're still using US Space-Navy comms protocols. Did you forget who I have on board the *Hercules* with me?"

I didn't need to think about it for very long. "Derrota."

"Uh-huh…Stephan's been monitoring everything you, in particular, have said since you arrived at the refueling outpost, or should I say *Sanctuary*? By the way, your singing in the shower sounds more like a cackling hyena."

"Can we get back to your war-winning idea…if there really is one?"

"First say you'll let us join your band of stinky marauders. At least in the interim. Let's call it a probationary period. I give you my personal word of honor that I'll never use what I learn from our time together against you."

"You already have…eavesdropping on our comms?"

"Well, that was before we'd come to any kind of agreement."

"Gail, everyone here on board the *Oblivion* has done so of their own accord. Humans, Pylors, even the Symbios. They believe in what we are doing. This isn't the military; if people don't want to be here, they can leave. With that said, we don't want anyone here that is doing so only for convenience because they have nowhere else to turn."

Her expression turned serious, and the look in her eyes was like nothing I'd ever seen before. "Galvin, playing by the rules has not served me well. Look at what I've lost. My attack group has been captured. Thousands of men and women, if they're not dead, are imprisoned on board a converted Varapin personnel carrier. With the exception of the *Hercules* and her crew, I've turned over everything to the enemy. Five fully operational warships, some of Earth's latest technology…and let's not forget dozens of senior officers with sensitive strategic knowledge. They surely will be tortured."

She swallowed and fought back tears. "As we speak, there'll be many within Space Command who might consider the *Hercules* leaving an ensuing battle as cowardice…or worse, the US Space-Navy Captain, me, as abandoning her duties."

"That's not how it was. You had no idea the other five ships in your attack group wouldn't make the jump along with the *Hercules*."

She shook her head. "You, more than most, should know the military machine is always looking for someone to place the blame for a fucktipated op. A scapegoat. Let's you and I not play that game, okay, Galvin? I'm screwed, and there's only one way I can crawl out of this hole I'm in."

"By showing them they're wrong. By blowing their doors off with a win so big, you'll shine brighter than a supernova?"

"And I can't do that from within the US Space-Navy. So, when I ask to join your personal crusade to make a difference, please believe me when I say I'm on board. It's more than that I have nowhere else to go…Galvin, I have something to prove."

"But this has to be more than that. You need to show you have something to prove."

"If you don't think I want to crush the Varapin-Grish alliance more than anything in the world, you don't know me very well."

There was another pregnant pause as I considered her words. "You can't speak for everyone on board the *Hercules*. This, what we're doing, is not the life for everyone."

I saw Pristy check her TAC-Band. "In less than ten minutes, three broad-beam shuttles will be leaving our flight bay. Three hundred and sixty *Hercules* crew members have chosen to return to Earth. Chosen not to become stinky pirates."

"Seems you've been planning this for some time now."

"No, not long at all. Just since I discovered the Third Fleet has been turned into space scrap."

I thought about her request. Was she bullshitting me? Maybe… probably. But did it matter? Could I leave her here to the ghouls? Of course not.

Akari interrupted our conversation, "Captain. The last two Grish warships have come under our control. Chen and Grimes are piloting the vessels over to *Sanctuary* now. Any further orders?"

"Yes…have SWM chief LaSalle get his people moving. I want all five Grish vessels permanently hard-welded to *Sanctuary*. Make it so they'll never break free, no matter what the external forces are."

I put my attention back on Pristy. "Let me ask you something. Was Derrota one of the crew members that opted to take one of those broad-beam shuttles back to Earth?"

She smiled at that. "Uh, no. Just look at the disheveled-looking man. Have you ever seen a more perfect candidate to be a pirate?"

I nodded, still thoughtful of the situation.

She pursed her lips. "So…am I to take it you've accepted my request?"

I shook my head. "No."

"Oh come on; you're just being pigheaded. What more do I have to do?" The corner of her mouth twitched upward. "Huh?"

"There is one thing…no, you'd never go for it."

"What?"

"You want to really prove you're committed to joining the stinky pirates?"

"I already said yes…what else do I have to do?"

"Make it permanent."

Any previous humor that had been in her eyes dissolved in that instant. "Galvin…"

"I'm sorry, but all of us here on the *Oblivion* are in it for the long haul. We are wanted criminals. We have no backup plan if we're caught or, well…killed."

Realization set in, and she slowly nodded. "What do you want?"

"Right now we have five jalopy Grish warships being hard-welded to *Sanctuary*. But the weakest link to making this refueling outpost a true mobile construct is her lack of aft thrust. One Grish destroyer was never going to be sufficient."

"No!"

"You haven't even heard what I'm proposing."

"You want *Hercules* hard-welded to the ass end of that fifteen-mile-long monstrosity! No, and double no!"

"I'm not even done with my stipulations."

"There's more? You want to take one of Earth's most powerful warships and make her an outboard motor for your Franken-ship and there's more?"

I didn't answer, simply waited.

"You are an ass. An ass of epic proportions. So, what else do you want of me?"

"You and your crew take an oath to our cause…that, and while I'm still captain, you answer to me. When you're not captaining *Sanctuary*, when we've found an adequate location to hide her, you'll be my XO on board Oblivion."

She closed her eyes for several beats. "Fine…in for a dime, in for a dollar. But you need to promise to get my people off that Varapin personnel carrier…alive!"

"Fine," I said. "I look forward to hearing your idea of how we're going to win this war."

Chapter 33

It took three days to secure all six warships to the hull of *Sanctuary*—it took Chief Porter and Derrota another two days after that to sync six mismatched propulsion systems to work in unison. *Sanctuary* would never be nimble, but she would be fast, and she was capable of manufacturing a jump wormhole on her own if necessary. Also, even on her own, she was highly defensible.

Those in any kind of leadership position were asked to convene on board the *Oblivion* within the captain's conference room. I was late arriving, having to deal with a pressing problem on board *Sanctuary*. Entering the conference room, I was surprised how crowded it was; in fact there was standing room only. It was the addition of what remained of the *Hercules's* crew that made all the difference.

A good half of the personnel here were still wearing US Space-Navy uniforms while I was wearing a white T-shirt, jeans, and tennis shoes. I wanted to make a point—we were no longer in the military. Wear whatever suited you.

Hardy was standing close to the conference table, and I used his shoulder as a grab-hold to lift myself up onto the table. Towering over the fifty or sixty people, I clapped my hands together several times to get everyone's attention.

"First things first. A warm welcome to the crew of the *Her-*

cules." I scanned the upturned faces and smiled. "Soon, each and every one of you will be giving your oath." I looked for Mr. Phillips and Vince and found them in the middle of the fray. They'd be procuring the individual oaths from each and every crew member, be it the *Hercules,* as well as those already on board. I raised my brows to the two little Pylors. "You have the Articles of Nine?"

"Aye," both men said. Vince lifted a tablet up to me.

"Don't need that," I said.

I looked to the awaiting crew members, attempting to make eye contact with everyone present. "People...we are all bound by the Pylor Articles of Eight. Which has been recently updated to the Pylor Articles of Nine." I continued to look about the room, seeing Doc Viv and Pristy at the back, talking in low tones to each other.

"Again, so there is no confusion...the Articles of Nine are basically our pirates' code of conduct. They were purposely made stupid simple as to leave no doubt for misinterpretation. I'll review them with you now. Please, if you have questions, wait until I'm done."

Article 1: All Pylors within a syndicate are equal and have an equal vote.

Article 2: All bounty is shared equally among a Pylor's syndicate.

Article 3: Captain's orders are to be followed—that or be charged with treason.

Article 4: Each year there will be a captain's vote. You want a new captain...vote.

"That or demand a joust in the ring." I noticed there was an ancient-looking parchment scroll showing on Hardy's face display. Each article was being highlighted as I progressed through the list.

Article 5: No fighting among the crew. Disputes are handled within the ring.

Article 6: Penalty for treason against a Pylor syndicate is being marooned or put to death—at the captain's discretion.

Article 7: The penalty for cowardice during battle is being marooned or put to death—at the captain's discretion.

Article 8: One found stealing within the syndicate, or guilty of dereliction on duty, will be marooned or put to death—at the captain's discretion.

I looked to Viv and Pristy and smiled. "And our most recent article…*Article 9: Pylor syndicate clansmen must bathe and practice good hygiene. Violators will spend a night in the brig.*"

No less than ten hands reached into the air. *So much for the articles being stupid simple.*

I gestured toward Bosun Polk. "Question?"

"If what you said, Pylors and everyone being equal, how's that going to work? Can I ignore an XO's orders just because I think he or she is a bilge rat?" Polk sent a sideways glance toward my new XO, Gail Pristy. Chuckles filled the compartment.

"Bilge rat? I see you're spending time with our Pylor crew members. The short answer is no. You and whomever you're referring to are equal…you both share equally in any bounty we collect. You have equal votes. That doesn't mean we have no hierarchy. You want to be able to tell the bilge rat XO to shove off? Get voted in as captain next year."

"Or challenge you to a joust in the ring?" Polk said with a crooked grin—one that looked more duplicitous than in jest.

I next chose Derrota. "Stephan, you have a question?"

"Yes. You mentioned, um…*Article 8. One found stealing within the syndicate, or guilty of dereliction on duty, will be marooned or put to death—at the captain's discretion.*"

"Yes?"

"While abandoning one's duty during times a battle is certainly a crime, I take it a crew member can leave? We are not obligated to stay…to be Pylor pirates indefinitely."

I smiled. "Already getting the itch to move on, Stephan? Even before taking the oath?" Before he could answer, I looked to the others within the compartment. "Look, any of you are free to leave. Preferably not within the heat of battle. Give me good notice, and I'll wish you well on your personal journey. But I hope to make your time here within our ranks the very best of your lives so that leaving the *Oblivion*, or any of our soon-to-be acquired vessels, won't even cross your mind. I mean to make each and every one of you rich beyond your wildest dreams, rich with camaraderie, purpose, and bounty."

I saw both excitement in their faces, as well as nervous anticipation.

"And speaking of bounty…before that can happen, we, as a syndicate Pylor clan, need to operate within Pylor space with impunity. And to do that we'll need a letter of marque."

"Where does that come from?" said a junior officer from the *Hercules*.

I saw that Pristy was listening for my reply with a furrowed brow.

"A letter of marque comes from the House of Lords back on Haven, and none other than Admiral Arlington McMasters himself. And before that can happen, we have a little job to do…let's call it what it is. A heist."

Pristy took a step forward. "What are we stealing, Galvin?"

"Hold out your fist, Gail."

Tentatively, she did as told.

"Your fist is a bit smaller than the actual Sultan's Fist. The name of one, very rare, very large gemstone. Alexandrite, to be specific. It is located within the Gliese binary star system, which is in the northern constellation of Draco. And we'll be absconding with that stone, if everything goes to plan, within the next week."

***

It took over an hour for Mr. Phillips and Vince to take everyone's oath and get their signatures. Next, they would be going from department to department within the ship for the rest of the crew to do the same. Before everyone cleared out of the conference room, I said, "XO Pristy has requested the following people stay behind—Stephan, Coogong, Wallace, Craig, Hardy, Viv, and…" I looked up, scanning the overhead crossbeams. *There he is…*I spotted the dark form hovering high up in the far corner. Coke.

With the room cleared out, we were able to take seats at the table, except for Hardy, who was too large for such a thing.

"Before we move on to planning for the heist, Gail has some thoughts she'd like to share regarding the war with the Varapin."

But all eyes weren't on Pristy; they were on the hooded form descending from above.

Ryder's hand moved to his holstered tagger.

I waved a dismissive hand. "No need for that. Coke here has no intention of starting anything."

Ryder didn't look convinced, keeping his hand close to his weapon anyway.

I said, "Okay, Gail…you have our attention. How are we going to win this war?"

She straightened her shoulders and looked to Derrota. "As you know, Stephan was able to, um, listen in to certain comms conversation here on board the *Oblivion*."

"Deceitful she is…no honor," Coke said in a rasp that put all of us on guard. "Execute the female and be done with it."

I looked to Coogong, the only one among us who seemed to have a relationship with the ghoul.

"I am sorry, Captain. Coke does not seem to be himself today."

"Oh, I think he's being more himself than you give him credit for," Ryder said.

Pristy eyed the hovering Varapin. "Tell me, Coke…if you could be anywhere else at this moment, where would you go?"

Coke, no longer stationary, was slowly moving counterclockwise around the table.

"My Ebom-Pod."

"Specifically where? You know what I mean," she said.

"Veilhall, of course."

Viv said, looking impatient, "Can someone clue me in…what's Veilhall?"

Derrota said, "Vivian, there is a reason Varapin spend so much time within their Ebom-Pods. Even though it is a forbidden practice, virtually all Varapin do it."

"Do what? You're talking in riddles here."

Coke interjected, "It is home…it is the Varapin kingdom of paradise."

Viv rolled her eyes. "Got it. It's your happy place. For meditations and such. Namaste."

The ghoul shot forward with such speed, no one had time to so much as flinch—that is all except for me. My reaction was near instantaneous—evident by the fact I already had one hand firmly gripped around Coke's neck. He hissed and jerked about, a wild badger with flailing claws.

I looked to my right and saw that Hardy had one weaponized metal arm extended outward—a Phazon Pulsar cannon pointed at Coke's head. It was good to know Hardy was still on his game.

Coogong raised his stick-fingered hands. "Please, Coke. Relax. We are here to help you. You and your kind."

I waited while the Varapin settled down then released him, more like tossed him away from us.

Hissing and spewing insults ten feet in the air, Coke rubbed at his neck. "I should never have agreed to come here."

While my attention was on the nearby dark specter of death, the others around the table were looking at me.

"You moved like a fucking cheetah," Ryder said. "How'd you do that?"

I looked to Viv.

"Let's just say Quintos here now has more in common with Gorvian physiology than any other human in the galaxy or the universe…" Viv shrugged, looking to the group. "Throughout his body, his neural synapses have been, um…well, kind of genetically tweaked."

"You agreed to this? Sounds awfully dangerous, Galvin, altering your DNA like that. Who knows what the long-term effects might be," Derrota said, looking concerned.

I let out an irritated breath, "We're getting far off topic here. It was that or die facing off with the Pylors down on Haven. Let's get back to Coke here and Pristy's idea."

She looked at me. "Well, after monitoring your conversation… the one where you, Coogong, and Hardy spoke of this Veilhall place—"

"Why do you keep calling it a place?" Viv asked. "It's a dreamworld…an aberration, right?"

Coogong spoke up. "No, Vivian…it is an actual physical place."

"How is that possible? The ghouls lie down in their little Ebom-Pods and actually go to this Veilhall?"

More hisses emanated from Coke.

Derrota said, "You've heard of astral travel and the like?"

Craig Porter spoke up for the first time, "Come on, that's all bullshit."

Derrota continued, "There is actually a considerable amount of data on the subject. MORROW was quite helpful. For thousands of years the Varapin have had the unique ability to travel to this place, this world. Granted, they need to be in a deep sleep. But it is a real place. Varapin, not all, but I suspect most, carry on two parallel lives, the Veilhall life being the far superior and gratifying one. And from what I've garnered from my research, from a Varapin's perspective, it's heaven-like."

"Why don't they just stay there?" I asked.

"Because we are tied to our physical forms here, stupid human," Coke spat.

Derrota said, "Certain human beliefs are similar. Called the *sutratma* or life thread of the *antahkarana*, the silver spiritual cord links the soul to the human form while one is still alive."

Craig said with a dismissive hand, "Fine. Why don't they all just go there? Point their little spacecrafts in that direction and rocket away…make a new life for themselves there in ghoul heaven? Good riddance to the lot of them."

"That's the thing, Craig…even though Veilhall is a real physical place, it is not on our own plane of existence."

That got everyone's attention.

"So why are we even talking about this?" Ryder said, moving to stand.

Pristy looked directly over to Coke. "Because we can send them there. Forget the life thread of the antahkarana and all that nonsense. We can send them there in their physical form, where they can stay and never have to return."

"That is impossible! You mock me, human, with your slanderous words. What makes you think after millennia, the Varapin would not have discovered such a possibility?"

Looking bemused, Pristy said, "As advanced as the Varapin are, they don't have what the humans have."

Coke scoffed, "Implausible…"

"We have a quansporter device."

That got the Varapin's attention.

Derrota took over for Pristy. "One that operates on the very premise of quantum entanglement, moving physical matter, be it here within our own quantum realm or within another quantum realm; it makes little difference. That is if you have the specific multiverse coordinates."

I waited for the rest of it.

Pristy said, "And we think we know how to get them." She looked up to Coke. "How would you like to go there? I mean really go there…to Veilhall?"

Chapter 34

The meeting broke up, and Coke had some things to consider. Namely, how far was he willing to go to help his brethren Varapin? Would he be willing to risk uncertainty? His life? He left wanting to further discuss things with his fellow stowaways. That was fine with me; right now I had a full plate dealing with the here and now.

While everyone else had left the conference room, both Doc Viv and Pristy had not risen from the table.

Viv said, "Sit back down."

I looked between the two. "This looks ominous." I sat back down.

Neither woman looked particularly happy with me. Which was nothing new. But a joined offensive was. "What is it? What have I done now?"

Looking more than a little pissed off, Pristy said, "I hear you have a young lady on board this ship."

I shook my head. "No, not that I know of—" then I remembered Sonya. *Shit!*

"She's fourteen years old, Quintos!" Viv scolded.

Pristy, drumming her fingers on the table, was shaking her head. "This is why this whole pirate crap is nothing more than male-oriented machismo bullshit."

I held my palms up as if that would help against this onslaught. "I'm not sure exactly what the problem is. Is she—"

"Sonya," Viv barked.

"I'm not sure what the issue is with Sonya. She seemed perfectly fine last time I saw her."

"And when exactly was that, Quintos?" Viv said, exchanging a quick glance with Pristy.

"I…um," then I remembered, "I talked to her up on the Symbio decks! She was coding…something."

"Listen to me carefully, Galvin," Pristy said in a soft voice, as patronizing as you could imagine, "Do you know the circumstances as to how the girl lost her family?"

I shook my head.

"That will be up to her to tell you…Let's move on. She's the lone child on a five-mile-long warship, a warship that is predominantly crewed by men. Many of them fucking pirates!"

I'd never heard Pristy yell like that. I stayed quiet because there was nothing I could say in my own defense. I had no defense. The two were right. I'd dropped the ball—big-time.

"Here's the kicker," Viv said, "You, by default, are the girl's guardian."

"Me? I'm the last person—"

Viv leaned forward in her chair. "Zip it, Quintos. This is the time for you to listen, not talk."

"Okay."

"We…Gail and I, met with Sonya."

"What did she—"

"Just listen…did you know she is living up on the Symbio deck?"

I shook my head.

"In that weird Palitine area with the muted lights and creepy chanting?" Viv asked.

I shrugged. "That doesn't seem so bad…Hell, I've been sleeping in an Ebom-Pod—"

Pristy slapped both her palms down on the table. "We don't want to hear it! And you're right; you are the last person who should be given guardianship of her."

"Wait. Who said anything about guardianship? I'm not her guardian. I only met her by accident."

I watched another glance go between them, and it was starting to piss me off.

Viv was holding something in her hand. A folded piece of paper. "We went through her things…which she was not all that happy about. Not that she had much. A spacer's travel pack filled with several changes of clothes…all worn and smelly. She had a few personal odds and ends, and she also had this…" She held up the slip of paper. "It's a legal Earth document."

"Okay…let me see it."

Viv didn't hand it over for several moments. "This changes everything, Quintos."

"Just give it to me." I snatched the paper from her clutches, opened it, and read what it said. Then read it again—and then again.

Pristy, her voice almost kind now, said, "Did you ever even ask her her last name?"

I looked up. Two sets of eyes—Phazon Pulsars burning holes right through me. "How is this possible? I've never been married. My brother never had children, as far I know…at least within our family tree, the Quintos name stops with me."

"Your father, Carl Quintos…he had a brother. Landers—Land—Quintos."

"If I had an uncle, one with a name like Landers, I think I'd remember that."

"I doubt it," Viv said. "Landers—Land—was a half brother,

and he was an off-worlder. He was a—"

"Pirate," I said, finishing Viv's sentence.

I wondered how much Sonya knew of all this. Then again, she was just about the smartest kid I'd ever met. She lived and breathed data. *Shit*, computer databases had been her childhood playground as much as that small farm in Clairmont was mine. Then I remembered how it had been her who had shown me where the Lori Quintos Symbio-Poth was sleeping, slumbering, regenerating… *whatever*, there in Palitine. She was trying to give me something—a connection to my past. Something she didn't even have herself.

I looked at the legal document in my hand once more, now noticing the details. Pursuant to a signed affidavit by one Landers Quintos, this child custody agreement was, in fact, real. So real it was signed off on by the Honorable Erving William Ringwald, second district court, the judicial branch of New Mexico. Then I noticed the date. It was two years ago.

I looked up. "She's been on her own since she was twelve?"

Viv nodded. "She ran away. Decided she wanted to stay with the same people she grew up with. Pirates."

I rubbed my eyes. "Has she been…"

"No," Pristy said. "Not that we can determine. If anything, the stinky pirates she's been traveling with have been watching over her. Apparently Land was a bigshot among the Pylors. These people may be criminals and scallywags, but they do take care of their own. Vince, as unbelievable as it sounds, has been as close to a big brother as she could hope for. He's never far from her, and he'd apparently die to protect her."

"That's at least something."

Pristy said, "Well, don't get too comfortable with that. This ship is filling up fast. With my crew coming on board, I'd like to say I can vouch for everyone…"

"I know," I said, refolding the document and putting it in my pocket.

Viv stood up. "You should have Sonya's guardianship formally transferred to—"

"Whoa! Who said anything about transferring guardianship?"

Pristy stood. Now both of them stared down at me. Both looked irritated and in no mood for my bullshit.

"Just let me talk to her. This is her life. Yes, she's a kid, but she's been forced to live as an adult for two years now. How about we give her a say in what happens?"

"Well, do something, Quintos," Viv said.

They both left, leaving me in silence and with my feelings of guilt.

My Jaadoo ring began to vibrate—it was Hardy.

Chapter 35

With the *Oblivion* parked and securely latched to *Sanctuary's* underbelly, I'd moved a select few of her bridge crew to the mobile refueling outpost's bridge. For the next week, at a minimum, I wanted them getting familiar with the operation of Franken-ship, as a number of the crew now referred to her.

I gestured to Pristy to take the makeshift captain's mount. "How about you do the honors, Captain? Figure it's best you two get properly acquainted."

She couldn't look any less thrilled. But she took the seat, took in the large halo display and the other smaller ancillary displays in front of her, then the various bridge stations, which were roughly set up like that on the *Oblivion*.

Pristy looked over to me with a raised questioning brow.

I said, "Let's do this…it's time to blow this dark, uninhabited crap hole area of space. And preferably before the Varapin get here."

She looked over to Grimes. "Helm…initiate jump protocol Delta 5."

The propulsion systems of all six hard-mounted warships came to life, causing the deck plates beneath our feet to vibrate.

Grimes said, "Interfacing with *Oblivion*…Initializing manufactured wormhole now."

Because *Sanctuary* had no jump technology of her own, we would be utilizing *Oblivion's* perpendicularity spheres. This was a crucial moment—the Gorvian ship needed to manufacture a wormhole of such magnitude that even a structure as large as *Sanctuary* would be able to pass through it.

The bridge lights flickered several times. Something loud clanged overhead.

"No worries…that should be expected," came a Mumbai-accented voice emanating from the adjacent CIC. Derrota appeared, offering a casual wave from the connecting passageway. "Just getting the bugs worked out." He disappeared back into the CIC, where he and Hardy were making last-minute adjustments.

Chief Porter's face suddenly appeared on the main halo display. "We'll want to take things slow, Gail. We've had too little time to fully test things. The *Oblivion's* P-spheres are already running hot. " He looked over to me with a scowl.

She said, "So no burning rubber at the starting line…and no doing donuts in the parking lot?"

Porter didn't look amused—he cut the connection.

Grimes said, "Propulsion is read…Perpendicularity spheres are charged; we have the first of our manufactured wormhole's endpoint locked in."

I marveled at the colossal-sized wormhole now taking shape before us. I wondered if this was the largest man-made manufactured wormhole in existence. I looked to Pristy to see if she was just as captivated as I was, but her expression was anything but captivated. I followed her gaze to that of the tactical station, where Akari James was standing with hands on hips. She was wearing the skimpy jeans short-shorts again—the ones where the bottoms of her butt cheeks peeked out.

Pristy's eyes swiveled to mine. Just loud enough for me to hear, she said, "Really?"

I shrugged and mouthed the words, *Welcome to pirate life.*

"Take us in, Helm," Pristy said.

"Aye, Captain."

Akari James said, "I've got multiple radiation spikes on my board." She turned to look at me and then to Pristy. "These are wormhole endpoint signatures…unidentified, but I'm guessing they're your Varapin pursuers…they've found us."

Pristy didn't hesitate. "Helm, full ahead. Don't worry about scratching the paint or denting the fenders!" She shot me a smile. We'd just dodged a bullet, and we both knew it.

***

Seven manufactured wormhole jumps later, and some one hundred and thirty light-years distance across the galaxy, we arrived just outside of the Milky Way. We were deep within a section of frontier space we were christening Lost Tombstone. Where we had recently come from a nameless area of space desolate and devoid of any nearby star systems, well, Lost Tombstone was just the opposite. This was a mostly uncharted area that Hardy, more specifically, LuMan, had a three-hundred-year-old reference to. One that was buried deep within his databanks.

According to LuMan, there were no, as in zero, other recorded interstellar visits, close passersby, or logged entries from any other starship. Why? Because this was a convergence point for no less than eight black holes. Eight black holes, moving closer and closer to each other so that, within the next few hundred million years, they would become one singular ungodly massive black hole. Even three hundred years ago, LuMan had noted this area of space as being a deathtrap.

So, these three hundred years later, it wasn't so much that this area of space was totally unknown, at least from afar—but it was not a place any sane pilot would want to jump close to. With a gravitational pull so strong that even light could not escape it, a black hole was something to steer clear of. So, eight black holes—don't even think about it.

But we did think about it. And for Sanctuary to be totally safe, or at least as safe as we could make it, we needed a place just like this one that was as off the beaten path as one could get. One that, even if the coordinates ever did become known to an enemy, they'd still think twice before visiting. But for now, with few exceptions, no one was to know what those coordinates were—especially the Pylors, no matter how much I'd come to trust them.

What we had going for us, that no one else would have going for them, was the ChronoBot's transport ship's jump entry and departure points. Like finding that lone life-saving oasis in the middle of the desert, LuMan's transport ship had found that equivalent in deep space centuries past. A self-contained, thirteen-billion-mile-long system of twelve worlds orbiting a white dwarf star—one nestled right there between three of the eight black holes. But these three were a strange anomaly. An anomaly first theorized by physicists Einstein and Maxwell, called the Einstein-Maxwell-Dilaton (EMD) theory, where we had three massive black holes that, strangely, "gravitationally" repelled—not pulled.

And it was there that we were headed. If the combined intellect of MORROW, Hardy, and Derrota was correct, we would survive this jump. We would arrive between those three black holes—a triangular area within its nestled star system. That is if things hadn't changed all that much over the last three hundred years. Derrota was certain, as was the ship's AI, that we had little to worry about. Hardy, less so. He gave the odds as seventy-thirty in favor of us being fine. I took those odds—we needed that interstellar oasis.

With Grimes's finger poised over the button, we emerged, ready to jump away.

Pristy said, "Tactical, tell me there's no one here…"

"There's no one here. Sensors picking up nada, nothing…no signs of technology."

Derrota came out of the CIC looking pleased with himself. "In three hundred years, this system has stayed stable. This is an amazing area of space. A virtual proving ground for Einstein and Maxwell's most fundamental physics."

I gestured to the halo display. "Stephan, what can you tell me about the twelve exoplanets orbiting that white dwarf?"

He brought up his ever trusty tablet and began scrolling through information. I made a mental note to get the Hercules crew members properly fitted with Jaadoo rings—making things like tablets obsolete.

"Eight of the twelve are nearly identical to each other in that they are not life-sustaining. At least life as we know it. Atmosphere's mostly carbon dioxide, but with dense clouds composed of sulfuric acid. Constant rains that would peel the skin right off an organic being in seconds…if you don't die from inhaling the fumes first."

"And the other four?" Pristy asked.

Derrota continued to scroll. "All four are different." He pointed to the halo display, which was now showing the star system in its entirety. Zooming in on four of the worlds, two of them were blue, the other two purple. All four showed the presence of fluffy white clouds and tan land masses contained within vast oceans. "All four are M-Class worlds and are suitable for life…we can breathe the air on those worlds, Galvin. We'd need to send probes to take samples…have Viv provide inoculations for any pathogens, viruses, or parasites."

Akari James stood, pulling up her short-shorts in the process. In my peripheral vision, I saw Pristy's annoyed glance my way.

Akari said, "Captain, or should I say captains…I'm picking up large life-forms on two of the worlds, the other two just microbial and rudimentary plant life."

Metatag information started popping into view next to each of the twelve worlds. Since none of them had actual names yet, MORROW had designated them long streams of alphanumeric characters.

Akari made a point to come around her station and approach the 3D halo display; at least as far as the males on the bridge were concerned, her backside was far more interesting than anything up on the display. She pointed to one of the purple worlds. "This one—she's the less dangerous of the two."

"Not so," Derrota interjected. "The immense size of the organisms is not the only factor, Akari." He glanced down at the tablet before joining her. "Yes, both of these purple worlds have evolved into a kind of Jurassic period. Both have dinosaur equivalents…but this world on the left has a more diverse arthropod phylum-type species."

I said, "Stephan?"

He smiled, "Insects, Galvin. Some as large as the dinosaur equivalents. So no, that is one world I do not recommend we visit."

"And the other purple world?"

Derrota looked over to Akari, back in her seat, and who'd had much of her thunder quelled by Derrota's peerless science knowledge. "Akari is right on point, though," he said, giving the young lieutenant her due, "This world is still quite dangerous. It would be hard to imagine, even with a ChronoBot at our side, we'd be safe to amble about, lest we be eaten down there."

A voice from the back of the bridge said, "How about if you bring along a fire-breathing dragon for protection?"

I knew that voice, the voice of a girl and not a woman.

I turned to face Sonya, who'd managed to stay unobserved up until now. "I don't remember inviting you onto *Sanctuary*, let alone her bridge, Sonya."

"Well, you didn't not invite me…and I could have just as easily hacked MORROW and watched from my tiny closet on *Oblivion*."

While I was still trying to come up with a clever response to that, Derrota said, "Sonya, you're speaking of Sadon, the Symbio-Poth dragon, yes?"

"Uh-huh…he's the biggest badass MF-er in the bunch. Hell, even Reggie craps himself when Sadon gets mad." She snapped her bubblegum. "Yeah, I'd take Sadon down there with you." She shrugged, "But who am I to make suggestions? I only update his core programming and know that particular Symbio better than anyone alive."

"It's more than that, though, Sonya," I said. "Don't we want to protect the Symbios from unnecessary injury, or worse?"

Pfft. "You're being naive, Captain Clueless…yeah, they are alive, in a sense, but they have the advantage of being totally recyclable."

"Hold on. Wasn't it you that was worried about the Symbios being taken advantage of?"

"Ah yeah…I've changed my mind on that. You should have seen how excited they were after that last battle with the Grish. Let's say Sadon gets himself in over his head down there. Well, what you would call his consciousness…it's all backed up within Oblivion's servers. And here's the kicker…he, they all, love this sort of thing…they're still talking, going on and on about fighting piglets and dronebots. Specifically the Symbio dragons and dinosaurs; they live for the fight. One thing, though…You have to make sure you don't leave him down there. To recycle Sadon, we'll need his body, dead or alive."

Pristy said, "I do have a simple question."

She had all our attention.

"Why are we going down there in the first place? Down to that all-too-dangerous world, when staying up here in this not-so-dangerous starship seems perfectly fine to me?" Pristy shook her head, "You've got what you wanted, Galvin. You have your hidden pirate hideaway that no one will ever find."

"Two reasons, Gail…one, because it's way cool to go down to an unexplored exoplanet, and two, as our clan grows in the months and years ahead, we'll need to think about building a settlement of our own."

"You mean like Haven?" Akari said.

I nodded.

Sonya said, "You planning on breaking away from the Pylors? What, have your own pirate organization, separate…and in competition?"

I'd purposely not invited any of the Pylors onto Sanctuary's bridge today. But Sonya was a Pylor. "I don't want to go there… get ahead of ourselves—"

"Don't worry; your secret's safe with me…for now."

The girl looked back at me with a strange expression. I thought of Landers Quintos and that Sonya was some kind of blood relative…maybe a distant niece of mine. I could see it in her eyes; she knew that too. Was blood thicker than water, or Pylor bonds in this case? I had no idea.

Chapter 36

Thanks to Coogong's continued tinkering, the quansporter pedestal now supported six individual containment field platforms or CFPs. As safe as the process was overall, according to the Thine scientist, even he admitted that utilizing quansporter CFPs was slightly more reliable, *safer* than, say, being quansported from one remote site to another. That was all the convincing I needed for us to go that route for this mission.

Outfitted in full combat suits, our away team of six was ready to quansport down to the smaller of the two purple worlds. The team included Max, Wanda, Derrota, Hardy, Chief LaSalle, and myself. LaSalle, our SWM chief, was needed to evaluate several construction sites for a potential dirt-side outpost. According to him, *Sanctuary* had ample construction materials and supplies on board for such an endeavor. The only one quansporting done remotely would be Sadon.

I gave Coogong the thumbs-up signal and immediately felt the now familiar queasiness that came with this unsettling process. We simultaneously quansported off *Sanctuary* at the same time, and within the blink of an eye, were taking shape down on the exoplanet, all six of us still together.

I was surprised to see Sadon was already there waiting for us. The Symbio-Poth dragon. He was obsidian black, his shiny, reflective scales mirroring the jungle-like landscape around us. The thought occurred to me how similar this was to the playing field of Caveman Glory. Only the overhead atmosphere here was a light purple shade instead of a sky-blue hue.

At our arrival in an oval, approximately fifty-yard open clearing, Sadon spread his wings wide and fluttered them as if making a mock attempt to take flight. A single burst of flames erupted from flared nostrils at the end of his long snout.

Over the open mission command channel, I heard Sonya's voice. "Tell me Sadon is okay."

"Aren't you looking at him yourself via my helmet cam?"

"Yes, but I'm not there…and the feed is distorted."

"Sadon looks fine. Relax. And if you're going to eavesdrop on the mission, keep quiet."

Hardy's energy cannons snapped out into position as he strode purposefully toward the edge of the clearing. Both Max and Wanda, several steps behind, flanked him right and left.

I, too, saw the approach of something there in the jungle via my HUD. Derrota joined me at my right. I said, "Can you determine what that is? Other than big?"

Sadon had moved forward and was flapping his wings—agitated.

"Just that I was wrong earlier, Galvin. Not some kind of distant relative of a dinosaur…these *beings* here are bipedal and—"

At that precise moment, *it* tore through the wall of vegetation—leaves and torn-away branches filled the air like shrapnel from a bomb. The creature loomed twenty-five feet over us.

With hands extended outward, I yelled, "Hardy, don't shoot! Sadon, just stay calm!"

"Oh my God…" Derrota said, taking a step toward the thing as if in a trance.

I placed a restraining palm on his shoulder. "Hold up, Stephan, until we know what we're dealing with here."

Sadon was making hissing sounds and continuing to flutter his wings.

Wanda said, "If I didn't know better, I'd say this was some kind of a joke."

Max said, "A joke on us…"

"Stephan? What are we dealing with here?" I said.

Sonya interjected, "Go on, just say it…it's a Sasquatch, a yeti; it's a fucking bigfoot."

"Language, Sonya," I said as if I wielded any kind of parental rights over the girl.

Derrota said, "She's right…what we're looking at is more mammalian-like than reptilian."

"You think?" Sonya said, heavy with sarcasm.

I continued to stare up at the beast. It was covered with dark red hair from head to foot. Definitely more human-like than ape-like. And its face was furrier than the rest of it. There were discernible features beneath that fur. A nose and mouth proportional for the creature's size, and two blue, all-too-intelligent eyes.

I said it again, "No one moves…" Then I said, "Stephan, is the atmosphere here, the air, dangerous to humans?"

"Uh, we've been inoculated. I think we're okay."

I uncoupled the securing latch beneath my helmet and slowly removed it. The yeti beast tilted its head from side to side, apparently fascinated by my actions. I said, "We come in peace…"

Sonya was the first to laugh, then the others followed. Sure, it was a stupid thing to say, but what *did* you say, as Sonya had so blatantly put it, to a fucking twenty-five-foot-tall bigfoot?

The yeti leaned down, hands on knees, and stared at me as if inspecting a curious-looking bug on the ground. He smiled, and then he laughed. Loud and haughty, the beast was laughing with an almost childlike innocence. He plopped down onto the ground, crossed his legs, and continued to stare.

Even without directly looking at him, I caught sight of Hardy—all of his weaponry was locked onto the beast—as were Max and Wanda's shredders. Behind me, Sadon paced back and forth. But the yeti seemed unconcerned with any of that. All of his attention was on me.

I said, "Can you speak?" and pointed to my own mouth and then up to him.

When the yeti spoke, his voice resonated deep, loud, and powerful. But not angry. That, and I was surprised—I understood what he said.

The yeti vigorously scratched under one armpit. "Little vermin, why have you returned?"

"Our auricular implants, Galvin," Derrota said. "They're able to translate his vocabulary."

I wasn't sure what the yeti was referring to. *Why have we returned?* Then the beast reached for me—no, not for me; instead he snatched up a nearby branch on the ground. Thick with green foliage, he began to tear at the leaves with his large bone-white incisors. He chewed, now taking in the others of the team. They had all taken off their helmets—something he apparently appreciated because he smiled and nodded approvingly.

In a guttural language not familiar to me but simultaneously translated to English by my implants, Hardy said, "We are visitors and not from this world. We are friends. My name is Hardy…what is yours?"

For the first time, the hairy beast assessed the ChronoBot with curiosity. "I am Botna. And I already know you are not from this world. You are a machine, the others…human."

The cold realization hit me. We were not dealing with an indigent, witless dullard—Botna might look similar to an oversized bigfoot, but he was far more than that.

He said, "You can put down your weapons, machine man… you, too, humans. I choose not to stomp on you today."

"Or eat us?" Wanda asked.

Hardy translated for her.

That caught Botna by surprise, and once again, his laughter filled the clearing.

I had a hundred questions for the creature, but top of the list was who, and when had others like us, come here?

Chapter 37

Botna leaned sideways while stretching out an unthreatening hand toward Sadon. Wary of the hairy beast, small flames billowed from the dragon's nostrils. Undeterred, Botna, showing surprising gentleness, began to pet the top of Sadon's head.

"Man…if I wasn't seeing this with my own eyes…" Max said.

I'm not sure what made me look into the dense surrounding jungle at that moment, but what I saw made me catch my breath. I froze.

Derrota said, "There are thirty-six of them." He had also noticed them.

I looked to Hardy. "Your sensors not working today or what?"

Hardy glanced over one shoulder. "No, I saw them. Tracked them as they approached. Even listened to their chitchat as they assessed us."

"And…"

"And they're not here to eat us. For one thing, they're omnivores. For another, they're apparently happy we're here. To paraphrase what they are saying…they are surprised, albeit thrilled, we've returned."

"Ask him about the others. The ones like us."

I listened while Hardy and the yeti conversed. Apparently, it had been some time since the others had come here. Close to two hundred years. When asked how long Botna had been alive, Hardy translated that into years for us. He was approximately six hundred years old, which was considered middle aged for his species. We also learned Botna was his tribe's leader.

Hardy pointed a mechanical finger toward me, "This human is our leader…He is called Galvin Quintos."

Botna looked down at me, his blue eyes taking me in. He let out a foul breath and motioned toward the jungle. Slowly, the others of his tribe emerged into the clearing. Some were similar in size and stature to Botna and carried makeshift clubs; others were obviously female, smaller, and had breasts and finer facial features. There were also eight children, who all ran toward an uncomfortable-looking Sadon. Just as their leader had done, they petted his head, and one young female enfolded the dragon into a tight embrace. A quick burst of flames singed the youngster's upper back, but she didn't seem to mind. Smoke and the acrid smell of burned hair continued to linger in the air.

Over the next hour we learned much about this small purple world—a world the Yuppa, their species, called Genoma. Apparently there were many Yuppa tribes around this world, but there were only two reasons to interact with any of them—to mate or to battle. Typically those two interactions took place during the same exchange. To the victors went the spoils, so to speak.

Derrota had already informed me there were a number of other large species here on Genoma. With Hardy translating, I asked, "Are there beasts on this world that attack the Yuppa? That are your enemies?"

The tribe went still, voices reduced to whispered murmurs between themselves.

Botna nodded. "We have three enemies, two of which are creatures, one that is mechanical." He sent a leery glance toward Hardy.

Botna described two large reptilian-type creatures; both

seemed to be very much similar to our Earth dinosaurs. And with a little prompting from Derrota, we figured Genoma had both a kind of T. rex and raptor, along with an assortment of slightly less aggressive species. While the T-rex didn't have much taste for the Yuppa—Botna thought it was their hair—the raptors certainly did.

"And the third? The mechanical enemy you spoke of?" I asked and waited for Hardy to translate.

A female came closer and sat down next to Botna. She said, "At the shore of the lake. Where the settlement sits. Four multi-legged robots. They keep us away from the wall."

"There's a settlement here…here on Genoma?"

Before I could look to Hardy, he said, "Cap…my sensors haven't picked up any kind of settlement. Maybe she is mistaken."

Derrota scratched at the stubble on his chin. "Hmm…as the old adage says, there are no straight lines in nature. About a mile from here, there is a kind of structure. It appears to be a rocky ridgeline, but it runs perfectly straight for about three-quarters of a mile."

The female, whose name we learned was Falla, said the four robot spiders had remained when the others, the humans, left some two hundred years prior. Obviously they had been left here to keep watch over the settlement.

I thought about that. An existing settlement? I looked to La-Salle. "What do you think?"

He shrugged. "That could save us substantial time and resources. And after two hundred years, it's probably a good bet the original inhabitants aren't coming back."

I said to Botna, "You want to show us?"

I figured it would take us an hour by the time we navigated through the thick jungle, but that was not to be. With fast hands, the Yuppa tribesmen gathered us up and carried us. Several carried two of us secured like small dolls in their oversized hands. At first it was somewhat humiliating, then I let that go and enjoyed the ride.

Above us, I saw Sadon circling, keeping a watchful eye on our trek through the dense wilderness. Within minutes we'd reached our destination. When we broke through the thicket of vines and leaves, a vast lake was spread out before us—one that reflected the deep violet color of the sky above.

We were not alone here at the shoreline. Six raptor-like dinosaurs, each with two ugly heads—both independent of one another and looking equally ferocious. They did not look like the raptors of Earth—heads wider, not as long. Turning to face us, they rose up, easily ten feet tall. They squawked and showed their teeth. Several made aggressive snapping motions.

Even if I could get to the tagger on my hip, I wondered if it would do much good against such a large, vicious animal.

From the bush behind us, club-yielding Yuppa tribesmen sprinted forward and attacked without hesitation. The closest two-headed beast got its head bashed in by the two-handed swing of a club, leaving it dangling upon a limp neck while the other head now had its jaws firmly secured over the Yuppa's upper calf.

With another swing of his club, the reptilian beast dropped to the wet sand, clearly dead. The injured Yuppa rubbed at his bloodied leg then rejoined the attack with the other tribesmen. It wasn't long before four of the two-headed creatures were lying dead on the sand, while two had scurried off into the jungle.

Looking up to Botna, still grasping me in an uncomfortably sweaty palm, I could see by his all-too-human expression he'd wanted to join in on the fight. I said, "Are there a lot of those… creatures?"

By now, my implants were better able to assist me with talking in their language. I'm sure it wasn't perfect, but Botna seemed to understand what I said.

"They outnumber us ten to one. This was a small pack…they usually run in packs of ten to twenty…then we have a real match." His bemused expression suddenly changed though.

My gaze followed his. There, down the sweeping curve of the shoreline about two hundred yards away, was clearly a man-made, more accurately, an alien-made wall structure. It was big—maybe thirty or forty feet tall—and made of large rocks and boulders.

And as if on cue, something massive crawled up from the other side.

Wanda said, "Great…it had to be a spider. I hate spiders."

Derrota, who was being held by Falla and somehow had retrieved a small tablet, said, "It's a machine. But highly advanced. Almost no electrical emissions. It's why we didn't pick up on it from orbit."

I was about to ask if it was weaponized when three bright red bolts of plasma shot toward us. While the Yuppa tribesmen instinctively ducked and scurried, it was too late for one of the smaller females. She now lay dead—half of her scorched body gently bobbing up and down at the shallow water's edge

Even while we took cover within the brush, sorrowful wails of anguish erupted from both male and female Yuppa. We were released to the ground as the giant beasts moved to comfort one another. I watched one tearful embrace after another.

But Botna would have none of that. He stayed close to the jungle's tree line, watching through vines and leaves down the length of the narrow beach to where the lone weaponized spider remained—standing vigil against any attempt to approach the settlement's outer wall.

Hardy, Max, and Wanda joined me, all of us crouching at the tree line.

"Tell me honestly, Hardy; are you up to taking that thing?"

His face display went active with a simple video animation, a nail being repeatedly hammered into a board. "Thing outweighs me by a factor of five. Even one strike from that big plasma cannon, and I'd be a goner. Sorry, boss…no can do."

Max said, "And there are three more of them? I say we let Sanctuary take them out from orbit."

I looked to Wanda and then Hardy. Both nodded. I thought about the alien proprietors of this settlement. *If they ever do come back, they won't be happy. Fuck them; we're pirates, aren't we?*

My helmet was still back in the clearing, so I removed the rest of my combat suit so I could have access to my Jaadoo ring. Within seconds I was talking to Pristy.

After giving her a rundown of the situation, she, too, was hesitant in making such aggressive action, but two hundred years was a long time. And the simple fact the thing looked like a spider… she was more than willing to target the bots with onboard Phazon Pulsars.

"MORROW's able to see three of the things, all standing along the various areas of the wall," she said, "but not a fourth. You sure there are four?"

"No, it's what one of the Yuppa said. Take out the three, and make a nice hole in that wall for us while you're at it."

"Roger that…stand by."

Chapter 38

Even though I was expecting it, seeing the three brilliant green plasma bolts, as if shooting down from heaven by an angered almighty God, was a spectacular sight. We watched, dumbfounded, as the unsuspecting spider bot sitting there atop the settlement wall took the direct hit. It exploded into a massive fireball. Its carapace-like outer shell detonated as if full of rocket fuel, propelling mechanical legs and scrap metal outward in every direction.

A moment later, not far from where the spider bot had been eviscerated, *Sanctuary* targeted the wall. It was far more robust than I'd earlier surmised—taking no less than ten plasma strikes to open up an eight-foot-wide gap.

We waited several minutes after the strikes—since that area of the wall was still glowing red, and great plumes of steam billowed up into the air.

As our away team headed off down the narrow beach, I noticed Botna and the other Yuppa were not following.

"You're not coming with us?"

The towering beast simply shook his head. And before I could tell him thank you for his help, he and the others had disappeared into the jungle.

By the time we reached the wall structure, although still scalding hot and radiating heat, we were able to enter the breached gap via a single-file line. Hardy took the lead. Only now did I realize the wall, here at the bottom, was about forty feet thick. The plasma strikes had melted smooth the inward-facing sections of rock into a kind of dark green glass. That and there was a five-foot-deep trench to navigate, and it was hot enough we had to move fast, feeling the soles of our boots going soft. As the team, enveloped within the forty-foot-tall cavern, scurried along—it was only then that it occurred to me we were more than a little vulnerable to attack at that moment.

I wasn't sure what to expect, specifically, as we emerged into the settlement proper—well, this was most definitely not it.

I reached out to Pristy.

"Go for Captain Pristy."

"Tell me…what are your zoomed-in optics providing for our current location? That, and what are *Sanctuary's* sensors telling you?"

"Actually, I was just about to reach out to you, Galvin…we can't see you. Looks like you moved through that wall structure into more of the jungle. The overbrush we're seeing makes it far too dense to, at least via optics, see you. Strange…no infrared signatures either. As far as sensors go…the six of you have completely disappeared. Although, we do see Sadon circling over that area."

Distracted, I said, "Let me get back to you." I cut the connection.

All six of us were looking up. Some seventy or eighty feet above our heads was the top crown of a glowing blue dome. a generated field of some kind that wasn't totally opaque since I could see a somewhat distorted-looking Symbio-Poth dragon circling around up there.

Letting my eyes settle to the structures around me, I was just as mesmerized. I counted twenty-four one- and two-story structures in all—all looked to be comprised of a dark grayish-blue metallic material. The sides of the structures were all dark glass. Curving pathways comprised of local rock, like cobblestones, connected each of the buildings. Ponds with active fountaining water features and strategically placed mature trees, each full of bright blue and pink blossoms, completed a kind of beautiful university campus feel to the place.

I said, "Hardy…I take it you've scanned our surroundings?"

"I've found our fourth spider bot." He pointed off to our right. "It's within the confines of that structure. It is not moving, and I suspect it is undergoing maintenance or refurbishing of some kind."

Hearing a noise from behind, I spun around while reaching for my tagger. There, just entering through the same cutaway cavern in the wall we'd just entered through, were three of those two-headed raptor beasts. I fired off multiple plasma bolts, hitting all three of them at least twice. They squawked and hissed with bared teeth and quickly retreated back the way they'd come. I turned to LaSalle.

"Chief, top of your list of things to do…we need a door or gate of some kind to keep out the riffraff."

Turning back to the others, Wanda, hands on hips, was standing before me. "You did it again."

"Did what?"

"Moved, took action before I could even twitch a muscle." She gestured to Max, who was still keeping a protective eye on the breached wall. "Cap, we're supposed to be the team's security. You're making us look bad." She offered up a smirk, but I could tell there was biting truth in her statement.

I shrugged, not knowing what to say.

LaSalle had wandered off and was now standing over by the gap in the wall and talking on his comms. My guess would be he was ordering up supplies and equipment from Sanctuary to get that gate constructed.

"Cap! Over here."

Both Hardy and Derrota had moved closer to the nearest building. I hurried over to them and saw that they were actually standing within a doorway's threshold.

"It just opened as we approached," Derrota said.

"Not true," Hardy corrected. "It opened for Stephan. I approached first, and nothing happened. Only when Stephan showed up did the wall, door, whatever, split apart for us."

"I believe there are DNA sensors, my human DNA being the trigger," Derrota said.

"Hey, I have human DNA," Hardy said, indignant, pointing to his head.

I chuckled, "Probably not much more than that of a small-sized rodent, though, buddy."

I signaled for the others to join us, including LaSalle, who waved me off, fully engulfed in his new construction project. "Wanda, stay out here with the chief. Maybe work on those reflexes of yours."

"Bite me," she said, turning her back to me and heading off toward LaSalle.

Moving into the structure, Hardy took point, while Derrota and I followed behind, and Max brought up the rear.

We were in a kind of passageway, but there weren't walls or bulkheads per se. Separated areas were divided by what looked to be projected energy fields, all various shades of blue.

"Seems the alien proprietors sure like the color blue," Max said from behind.

Peering through the translucent fields from one area to the next, I could see there was an abundance of technology here. There looked to be fully active 3D displays, consoles with active control boards, and a whole lot of equipment whose functions I had no clue of.

"I believe we are within the settlement's command and control center," Derrota volunteered.

Max said, "Uh-huh," with just enough sarcasm to make me smile. Derrota did sometimes state the all-too-obvious.

I stopped, having noticed one particular display in an adjacent area had come alive with motion. Stepping closer to the energy field partition, a four-foot-wide door-like opening offered me access. I stepped inside. Max stepped up beside me—and we both stared at the now unobstructed display.

"They look like us…just like us," Max said.

What we were looking at was an immense deep space structure—a space station—one with a heavy amount of localized moving starship traffic.

Derrota moved past us and began assessing the control board. "Ah, similar interface to Gorvian, perhaps a little more advanced." He reached out, and both Max and I yelled, "Stop!" at the same time.

Mid-motion, Derrota held fast. Looking over his shoulder, wide-eyed, he nodded. "Yes, yes…best we don't make ourselves known to them. I will be more careful." He turned his attention back to the board, now keeping his hands clasped behind his back.

I saw that Hardy was still standing outside in the passageway. As with the entrance to the building, it seemed as though he couldn't gain access to these individual compartments either. "That must be frustrating for you," I shrugged.

"Galvin…this is interesting…"

I took a step closer, looking at the control board before Derrota. My eyes swept over the myriad multicolored readouts and indicators. And then it hit me. On several smaller integrated displays was the presence of alphanumeric characters. I made eye contact with Derrota. "What does this mean?"

Hardy was now pacing back and forth in the passageway. His

loud stomping was a statement in and of itself.

"I would say, Galvin, there are just two possibilities."

"I'm listening."

He shook his head. "No…there can be only one explanation. Time travel."

I rolled my eyes. "Don't be ridiculous, Steph—" But my words got caught in my mouth as a newly activated 3D display popped into view. There, clearly observing, hell, listening to our conversation—was a life-sized person—a man to be specific. Just standing there, arms crossed, he was looking more than a little irritated.

Chapter 39

"You're trespassing," the man said.

I nodded. "Texas? Maybe Oklahoma?"

"Texas…grew up outside Dallas, and apart from my accent, you're still trespassing."

"What is this place? And who the hell are you?" I asked.

The man was about my height, close to six feet. He had a small zigzagging scar beneath his left eye. *Perhaps a battle wound?* His hair was black and short, a military cut. That and he was wearing a dark maroon uniform. There were four angled gold officers' stripes upon his left sleeve. But it was not a uniform I was familiar with— certainly not US Space-Navy or any of the other Earth forces that I remembered.

"Captain Quintos…you need to leave that compound…leave now, and I'll let this…intrusion go."

"You know who I am then?"

He smirked. "I know who you were, who you are now, and who you will be ten years from now."

I glanced over to Derrota. Perhaps my Mumbai friend was right about that whole time-travel thing.

The man continued, "I am General Clive Resnick. And yes, I am from Earth." He turned his gaze toward Derrota. "Good guess, but no…I am not a time-traveler. Although that is not outside the realm of possibilities."

"Then what…how do you know where I'll be ten years from now?"

"Predictive assessments…Quantum modeling. Things human, Pleidian Weonan, Thine, Grish, Varapin, or even Gorvian tech have yet to master."

"And who are you with there…wherever you are? I imagine that's a story worth hearing."

He smiled. "Well…if I told you, I'd have to—"

"Yeah, yeah, you'd have to kill me. Funny. Look, I have no intention of leaving here. From what I understand, this place has been uninhabited for at least two hundred years. And it just so happens, I need a place like this. One that is off the beaten path, so to speak. I promise not to…" I looked around, "Break anything."

"You already did. Three advanced security rovers…the compound wall…" Resnick scratched at his chin, looking thoughtful for several more moments. "I am not unsympathetic to your… shall we say, cause? Yes, the Varapin were a plague against every-thing…decent. The first of many."

"You said were. As in past tense."

Resnick waved off the comment. "A figure of speech. Don't read too much into that. Let's get back to you and your…predic-ament."

"What predicament? I don't see that there's all that much you, or anyone else, can do about us being here." Out of the corner of my eye, I caught sight of Hardy standing there behind the project-ed energy field wall. He was waving his hands like a lunatic. Then he made a rapid slicing motion across his neck as if to say, *Shut the fuck up!* It occurred to me then that Hardy wasn't able to contact me via our open comms channel.

Resnick was talking again. "Look about, Captain Quintos… take in the level of technology."

I nodded and then shrugged. "Yeah…advanced. But I think we can figure it out."

"Oh, I'm sure with the help of Stephan Derrota there and Coogong up on the Oblivion, you most certainly could. But then you would discover the other embedded security measures installed at that facility. Ones that, if I so ordered, would reduce all of you, including that ChronoBot, to your most basic molecular constituents."

Is he bluffing? I suspected not. "What is it you want, Resnick? Threats are one thing, but if you were going to do that, kill us, you would have done so already. So, again, what do you want?"

I took in the scene behind the general; there were others there, and not all were human. I suspected he was on board that space station, but it just as easily could be a starship.

"I'm sure you have come to a similar conclusion in life, Captain…there is a price to pay for just about everything. Every decision comes with consequences. Some good, some not so good. You want to hole up there at Stratham Hold…yes, that is what it is called…there will be a price to pay."

I thought of Admiral McMasters and his ridiculous gemstone—his damn price to pay for a letter of marque. Now I was going to owe this General Resnick too? "And what type of payment are we talking here? We're not exactly flush with spacer's credits."

"The payment due will not be one of credits, currency, or oversized jewels."

I felt the hairs on my arms stand up. This guy knew way too much about our situation. About me.

"The payment will come in the way of a personal favor to me at some point in the not too distant future."

"You want me to agree to this…favor, one that has no specific due date, and one that has not even been decided upon yet? Hell, you may ask me to fly my ship into a core-collapsing supernova or to pillage a village on some backwater frontier world."

"I could, but I won't. The…organization, the people I work with, are of high moral fiber. As am I. But, let me be clear here: you will owe me…and payment will eventually come due."

"What is this organization you speak of? Who are these people you work with?"

"Let's just say there is a galactic-level consortium currently in place. One that is above all the interstellar turf wars and petty disagreements. There are far more significant concerns, Captain. Ones that have far-reaching implications for the very survival of not just our species, of all our species, but our universe as a whole."

"Fine. I'll agree to do you this favor. In return we can use Stratham Hold for—"

"An indeterminate amount of time. It could be a year; it could be several years, but in time, we will return, and you, my friend," he hitched a thumb sideways in the air, "…will need to amscray."

I said, "Deal. Now, if we need to contact you—" But General Clive Resnick was already gone. The communications channel closed.

There was an opening in the projected wall, and Hardy stepped through. Apparently he'd now been given the necessary clarence to do so. More importantly, it showed me that this consortium still had ultimate control over this compound. I didn't like that, but there wasn't much I could do about it at the moment.

Derrota said, "Hardy, what were all those antics about…the waving hands and such?"

"I know who they are. At least I think I do," Hardy said. On his face display was a slowly turning white geometric symbol—the omega symbol.

$$\Omega$$

"The builders of this settlement compound, those people you

were just talking to…they're about as close to god-level beings as you can get, at least in the physical realm. One needs to be careful when dealing with the Grand Consortium. Be careful what you agree to." Hardy looked at me. "Wait…tell me, you didn't make any promises or anything like that…"

"Nothing in writing, if that's what you mean. In appreciation for this consortium letting us borrow this facility for a while, I've simply agreed to return the favor…sometime. No need to get your panties in a twist, Hardy."

Max found that funny, but stopped laughing when Hardy stared back at him with a blank face display.

Totally absorbed in what he was doing, Derrota was now tapping away at another control board. "Galvin…this is quite amazing. The technology. The capabilities…" he looked over to me. "We have full access to…well, everything."

"Just be wary of these new landlords of yours, Cap," Hardy repeated.

"Anything you want to share? Perhaps some personal history with the consortium?"

He shook his head. "No. It would be LuMan's story to tell, and he's not talking."

Chapter 40

Seated at my desk within the *Oblivion's* captain's ready room, I was finishing up with more than a week's worth of virtual paperwork. Transfer requests, maintenance and new construction sign-offs, promotions and demotions—yes, we were pirates, and everyone was equal when it came to the sharing of bounty, but there were still job positions and ranks. Crew members needed to feel appreciated for a job well done—be recognized for such.

Movement caught my eye, and I looked up to see Hardy across the compartment. He was goofing around with Iris. Maybe it was a game of tag; maybe it was hide-and-go-seek. All I knew was that it was distracting. Apparently, Hardy's inner LuMan had raised the threat level that *something* could happen to me. When asked specifically what that threat was, he only said that it was a combination of things. And since LuMan's prime directive, if you will, was to keep me safe, at any moment in time it would override any of Hardy's wants or inclinations. Thus Hardy would remain close until this nebulous threat level subsided.

It had taken four days to make Stratham Hold a functional dirt-side base of operations. LaSalle, with the help of Coogong, had implemented a kind of virtual drawbridge for the breached wall—one that utilized Gorvian technology. Similar to *Oblivion* and *Sanctuary's* ZEDS, constrained within the wall's gap was now an impassible energy lattice web, which, when powered on, would make physical access into Stratham Hold impossible. No more uninvited raptor-like beasts making their way into the compound.

It had been some time since we started moving crew members down to the planet. It took some convincing, but eventually Pristy came around. Her *Hercules* crew consisted of twenty-five hundred remaining crew members. Today, about half of those had already transported down to Genoma and were making Stratham Hold their new home. To give you a sense of the sheer size of the settlement, only about one-third of barracks building number four was filled. There were four other still completely empty barracks buildings within Stratham Hold.

Although much of the time Sanctuary would remain in orbit around Genoma, there would be times when the massive refueling Franken-ship would be needed to support one particular mission or another. And the one coming up, our gemstone heist mission for Admiral McMasters, would be one such mission.

I was feeling relatively good about things—although I did have several growing concerns, the first of which was my limited band-width when dealing with the settlement. Typically, I would be cap-taining the *Oblivion*, and Pristy would do the same for *Sanctuary*. That left the management of Stratham Hold still up in the air.

About to ask Hardy, who was now crouched down, apparently hiding behind one of the armchairs; instead I said, "MORROW, where is Chief LaSalle at this moment?"

Chief LaSalle is on Genoma within Stratham Hold.

"I already know that. Specifically, where is he?"

Chief LaSalle is speaking with Vince Monroe at the southern wall.

It occurred to me that I hadn't known that Pylor pirate Little Vince's last name was Monroe.

I stood up and hurried toward the exit. By the time I was out in the passageway, I felt Hardy's heavy footfalls behind me. I'd already talked to Coogong to have him on call, so to speak, and he was there waiting for me within the quansporter compartment.

He smiled as I entered. "Captain. I so wish you would let me show you how to use the automated functions of your Jaadoo ring for this."

"Sorry, Coogong. I know it must be a distraction having to stop what you are doing each time I want to go somewhere."

"It is no bother. I only mention it to save you time."

I stepped onto the large pedestal and moved to an individual containment field platform. Within several seconds, Hardy was standing on the one to my left. I nodded to Coogong, standing behind the central console.

He said, "Quansporting now, Captain."

We arrived near Stratham Hold's most southern wall, not far from the gapped opening with the installed ZEDS. Just as MOR-ROW had indicated, both LaSalle and Little Vince were there, along with others including Sloppy Joe; even Wendy and Grip were among the crowd of twenty or so. I saw crew members from both the Oblivion and Sanctuary. It was as if everyone was watching an action thriller movie, all eyes glued to the eight-foot-wide gap in the wall.

I stepped up to LaSalle, and only then did he notice me.

"Captain…I…um, didn't expect you down here until morning."

"What's going on here?" I asked, gesturing toward the wall. "Why all the interest?"

LaSalle gestured with a raised finger. "Wait. You'll see in a moment or two."

It was dusk, and the compound's decorative indirect lighting had come on. I waited another thirty seconds and said, "Chief…I have a lot on my plate—"

That's when it happened. A shape, or maybe it was a shadow, appeared at the far side of the wall—something was coming in at the opposite entrance to the gap. I leaned forward and squinted my eyes. "What is that? One of those two-headed raptor things?"

It started with a cacophony of loud zapping noises. Then, brilliant blue lightning bolts flashed—crisscrossing the entirety of the opening. Only then did I see the beast standing there, all lit up as if it was glowing. I flinched. There was a blinding white explosion—one that made no sound at all. Now, seconds later, only the occasional errant spark flashed—reminding me of fireflies when I was a kid back home in Clairmont. I took a step forward. Clearly, there was nothing left of the beast.

"Obviously, this is a problem," LaSalle said. "ZEDS are invisible…as far as the local wildlife is concerned, that's an open chasm."

Little Vince said, "May as well put out a welcome mat that says, 'Come on in!'"

Sloppy Joe added, "Then again, two-headed lizards probably can't read."

Ignoring the Pylor, LaSalle said, "Coogong mentioned something about ZEDS having a menu setting…one that will keep the charged webbing illuminated."

"Good idea," I said, "considering one of us could have just as easily wandered into that gap and gotten atomized. Those mounted little red warning lights you have at the two entrances could easily be missed."

LaSalle let out a breath, looking crestfallen. "I'll have it fixed by morning."

"Hey, these things happen. No harm, no foul."

"Tell that to the Jackaboo."

"Jackaboo?"

"Uh, yeah…that's what we're calling the two-headed beasts. They're not raptors. Wanda came up with the name. Anyway, I feel bad. That animal didn't need to die like that."

I shrugged. "I get it…but, keep in mind, it was coming in here in search of its next meal…namely one of us."

LaSalle nodded. "You wanted to speak to me, Captain? The reason for you coming back down here?"

I nodded. "How about we take a walk?" Together we headed off down one of the softly lit pathways. Although I didn't hear him, I knew Hardy would not be too far behind us.

"Chief, I've got a question for you—"

He cut me off, "I'm sorry about the ZEDS fiasco, sir. It was unacceptable. If you want to reprimand me, maybe demote me, I fully understand." His southern New Orleans drawl became more pronounced.

I stopped and looked at the man. He was somewhere in his mid-fifties. His dark skin seemed to glisten in the evening light. And he looked both discouraged and humbled.

"Reprimand you? LaSalle…Chief, you did nothing wrong. The reason I'm here is to ask you a favor. To ask you if you would agree to run this place. Be the superintendent of Stratham Hold."

At first confused and then bewildered, he looked away as if mentally putting the last few puzzle pieces into place. "I did not expect…superintendent…Stratham Hold?"

"You'd be the counterpart to Captain Pristy on *Sanctuary* and myself on the *Oblivion*."

"But I have no command experience…I'm not educated—"

"What you do have is far more important to me. You're honest. You're fair. I can trust you…know that while I'm away, this place would be in the best of hands."

Standing a tad taller now, he scanned our surroundings—the twenty-four large ultra-modern structures, the tall surrounding walls, the sky-like dome overhead.

"There's a lot that needs to be done here, Chief," I continued. "Over the next few months, I plan to bring others here. Others that want to be a part of what we're about. In time, there will be ten thousand or more here at Stratham Hold…just as many as up on *Sanctuary*."

He looked at me. "And be a part of what, sir? What are we about?"

"We're about change. But number one, we're about ridding the galaxy of the Varapin, and to a lesser degree, the Grish. I, for one, am not willing to see Earth become overrun by those hooded fuckers. Thus far, it's been the Alliance shouldering the weight… the fight against the ghouls…while hundreds, thousands of other fat and happy technologically advanced worlds, keep to themselves, watching from the not-too-distant sideline reaches of space, not realizing that all too soon, they, too, will become Varapin prey. If they're not going to join with us in the fight, then we're going to make them pay, be it spacer's credits, starships, technology, or anything else we can steal, embezzle, pilfer, ransack, or heist… anything that will enable us to win this war."

"And you really don't think Earth's forces, namely the US Space-Navy, can do that along with the Thine and Pleidians?"

"The Alliance is well intended. But no. One way or another, we'll be bringing those sideline freeloaders into the fight. First with their wallets, later with their militaries."

"That's quite a speech, sir. Nothing I didn't know already, but it was nice to hear you still have the passion…the will to defeat the enemy. And yes, I'd be honored to run this place. I already have a few ideas on how to improve things."

Chapter 41

On the morning we were to leave Genoma's orbit and head out of Lost Tombstone's star system, I made another impromptu quansport down to Stratham Hold. Chief LaSalle had something he wanted to show me.

I arrived with Hardy near the southern wall and immediately saw that ZEDS were all aglow with bright red zigzagging energy vectors within the wall's gap. If that wasn't an obvious deterrent, then who, or whatever, attempted to breach that area of the wall would get what it deserved. I saw the chief speaking to a small gathering of still-uniformed *Hercules* crew. Hardy and I made our way over.

LaSalle glanced up as we approached.

"Nice job with the ZEDS. Seems you didn't waste any time."

"Thank you, but that's not why I asked you to return. I know you have a tight departure time."

"What is it then?"

Hardy spoke up before the chief continued, "Oh crap…that can't be good."

I followed the directed gaze of Hardy's teardrop-shaped head. There, moving slowly along the distant perimeter of the east wall, was spider rover number four. Apparently, whatever maintenance or repairs it was undergoing had been completed.

"My concern is the inhabitants of the settlement may be in danger," LaSalle said.

I nodded. "And rightly so. Those things are incredibly dangerous."

"I mean, how do we know it won't attack one of us?" the chief said, scratching the back of his head.

"Well, according to our landlord, General Clive Resnick, we're no longer trespassers here," I said. "I assumed he informed the compound's security."

"You trust him? That thing's a killing machine."

I waggled a hand in front of me, "Yeah, kinda sort of." I gave Hardy's shoulder a couple of pats. "Best way to know for sure… we put our own killing machine right in front of it."

"Me?" Hardy said, his face display now depicting an animated cowering, shaking kitten.

"Go. See if that rover means any of us any harm."

"You mean if it means me any harm."

"That too. Go!"

We all watched as the ChronoBot reluctantly headed off toward the east wall. Iris, a glowing dot, was making slow figure eights over his head.

There were very few times over the last few years, if any, that I could remember Hardy being unsure of his capabilities to handle virtually any confrontation. As goofy and playful as Hardy could be, ChronoBots were known throughout the galaxy as being devastating killing machines in their own right.

Hardy came to a stop no less than twenty paces from the rover. The giant metal spider suddenly jerked up higher, its primary energy weapon turret swinging around and locking onto Hardy. There the two robots stood, assessing each other. And for a moment, I regretted sending Hardy over there. What would life be like without him in it? I didn't even want to consider that. I yelled, "Come on back…it's not worth—"

The rover lowered back down and, assessing there was no threat, continued its slow amble along the curvature of the wall. It continued right on past Hardy, who watched its creepy eight-legged progress as the rest of us did. I wasn't sure I could ever get used to that thing.

***

I was pacing back and forth in front of the captain's mount. I'd already given orders to the helm to get the wormhole manufacturing process started. We would be jumping out of the Tombstone star system within minutes. Even now, I was still on the fence about taking *Sanctuary* along with us.

The truth was there was little practical reason to jump both vessels. The *Oblivion* would be doing the heavy lifting for this mission. I looked up to the segmented halo display—Genoma, violet and beautiful, was slowly spinning on her axis. Another segment showed Sanctuary, also in high orbit over Genoma. The last display segment showed the interior of *Sanctuary's* bridge, where Captain Pristy, looking thoughtful within her own captain's mount, was awaiting further orders. I had mentioned to her I'd yet to fully commit to bringing along the massive refueling outpost-turned-starship.

I watched as Derrota joined Pristy at her side—the two now conversing just as he and I had done a thousand times prior. Neither of them had fully embraced what I was doing here—the whole pirate thing. Had they joined me only out of necessity? I wasn't sure. And there was my answer. What better way to test that ship—test her crew—than a mission? Better to know now than later when Sanctuary's involvement really did mean the difference between success and failure—life and death.

I said, "MORROW, open an announcement channel…*Oblivion* and *Sanctuary*."

Channel is open…

"Good morning, crew members…this is your CO speaking."

I saw Pristy and Derrota look up to their own halo display.

"Today we embark on our first pirating expedition. After our fourth wormhole jump, we will be exiting into the Gliese binary star system, which is in the constellation of Draco."

Glancing around the bridge, I saw several heads nod. The crew of the *Oblivion* already knew where we were going and what we would be doing there. This announcement was mostly for those on board *Sanctuary*.

"Once we're there, if you have the chance to look out a porthole window or get in front of a view display, you'll be witnessing one of the most beautiful sights in the known universe. A once-in-a-generation spatial anomaly called an ionic swirl. It started about a week ago and will continue maybe for another week or two. The ionic swirl spans a distance of over two hundred thousand miles…" I recounted how Admiral McMasters had described the anomaly. "Picture multiple constantly swirling rainbows upon the black backdrop of deep space. A dazzling exhibition with every prismatic color you could possibly imagine."

Catching movement, I was surprised to see Doc Viv had joined me on my left. She smiled. In a lowered voice, she said, "Thought I'd come and give you a little moral support. This is a big day for you."

I put my attention back to finishing my announcement. "Folks…our quarry today will be the luxury starliner Pecunious. On board that fine vessel is a certain very large and very rare Alexandrite gemstone called the Sultan's Fist. Acquiring this rock will go a long way toward us receiving our letter of marque to operate, to pirate with impunity within this quadrant of space, ultimately putting us in a better position for building our forces…an armada of advanced warships unequaled by friend or foe. Look, we're in this together, people. All I can say at this juncture is good luck and be prepared for anything and everything. I suspect we're in for a bumpy ride."

I looked over to Viv. "That okay?"

She didn't answer right away, giving it some thought. "Quintos, it's not a bad thing that you have high aspirations…maybe even visions of grandeur. If not our leader, then who? Just don't lose sight of the fact you have a whole lot of people coming along with you on this adventure. Not so much because of your lofty intent, but because they would follow you anywhere…they'd follow you into the fires of hell if you asked."

"I appreciate that, Viv."

"Uh-huh…I know you do."

I said, "Chen…ask Captain Pristy if she would like to take *Sanctuary* into the wormhole first."

Chapter 42

Gliese Binary Star System
Captain Galvin Quintos

We arrived three light-seconds from the Gliese binary star system, well outside of the most commonly used commerce and shipping lanes. Up on the halo display was a magnified view of the distant star system and the colorful ionic swirl spatial anomaly now fully active. Only now was I realizing what all the hubbub was about. The visual spectacle, say in comparison to Earth's aurora borealis, well…it would be like an early twentieth-century black and white TV comparison of today's ultra-high-res 3D halo display. To say it was breathtaking, the constantly moving rainbow of colors, like a choreographed dance, would be a gross understatement.

Forcing myself to look away, I said, "MORROW, inform each of the Sultan's Fist team members we'll be assembling within the captain's conference room in ten minutes."

***

I entered the conference room fifteen minutes later to ensure any late stragglers would have time to get there. This was now the fourth time the entire team had assembled, although smaller break-off teams had met on their own to go through the various heist segments with mock simulations. Everyone was well aware of the part they would be playing for the heist. Thanks to Sonya's hacking capabilities, we had an excellent feel for the type of passenger that would be vacationing on the *Pecunious*—from ruthless investment traders, those willing to put profits before loyalty to planet and country, to overindulged and egocentric media stars and starlets, to the wealthiest of today's intergalactic criminal element.

While I moved to the front of the table, Hardy took up a position standing at the far bulkhead. I looked at my luxury *Pecunious* heist team. I was happy to see the four Pylors among them—they being the most adept and practiced at the type of thing we'd been planning. Directly to my left were Little Vince, Sloppy Joe, and Hock. They were dressed as below-deck maintenance/engineering workers in pristine stark white overalls. Next was Mr. Phillips, dressed in a *Pecunious* crew uniform, a smart-looking light blue jacket and matching slacks. Next came Max and Ham, who, like me, were dressed in the kind of high-end and slightly garish business suit attire appropriate for intergalactic mobsters such as we would be playing. Next, going around the table, were Wanda, Grip, and Pristy, each dressed appropriately as guest server stewards in fitted black tuxedos.

Looking to my right was Sonya, who was currently tapping upon a fathom projection tablet, or FPT—the most advanced AI device on board the ship, that was, next to Hardy and MORROW. Sonya had yet to look up from whatever she was doing. Next to Sonya was Coogong, who was currently looking over Sonya's shoulder at her FPT and who would be responsible for quansporting duties and basic technical support.

And finally, next to him was Doc Viv. She, playing the wife of my mob boss character, was dressed in a fetching, low-cut, glittery gown. She would be assisting Coogong and, of course, would be ready for any medical issues that arose on board the *Pecunious*.

Pristy, down near the far end of the table, with puffed-out cheeks, expelled a long, weary breath. Glancing up, she looked as if she'd rather be anywhere else. "Why am I here? And why did I have to put on this silly outfit?" She gestured down to her guest server steward's tuxedo. Her blonde hair was piled high atop her head and attractively secured there with two gold chopstick-like spikes, her face made up with a tad more makeup than usual. She looked stunning, and I had to force myself to look away as if disinterested.

Viv said, "This is it…the last meeting for the fourteen of us before it's go time. Gail, we've gone over this with you."

I said, "For Captain Pristy and all of our benefit, who'll give us a quick refresher of what we're walking into…one more time?"

No one volunteered, so I said, "Mr. Phillips, how about you?"

Looking put out, Mr. Phillips stood up.

But before he could say anything, Grip said, "You should probably stand up for this."

Mr. Phillips ignored the jibe. "I'll start with the ship…the *Pecunious*…well, it is one of an exclusive fleet of ultra-luxury pure pleasure starliners. It caters to the ultra-rich, who expect their every whim and desire to be fulfilled. The amenities on board this vessel are beyond extravagant…trips to the rarest celestial phenomena and most thrilling parts of known space. Guests will see galactically renowned entertainment. Meals of rare, endangered, and thought-extinct species are available at any time, day or night. Oh, and of course, there'll be high-stakes gambling tables on multiple decks. As for accommodations, the guests reside in palatial, mansion-sized, multi-cabin suites.

"Crew member waitstaff are there for the guests in any capacity necessary, and I mean any. They are paid an exorbitant wage and know what they have signed up for. As for the guests…as one might expect with the ultra-rich, most, if not all, have acquired at least some of their wealth in shady ways. These people are a part of or simply love to hobnob with the galactic underworld. Thus the passenger manifest includes the criminal element. We're talking major organized crime figures and their entourages. There go our mob boss, his wife, and security team." Mr. Phillips gestured to me and then Viv.

Pristy said, "Thank you…I already know all this."

"I'm in!" Sonya exclaimed with two fists thrust high over her head. "Sorry, got overexcited there," she said, looking a little embarrassed.

"Explain," I said.

The teenager glanced about the table. "Up till now I've been getting my information from several sources—MORROW's databanks, always updating from the galactic web when it's available or in range, and Hardy's knowledge base. But until just now, I didn't have the most current and accurate information."

"What changed that?" Viv asked.

Sonya smiled. "I just hacked into *Pecunious's* onboard, highly encrypted, uber-secure server farm. I don't think anyone's ever done that before." She looked somewhat astonished by her own achievement. She popped a bubblegum bubble and resumed tapping.

"Excellent job, Sonya. So…what have you found out?"

Tapping away, she said, "Uh, didn't I just say I just got access? But…as we speak, I am updating the crew and passenger manifest…I was able to do most of that last week via the galactic web without hacking the system. Now I'm making a few tweaks…and adding our latest heist team member." She glanced toward Pristy. "But there's something that may be a problem. Hardy, I'm guessing you're already evaluating the latest data I sent you?"

The ChronoBot took a step forward, gesturing to the halo display now projected above the center of the table. It was a detailed schematic of the *Pecunious*.

I said, "Guys, we already have this memorized. We know the layout of that luxury liner like the back of our own hands."

"Not so fast, Mr. Shiny Suit Mob Boss…the old and new schematics don't jive. Not completely, anyway," Sonya said. "There's a discrepancy…there's an extra space…the size of a small compartment. Maybe a vault?"

The halo display now showed the zoomed-in area, which hadn't shown up on the old drawings. Hardy said, "Yeah, this area looks to be over the top…crazy secure. And I can't see into it."

Wanda pointed to the display. "Didn't you take a look at the small type…the actual description? It's called the Sultan's Gauntlet. If that's not a clue, then I don't know what else would be. And look, this room, or vault as you put it, is right off the royal family's cluster of suites…perhaps even the sultan's bedroom."

I said, "You're right. And it's clearly inaccessible to the *Pecunious* crew, with no direct passageway entry point. More importantly, no access for any of us unless we quansport—"

I saw that Coogong was shaking his head.

"What is it?"

"I am sorry, Captain…but I do believe quansporting to that part of the ship would be problematic."

Grip interjected, "What's unique about that part of the ship?"

Coogong made a hand motion in the direction of the halo display, and the schematic zoomed out to show the decks directly above and below the vault area. He used a spindly black finger to draw a red circle around the area below. "This area of the ship, let's call it a subdeck, sits between the vault and the vessel's prime galley…the kitchen. These eight rectangles are the power converters for the food replicators."

"Why does that matter?" I asked, wanting to move things along.

Before Coogong could answer, Hardy said, "Because those things put out a nominal amount of radiation. Not dangerous or anything…but maybe enough to influence the quansporting process."

Coogong said, "It may be perfectly fine. But I would recommend we not take the chance."

I remembered that radiation was one of the reasons why nukes or fusion bombs couldn't be transported, which would have been advantageous during space battles.

I said, "So, quansporting to that part of the ship is out. And with the exception of the family…or maybe the ship's captain, no one's getting inside that vault."

No one spoke for a full minute.

"This complicates everything. Maybe just forget it all," Pristy said. "Your plan…does it even work anymore?"

"What are you talking about?" I said, getting annoyed. "We're not going to just forget it all. We have too much at stake here. Have invested too much time and expense."

I took a breath. *Why is she being like this?* "And maybe we don't bother with the vault. Our mission is to get the gem up on the promenade deck."

She shrugged off my words, then gave Hardy a hard stare. "You know, there's a good reason no one else has attempted something like this…your twin ChronoBot doing laps around the promenade deck." She looked at me with a condescending smile, "But hey, Galvin…this is your circus. We're just the clowns making the kiddies laugh…we do whatever you tell us to do."

Before I could object, Viv changed the subject. "There could be another good reason for that vault. Maybe that's where the real Sultan's Fist is stored."

"So the one on the promenade deck is what? A fake?" I said,

unconvinced.

Max joined the conversation. "Unless Sonya can hack out more information, there's no way to know. Sure, that vault may hold the real Sultan's Fist while a fake is up there on the promenade deck. Or it may be used for other family jewels or even the sultan's favorite sexbot. Only way to know for sure…break in and see for ourselves."

Sonya raised a finger while still not taking her eyes off her FPT device. "Going through the ship's passenger manifest. I see it's been updated. I mean, other than by me. The sultan's son is on board."

"Okay…why do we care?" I asked.

Sonya continued, "He would have access to that area of the ship…to the vestibule leading into the vault. And I'm now seeing the latch electronics. Hmm, looks to be some sort of biometrics lock. I don't know; perhaps he could be the actual key to opening the vault?" Sonya shrugged and shook her head.

"Bingo!" Hardy said. "Good catch; that is exactly what it is. A state-of-the-art bio-reader that requires actual organic DNA. And nope…pre-scanned electronic samples won't suffice here."

Sonya, smiling, added, "Ah! Here he is, the sultan's son… Jucahn Shun Enthor, quite the gambler and a playboy. A spoiled brat from what the interplanetary gossip posts are spewing out."

Sonya sent the picture of the man to the halo display. The room went quiet. Then Little Vince said, "Am I the only one that sees the obvious similarity to someone sitting in this room?"

All eyes went to Grip, who just so happened to be a dead ringer for the sultan's son.

Grip squirmed in his seat. "What?"

"It's uncanny," Wanda said. "You look just like this Jucahn Shun Enthor character."

Coogong said, "Excuse me…would it be possible to get a

moist sample of the sultan's son's DNA? Perhaps somehow we could get a swab?"

The faces around the table contorted into various forms of a grimace. Even Little Vince and Sloppy Joe didn't look thrilled at that prospect.

"Let's put a pin in that for now," I said.

Moving forward, the team went back over all the various obstacles pertaining to the promenade deck heist.

Hardy said, "The Stinemark Lattice security system…the case I'm seeing is more advanced than we originally thought." He looked over to Coogong.

"Yes…palladium micro-alloy glass. I need an hour in my lab to formulate a better method to breach that material."

Pristy said nothing, but her bemused expression, one that said that this was one big clusterfuck of a job, was starting to make my blood boil.

"Go now, Coogong; get back to us ASAP," I said.

Coogong hurried from the room.

As Sonya tapped in updates to our heist itinerary, we continued our discussions—those dealing with the roving promenade deck ChronoBot, the electronic security measures, the overall down-to-the-second timing of everything, and finally, we recapped what each of our respective jobs will be. Thanks to Sonya, the halo display was now providing the respective characters each of us would be playing and our basic job functions:

MOB CHARACTERS

Quintos – Mob Boss (Handles the display case break-in after Max creates ChronoBot distraction)

Viv – Mob Boss Wife (Helps Quintos with display case break-in)

Max – Mob Boss Chief Security/Enforcer (Creates the distracting ruckus that pulls ChronoBot from promenade deck)

Ham – Mob Boss Security (Lookout during display case break-in)

STARLINER CREW
Mr. Phillips – Head of *Pecunious* Security (Receives Max the enforcer from ChronoBot)

Pristy – Steward (Updated responsibility – Get close to sultan's son to collect moist DNA sample).

Ham – Steward or Purser (Supposed to be match for sultan's relative)

Wanda – Steward (Helps w/display case break-in)

VAULT BREAK-IN CREW
Grip / Little Vince / Sloppy Joe – Below Decks – Maintenance/Engineering (Vault Break-In)

Hardy – Security/Muscle

HEIST SUPPORT
Sonya – Network Intel/Hacking

Coogong – Quansporting/Technical Support for vault and display case heists

Once confident we had those aspects of the heist down pat, we turned back to the subject of the Sultan's Gauntlet vault.

We formulated a second team from those that had less demanding jobs from the promenade deck heist. We were going to have less backup security, but I was fairly confident we'd be able to handle both jobs in parallel. The truth was, we really didn't have much choice.

Chapter 43

One hour later we had assembled within the quansporter compartment. Everyone was talking at once, and I had to clap my hands several times to get the team's attention. "Listen up, people. Yes, it's go time. I know you're excited. I am too. We have a lot riding on making this a success. Hours and hours, days and days of planning and preparation will come down to what happens within a time span of no more than twenty minutes. That's it, twenty minutes to not only grab the Sultan's Fist from the promenade deck but break into the vault, the Sultan's Gauntlet, as well. If we, any of us, are still on board that luxury liner after that, we're in trouble."

The compartment went quiet.

Pristy said, "Wait, you never mentioned a hard time limit before…"

"Well, I'm sorry about that. You must have missed that from our earlier meetings," I said. "*Pecunious's* security sensors will override what it sees on the manifest right off the bat. When it's not able to reconcile our twelve, nearly simultaneously added bio readings, an internal timer will start. After twenty minutes a ship-wide alarm will sound…the ship will go into lockdown. It's the only security measure Sonya won't be able to avert."

"What do we care?" she said. "We'll be done. We'll quansport off—"

"Not so fast, Gail. Once Pecunious goes into security lockdown, all windows and hatch doors close. That and the ship's shields come on. Unlike most modern warship shielding, this luxury liner uses old-fashioned thorium-232 as a power element. That kind of radiation will make quansporting off the ship impossible. Now, Coogong says he'll have a fix for this within a few weeks, but as of right now…"

"We have a twenty-minute hard time limit," Pristy said.

I nodded, "We know exactly where the sultan's son, Jucahn Shun Enthor, will be. We're going to be putting you right in front of him. All I can say is you'll need to catch his attention."

She made a disgusted expression.

"You have the bio swab?"

She nodded and held up an index finger—one fitted with a special Coogong-devised swab appliqué. "But I might just throw up having to use it."

"You'll be fine," I said, noticing she was now also wearing a Jaadoo ring.

"Unless there are any more questions, it's go time," I said. "We'll all be quansporting from the pedestal here." I stepped down. "First six, come on up."

I waited for the first group to quansport to situate themselves onto the six individual containment field platforms.

***

Mario Bianchi Mob Boss Team

Coogong quansported the four of us—Viv, a.k.a. Maria Bianchi, and myself, aka Mario Bianchi, along with Max and Ham, my enforcers. As part of my recognizable attire was a wide pink necktie with matching pink pocket square. Mario Bianchi was a real person and a real, quite diabolical, interstellar gangster. His reputation, other than for wearing the pink tie and pocket square, was that of a ruthless killer—one suspected of the recent systematic killing of a rival gang's family of twenty-six, men, women, even children, vacationing together on a tropical world within the Nubian system.

We arrived within a narrow passageway right outside an upper-deck gambling hall. With Max in front of us and Ham behind, I held out an elbow for Viv to take. "Shall we?" I couldn't help but notice the cleavage revealed by her low-cut gown.

She smiled and took my arm. "You may want to stop staring at my tits…we have a job to do, Mario."

The four of us entered the main gambling hall with all the pompous confidence one would expect from this quadrant of space's most ruthless and powerful mob bosses. The hall was packed with formally dressed passengers. And like all gambling halls, the assault on the senses was the same—the loud dinging of slot machine payoffs, croupiers at the roulette wheels yelling, "Place your bets!"

Through the wafting cigar smoke—a thick, lingering haze that was already making my eyes water—I caught sight of the open French-style doors along the port side of the promenade deck. Right outside those doors was the display case for the Sultan's Fist.

As we strode farther into the hall, I could see we'd caught the attention of the passengers. My auricular implants picked up much of it: a woman leaning in closer to her husband, "Look…it's Mario and Maria!" A man at the bar, "Hey, isn't that Mario and Maria?" Two servers coming out of the kitchen, "Oh my God…look who's here."

The just barely audible murmurs rose in cadence as we approached a crowded craps table at the center of the room. The dealer yelled, "Dice are out!" and a moment later I heard the thrown tumble of dice. The crowd roared with excitement. "Player rolls a seven!" came the dealer, or maybe it was the stickman's voice.

With all the people gathered around, I couldn't see a thing. I checked my diamond and gold watch. Thirty-eight seconds had transpired. Time to make a scene.

I turned to look at Viv and nodded. She drew her hand back and let loose with the slap of all slaps. A loud, open-palmed whack that nearly took my head off.

"You son of a bitch!" she yelled, already winding back for another strike. A strike I could easily duck or step back from, but I didn't. I had to take it again for the team. The slap was louder and harder than the first. And from the look on Viv's face, she was enjoying this a little too much.

"How dare you!" she bellowed. Pointing to a nearby stunned and paralyzed-looking server in a short skirt, Viv yelled, "Why don't you just screw the little bitch right here in front of me! So, I'm not hot enough for you anymore? You think these tits aren't as perky as hers?!"

Here's the unscripted part: that was when Viv pulled down her lovely sequined gown, exposing the perfection that Mother Nature had endowed her with.

There wasn't a pair of eyes within the gambling hall that weren't looking at her. My bet? The men mostly coveted her…the women, for the most part, were jealous of her.

Viv looked back at me with wide *Do what you're supposed to do!* eyes. Dragging my attention back to the moment, I took a step forward and, not liking this part, in fact hating this part, I slapped her back. Not hard, but hard enough that everyone could hear it. Viv, evidently quite the aspiring actress, screamed and flung herself onto the floor.

And that's when all mayhem erupted. A beautiful damsel—no, a half-naked beautiful damsel in distress—would be a call to arms for the type of people in this room. And come they did. Although personal weaponry was discouraged on this type of cruise, as it turned out, no one cared. Everyone, men and women alike, looked to be armed and was now pulling a pistol of one sort or another. Some were small energy weapons, others old-fashioned projectile-bullet-firing guns.

As the barrels of no less than one hundred weapons pivoted in my direction, well, that was when I truly hoped Doc Viv's neon green Gorvian plasma shit would do its thing and would one more time make me faster than greased lightning. I dashed left then right, doing so while pulling one of those same old-fashioned pistols from an under-jacket holster. Now full-out running through the throngs, I raised the gun and pulled the trigger—twice. Screams and yells erupted as everyone dove for cover.

With a quick look over my shoulder, I saw what I needed to see: a seven-foot-tall ChronoBot just now striding in through the promenade's open French doors. Hardy would be jealous; even from this distance, I could see this robot's chrome was immaculate. Shiny enough I could shave by its reflection.

In my ear I heard Sonya's voice, "That took a minute and forty seconds. You're running behind, boss."

"I got distracted," I said, running for the exit on the opposite side of the hall.

"I saw…I hacked the security feeds. Man, that woman sure doesn't hold back playing her part."

"Can't talk…have a ChronoBot on my ass…"

And right on cue, Sonya's intercepted call for ship security brought none other than Mr. Phillips in his tidy blue uniform, heading a small and slightly confused-looking security detail along with him. Sure, they would have gotten the last-minute memo—*thank you, Sonya*—that there was a new head of security, but it would be weird—out of the norm. I didn't care—for the twenty minutes that we'd all be here, they could think whatever they wanted.

It was now Max's turn to catch everyone's attention, including the ChronoBot's. Max leaped up onto the craps table, brandishing the stickman's curved wooden stick. Looking crazed, Max whacked the dealer a little harder than I would have liked in the side of the head. "Get back! All of you…get back! I know how to use this… back, I say, back!!!"

And right before the ChronoBot was able to reach out one of his metal articulating arms to grab him—as if by magic, Max was quansported away. Now he was on top of the roulette table. On the wheel itself. "Spin me! Someone come and spin me!"

I stifled a laugh. *What a nut.* Viv was now at my side, and together we hurried out onto the promenade deck.

***

Heist Support Team
Sonya watched the feed as all the turmoil within the gambling hall erupted. She laughed out loud as Quintos and the bare-chested Viv smacked each other around.

She was ready when the emergency call came in from the ChronoBot. Intercepting it, now she was the one to dispatch the Pecunious security team—one led by Mr. Phillips, the ship's newly hired head of security.

She watched the promenade deck feed as Quintos and Viv ran toward the now-unattended display case. Sonya had already defeated the ship's security measures, leaving only the Stinemark Lattice and palladium micro-alloy glass case for them to deal with.

She nervously chewed and snapped bubbles unconsciously. She already knew the Stinemark Lattice was powered by a source separate from the general ship power supply. *Of course it is. They're not complete idiots.* She was about to cut the power.

Her raised finger hesitated. She stared at the confluence of thousands of characters and symbols on her display. Getting to this point, cutting the auxiliary power, had been no small feat, which no one would ever appreciate, but *something* wasn't right. She leaned in and assessed the code again. Her brow furrowed. "Redundancy! I see you there…"

It was a kind of "domino" failsafe power backup system in place. Well hidden, but it was there. Her fingers now flew over the input device in a blur of motion. *Chew-chew, snap, snap*…She'd seen the preprogrammed embedded delay between the shut down and power up of the failsafe. *Shit, that could have really screwed the pooch.* The case had to disintegrate during that blackout window.

Sonya whipped her head around to the left toward another display. She'd been forced to listen to the ship's piped-in elevator music, and if she didn't figure out how to turn down the volume like right-fucking-now, she felt her head would literally explode. It was the same music perpetually playing within the many corridors and passageways of the Pecunious, but most importantly, the promenade deck.

Switching to an adjacent input device, she now began editing the so-very-annoying track and began modifying its low-frequency resonance. Modifying it so that it was at just the right frequency to disintegrate the display's palladium micro-alloy glass case.

Sonya grimaced, just thinking about what she was about to do—cause real havoc with the Pecunious passengers' eardrums. Only those with nullifying auricular implants, like the Oblivion's team, would be spared. But the impending low-frequency blast would only amount to half of what would be needed to get the job done. They still needed Coogong's reengineered chemical brew.

She hailed the Thine scientist over a separate channel. "Coogong, you there?"

"Yes, Sonya, I am here."

"I'm about to cut the aux power and start playing the altered music track. Viv and Quintos are almost to the display case." She realized she sounded desperate and supposed she was. Quintos was all she had in the way of family now. She wasn't sure how she felt about that. Not that he would give a rat's ass. Who was she to him? Just one more dirty, unruly Pylor.

"I am quansporting the canister over now, Sonya. Oops…oh no!" *Clang!*

She heard something drop onto the deck. "Coogong? What happened?" She closed her eyes and tried not to think of the implications if Coogong's formula had shattered onto the quansporter compartment's deck.

On the video feed she saw that Viv and Quintos had reached the display case. The latter, not seeing the promised canister waiting for him, looked up toward the security camera. Hands splayed, he said, "Where's the spray canister?"

Chapter 44

4 Minutes Earlier…
Starliner Crew

Pristy listened as Sonya, via comms, directed her through a maze of inter-ship passageways.

Sonya said, "Okay! I got him…he's coming to you; be ready. Wanda and Ham have secured the corridor…taking up positions forward and aft respectively. Keep in mind, if things go wonky, they're two minutes away."

"I'm as ready as I'm going to get," Pristy said. "I still can't believe Quintos talked me into this shitshow."

Sonya didn't say anything.

"I mean, I had a perfectly fine career…right?"

"I don't know. I'm just—"

Pristy continued talking over her, "I mean seriously, pirates? I'm now a damn pirate?"

"Um…Gail…Captain Pristy…he's coming your way. At the next intersection—"

"Oh crap," she said in a lowered voice. "There he is…Huh, he really *does* look like Grip. Maybe even better looking."

"Hey, I heard that," Grip said, his voice coming in clear over her comms.

"Sorry, Grip…forgot I was back on the open channel."

Pristy saw the tall black man about thirty paces ahead—and coming her way. "He's wearing some kind of long, flowing gold garment. I didn't know he'd be wearing a dress—"

"It's called an agbada, and it's not a dress," Grip corrected. "It's an indication of his heritage and high society standing."

"Okay…sorry. It's not like I'm making fun of him…it's just unexpected."

"Fine. Just try to catch his eye," Grip said. "A lot is riding on this…on you being…well, somewhat inviting. And as long as you're griping and complaining, that's not likely to happen."

"Grip, why don't you do your job and I'll do mine…okay?" She put on a smile as the sultan's son was ten yards away. Casually, Pristy pulled on one of the metal spikes holding her hair atop her head. As the gold chopstick dropped to the deck, her blonde locks fell down around her shoulders.

"Oh my," she said, feigning embarrassment, and bent down to retrieve her chopstick.

Jucahn Shun Enthor, son of Sultan Enthor, was quicker than she was and had already snatched up the hair implement. He looked at it as if he'd never seen such a thing before. Both were crouched, their faces mere inches apart. The man, big and tall, loomed.

Dewy-eyed and acting coy, Pristy fumbled for something to say. "I…I'm so sorry. Clumsy of me…please forgive me, sir."

"Nonsense. It is I that caused this." His voice had a heavy Nigerian accent—was stern, almost indignant. "I am to blame, and I must make reparations."

Now Pristy really was fumbling to say the right thing. "No, no. I…"

He waved a dismissive hand. "You will allow me this small thing." He gently touched Pristy's elbow, prompting her to stand.

She did, as did he.

She watched as his eyes moved over her body—taking her in like a prized heifer at a county fair. He moved closer, reclaiming the lost distance when standing. "Tonight we will dine together. You select the establishment. There are many on board this fine vessel to choose from."

Lowering her eyes, she took in the sultan's family crest embroidered into the fabric of his agbada. Pristy reminded herself, *Be demure. Be innocent.* "Oh, I don't know, sir. Only certain members of the crew are allowed to fraternize with the guests." She knew that wasn't true but went with it anyway. The truth was, she was starting to feel a little warm around the collar. That, and she was getting more than a little lost in big and brawny Jucahn Shun Enthor's seductive gaze. Wow, the man had a certain magnetism about him. The attraction she was feeling at the moment was no longer just an act.

In her ear, she heard Sonya's voice, "Uh, did you forget why you're standing there in that passageway? It took a lot for me to arrange this. You do know I'm like watching you right now, right? Date the son of a sultan on your own time."

Pristy flashed a narrow-eyed glare up to the security camera. Adequately humiliated, she forced herself to get a grip. *I need him to try to kiss me.* She pursed her lips, as if considering the man's proposition, then she smiled. "Maybe…"

He shook his head, confused. "Maybe? What is this maybe? I insist."

How do I get him to kiss me? She looked past him, then stole a glance over her shoulder, as if making sure there was no one around. She stepped in close to where their faces, their lips, were almost touching. Just above a whisper, she said, "I want to…but I'm afraid."

His arm came around her lower back like a vise, pulling her in close. Then he kissed her hard—too hard. The brutish advance made quick work of any attraction Pristy might have had for the man. She tasted blood and wasn't sure if it was hers or his. Instinctively, she tried to pull away. He was too strong. Then his tongue was forcing its way halfway down her throat.

Squirming an arm free, Pristy reached up and pushed his face away from hers—penetrating his mouth with one Coogong-devised swab-appliqué finger. Relieved, she had her sample, but she also wasn't having any luck getting this sultan's son to back off her.

This Nigerian prince, or whatever the hell he was—once seeming nice, a gentleman even—was now palming her chest with one hand and groping her backside with the other. Again, his mouth covered hers. Now, Pristy was feeling real fear—a real threat of what was to come. Off balance, she was manhandled down to the deck.

God, please, someone help me…She wanted to scream, to let Sonya know she needed help. Couldn't Sonya see on the feed that this brute was intent on doing whatever he wanted to her—like right here, right now? Where was Wanda? Where was Ham? *I can't breathe…Oh God, help me!*

He was on top of her now, the weight of him crushing. Fists had ahold of her blouse—Pristy felt and heard the thin fabric rip apart. She tried to blank her mind to what inevitably was going to happen next. She only hoped he wouldn't kill her when he was done. She closed her eyes.

Suddenly, the weight was off her. How…? She tried to make sense of it. One second he was on top of her; the next he was not. She opened her eyes and tried to reconcile what she was now seeing. It didn't make sense. There were two sultan sons, two Jucahn Shun Enthors. No. The other one was Grip, and yes, they were about the same size, both big, brawny, and powerful, but Grip, well, he was a marine and…

Pristy winced as her friend and now savior repeatedly hammered his fist into Jucahn Shun Enthor's mouth. She turned her head as blood splattered. Looking down, she counted no less than three dislodged teeth lying on the blood-soaked deck.

The Nigerian now duly pummeled and clearly on the verge of unconsciousness, Pristy yelled, "Grip! Stop, I'm okay...you're killing him!"

"Yeah? And your point?" Grip said, out of breath and pulling the half-dead man to his feet and throwing him up against the passageway bulkhead. Holding him with an outstretched arm, he cocked back his other arm—an arm primed like a jackhammer—his white-knuckled fist ready to end the man's life.

Pristy saw both Wanda and Ham were running toward them from opposite ends of the passageway. She said, her voice just barely above a whisper, "Please, Grip...stop. We have a job to do. Let's get to it."

Grip's eyes found hers, "If Coogong hadn't quansported me here when he did...he would have raped you, Gail. That's unacceptable."

"Yeah, well, he didn't, and I don't want you to kill him."

Grip took a breath, released his hold on the sultan's son, and let him crumple to the deck.

Pristy said, "Coogong? I have the sample. Quansport me back to the *Oblivion*."

***

Mario Bianchi Mob Boss Team

The promenade deck was empty with the exception of Viv and me. The two of us were crouched down low behind the five-foot-tall Sultan's Fist glass display case. We watched as Max disappeared and reappeared throughout the gambling hall. Atop a poker table, then the ornate mahogany bar, back to the craps table, then atop a bank of $300-a-pull slot machines. At one point Coogong must have misjudged where to quansport the agile marine to, because Max took shape mere feet in front of the obviously irate and more than ready to kill robot.

The ChronoBot's energy weapons pivoted, now tracking Max's movements. Fortunately, no clear shot was possible without injuring, more likely killing, passengers in the process. Max disappeared a millisecond before the ChronoBot fired off a couple of quick plasma bolts.

Viv elbowed me. "Isn't that what we're waiting for?"

I followed her gaze to the object sitting atop the display case. A glass spray bottle with clear liquid inside. There were a few wrappings of tape where the canister was cracked.

I said, "Sonya…you there?" I heard the snap of a bubble. I handed Viv the canister.

"Uh-huh. I'm here. Where else would I be?"

Viv began spraying the liquid onto the palladium micro-alloy glass case.

"Okay, Sonya…play that modified track. Go ahead and do that now."

Almost immediately the case started to sizzle and steam. Both Viv and I took a step back, blinking away the stinging in our eyes. For the first time we could see the intricate, laser-like crisscrossing beams of the Stinemark Lattice. I was well aware that contact with any one of those beams, say with a finger, would slice through flesh and bone like a hot knife through butter.

Startled, I heard nearby yells and shrieks of pain. On the other side of the French doors we saw a mélange of whirling and flailing passengers—all of them had elbows raised—hands covering their ears from omnipresent mind-splitting vibrations.

Although well aware of the discomfort within my own ears, I

knew my implants were doing their job.

Sonya said, "Captain, the Stinemark Lattice needs to be shut down at just the right moment. Right when the palladium micro-alloy glass case starts to crack."

I didn't have to wait long. The first crack appeared midway up the display. "Now! Sonya, shut down power to the lattice!"

Grabbing a fistful of my jacket, Viv pulled me backward as the entire display case began to crumble. Truth was, it was a tad anti-climactic considering all the trouble we had gone through. I saw the web of bright lattice beams falter, more like a flicker, and then come back on. But it was too late because what we'd come here for was already lying on the deck.

Viv knelt down and reached for the spectacular, bluish-purple, fist-sized Alexandrite gem.

"Careful. That spray shit's corrosive," I said.

She paused, mid-reach, and looked back at me over her shoulder. "I'm also a chemist, remember? The corrosive half-life of Coogong's spray is kaput...Done. It's no more caustic than plain drinking water now." She plucked the gem from atop a small mountain of glass chips. "Got it!" Viv stood while admiring the brilliant stone.

She looked at me and smiled. "We did it!"

But I wasn't looking at Viv; I was looking at the seven-foot-tall ChronoBot now bursting through the splintered wood and glass shards of the fancy French doors that only a moment before had separated the gambling hall from the promenade deck.

Chapter 45

Vault Break-In Crew
Current Time…

When the sultan's son, Jucahn Shun Enthor, burst into the sultan's luxury suite of rooms, his startled family members—little brother Thamian, sister Armanna, and mother Cupra—all jumped to their feet, relieved to see Jucahn's return. There had been earlier reports of some kind of promenade deck attack. Against Cupra's warnings, Jucahn had gone to investigate. But now, seeing Jucahn's torn and bloodied agbada…

"You are not Jucahn!" little brother Thamian shouted, trying to sound far braver than he really was. But it was older brother Jucahn who was the brave one, the protector of the family when Father was away.

Sister Armanna and mother Cupra both gasped, taking steps backward. Thamian held his ground but was too afraid to do anything else.

Grip took in the family scene. Pointing to Thamian, he said, "You. I take it you want to see your big brother again? That and you want him to continue breathing?"

Before he could answer, the entrance door swung open again,

and two men in white overalls entered the suite. Both were un-kempt-looking; neither looked to be a typical Pecunious crew member. The third to enter the suite was none other than Hardy, his unexpected appearance causing frightened whimpers from all three family members.

Little Vince hurried over to Grip. "We're running late. Maybe I should be doing the interrogating." Vince glanced toward the little sister, offering her his most sinister sneer.

At the sight of his discolored teeth, the girl whimpered and took protective sanctuary within the arms of her mother.

"What do you want with us? Do you know who we are…who my husband is?" Cupra shouted.

"Yes, we know who your husband is, and we want nothing from you other than information. Tell me…how do we gain access to the vault? The outer room to the vault?"

Little sister Armanna was the first to glance to her left, toward an inset floor-to-ceiling bookcase.

Cupra, pulling her daughter behind her and looking defiant, said, "You are wasting your time. The vault is impregnable. Only the sultan himself and his eldest son can gain access to the vault. The sultan is away on business, and his son would die before al-lowing you access."

Grip said, "We know that, lady. Look, nobody needs to get hurt here. We're just here for the vault." He gestured to the book-case. "How do we access the outer room?"

Cupra looked to her son and nodded. "Show him."

"Mother, no!"

"Show him now, Thamian."

Reluctantly, the young man moved to the bookcase, flipped down two of the books, and reached a hand inside. There must have been a hidden switch, because the entire bookcase now si-lently slid sideways.

Grip said, "Sloppy Joe, stay here and watch the family. Hardy, Vince…you're with me."

The three of them crossed the room and stepped in through the opening.

The vault's ten-foot-by-ten foot antechamber was small and nondescript. The door to the vault itself was polished metal, and, as expected, massive. The thing was easily twelve feet tall and as wide as the room itself. To Grip, it looked like something from an old-time heist movie—only more daunting and even more impregnable.

Both Grip and Little Vince looked to Hardy, who had stepped up close and was knocking at various locations with an oversized fist.

"What's that all about…the knocking?" Grip asked.

"Just getting a feel for the door's thickness."

"And?" Vince asked.

"It's pretty thick," Hardy said. He bent over, taking in the heavy locking mechanism and then the glowing blue electronic access panel.

Sonya said, "Okay, it's all up to your team, Grip. The heist team on the promenade deck team was successful. You have seven minutes to get into that vault, retrieve what's in there, and get back to the *Oblivion*."

"Copy that. I take it Gail got the sample to Coogong? We need the bio-samples—"

Sonya cut in, "Samples are already done. She's quansporting now."

"She?"

Pristy walked in through the hidden bookcase opening. Her left cheek was already showing purple bruising, and her lower lip was somewhat swollen. "Here you go. Coogong is confident this should gain you access."

Grip said, "Gail…you didn't have to—"

"Yes, I did." She held up a clear plastic bag. Inside, slopping around in a pinkish goo, were two distinct fleshy objects. A man's thumb and an eyeball with an attached, hanging optic nerve. On closer inspection, Grip saw the eye was connected to a small black box.

"The box is a pump…electronics will be checking for proper retina blood flow," she said.

Vince said, "Were those taken from the guy…the sultan's son?"

Pristy shook her head. "No, of course not. Coogong did a rapid regrowth based on the wet DNA sample I delivered. Only took a minute."

Sonya's irritated voice was in Grip's ear, "Did I mention you're running out of time? Enough of the chitchat! Get going!"

Grip looked to Hardy. "Any idea which goes first, the eye or the thumb?"

Hardy said, "Go with the thumb."

About to question the robot's not very resolute answer, Grip opened the baggie, fished out a disgusting wet thumb, and handed it to Hardy. "Here you go."

Hardy didn't hesitate, placing the thumbprint area onto the sensor. Immediately, something metallic clicked within the mechanism. "Now the eyeball," Hardy said.

Grip handed him the eyeball with the attached pump. Hardy placed the eye in front of a secondary scanner higher up on the access panel. Again, more metallic clicks, then a much louder clang! The vault door began to swing open.

Grip and Pristy exchanged expressions of relief. They all had to take a step back to let the vault door complete its slow swing open. Inside, the vault itself was completely dark. Hardy stepped inside, and then an overhead spotlight came on.

Hardy froze in place. As for Pristy, Grip, and Little Vince—no one took a breath. There, eight feet in front of Hardy, was an all too familiar-looking seven-foot-tall robot.

Little Vince couldn't help himself; he had to say it… "Oh shit, a second ChronoBot."

That was when the faceplate on the thing became active—displaying the same sultan's family crest as the one currently on Grip's stolen agbada.

Chapter 46

Vault Break-In Crew

Current Time…

Hardy had time for just seven words. "Coogong, get the others out of here!"

After that, he had no time to verify they were indeed being quansported off the *Pecunious*—no…the sultan's ChronoBot was charging.

Hardy immediately didn't like this brethren battle bot. Not so much as a scratch, a nick, or a smudge was visible upon its gleaming, highly reflective chrome surface.

Hardy managed to dodge, sidestepping a punch to his head. He countered with a punch of his own to the chest area of his opponent. The metal-against-metal clang was gratifying, but not nearly as much as seeing the fist-sized dent he'd left behind.

The sultan's robot spoke, his voice identical to that of any factory-default ChronoBot and LuMan. "You are battered and old…not to mention, you have pink chrome. I will enjoy defeating you…"

Hardy wanted this dark closet tin can to see that there was far more to him—that they were very, very different. Hardy's face display changed to his retro 3D John Hardy face. He smiled and winked while blocking another punch—quickly countering with a punch of his own to his opponent's faceplate. He said, "And it's not pink; it's rose gold."

The sultan's ChronoBot staggard backward.

"Do you see the problem?" Hardy asked. "Hiding in here in the dark, day after day, like some kind of antisocial bridge troll, clearly you've lost your edge. You're a disgrace to our kind—"

Infuriated, the sultan's ChronoBot lunged for him, articulating arms outstretched, fists tightly clenched. Hardy went down to one knee and, grabbing the attacking bot around his lower torso, used the attacking robot's forward momentum to send it up and over his head—out through the vault's open door. A thunderous racket followed, and the vault vibrated as a thousand pounds of robot hit the deck out in the antechamber.

Feeling pretty good about himself, Hardy stood and sauntered out through the vault's open door with all the confidence of a matador having just dodged a powerful charging bull. *Now it's time to finish the job.*

Entering the antechamber, Hardy abruptly stopped. *This is unexpected…*Before him, the sultan's ChronoBot was back on his feet and looking no worse for wear. That, and all of its hidden weaponry—one shoulder-mounted pivoting energy cannon, two forearm energy cannons, and two upper thigh energy cannons—was now pointed directly at Hardy's center mass.

Hardy said, "And here I thought you wanted a fair *mano a mano* fisticuffs fight."

Hardy did the only thing that came to mind—he dove.

With an explosive onslaught of plasma fire erupting all around him, Hardy figured, of course, it was the sultan's ChronoBot who'd engaged the weapons fire. Coming up fast from his tumbling roll, Hardy's own hidden cache of energy weapons was now deployed.

But Hardy found his target was already laid out, lying prone on the deck several paces away from him. Where its chrome surface had been so pretty, bright, and flawless, it was now blackened with hundreds of small charred craters.

Pristy was the first to step into the antechamber via the bookcase opening, holding a still-smoking shredder. Vince, Grip, and Sloppy Joe, equally armed, stepped in beside her.

Pristy said, "No, Hardy…we didn't quansport away. Come on, you thought we'd just leave you here on your own?"

He pointed. "And those shredders?"

"You can thank Coogong for these," she said. "Now, how about we see what's in the vault before that other ChronoBot shows up?"

Chapter 47

Starship *Oblivion*, Gliese Binary Star System
Captain Galvin Quintos

Fortunately, Viv and I had been quansported off the *Pecunious's* promenade deck just moments before that attacking Chrono-Bot would have incinerated us. The only injuries we sustained were a few small cuts to our faces as those French doors blew apart. Patched up with sprayed-on AugmentFlesh, we left HealthBay together and headed for the bank of StreamLine lifts.

"Well?" I said, scratching at my face with a fingernail.

"Well, what?" Viv replied, slapping my hand away, "Augment-Flesh only works if you leave it alone."

"It was your first pirate raid…what do you think?"

The corners of her lips ticked up. "I think you nearly got us all killed."

About to protest, I held my tongue. *She's right.*

Together, we stepped into the lift and within moments felt increasing g-forces as it picked up speed. She was still wearing her long, sparkling, sequined gown. She shivered and crossed her arms over her chest.

Trying my best not to gawk at her now somewhat exemplified

cleavage, I removed my suit coat and draped it around her shoulders.

She said, "Thanks." She pulled the coat in close around herself. "It was exhilarating, to answer your question. That, and I'm a bit surprised we pulled it off."

Minutes later, we reached the captain's conference room and walked into a round of enthusiastic applause. The others were all here—Hardy, Max and his marines, the three Pylors, Sonya and Coogong of the support team, and Pristy.

Raising our own hands, Viv and I both returned the applause back to the group.

"Well done, people," I said over the continued clapping. "Amazing job, all of you."

I headed in the direction of Pristy, who was standing beside her savior, Grip. Approaching her, guilt weighed heavy on my shoulders. I'd expected way too much from her and worse, put her in a situation that could have led to a far more consequential result. Dammit, she'd almost been raped—and that was on me. It was my fault, and I had no excuse. Pristy had already been on the verge of leaving us; anyone could see how unhappy she'd been these last few days. I'd taken her away from a promising career within the US Space-Navy. There was a lot I had to account for with this woman, and I knew a simple apology was going to fall short.

"Gail, I am so sorry. Things should never have gotten to that—"

She held up her hands. "Stop right there. Don't even think about it."

Stymied, I didn't know what to say—she looked more than a little angry.

"Look, I knew the risks. I knew exactly what I was signing up for. So you don't get to take ownership of that."

About to object, I saw her glaring back at me. I closed my

mouth.

"I've come to a realization. Sure, you are indeed a pompous, self-absorbed ass."

"Oh, snap!" Sonya said from across the room.

"But you're also someone who gets things done. Who inspires his people to do things they normally wouldn't do. And you are a leader that doesn't command from the sidelines; you jump right into the fray with everyone else. And when you risk it all like that, put your own life on the line, the result is a kind of loyalty I could only dream of achieving someday...no, of deserving someday.

"Galvin, you may no longer be that same ultra-successful captain in the US Space-Navy, but you are still the kind of captain I can learn from. And I'll learn far more from you here, with this bunch of misfits, than anywhere else." And with that, she reached a hand into her tuxedo's side pocket and came out holding a brilliant blueish-purple gem. "And here's your real prize. The authentic Sultan's Fist."

She reached for my hand and took it in hers. Smiling, she placed the Alexandrite gemstone into my open palm. She leaned in and kissed me on the cheek. In a voice only I could hear, she whispered, "You're not getting rid of me that easy, Galvin." We held each other's stare for a long moment before I turned and headed toward Coogong and Sonya, who were standing together across the room.

"Okay...everybody, let's talk about who else saved the day. Two that went way beyond the call of duty. Coogong, thank you for all that you did today. Quansporting us in and out and all over the place with the deft precision of a neurosurgeon. The way you put Max on top of that roulette wheel...well, that was impressive, to say the least."

More applause and cheers came from around the room.

I held up a hand to quiet everyone down while turning to the young girl with streaks of purple in her hair. "And finally, I would like to give a very special thanks to this one. To my niece, Sonya Winters. I am so, so proud of this young lady."

Sounds of the most enthusiastic applause yet filled the room.

Tears welled in her eyes. Embarrassed, or just feeling awkward from all the attention, Sonya turned away to face the bulkhead. Then, head in hands, her shoulders began to shake as she wept.

I stepped in, putting my arms around her. I said, "I am so proud of you, Sonya. You are an amazing young lady, and today's success is as much your doing as anyone else's here." I kissed her cheek. "Now turn around and accept the round of applause you so deserve."

Reluctantly and with splotchy, reddened cheeks, she did as asked. The applause continued for a full minute, then was interrupted by MORROW's overhead announcement.

Wormhole jump Successful…
Starship Oblivion has arrived and is moving into high orbit around Haven.

I looked up. "Seriously, Franken-ship?" I repeated. Okay. "Sonya, please tell me you can do something about MORROW's wise-ass programming component."

She laughed. "Not a chance…if anything, this ship needs more wise asses, not less."

Chapter 48

**Starship Oblivion— Hidden Lost Tombstone
Star System
High orbit over Genoma**

Captain Galvin Quintos

It had been two days since we'd left the Gliese binary star system, the *Pecunious*, and that wondrous ionic swirl. With a quick one-day stopover at Lost Tombstone star system, I checked in with LaSalle down on Stratham Hold, then met with Chief Porter and Captain Pristy on board *Sanctuary*. Both Pristy and I wanted that vessel, if you could call it a vessel, to have the capability to, at a minimum, make short-range jumps and eventually be able to manufacture the kind of long-range wormholes that *Oblivion* was capable of. It was a big ask, but one Porter felt confident he could manage…in time. For now, *Sanctuary* would remain in orbit around Genoma.

It was time to leave. I had a scheduled meeting with Admiral McMasters back on Haven that I didn't want to be late for. Pristy walked me out of Sanctuary's engineering area.

"So…you're just going to leave us here over Genoma?"

"You have your Sir Louis de Broglie quansporter unit. I know it's the older model, but it still works, right?" I said.

She shrugged. "You're also taking Coogong with you. Not real sure anyone will have confidence using that temperamental old thing, but yeah…it's an option."

"You have shuttles on board *Hercules*, not to mention any shuttles still on the Grish vessels. You have ample means of getting down to the planet."

She nodded. "Speaking of the Grish. We have their crew still on board. They're taking up resources. Food. Around-the-clock guards. And they shit on the deck wherever they please. I don't want them on Sanctuary long term."

"Nor do I—"

She held up a finger. "I'm not done. You promised you'd help me free my attack group crews. Every day, every hour that goes by makes a rescue more unlikely. I can't stop thinking about them. While my crew and I are alive and free, they are suffering. Probably routinely tortured. So you either help me, or I have Hercules ripped from her moorings, and I go save them myself."

"I promise. That is my number one priority when I return. Come up with a plan…Between *Oblivion* and *Sanctuary*, we may have a fighting chance of getting your people freed."

She nodded but didn't look satisfied.

"What else is bothering you?"

"Have you considered the repercussions if something happens to the *Oblivion*, to you and her crew while you're away?"

I stopped to look at her, not getting what she was saying.

"We'll be stranded here, Galvin. No one else in the galaxy knows about this place. We'd be marooned."

I slowly nodded. She was wrong about that. The mysterious general Clive Resnick and his organization, the original inhabitants of Stratham Hold, knew about our habitation of the compound—

would he send help in a time of need? I had no idea.

"If you had to, you could do what you said and rip *Hercules* from her moorings. But it won't come to that. I'll be back within a few days."

We said our goodbyes, and I quansported back to the Oblivion. Twenty minutes later, the Oblivion jumped away.

***

Our arrival into the Eta Carinae star system was noneventful. I was grabbing a few hours of needed sleep when my Jaadoo ring vibrated. I had a message. Admiral McMasters was now on board the Oblivion—he was waiting in my ready room.

With Coogong's help, I'd been practicing using my Jaadoo ring's quansporter interface menu, making direct inter-ship jumps, bypassing the quansporter compartment completely. Doing this still made me nervous, but if I wanted the rest of the crew to start using this new technology, I needed to set a proper example.

I quickly sent a message to Hardy, who was already on the Oblivion somewhere, to join us in my ready room. With that, I called up the projected ring's visual interface, entered in my desired Q-destination, and tapped the **Quansport** key.

I materialized in my ready room to a startled-looking Admiral McMasters. He had been seated in one of the two armchairs; in the other was none other than Mr. Phillips. That, I had not expected.

"Ah, Captain Quintos," McMasters chuckled, "You certainly are one for dramatics."

"Good to see you too, Admiral," I said, ignoring Mr. Phillips's presence in the room. The implications were disturbing. Yes, the little pirate was a Pylor—we all were—but I had assumed incorrectly that he'd aligned himself with my own small clan and me. It brought to mind the pertinent question, which other Pylors on board the Oblivion, as well as Sanctuary, also had mixed allegiances?

McMasters, now standing, said, "I understand your mission, as it were, was an astounding success. That, and you have something for me?"

The admiral looked as excited as a six-year-old on Christmas morning. He went so far as to rub his hands together in anticipation.

Only now did I glance over at Mr. Phillips. How much information had the man conveyed? I should expect everything, including my acquisition of the now mobile refueling outpost *Sanctuary*, not to mention the Stratham Hold compound within the hidden Lost Tombstone star system. Two pieces of information I would most definitely not want McMasters to have any clue about. The Pylor rule of law to share all bounties—that was something I had no intention of doing.

Hardy entered the ready room carrying an approximately twelve-by-twelve-by-six case in one mechanical hand.

McMasters took in a deep breath and held it. "The stone?"

Hardy came to a stop in front of my desk, put the case down on top of it, and opened it. There, secured within a foam cut-out, was indeed the Sultan's Fist. It sparkled beneath the overhead lights.

I said, "The letter of marque?"

Irritated, McMasters tapped at his coat's breast pocket. "I have it with me."

"May I?" McMasters said without waiting to grab for the large gem. Now smiling from ear to ear, he plucked it from the case and held it up to the light. "Oh my…just look at it. Simply magnificent!"

Turning serious, he snapped his raised fingers several times. "Mr. Phillips…will you do the honors?"

Retrieving his own case from beside his chair, the small man unlatched and opened the case upon his lap. After a few taps, up came a projected display. The word

READY

hovered several inches in the air. Clearly the thing was a kind of test device.

McMasters handed the gemstone to Mr. Phillips, who then inserted it into a raised, three-pronged cradle. Indecipherable characters and symbols scrolled for several seconds, before one oversized word locked into place.

FAKE

Admiral McMasters continued to stare at the hovering word. Like an actor in a movie, a bit melodramatically if you asked me, McMasters slowly turned to look at me. "What is the meaning of this?"

Keeping my face expressionless, I slowly walked around to the other side of my desk, opened the top drawer, and retrieved the real Sultan's Fist. I held it up for McMasters to see. "Am I not a pirate? Would any real pirate worth his salt not at least try?"

The corners of the admiral's lips pulled upward.

I tossed the priceless gem over to Mr. Phillips, who deftly caught it in one hand. Hardy quickly reached in and removed the fake stone from its cradle before Mr. Phillips could insert the real one. After more tapping and more scrolling characters and symbols, a lone word appeared suspended over the test device.

REAL

Mr. Phillips handed the stone to Admiral McMasters. He looked at the shimmering gem for several moments before saying anything. "You did it. You actually did it." He looked at me.

"A team effort," I shrugged. "Any possibility you're going to tell me why you need that stone? What you're going to use it for?"

"No. That is a secret I will not divulge." He hesitated. "Secrets are a funny thing. They can be both an advantage or a disadvantage, depending on the disposition of the holder. I choose to keep my advantage concerning the stone. But it seems you have your own secrets, Captain Quintos. Secrets I have commanded Mr. Phillips here to relinquish to me."

I tried to read Mr. Phillips's expression but could not.

McMasters continued, "He has chosen…not to do so. It seems his many years of loyalty to me have been for naught."

Even with my much faster than normal reflexes, I wasn't fast enough to do anything when McMasters took me completely by surprise by pulling a small energy pistol from a hidden holster inside his coat, pointing it at Mr. Phillips's head, and pulling the trigger twice. The sound was barely audible—*Zip zip*.

Hardy's arsenal of weaponry snapped into view—five lethal energy weapons directed at the admiral's chest.

I held up a restraining hand. "Hold on, Hardy." I moved to the slumped-over body of Mr. Phillips and checked for a pulse at his neck. I already knew the man was dead, but I wanted a few more seconds to think. "You didn't need to do that, Admiral. He was a good man. I suspect he was as loyal as they come."

Looking pleased with himself, McMasters splayed his palms and repeated my own words back to me. "Am I not a pirate?"

Hardy's forearm cannons rose a bit higher, now leveling on McMasters' head.

"Let this be a warning to you, Captain Quintos. I am allowing you and your small clan to operate under the Pylor flag. I request…

no, demand, loyalty." His eyes flicked to Mr. Phillips's corpse. "You want to test me…you will face a similar fate as the little man currently voiding his bowels on that pretty armchair."

McMasters would pay for what he'd done. But not today. I watched as McMasters reached a hand into his coat and withdrew what looked to be an old-fashioned rolled piece of parchment. A tied red ribbon held it secured. The admiral held it out to me. "Here is your letter of marque."

I took it, untied the ribbon, and glanced at it. The page was filled with handwritten cursive text. I handed it to Hardy, who looked at it for about one second.

"It's in order," Hardy said. "No surprises. Speaks mostly of shared bounties…percentage splits, rules of conduct, and loyalty to the Pylor flag."

Walking toward the exit, McMasters said, "You'll learn I am a man of my word, Captain. That's all I ask for in return. Now go forth and pirate to your little heart's desire."

The Oblivion's loud klaxon blared from overhead. McMasters stopped just short of reaching the exit.

ALL HANDS…INCOMING! ALL HANDS… INCOMING!

My Jaadoo ring vibrated—the projected form of Akari James came alive. "Captain! We're under attack. They're coming in through various points within the asteroid field. Missiles, hundreds of them, are inbound!"

Chapter 49

I ran onto the bridge with Hardy and McMasters following close behind.

"Situation report!" I yelled, trying to comprehend what I was seeing up on the halo display. I was seeing the faint, ghostly outline of a number of cloaked ships.

Other crew members were just now hurrying onto the bridge. I'd kept a minimal crew posted overnight, feeling confident there were few places more secure than high orbit over Haven here within the Eta Carinae star system's asteroid belt. But I'd been wrong.

Akari James was at Tactical, Grimes at Helm, and Chen on Comms. I caught sight of Bosun Polk hurrying to her station behind me.

Akari said, "They found us, Captain. I don't know how…but they found us."

I looked at her. "Who the hell are they?"

"The Varapin armada. The same ones who took out Pristy's attack group with relative ease."

I remembered. "Vanquishing Shadow Strike Force."

"You did this!" McMasters bellowed at my side. "You brought them here…they must have followed you!"

I shook my head. "No way. We emerged directly from a man-ufactured long-range wormhole. No, Admiral, you've conveniently forgotten the Grish were already attempting to breach that asteroid field. They simply passed on the information to the Varapin. They pinpointed the location of Haven. Then, very well cloaked, with their more advanced sensor technology, the Varapin were able to weave their way through that maze of asteroids." I looked over to Hardy.

"Yes…impressive."

McMasters scoffed toward the ChronoBot. "That's all you have to say? Useless tin can…no wonder they stopped manufacturing your kind three hundred years ago."

Hardy was back to wearing his black leather vest. A soft glow emanated from the top of his breast pocket. Iris stuck her head out—little brows furrowed, she glowered toward the admiral. The Symbio-Poth fairy might be small, but I for one wouldn't want to make an enemy of her.

"You should get back to Haven," I said. "You must have close to a hundred Pylor vessels in orbit. Mount a defense."

He rolled his eyes. "I have officers to do that…have no doubt, they're already targeting—"

"Captain, those incoming missiles," Akari said with concern in her voice.

"Fine. We'll need to take them out."

"There are hundreds of them. I suggest we jump out of here," she said, avoiding the admiral's now angry glare.

The halo display came alive with three consecutive flashes.

McMasters stepped closer to the display, his mouth hanging agape. "Those were my three heavies…advanced battle cruisers. The *Harpoon*, the *Canton*, and the *Recluse*." Turning back to me, there was genuine fear in the man's eyes. "Good God! Those were my biggest and baddest warships!"

Hardy said, "Then it makes sense they would have been targeted first."

I stared up at the display as more enemy warships emerged from the asteroid field. Certainly, Akari had made a perfectly sound proposal—jump out of here to fight another day. A day where we'd have better control over the playing field.

McMasters was nearly apoplectic now. "You can't abandon us, Quintos! Those ghouls…it won't be long before they've destroyed all of my warships…then…well, they'll send down those, those smaller attack vessels…"

Hardy said, "Called Ravage-Class Landers."

"They'll infiltrate the populace; thousands of civilians will have their life forces—"

"Ghan-Tshot. It's called Ghan-Tshot," Hardy interjected.

"Hardy, you're not helping," I said.

There was no way I would abandon the Pylors. But could *Oblivion* defeat this armada? I didn't think so.

I had to concentrate. Turning to the tactical station, I said, "We have our badass Gorvian tech. Maybe it's time we put it to use. Akari, what exactly is inbound?"

She checked her board. "Roughly two hundred and thirty smart-missiles. Fusion-tipped…nukes. ETA…three and a half minutes."

I thought of Oblivion's ZEDs. Would they hold up against that kind of barrage?

As if reading my mind, Akari said, "Shields…sure, our ZEDS are online, Captain, but nothing could withstand two hundred plus consecutive nuke strikes."

I said, "Hardy, get up there and help on Tactical. Akari, target the rest of those enemy ships coming out of the asteroid field. Deploy nullifier missiles. I know we don't have an endless supply of those, but they'll cause the most damage to Varapin shields. Fire at will. As for the incoming missiles, let's use our Dual Pion Pulsar Beams. As soon as incoming are within range, let 'em rip."

Hardy said, "You're referring to the DPPBs or Baby Pulsars."

"Whatever. Take out as many of those bogies as *Oblivion* can handle."

I turned to Bosun Polk. "Can you mirror another Tactical board onto your station?"

"Absolutely."

"You're on hydro-missiles and Phazon Pulsars!"

"Roger that, Captain."

I looked to the helm station. "Crewman Grimes, you'll need to keep us moving. Jump us around…Remember, our perpendicularity spheres need a chance to recharge!"

"Copy that, Captain."

"Captain. We're being hailed by the *Bow Before Me*," Chen said. "A Captain Flinth Shap."

"Open the channel on display."

The armada's commander looked no different from any of the other ghouls I'd come across over the last year or so. He was hovering—had an obsidian black skull of a head, with jutting, exposed white jaw area. But his robes were not black; they were a shimmering midnight blue. Behind him was a highly advanced-looking bridge compartment. Perhaps not compared to that of the Gorvian-designed *Oblivion*, but still on an advanced order of technology.

"Captain Quintos…I have looked forward to this day. You are a difficult human to track down."

I watched as my frenzied bridge crew combated the enemy armada. Nine Varapin warships had now emerged from the asteroid field. That, and not one of them had been destroyed yet by *Oblivion's* weaponry.

"I have come for my ship, for the Oblivion. You will give her to me."

"Not likely, Shap. As you can see…we're holding our ground quite well here."

I watched as Captain Flinth Shap signaled to one of his crew.

"I take it you are observing the lone green world below?"

I didn't answer.

"And thus I know you have the capability to track the dozens of Ravage-Class Landers leaving three of my ships…all en route down to the surface?"

Again, I didn't answer.

"It has been a long journey, Captain…Soon, my warriors will commence a mass Ghan-Tshot feeding…I take it you are familiar with Ghan-Tshot?"

McMasters brushed past me. "What do you want? Stop those landers, and I'll give you exactly what you want."

"I want three things…the *Oblivion*, of course, the refueling outpost you recently absconded with, as well as your fully operational quansporter technology. I receive those three things, and the inhabitants of this world go free…unharmed. And I'll take it a step farther…your crews, Captain Quintos…will all go free."

I shook my head. "Just like the crew members of that US Space-Navy attack group were freed?"

"This is war, Captain…no one said it was pretty. But rest assured, the crew of that attack group is still alive. For now."

Hardy said, "My sensors are picking up a lone personnel transport just outside the asteroid field. It just went visible…no longer cloaked."

The deck began to vibrate beneath my feet. Glancing at Akari, I saw she looked concerned.

She said, "We're not able to take out all of their missiles. Too many…they're just now impacting our ZEDS."

The alarm klaxon was mind-numbingly loud overhead.

McMasters was pacing now. He had both hands on his head. "This can't be happening…this can't be happening!"

The display flashed. "Got one!" Akari bellowed.

If I was reading Captain Flint Shap's expression right, he was smiling. "A smaller destroyer…an insignificant component within our arsenal."

Hardy nodded. "He's not wrong."

I said, "Your concern for your lost crew—what was that, several thousand souls? Touching."

Before the commander could answer, Bosun Polk said in a lowered voice, "Shields and ZEDS are heating up, Captain. Down to 70 percent effectiveness."

It made sense. I'd noticed that the *Oblivion* had ceased her erratic and unpredictable jumping. I didn't need to look at Grimes to know our perpendicularity spheres required recharging. The *Oblivion* was taking more direct hits now, and the enemy was steadily advancing on us—we were bloody meat within a piranha-filled river.

McMasters stormed over to me, took me by my shoulders, and shook me. "You have to do as he asks! Relinquish this damn ship! Those landers…they're landing! Can't you see that?"

"And you honestly think that ghoul will keep up his end of the bargain? He won't. But more importantly, we hand over our quansporter tech, and this war is as good as over."

"It's over anyway!" McMasters roared. "The Alliance has been losing for months now…it's inevitable. You're only prolonging the unavoidable."

The halo display was now flashing on a regular basis. It was the in-system Pylor ships, mostly warships, but many simply commercial vessels, now erupting into fireballs.

"Chen, cut the channel. We're done talking to the ghouls."

"No!" McMasters objected. "We can negotiate…For God's sake, Quintos, you're signing a death warrant for Haven's populace. My family is down there! My wife, my children!"

There were now thunderous poundings emanating from the hull. Continuous missile strikes.

"I'm sorry, Admiral. Truly I am. But I think it's best you be with your family in their time of need," I said. "MORROW, ask Coogong to quansport Admiral McMasters to his residence on Haven."

Within eight seconds, McMasters was gone, a distraction I could no longer tolerate. I lowered myself into the captain's mount and watched as my bridge crew worked at their respective stations.

I sat up straighter. "We're not cloaked."

"Correctamundo, Cap."

Akari added, "Why bother…Varapin tech's been able to see through US Space-Navy cloaking for months now…" But her words fell short, and she turned to look at me. "But this isn't a US Space-Navy ship."

She tapped at her board, and almost immediately the thunderous booms began to lessen.

"Hardy…you of all people should have realized the obvious."

"Agreed. And just as you're blaming me, I'm blaming LuMan."

Ignoring him, I said, "Grimes, please tell me our perpendicularity spheres have sufficiently recharged."

"I can give you one, maybe two short jumps."

"All I need is one. Get us up close and personal with the *Bow Before Me*. It's time we take the offensive. Akari, Hardy…be ready to throw everything we have at that heavy."

"Jumping now, Captain," Grimes said from the helm station.

Within the blink of an eye, the halo display was now showing the up-close faint, ghostly outline of the *Bow Before Me*.

"Three miles between us, Captain," Grimes said, sounding proud of himself.

Even before I could give the order, Hardy and Akari were firing our nullifier missiles. The smallest elements, the very molecules of that warship, were now imploding upon themselves. There were no dramatic explosions, no great flashes of light. And in mere moments, the *Bow Before Me* simply ceased to exist.

"Take that, you son of a bitch," I said.

Hardy said, "Interesting…we have new visitors."

"Crap!" Akari said. "We're in trouble. Big trouble."

But I already saw what was happening. What remained of the Vanquishing Shadow Strike Force, seven still highly capable warships, was now closing in on us and not holding back with its own unrelenting assault upon us.

"Shields down to 30 percent and falling fast," Bosun Polk said.

"Helm, get us out of here!" I yelled.

"Working on it, Cap—"

Suddenly the *Oblivion* jarred so violently, anyone on their feet was thrown to the deck. Bridge lights flickered out, then came back on. MORROW announced:

Breaches Detected…Deck 3, Deck 12, Deck 42, and 43. Atmosphere Venting…

Hardy said, "Not just visitors…"

"What the hell are you talking about? Hardy, just keep on the attack for as long as we can."

"He's right, Captain," Akari said. "Coming in from the asteroid field. Three more warships…and they're big M-fers."

Chen said from Comms. "Um, the visitors…Captain, we're being hailed."

Before I could respond, a familiar alien and oh-so-beautiful face appeared upon the halo display.

"Hello, Galvin. Sorry to arrive to the party so late. As promised, I'm delivering what is rightfully yours. I hope you don't mind that I came along to make the delivery myself."

I stared back at Empress Shawlee Tee and didn't even try to blink away the tears welling up in my eyes. "Shawlee" was all I was able to croak out.

Hardy said, "Looks like we have a few familiar vessels coming inbound."

I nodded, unable to speak. My breath, all our breaths, caught in our chests. There, up on the halo display, was the most beautiful sight I'd ever witnessed or probably ever would. The USS *Hamilton*, the USS *Jefferson*, and the USS *Adams* were on approach at full speed—guns ablaze.

Now that's a last-minute rescue for the books.

The End

Thank you for reading Starship Oblivion—USS Hamilton Series Book 5
If you enjoyed this book, PLEASE leave a review on Amazon.com—it really helps!
To be notified the moment all future books are released—please join my mailing list. I hate spam and will never ever share your information. Jump to this link to sign up:
http://eepurl.com/bs7M9r

Acknowledgments

First and foremost, I am grateful to the fans of my writing and the ongoing support for all my books. I'd like to thank my wife, Kim; she's my rock and is a crucial, loving component of my publishing business. I'd like to thank my mother, Lura Genz, for her tireless work as my first-phase creative editor and as a staunch cheerleader of my writing. I'd also like to thank Margarita Martinez for her amazing, detailed line editing work and Daniel Edelman for his prerelease review. Others who provided fantastic support include Lura and James Fischer and Eric Sundius.

Check out the other available titles by Mark Wayne McGinnis at the beginning of this book.

Made in the USA
Middletown, DE
05 November 2021